7/18

Every Secret Thing

Rachel Crowther trained as a doctor and worked in the NHS for twenty years, writing fiction on the side between babies and medical exams until her first novel was published after winning a competition. She has five children, two mad dogs and a kitten, and is also a keen musician and cook. This is her third novel.

Also by Rachel Crowther

The Things You Do For Love
The Partridge and the Pelican

Every Secret Thing

Rachel Crowther

ZAFFRE

First published in Great Britain in 2017 by

ZAFFRE PUBLISHING
80-81 Wimpole St, London W1G 9RE
www.zaffrebooks.co.uk

A CIP catalogue record for this book is available from the British Library.

ISBN: 978-1-785-76212-3

also available as an ebook

1 3 5 7 9 10 8 6 4 2

Typeset by IDSUK (Data Connection) Ltd

Printed and bound by Clays Ltd, St Ives Plc

Zaffre Publishing is an imprint of Bonnier Zaffre,
a Bonnier Publishing company
www.bonnierzaffre.co.uk
www.bonnierpublishing.co.uk

For my friends in Clare College chapel choir, 1983–86

For God shall bring every work into judgment, with every secret thing, whether it be good or whether it be evil.

Ecclesiastes 12:14

Prologue

Cumbria, September 2015

It was almost dusk when the taxi reached the top of the pass and Nag's Pike came into view. Judith had forgotten the drama of it: the way it cleaved the horizon with the sharp double peak of its pricked ears, asserting its dominance over the gentler curves of the surrounding fells. She hadn't, of course, forgotten the part it had played in their own drama all those years ago, but as it rose up now, dark against the silvered sky, the details came rushing back.

On the evening they'd arrived, in the summer of 1995, Fay had named the peaks that circled them as they gazed from the terrace, wonderstruck by the view. Place Fell, Fairfield, Helvellyn – and Nag's Pike, rearing its uncanny horse's head centre stage. She'd recounted the legend of its creation, pointing out the features local tradition conferred on it: the shaggy mane of woodland running down the straight slope of its neck, and the broad saddleback plain below. That was the way up, Fay had told them. They hadn't imagined, then, that they'd find themselves climbing Nag's Pike a few days later. Certainly there had been no whiff of foreboding about the consequences of that expedition.

The five of them had been invited to High Scarp that summer to sing in the village music festival – a perfect coda to their three years together in Cambridge, singing in the chapel choir, and to the extraordinary closeness of their friendship with each other and with Fay. The weekend had been filled with rituals which they'd found charmingly quaint, Judith remembered. The National Anthem in the solid little church; the games of charades and consequences by the fire; the fond way Fay spoke of the traditions of the place. If Fay had been a little different that weekend at High Scarp, they had all been too preoccupied to wonder much about it. And if there had been a quiver of disquiet before the Nag's Pike outing, it had been because of the way Fay had insisted on it, as though she expected dissent. As though, Judith thought now, she'd known the expedition would change things irrevocably, and feared they had an inkling of it too.

But that wasn't possible, she told herself, as the taxi dropped down into the valley. Fay couldn't have foretold how much would be exposed that day, even if she'd known more about them all than they realised. Even so, as the turning to High Scarp appeared at last, she couldn't help wondering if there had been some malevolence in it all. In Fay's invitation twenty years ago, and in the posthumous summons they were answering now.

Cambridge, October 1992

The entrance to the chapel was tucked away in the corner of First Court, easy to miss if you didn't know it was there. Crossing the square of grass and cobbles, already familiar after three days at St Anne's, Judith felt a twinge of doubt. Not so much about the religion as the belonging, she thought. That was complicated: whether she wanted to belong, and what to. She loved singing, she wanted to sing, but she could tell from the way people talked about it that there was more to this choir than that.

While she hesitated, two people came across the courtyard from the other corner – a tall, spindly looking boy with dark hair smoothed flat and a blonde girl of the kind there'd been lots of at Judith's school.

'No!' she heard the girl say. 'You must, of course. Nothing ventured . . .'

At that moment she glanced in Judith's direction and smiled, a more straightforward smile than Judith expected, and Judith found herself smiling back. Nothing ventured: well.

The Director of Music was waiting just inside the chapel. Lawrence; not Dr Watts.

'Welcome!' he said. 'Judith – Cressida – Stephen. The others will be along, I'm sure.'

It was still light outside, but the chapel was filled with a muted, dust-moted stillness that seemed to set it apart from the day, from the warm stone of the courtyard and the world beyond. The floor stretched away in a pattern of black and white tiles, flanked by oak panelling, towards the choir stalls facing each other at the far end, and the air was thick with smells Judith recognised from other occasions when she'd been in a church. Wax candles, old hymn books. A hint of lilies, perhaps.

'You're joining a wonderful group of people,' Lawrence was saying. 'And we're very lucky, of course, with the organ.' He glanced up towards

3

the organ loft as he spoke, and his last words were caught by the acoustic, echoing back from the gilded ceiling. The building, Judith thought, was flaunting itself. Doubt surged again, more sickly than before.

'Lucky with the architect, too,' said Cressida. 'Adam at his best. A late gem.'

She might have said more, Judith thought, but just then the door opened to admit a squarely built, red-haired boy wearing a No Fear T-shirt and faded jeans.

'Hello,' he said. 'Am I last?'

'Not quite,' said Lawrence, as the boy shook his hand. 'Do you know . . .?'

'I've met Cressida,' he said. 'But we haven't . . . I'm Bill.'

'Stephen,' said the tall boy. 'I'm a late recruit.'

'And . . .' Bill turned towards Judith, and then he paused, the momentum of his arrival halted for the first time. The sickness in Judith's stomach curdled, twisting into something both familiar and entirely unrecognisable. Bill was smiling at her, a wide grin that seemed to take in the whole group, the whole occasion, and at the same time to be directed exclusively at her. He was so full of geniality as to be almost hateful, she thought, one of those cocksure musicians who don't even realise they're . . . but there was another feeling rising inside her too, altering the light.

'I'm Judith,' she said. 'Hello.'

'It's very nice to meet you.' Bill hesitated for a moment, appraising her, and Judith was grateful she'd got the words out before they dried in her chest. 'Are you –' he began: but then someone else was bursting through the door.

'Ah!' said Lawrence. 'Marmion, welcome!'

'Sorry.' The girl called Marmion grinned apologetically, clattering towards them across the marble floor. Judith recognised her: she was the kind of person who stood out in a crowd without meaning to, her face beaming in the centre of the Fresher's photo, carrying across the

4

bar above the beer and the shouting. 'I'm so sorry. I was with my tutor. I lost track of the time.'

'Never mind,' said Lawrence. 'You're here now.'

As he made the next round of introductions, Judith looked back at Bill, with a tiny dart of anticipation about meeting his gaze again. But his smile had moved on to Marmion: not the same kind of smile, not at all, but even so Judith felt a shock of betrayal. Ludicrous, she told herself. Ludicrous. When Lawrence gestured them towards the choir stalls, she hesitated before following Bill and Marmion. Two wholesome people, she thought, chattering away in the way people who have things in common do; people who recognise themselves as part of the same tribe.

But after a few yards, Bill glanced back.

'Judith,' he said, 'Marmion says you play the flute.'

'Your room's above mine,' Marmion said. 'I heard you playing last night. *Syrinx*, I think. Was it *Syrinx*?'

'Possibly.' Judith forced a smile, avoiding Bill's eyes.

'I do too,' Bill said. 'We could play duets.'

'Possibly,' Judith said again. 'My flute needs a service, though. The keys are sticking.'

Bill looked at her for a moment, one eyebrow lifting almost imperceptibly, and Judith felt a flush filling her cheeks. Shit: what was she doing? What could she possibly want with someone like Bill – or with the chapel choir? Perhaps she should cut and run. There was so much else on offer in Cambridge; so many people.

But the others were in the choir stalls now, and Judith found herself following. Her arm brushed against Bill's as she took her place, and she was absurdly conscious of it, of the prickle of excitement that seemed to fast-circuit from her skin to her belly. She kept her eyes on the folder of music in front of her, the fall of light from the tall windows that straked the floor with bright narrow lines.

'Ah, good!' Lawrence said, as the door opened once again. 'Ladies and gentlemen, can I introduce Deep Patel, our organ scholar?'

Patel, Judith thought. So she wasn't the only … but she hated herself for the thought. That wasn't her tribe either. She didn't have a tribe. Deep looked nice, though, slight and shy and quick-gestured. He darted up the chapel to say hello, then whisked away towards the organ loft. After a moment they heard the faint wheeze of air in the pipes, then a declamatory arpeggio.

'Let's start with a hymn,' Lawrence said. 'Number 137, please.'

And then Deep was playing the introduction, and they were all singing, and the sudden shock of the sound made every hair on Judith's body stand on end. Only five of them, but they filled the chapel, flaunting themselves back to that big-hearted acoustic. Beside her, Bill's rich tenor soared up to the high notes, and she revelled in the pleasure of it: the chaste, suggestive pleasure of singing together.

This was something worth having, she thought. This was something she could do. Perhaps she wouldn't run away just yet. But, she promised herself, she would resist whatever it was that Bill kindled in her. Plenty of fish in the sea, as her father would say: why choose one who disconcerted her so much? Why deny herself the delicious, tantalising diversion of pretending she didn't care?

Part I

June 1995
Marmion

From the bath, Marmion could see the fells through the window, dazzlingly vivid in the sunlight. They looked grander than they had last night, when they'd all surveyed the view for the first time in the soft haze of dusk – although that had been a magical moment, standing together on the terrace after their long, long journey and gazing out at the valley, not being quite sure what was empty space and what solid rock, or whether the glints of silver were stars poised above the tops or moonlight caught in the tumble of a waterfall. An enchanted landscape, she'd thought then: the kind where dragons might lurk. Where anything might happen in the fold of a hill or the tangle of a thorn bush.

Closing her eyes, she let her mind fill with the joy of the moment. The shapes and colours of the fells beneath the placid blue of the sky, and nearer at hand the smell of frying bacon mingling with the astringent scent of Fay's bath salts; the plain white tiles, soft with steam, and the voices of the others in the kitchen. Even the chipped edges of the old-fashioned bath and the whale song of the pipes, which you could hear when you ducked your head underwater, as though the house had a language of its own and would share its secrets if you knew how to listen.

It all represented, she thought, both the pleasure of this particular day and the more nebulous and enchanting possibilities that lay beyond it. In this wide landscape she could see the world opening its arms, the breathtaking sweep of adulthood laid before them. Wriggling her toes in the warm water (not much of it: High Scarp's plumbing arrangements were not among its chief strengths), Marmion felt a wash of gratitude to Fay, who had already done so much for them all, and had now laid this new gift at their feet.

The invitation had first been mentioned several months ago, when life beyond Finals had seemed impossibly distant. The timing was perfect, Fay had said, since the little music festival in Griseley fell between May Week and graduation, and a few days away from Cambridge would be just what they all needed by then. Marmion didn't remember it being mentioned again, but two weeks ago Fay had produced a programme for the festival, and there had been, then, a little jolt of guilt because they'd almost forgotten about it in their preoccupation with exams and celebrations.

When it came to it, none of them had been as keen to leave Cambridge as Fay had predicted, and the journey had seemed endless – almost a whole day, driving up the A1 and across the A66, the five of them and Fay crammed into her old Volvo with their luggage, and Marmion, for one, feeling too sick to enjoy the views as the flat plains of Lincolnshire gave way to Yorkshire and the Dales. But there had been an irresistible drama to the final approach, the fells looming up on either side, the trailing lines of dry-stone walls, the glimpses of lakes and tarns and then the final steep climb to High Scarp – which was, as its name suggested, built on the side of a mountain – a fell, rather – above the village of Griseley and the shores of Ullswater, in a wilderness of gorse and sheep and soaring heights.

None of them had been to the Lake District before, and as they stood on the terrace yesterday evening it had felt like a revelation. They'd shared in a smug kind of pleasure, Marmion thought, as if this was a reward they had earned: not just by enduring the car journey, by surviving all those exams, but by honouring the friendship Fay had offered them. But she felt a dart of conscience, now, as she gripped the curved enamel rim and heaved herself out of the bath. This was a blessing bestowed rather than merited, she told herself firmly. She mustn't take the delights in store for granted.

The towels were plentiful, but of the flimsy, well-washed variety, and not quite big enough for any combination of them to cover her properly. As she rubbed her hair, she caught sight of herself in the long, thin mirror on the back of the door. Designed for Fay, she thought. Marmion was almost as tall as Fay, but differently constructed: no sparing of materials, her father used to say when she was a little girl. For a moment she stared at her reflection, the collage of pink flesh and white towel undeniably erotic, with tendrils of hair falling damply over her shoulders. It wasn't Quakerly, she knew, to admire herself, but surely it was a good thing to be happy with the form she'd been blessed with: to be happier with it than she'd been as a teenager. She had Bill to thank for that. Smiling, she rearranged the towels around her hips and emerged into the corridor.

As she passed the kitchen, she could hear a babble of good-humoured banter. It showed how well they knew each other, Marmion thought, that she could tell through a closed door not only who was speaking, but what the expressions on their faces were, and indeed – within a whisker – what they were going to say next. Their catchphrases, at least: Bill's 'quite', amused or terse or approving as the situation required, and Cressida's colourful exclamations of disbelief, and Judith's profanities, which Marmion was used to by now but which still raised a frisson sometimes. And Stephen's deadpan contributions, hard to place between the philosophical and the utterly practical. 'That's an interesting way to toast bread,' Marmion heard him say now, and then there was Cressida's loud flusterment as she retrieved a slice that had evidently caught fire, and the running of a tap, and the peaty smell of doused charcoal. 'How did that happen?' wailed Cressida's voice. 'Please don't tell Fay: I can't believe I've burned it all.'

They had met Fay soon after they'd arrived at St Anne's, a new cohort of choral scholars for the chapel choir. Two men and three women, surprised to find themselves elevated to those adult titles from the girls and boys who had left school a few months before. Marmion was an alto, Judith and Cressida sopranos, the three of them as different, at first glance, as it was possible to imagine. Cressida was small and slight and fair, the product of a famous girls' boarding school who'd grown up with horses and brothers in the Home Counties. Judith – a Jewish Hindu atheist, as she called herself – was the only daughter of two doctors from Bristol, strikingly beautiful and ferociously strong-minded. The men were unalike too: easy-going, ginger-haired Bill, whose parents ran a small hotel on the outskirts of Birmingham, and Stephen, tall and gangling and less at ease with himself than the others, who had rarely spoken of his family since that evening in their first week when they'd all talked about home and he'd revealed, in an uncharacteristic confiding rush, that he was adopted, and had a brother who was severely disabled – as though he wanted them all to know that much, and to understand that those topics were off limits thereafter.

None of them, anyway, remotely resembled anyone Marmion had met at her North London comprehensive, where her placid Quakerism had made her an oddity even among the ethnic and social mix of her classmates. None of them remotely resembled her family, either, which came as more of a surprise. Marmion had imagined Cambridge as a world full of Hayters, earnestly committed to a life of intellect and art.

But they had got along from the start, the five of them. A motley crew, Fay had called them, when she'd invited them to dinner a couple of weeks into their first term. It seemed aeons ago now, that time when they were still getting to know each other. Fay had some connection to St Anne's, and to the choir – she often came to evensong, and had a seat reserved for her at concerts and carol services. But she had taken a particular interest in their little group. She'd adopted them, people said, sometimes enviously – because there were certainly benefits to Fay's friendship. She had a beautiful house in Newnham, and membership at Glyndebourne. And she was interesting, too. Fascinating, at least in the sense of being a puzzle. She wasn't well-preserved in the conventional sense – her hair was being allowed to go grey without resistance, and she rarely wore make-up or jewellery – but it was obvious that she had once been beautiful, and when you saw that, you had to admit that she still was.

As to who she was, that was less easy to tell. She hinted at having been a professional musician, but none of them had ever found any record of her career. She sometimes mentioned business commitments, but they never saw her occupied with them. She seemed to be alone in the world, but she often spoke as if there were other people in the shadows, an extended family of ghostly siblings and cousins and retainers who filled the house when they weren't there. Her generosity was lavish, but every time they began to be sure of their importance to her, there would be a casual reference to other calls on her time that made it clear they weren't by any means at the centre of her world. And then, as graduation approached and they could feel their association with Fay waning, the trip to High Scarp had been proposed, and they had understood that the invitation was a compliment she rarely extended, an honour they couldn't refuse.

Fay herself was both the same and different up here, Marmion thought, crossing the garden now to the wooden outhouse where she and Bill were sleeping. Her hair was swept up in the same unfashionable bun she wore in Cambridge, and the colour and style of her clothes was the same, although the skirts had turned into trousers for Cumbria and a thick jumper had replaced the famous long grey cardigan. It was as though someone had designed her, an art director in a theatre or an opera house, with wardrobes for town and country. A Britten opera, perhaps. The powerful matriarch without a family to rule over.

That thought made Marmion smile: it was the kind of thing Bill would say, she thought. Well, perhaps after three years you did start to think like each other. She let herself imagine Bill saying those words and looking at her with a grin that suggested he saw her as a different kind of matriarch: a happier and more fruitful one. She halted for a moment to enjoy the view, and to savour her own good fortune.

*

The atmosphere in the kitchen owed as much, Bill thought, to the four people crammed into it as to the efforts of the elderly range. The window had long since steamed up, and the smell of bacon and toast was making his stomach rumble pleasurably.

'Plate,' said Judith, and he grabbed a dish from the table and held it out to receive fried eggs from the pan. There was a sizzle of fat, a flare of steam in their faces. Judith smiled, nudging a lock of hair off her cheek, as he slid the plate into the oven. 'Good boy.'

'At your service.'

This was fun, Bill thought. At home, the hotel kitchen was out of bounds, and in the family's poky little kitchenette cooking was a chore, not a pleasure.

Cressida, flushed with heat and exertion, thrust a handful of cutlery at him.

'The table needs laying,' she said.

'Right-oh.' Bill saluted, suppressing the unreasonable feeling that he liked being bossed about by Cressida less than by Judith, and pushed through the door to the dining room.

This was the nicest room in the house, he thought, as he set the silverware down. It doubled as sitting room and dining room, and apart from the long table which ran beneath the window, there were several shapeless chairs and sofas, grouped around the wide hearth, and a rather battered piano. Everything about High Scarp spoke of a long history in the same clan: the once-elegant china that was stained and crazed with age; the black-and-white photographs on the walls; the antique radiators that were never more than lukewarm, despite the chill of the summer nights. The traditions of the place were clearly long-established too – the ancient walkers' maps, and all the music in the village church that High Scarp visitors had contributed to over the years. *We always*, Fay kept saying. Bill liked the sense that they were part of a pattern.

He looked out of the window, letting his gaze roam over the hills and the serene blue of the sky above. A feeling he'd first noticed a day or two ago gathered in his belly: a tightness, a density, that might be pleasure or pain. He was filled with an inexplicable mixture of contentment and impatience – as though he wanted to prolong this moment, this weekend, forever, but also to seize what it held for him and devour it in a greedy rush. That landscape, he thought – that great empty space out there – was all his, just now. Everything was possible. Anything he might want.

That thought caused a lurch of uncertainty. *Anything he might want.* Was that really true? In his mind's eye he saw the sheen of sweat on Judith's neck, the sudden flash of her smile, and something else stirred in his memory. Buried deep beneath the rich silt of the last three years there was another image he had never quite forgotten. His first sight of Judith, that day in the chapel. Her fierce, see-if-I-care gaze, and the sense he'd had ... No, it was impossible to be sure, now, what he'd thought or felt back then. It was impossible to untangle the threads of the years that had followed, the way their paths had all unfolded. But as his eyes swept down across the garden to the fells and the sky beyond, there was another lurch in his stomach. Marmion was standing on the lawn wrapped in a towel, staring out at the same view as him, with her head lifted to the early-morning sunshine.

*

Gazing out at the valley, Marmion wondered whether you'd ever get used to this scenery if you lived up here: to living among hills rather than people. This valley must be almost the same size as her corner of

London, the densely packed streets between Crouch End and Archway, and there seemed to be absolutely no one else in it this morning.

But as she scanned the distant fells for the moving dots of walkers she caught a glimpse of someone much closer at hand, down in the lower part of the garden. Not exactly hiding, but – lurking, she thought. A hiker, perhaps, who had strayed in through the gate? But as she watched, the figure moved, and she saw that it was Fay. Unmistakably Fay, who had every right to lurk in her own garden, of course, but even so Marmion felt a flicker of unease. Something about Fay's stance, the way she lifted her hands now to cover her eyes, seemed odd. Had Fay seen her? Was she all right? For a moment longer Marmion hesitated, then she pulled the towels more tightly around her and hurried on towards the cabin with the disconcerting sense that she'd been caught spying.

She dressed quickly, impatient now to be with the others again. When she came into the house, Fay was standing in the hall beside the phone.

'Hello,' Marmion said brightly. 'What a beautiful morning.'

Fay smiled in an unfamiliar way: a little distant, as though she was disappointed by something. *Had* Fay seen her, then, out in the garden? Had she thought . . . Marmion felt a flush around her ears. She was being idiotic, surely; imagining things. But she was grateful when the others appeared, their noise and bustle filling the little gap of awkwardness.

'This bacon looks delectable,' Stephen was saying, and behind him Bill raised his eyebrows and said, 'Ah! Is madam ready for her breakfast?'

Marmion mimed guilt. 'I'm completely ravenous,' she said. 'I've been smelling it for the last half an hour. What marvellous people you are.'

And then, as they found their places around the table, there was a sudden moment of silence – the result of chance, not intention, Marmion thought, but even so it seemed to fall upon them like a gift. At home, this would have been the moment for the Quaker form of grace – a few minutes of quiet thankfulness – and she shut her eyes and reached for that sense of calm and sanctity she had been used to having within her grasp her whole life.

When she opened them again, she smiled at Fay across the table. It was too nice here to let shadows trouble her. But in the moment she held Fay's gaze, it occurred to her to wonder what Fay might expect of them all after they graduated this summer, when what they'd offered her until now – a share in the closed world of the choir and their undergraduate life – was over. It occurred to her to wonder whether this trip was supposed to signal a reckoning of some kind.

September 2015
Stephen

Stephen Evans sat at his desk, sifting papers. He was conscious that his mind wasn't entirely on the task in hand – a rare occurrence, but it didn't much trouble him. There was time enough before Monday to address the few issues in this sheaf of documents that required some thought. He liked to have a teaser or two at the back of his mind: the mental equivalent of a chewing-gum habit, he thought. Certainly the question of alternative financing models for the Balkan consortium would be good fodder for motorway driving. He glanced at the clock, then shut his briefcase.

His PA looked up as he passed. 'Off now?' she asked. 'Do you need me to print out the route for you?'

'I know the way,' he said. 'From years ago.'

'Fell-walking?'

'A bit of singing, too.' Stephen smiled briefly. 'I'd prefer not to be called, this weekend.'

Jenny nodded, her eyes lingering on him for a moment before her attention returned to her computer.

Stephen had developed the habit of representing his past as a series of facts and anecdotes that he produced at apposite moments, like scout badges or souvenir pins. There was his adoption, his humble upbringing, his brother. There was his Cambridge educa-tion, and an occasional tantalising refe-rence to his life as a choral scholar. There was the period in the Middle East, the immersion in Arabic and Islam and the upper echelons of society in the Gulf States; the MBA at Stanford and the spell in Silicon Valley; the dot-com years in India. The story was never spun out as a narrative

18

whole: just the relevant credential, the apt reference, to advance his case or to throw an adversary off course, or simply to amuse. He was, people said, a likeable man – he knew that that was his reputation. In certain circles he was known as a competent tennis player, and as a jazz enthusiast who still, very occasionally, played the trumpet in a pick-up band. He knew he mystified people, though. He didn't set out to be a puzzle, but neither did he trouble to explain himself. Not for him the profile in the weekend broadsheet or the financial press: never the spinning out of a drink in a hotel bar into confessional territory.

These days, what perplexed people most was that he showed so little interest in the trappings of achievement, and that he had never repeated the early, unsuccessful experiment in matrimony. There was a modest-sized flat in a far-from-modest building in Kensington, but no manorial pile in the Cotswolds nor chalet in Verbier. There was a nice car, but only one. He was regarded as an ascetic, and he was happy to endorse that impression. It was true that his emotional life was carefully controlled, his passions most likely to find expression in an overhead smash or a jazz riff. Or in the boardroom, of course. The thrill of drawing together the threads of a deal, or getting to grips with a new market, never palled.

He told himself it was a logical choice he'd made; that putting his professional life first accounted for the sparseness of his personal life, and that he was happy to pay that price. But it wasn't that simple, of course. It was neither entirely true that he was an ascetic, nor entirely true that he'd made a choice. Circumstances, timing, context – those things weren't all within his control. The cards had fallen in certain ways: everyone could say that, presumably. He had lived for so long in the Middle East that self-discipline had become a virtue, but it had always come easily to him. He'd always liked his own company.

He was glad, though, that the matrimonial experiment had taken place. Suky was still important to him. He hadn't been rich when they were married, but he'd been generous afterwards, and she'd been grateful. She had a husband and a child now, and a flourishing psychotherapeutic practice, but she repaid his liberality – and his affection – by finding time for him when he asked. A civilised arrangement, Stephen thought, as he collected his car from the underground garage and pointed it towards Regent Street, and thence the west. Suky was by no means the least of the reasons he was glad to be back in London for the time being. He was sorry that she'd been on holiday for the last few weeks, so that he hadn't been able to talk to her about this High Scarp business. Should I go? he might have asked her. Is it the right thing to do?

Suky knew most of the narrative that filled the gaps between the scout badges: she would have advised, inferred – understood. Though not everything. Not the close bonds, back in Cambridge, and the intensity of it all. No, certainly not everything.

He'd left the office early enough to be ahead of the rush hour, but even so the queues heading out of London were heavy. Unfazed, Stephen studied the imposing Victorian façades along the Marylebone Road. Another thing people might find surprising, he thought, was his patience in the face of wasted time – or what many of his colleagues would see as wasted time. Perhaps it was all those years living in places where time operated in a different fashion to the what's-next English-speaking culture; where there was a more graceful, a more ritualistic rhythm even to business life. Certainly he'd lived in many cities where the traffic was worse than London, and he hadn't been back long enough yet to be inured to the capital's charms. Crawling towards the Westway, he counted up the years. It was well over a decade since he'd spent more than a month in the UK. The next thought came unbidden: his mother had still been alive then, and now even his brother was dead. Robert had hardly been a bulwark, of course, but he had been an anchor, something to tie him to England.

Stephen caught a strain, then, of an emotion that had haunted him recently: a yearning he hadn't felt in all those years abroad. It was more complicated, being home. It raised expectations, exposed illusions. He'd made a virtue of fitting in where he didn't belong, all over the world, but being back here begged questions he'd rather have avoided. *Was* this home – England, London, the penthouse flat that had sat empty for so long that it looked more like a rented pied-à-terre than a welcoming hearth? Where did he belong, after all?

He wondered, as the traffic accelerated at last, whether he was going to High Scarp in search of answers. One particular question still lurked in his mind, of course – but there were others, too. Did he imagine the weekend would satisfy a curiosity he hardly knew he had? Did he really think he'd have more in common with his long-ago friends than with the sharp-eyed divorcees who roped him into mixed doubles, or the dyed-in-the-wool City types who filled London's boardrooms? Three years of singing Howells and Tallis together, peppering their conversation with lines from the psalms, seemed a flimsy basis for intimacy, two decades later, with people whose lives he knew nothing of, and from whom he'd parted in such uncomfortable circumstances.

Shielding his eyes against a shaft of late-afternoon sun, Stephen frowned. It was unlike him to be susceptible to sentiment, he thought. He was usually more suspicious, more scrupulous about his motives. Was it a mistake, this trip?

Well, he was going, anyway. Driving all that way on a Friday evening. Let it be a pilgrimage, an *hommage* to the past, and let the sacrifice of time and effort be part of it. He could have taken a train or a plane, could have hired a chauffeur or even a helicopter, but if he was going, he was going under his own steam. He liked the idea of arriving late, by moonlight: he remembered how wonderful the stars had been up there.

June 1995

Marmion

The little church felt cool and hushed after the open spaces of the fells. They had it to themselves this morning: they'd been allocated two hours of rehearsal time to get used to the acoustic and finalise their programme before the opening concert of the music festival tonight.

'Ha!' Bill sang out, as he walked up the aisle; and then, as the echo died away: 'Nice acoustic. Good solid walls.'

The others followed, laughing at some quip of Judith's, their voices rising like bursting bubbles through the still air. It was odd, Marmion thought – endearing, but strange to her – that their first reaction when they came into a quiet space was always to make a noise. To fill it with themselves, rather than letting it fill them.

Far above, the roof was braced by thick rafters, and near the door hung two large banners made by local schoolchildren. She liked this church, Marmion thought. Liked it better than city churches with their gilt and incense. She felt a hum of pleasure in her chest as she caught up with her friends, her footsteps soft on the old stone.

The five of them arranged themselves in a semicircle below the altar rail. Judith, Cressy, Marmion, Bill, Stephen: sop, sop, alto, tenor, bass.

'Byrd first, or Bruckner?' Bill squatted in front of the box he'd carried down from the cottage, humming as he sorted the music into piles. He'd been singing this repertoire longer than any of them, having started at the age of eight as a chorister at Birmingham Cathedral, and he still slipped across to the treble part from time to time, soaring up to enjoy the top notes in his piercing falsetto.

Although they'd both grown up steeped in music, Bill was in many ways an unlikely partner for her, Marmion thought. He was handsome, in a boyish, twinkly, teasing way, as well as being the choir's star tenor: she still couldn't quite believe that he'd chosen her rather than Judith or Cressida or any other girl in the world. His sense of humour still surprised her sometimes – that flippancy that was unexpected in someone who was otherwise kind and reliable and serious-minded. But it was good for her, she knew, to have fun poked at her. It gave her a little thrill of pleasure and possession, making her think of the other things they shared. Things she probably shouldn't think about in a church.

'Which Bruckner?' asked Judith. '"*Locus iste*", I suppose?'

'That seems pretty apt,' said Stephen. 'This place was made by God.'

'An inestimable mystery, beyond reproach,' said Bill. 'Just like you, Judith. But God is fairly central to our repertoire, I fear.'

'I don't object to God,' said Judith. 'I like his music, anyway.'

'Good-oh.' Bill grinned in his characteristic way, as though he could barely suppress his high spirits. 'Ah, but maybe something else to kick off with . . .'

Judith and God was a running gag. Of all the places for her to end up, she often said, a Christian choir was the last you'd expect for the daughter of a Jewish mother and a Hindu father. A chapel choir was a strange place for a Quaker, too, but Marmion was used to the idea that music got everywhere in life. Early on she'd tried to probe Judith about the traditions she'd grown up with, and how her parents had reconciled their beliefs, but Judith had laughed. 'Medicine is what my parents have in common,' she'd said: 'medicine and me. The rest of it doesn't worry them.'

Not much seemed to worry Judith, either. She was blessed with apparently unassailable self-confidence and quite enough brains and beauty to live up to it. *Hybrid vigour* was another of her favourite phrases: Marmion, who'd been brought up to value diversity, was awed by the richness of Judith's cultural heritage. She had relatives in Tel Aviv and Delhi, and she talked about her travels in the Middle

East and the Indian subcontinent as though they were no more exotic than the Hayters' family holidays on the Isle of Wight. If the absence of God from Judith's life didn't trouble her, Marmion thought, it was perhaps because the promise of this life was plenty to be going on with. She would make a wonderful lawyer, with her quick wits and her feisty determination. But she was also generous with her time and her vivacity, and when she paid attention to you it felt like a blessing.

That made things harder for Cressida, Marmion thought now, as Bill handed round the first sheaf of music. There were several sides to Cressy, not all of them easy to live with. There was Cressy the private-school girl, who understood a certain order of things – moral and intellectual as well as social – and held fast to it. There was Cressy the girlish waif, sweetly pretty and perfectly designed to encourage the protective instincts of men. Women often disliked that Cressida, although Marmion could already see that she had the kind of prettiness you needed to capitalise on before it faded, and that Judith's looks would last much longer. And then there was Cressy the English student, astonishingly well read and deadly serious in her academic aspirations.

Marmion was studying for a degree in music – what else would the daughter of two professional musicians do, armed with a string of Grade 8 distinctions and a just-passable collection of A levels? – but Cressy's knowledge of music as a cultural phenomenon, of the overlaps with literature and art and social history, was vastly greater than hers. She could ignite a spark of interest with a chance remark and follow it through with a dazzle of detail. When 'The Lamb' appeared on the service sheet at Advent, Cressy had talked, on the way over to chapel one evening, about how John Tavener's twentieth-century spirituality related to William Blake's, two hundred years ago. After that Marmion had sung '*Little lamb, who made thee?*' with the pleasing sense that she'd grasped something complex and satisfying.

Cressida, of course, was staying on in Cambridge next year to do an MPhil, and looking at her now as she inspected the stained glass windows Marmion felt an unexpected pang of envy: a sudden sorrow for the changes ahead, the end of this carefree era. Had the rest of them ignored that fact as recklessly, as determinedly, as she had?

*

Staring up at the wonderful glass, Cressida was conscious of a familiar sense of surprise, even anguish, at the way everything was so compromised by the banality of life. Things like art and poetry, and the fine threads of emotion you could draw from them, ought to illuminate human existence – but it was so hard to find any objective correlative, in real life, for the purity of feeling that art and poetry inspired. Not that she meant – oh, human feelings were real enough, and strong enough, of course. Not just hers: she didn't need her friends to rhapsodise over a rock or a tree, or even a stained glass window, to prove that they felt things deeply.

No, it was more the pattern of things: wanting to believe that there *was* some pattern, some point, to the great billowings of passion that art inspired. Poetry didn't require love to be requited, of course, but it led you to believe there was some purpose to it; some lesson to draw, or higher plane to perceive. There was a terrible amount of waste in human life, in Cressida's view. Wasted emotion. Wasted suffering that had no benefit, no rationale.

She was thinking, of course – she hated to be so blunt, even in her private mind – of Stephen: of her and Stephen.

With only the five of them singing, she and Stephen would be close enough to touch all weekend, a fact which both delighted and tortured her. Not that it was simply . . . It was impossible to tease out the physical from the intellectual, she thought. Stephen's awkward, mobile face, with that long nose and high cheekbones, but also the light that came into his eyes sometimes when he spoke – and the things he said, cleverer and more tantalising than any of the others. The way his body was

26

a secondary thing, a container for his mind, but also gave him pleasure – and her, too. Taking her breathlessly by surprise by running up a hill, or cocking a cigarette from a packet with such careless grace. Smoking at all, when he was otherwise so measured, so controlled.

Oh, there was plenty of objective correlative for her infatuation (a painful word, but she insisted on it). There had never been another man to match him, despite all her efforts to divert her affections. But what was the point of it? And what, more troublingly, was the point of his resistance? *Was* it resistance, or simply ignorance, or reticence, or uncertainty? What would happen if she seized her courage and . . .?

Being up here, away from the place where they'd been familiar friends, might help him to see things differently, Cressida thought – as might the sense that there was an open door ahead. Men his age preferred to have an escape route clearly in view, she knew that, and she didn't mind. It was the intensity of intimacy she craved. She didn't want to possess Stephen in the way Marmion possessed Bill. She could see how dulling constancy might be – and even if there was a niggle of self-deception in that thought, she certainly understood quite clearly that continuity was a different matter, an entirely different matter, from the sublime moment. She understood, for example, that the continuity of Marmion and Bill's relationship was a different matter for each of them.

She looked at Marmion now, a smile on her round, open-featured face. Had Marmion seen the way Bill looked at Judith sometimes? she wondered. Was her childlike belief in happy-ever-after justified, or did her serenity derive from a higher, a more reliable, source than that?

*

'Are you with us, Marmion?' asked Bill.

'Sorry.' Marmion smiled, dragging her attention back to the moment. 'What are we starting with?'

Bill skipped across to the piano and played a sequence of four notes. Marmion recognised the opening phrase of the Walford Davies setting of Psalm 121.

'Good,' she said. 'That's a good way to begin.'

Turning back from the piano, Bill raised one finger to bring them in.

I will lift up mine eyes unto the hills: from whence cometh my help.

The chant was simple, filled with a joyous assurance that always felt like a salve to the soul. Their voices resonated together, five parts moulding into a glowing whole. Marmion could feel the music washing through them and rising through dust and sunlight to the distant rafters, banishing the flutters of doubt that had assailed her earlier, the whispers of anxiety and self-consciousness.

My help cometh even from the Lord: who hath made heaven and earth.
He will not suffer thy foot to be moved: and he that keepeth thee will not sleep.

Wonderful, Marmion thought, as they reached the last line and began on the Gloria. If there was any need to justify her affection for the Anglican liturgy, let it be because of the psalms, the pleasure of bringing this ancient poetry to life. Looking round at the faces of her friends, she thought that the thrill of singing with this group of people would never leave her. Making something together, she thought in a moment of startling clarity, in the same way as sex, and with the same effect of rendering you completely alive.

September 2015
Judith

Judith was keen on trains, not just for ecological reasons but because she found them – even the fraying, fetid variety that still ran on some lines – inexplicably exciting. And quick, if you were going a long way. Less than three hours from Euston to Oxenholme, and then a taxi at the other end to whisk her up to Griseley. Perfect. Let lesser mortals stew in the weekend traffic on the M6 while she sat in her window seat and enjoyed the view.

But even as the train pulled noiselessly out of the station, a glimmer of doubt began to filter through her jubilation. She'd focused on the practical arrangements, of course, in order to maintain a degree of ironic detachment about the purpose of this weekend. There was no getting round the fact that this was a very odd thing to be doing: going to meet her closest friends from university – none of whom she'd seen for donkey's years – because the older woman who'd taken an interest in them all twenty years ago had left her house in the Lake District to them in her will. And left it wrapped in a complicated legal bow whose details were to be revealed, in suitably melodramatic fashion, when they had all gathered in the house again. However you looked at it, this wasn't exactly a weekend mini-break without strings.

As the outskirts of London swept past, Judith pondered. Her view of the past was shrouded by something rather more heavy-duty than ironic detachment, but she prided herself on her ability to see almost anything clearly when she put her mind to it. Start with Fay, then. It was because of Fay that she was on this train, after all.

Fay had known there were good reasons why they'd all lost touch. Indisputable reasons. Was it really possible that she'd had no one else to leave High Scarp to? No nieces or nephews; no other students she'd got to know in the decades since they'd left Cambridge? Were they supposed to feel guilty about neglecting her all this time? Judith hadn't thought about that before – not that she'd thought about any of it more than she could help. Not at the time, when ploughing on with her life had seemed the only way forward, and not later, when Cambridge, Cumbria and the collective consciousness of the choir had been at a safer distance. Even Bill – she'd buried all that, as well as she could, and as for the rest . . .

She leant her head back against the seat, conjuring up Fay's face, and that rather deep voice. *Have you forgotten?* Judith heard her say, with a twitch of a smile. *Have you forgiven yourselves?*

Was it fanciful to imagine Fay as a kind of Svengali figure? To recall a sinister shadow about her? She'd been generous almost to the point of embarrassment, for the three years they'd known her, with barely a hint of expectation to accompany her largesse. But there had been twinges of discomfort that last summer, Judith remembered. Moments when things hadn't made sense, or the familiar order had felt unsettled. Had she read too much into them, then, or too little? And what on earth might Fay have in store for them all at High Scarp this weekend?

Them. The *them* she hadn't considered properly for years. That was the real thing, of course.

She was curious, Judith admitted. Almost ghoulishly curious, now, to see what they'd be like, and what they'd make of each other. She'd done a bit of ferreting, but only half-heartedly. The things she really wanted to know, really dreaded finding out, were impossible to discover on the Internet.

'Hello, Judith,' said someone.

Judith turned to find a man smiling at her from the aisle. For a wild moment she thought it might be Bill, swimming out of her thoughts and into fleshly form, but only for a moment.

'Hello,' she said.

'It is Judith, isn't it? Judith Malik?'

'Absolutely.' She smiled, half her mind still elsewhere. She couldn't remember his name, this man, but she had a fair idea where she'd seen him before. A conference hotel near Peterborough, about a year ago. 'How are you? Off for the weekend somewhere?'

'I live in Preston,' he said.

'Oh, right.'

'Are you heading that way?' His smile was more hopeful than she liked.

'The Lakes,' said Judith. 'Staying with friends.'

The woman opposite was following this exchange with an active attention which was presumably justified by the sign on the window that read: *Quiet Carriage*. Seeing a way out, Judith nodded at it with a shrugging, regretful smile.

'I'm off to the buffet car,' he said.

Judith nodded again; and then, to make it clear that she had no need of the buffet car, she opened the lurid bottle of juice she'd bought in Pret at Euston and took a tentative sip.

With a final wistful smile, the man ambled off, leaving Judith conscious of a blush about her cheekbones. The juice was disgusting. She stuffed it back into her briefcase. This wasn't the weekend for purgatorial health fads – nor, indeed, for additional complications of any kind. Damn the interfering tentacles of coincidence.

The irony was that Preston Man was the only indiscretion she'd had for years. But getting by, as she did, on a somewhat unorthodox set of arrangements, the odd dash of novelty was tempting. She wasn't old enough yet for such things to be undignified, she told herself, and she wasn't answerable to anything beyond her own liberal sense of propriety. She held fast to that mantra, despite the occasional flashes of a morality more conventional than she liked to accord herself; the occasional glimpses of a life in which she was safely tucked up with the same man every night.

Instead she had two men, neither of them exactly safe and each with a wife of his own to be tucked up with at night. Arvind was a colleague – a member of her chambers, several years her junior – and Jonty had been a client. That was the risqué part; that and the wives. But both had their merits as bed-mates and companions, and Judith had known all along what the score was with each. It might look as though she'd drawn two short straws, but it suited her not to be properly spoken for: if she needed proof of the satisfactoriness of her sex life, surely it was that Preston Man and his ilk were a rare diversion. But it was unsettling, even so, to have them appearing unsummoned from the ether, especially just now. It seemed to raise questions, to draw attention to things that would be better kept submerged this weekend.

Judith sighed. God, three hours was a long time to spend on a train, especially one that leant and weaved like this so you couldn't forget you were hurtling towards a destination you'd tried hard to forget. Staring out of the window at a cine roll of twenty-first-century Britain, she told herself that she wasn't going to let the past ambush her. She was neither victim nor transgressor, and she wasn't in thrall to anyone. Not even to herself.

June 1995
Marmion

Fay had laid out lunch on the terrace when they got back from the church: plates of cheese and cold meat, jars of pickle, a basket of bread and two bowls of salad. She'd always been the master of effortless catering, Marmion thought. All those meals – the summer picnics and winter stews and set-piece fondues, with molten cheese drawn out in strings across the table and candles flickering among the bowls of roses. All those happy times Fay had given them.

'Thou shalt prepare a table before me,' said Bill. 'We shall all be fat upon earth indeed.'

Fay smiled. 'How was St Cuthbert's?'

'We liked the windows,' said Cressida.

Marmion grinned. Cressida had explained the stained glass to them after the rehearsal: the three windows designed by a local artist which showed Christ preaching in the valley, blessing the flock, baptising in the lake. Marmion felt a Quakerly squirm of discomfort about iconography, but these images were heartfelt, designed to show God among ordinary people, not to scare them with His grandeur. Although up here, stained glass was hardly necessary. The fells spoke for God, in her view.

For an hour or so they all sat around the wooden table, amusing each other with anecdote and reflection and teasing, watched benignly by Fay. The shadows of the morning seemed now like a figment of Marmion's imagination. Bill sat opposite her, and Marmion basked in the knowledge that she could lift her eyes to his face any time she wanted; that he was just there, just a few feet away. As were the others, of course. It had always been hard to disentangle the specific, sharp joy of her relationship with Bill from the pleasure of the group and their shared friendship. Part of knowing Bill so well was seeing him in different contexts: not just alone but in the choir, among their friends, and even, a couple of times, at home.

Bill's family was in some ways rather like hers – similar enough, anyway, for Marmion to feel at ease with them. Like the Hayters, the Devenishes were a tightly knit clan. Bill's older sister Mandy lived at home with her baby daughters, who'd been born prematurely and had spent several weeks in the special care unit. The twins' father was never spoken of, at least in Marmion's hearing, so they, like the hotel, were a family project. But – and this was perhaps how the Devenishes were un-Hayter-like – it seemed to Marmion that the babies were more a burden than a joy. Of course she couldn't be sure how her parents would react to the arrival of two unsupported grandchildren, but she'd felt, sometimes, that Mia and Grace were seen as part of a pattern of adversity. Bill's father was musical, and Mandy had read English at university, but there never seemed to be time for such distractions in the Devenish household. There were always so many practicalities to deal with: bookings, guests, complaints, bills, medical appointments. Marmion could see that Bill longed to escape from all this, but that he was ashamed of that impulse too – and she could sympathise with both those feelings. Certainly a weekend with Bill's family made her own seem almost frivolous.

A loud laugh from Judith drew her attention back to the group gathered on the terrace. Stephen was regaling them with an account of a dalliance he'd conducted in the University Library in the weeks before Finals. Marmion smiled. Stories of unrequited love were part of Stephen's stock-in-trade, produced to amuse them all. The fervency of his devotion was always less convincing than his willingness to cast himself as a comic character.

'I must have bought her a dozen cheese scones,' he was saying now. 'I even buttered them for her,' and they all hooted with laughter, imagining long-limbed Stephen demonstrating courtly love with a butter knife in the fervid atmosphere of the library's tea room.

'What was her name?' asked Judith.

'Sarah,' said Stephen promptly. 'Or perhaps ... Clare, actually, I think. No, she was *at* Clare. A medic, anyway. She told me all about her skeleton.'

'I didn't think medics went to the library,' said Bill. 'Don't they lurk in dissecting rooms and anatomy museums?'

'There are books to be read about medicine,' said Judith. She stretched her arms luxuriantly, letting one of them fall on the back of Bill's chair before folding them behind her head. 'More of them than you might think. Didn't you have a fling with a medic last term, Cressy?'

'*He* lurked in dissecting rooms,' said Cressida, mock-reprovingly. 'Didn't let me near his skeleton, anyway.'

Marmion watched her for a moment, catching her glance at Stephen. Sometimes she thought Cressida's crush on him was over; sometimes she thought she'd imagined it. She was always the last to pick up on romantic intrigue, she knew, but there had been times when she'd been sure that Cressida was unhappy, and that Stephen was the cause. She wondered now, batting at a fly which had settled on her arm, whether she was right, and whether her clumsy intuition about the reason for Stephen's indifference was anywhere close to the truth.

As another ripple of laughter went round the table, Marmion thought for the second time that day how hard it was to believe that all this – the habit of seeing everything through the prism of their little circle – would be over so soon. She hadn't begun to imagine how she'd do without it. But she dismissed the flutter of melancholy before it could settle, swatting it away like that bluebottle a moment ago. It was silly, she told herself, to waste the time they had left being maudlin.

'Do you realise,' she said, 'that we've sung evensong three times a week for three terms a year for three years? Not counting all the extra services and concerts.'

'How many is that?' Cressida raised an eyebrow. Marmion's maths was on a par with Judith's godliness: another standing joke.

'Well over two hundred,' said Stephen.

'It seems more,' said Marmion, disappointed. There were the rehearsals too, of course, hundreds of hours of singing together, but even so: she'd wanted the total to startle them.

'Two hundred's a lot,' said Stephen. 'Two hundred Magnificats. Two hundred evening collects.'

'Do you remember the compline when Bill set fire to the service sheet?' Cressida asked.

'No one noticed,' said Bill.

'Or the nude service?' said Judith.

Marmion grinned. Deep, the organ scholar, had dared them to wear nothing under their cassocks one Tuesday evening, and they'd all processed solemn-faced up the aisle, feeling deliciously childish and a little chilly, in the depths of the cold Cambridge winter.

'No one noticed that, either,' said Bill. 'More's the pity.'

'No one except God,' said Marmion.

'I thought God wanted us naked,' said Judith. 'Wasn't that his beef with Adam and Eve?'

'I rest my case, m'lud,' said Cressida.

'I rather thought God could see past our outer vestments anyway,' said Stephen.

Marmion was never sure, when God came into the conversation, whether she was being teased. 'Of course He can,' she said. 'You can't hide anything from Him. For God shall bring every work into judgment, with every secret thing.' She smiled, trying to convey both sincerity and light-heartedness. But no one replied, and after a moment Fay pushed back her chair.

'On that note,' she said, 'it's time to go. Rehearsal at three.'

'Another rehearsal?' asked Judith. The others looked from her to Fay, surprised by the change of plan.

'I told you this morning,' Fay said. 'With the church choir, for the service on Sunday morning. They'll be glad of your help.'

'Good,' said Cressida – with more conviction than any of them felt, Marmion thought. There had definitely been no mention earlier of another rehearsal: the confusion, the oversight, embarrassed her a little. She stood up, smiling at Fay.

'Shall we bring all this in?' she said. 'Wonderful lunch; thank you.'

*

The church was fuller than Judith had expected. She was sure that most of the audience had come for the local performers in the second half (including an elderly barbershop chorus who promised to be hilariously bad), but even so they applauded the High Scarp group enthusiastically, and didn't seem to notice when Stephen got the words wrong in an exposed section of a Stanford motet, substituting something vaguely erotic, and all five of them came close to corpsing.

After Byrd and Bruckner and Britten they sang some close-harmony arrangements: 'When the Swallows Come Back to Capistrano' and 'Blue Moon', and then 'In the Still of the Night' – a final luscious solo for Bill.

The lights hadn't been put on yet in the church, and Judith was very conscious of the music swirling around them in the dusk, the audience reduced to a faint rustle. *Do you love me as I love you*, Bill sang, with a little exposed lift on the *I*, while the others filled in the background of the moonlit night and the open window with their swooning harmonies. As the last note died away, there was an audible sigh from the audience, and Bill turned to grin at the others with a mixture of pleasure and amusement and bashfulness.

Her heart still racing from the thrill and concentration of the singing, Judith felt a quiver of shared pride, and of something sharper. Smiling stupidly like this, feeling the prick of tears, wasn't like her. She was more in love with all this than she'd ever admitted, she realised now. More in love with the careless professionalism, the taking-for-granted of each other's skill. She watched each of them step forward to acknowledge the applause: Marmion glowing with pleasure, Cressida holding tight to her self-possession, Stephen betraying more than usual in an unguarded smile, Bill grinning broadly. They bowed together, and then Bill was murmuring something and a hush fell over the church again as he looked up, their self-appointed spokesman, and announced, 'The Silver Swan'.

This was Judith's moment of glory – the top line gliding effortlessly, swan-like, above the close-knit texture of the part-song, while the others took turns to press forward with the quaver runs that drove the piece towards its last, painfully drawn-out cadence. As they settled on the final F major chord, Bill looked across at her, raising an eyebrow and making the little wobble of a hand gesture that meant *marvellous* or *fabulous* or whatever word – inevitably less powerful than that almost invisible shimmy of the fingers – each of them might choose.

The tremble of pleasure and longing Judith had felt a moment ago flared again. For the sweet sadness of the song and the shared experience of the singing, but also – and here was the dangerous, the almost unthinkable thought – for the pleasure of Bill's admiration. Unthinkable because Bill was Marmion's boyfriend, and Marmion was her friend, and Bill mattered more to Marmion than any man had ever mattered to Judith. Because she'd promised herself to relinquish him, to resist him, three years ago, and she'd stuck to her promise.

While the audience clapped again and the others smiled out at the crowd, Judith's eyes stayed fixed on Bill. She knew him so well now, every nuance of expression familiar, but just now she felt she'd never really looked at him before. His solid, straightforward face, that look of unplaned wood, wasn't her usual style at all. There was something almost ridiculous about him, she thought; about his defiant disregard for sophistication, despite the subtlety and sensitivity of his singing. It made the kick of attraction all the stronger – but she could resist, still. For sure she could resist. There was no harm in a quiver, a catch, that no one else saw. But as Bill turned to lead them off the platform, his eyes rested on her for a fraction of a second and her heart stumbled. He knew, she thought. He might not have admitted it yet, but he knew.

*

Back at High Scarp, Marmion settled happily on the sofa as Fay opened a little cupboard set into the wall beside the fireplace.

'Whisky?' Fay asked. 'Cognac? Or sloe gin, or ... there's some absinthe, and some chartreuse, even. Poisonous stuff, chartreuse, but you ought to try it once.'

'Chartreuse for me,' said Judith. 'Too *Brideshead* for words. I shall be Anthony Blanche.'

Marmion chose sloe gin, which sounded less lethal than the alternatives, and which tasted like rather delicious cough mixture. Bill and Stephen accepted a glass of Glenfiddich apiece, and Cressida a tot of brandy.

Armed with glasses that shone green and purple and amber in the firelight, they settled down to Fay's programme of entertainment. Marmion was victorious in the charades with 'Hold Me, Thrill Me, Kiss Me, Kill Me' – playing successfully on the others' assumption that the pop charts were, as Bill put it, uncharted territory for her, so that they were too busy guessing Monteverdi operas to remember that she'd been to see *Batman Forever* on her own one afternoon after exams.

After that there was a party-piece game which involved making sound effects the others had to identify. Fay went first, blowing out her cheeks to produce a convincing imitation of a bullfrog. Bill – playing up to the spirit of the occasion, Marmion thought – suggested a cow, and then a fart, before yielding the right answer to Cressida.

'You next, Bill,' said Fay.

'I didn't guess it, though,' said Bill.

'Even so.'

After a moment's thought, Bill put his hands to his lips and produced a stream of birdsong.

'Goodness,' said Judith. 'That's an unsuspected talent.'

Bill grinned. 'What is it, then?'

'Nightingale?' suggested Judith. 'Lark?'

Bill shook his head.

'A gap in my education,' said Judith. 'What about you, Cressy? Wasn't birdwatching on the syllabus at Benenden?'

'Sadly not,' said Cressida. 'Squeezed out by all that flower arranging and decorative sugarcraft.'

'Wren?' offered Marmion, although she had no idea what different birds sounded like. The downside of a city childhood, she thought. 'Thrush? Robin?'

'You're an ignorant lot,' said Fay. 'It's a blackbird.' She looked enquiringly at Bill, and he nodded. 'You must all have heard a blackbird sing.'

'The trouble is, they don't introduce themselves,' said Judith. 'And I hesitate to say they all sound the same, but . . .'

'Don't encourage him,' said Stephen. 'Can't you see he's got dozens more up his sleeve? We'll be here all night.'

'Bill's birds,' said Judith, and she laughed briefly.

'Your go, Marmion,' said Fay.

'Is it the person who makes the silliest suggestion?' said Marmion. 'I'm afraid it is. And I'm afraid I'm going to be no good at this.'

It ought to come with having a musical ear, being able to reproduce sounds, but she wasn't sure it did. But then she remembered one of her father's party tricks, produced to tease or amuse her into practising when she was little, or to hint that her fiddle was out of tune. She took a deep breath and produced a whining string sound, just below an A, then tweaked it down and up and down, never quite centring on the right pitch.

'A siren,' said Judith.

'No.'

'A baby crying,' said Stephen.

'You've clearly never heard a baby crying.'

'A baby animal?' suggested Cressida.

'Call yourselves musicians,' said Marmion. 'Listen again.'

This time she sang a spread D minor chord, the one most violinists tune to, before launching into her pitch-twisting routine, then mimed holding a violin on her shoulder and twiddling the pegs.

'That's cheating,' said Fay, as Bill and Cressida shouted out the answer together. 'Stephen next.'

Stephen didn't hesitate. Screwing up his face, he produced a fizzing sound that made Judith snigger again. She'd had a couple of glasses of chartreuse by now, and there was some colour in her cheeks.

'Alka-Seltzer,' she said.

'Nope.'

'One of your 78s?' offered Bill.

Stephen shook his head, and repeated his performance with greater vigour.

'Oh, I'm not sure I want to know what this one is!' said Marmion.

'A waterfall?' said Cressida.

Stephen waggled his fingers in front of his face like fronds of seaweed.

'I have absolutely no idea,' said Marmion. 'Something crumbling apart?'

'A fire,' said Fay. They all looked at her. 'Is it a fire?'

'Yes,' said Stephen.

'How on earth did you know that?' asked Bill.

'Fay knows everything,' said Judith.

They ought to be laughing, Marmion thought, at Fay's luck or intuition or at Stephen's absurdity, but somehow they weren't. Something seemed to have shifted in the room. Something to do with Fay, perhaps: had she been in a fire, or lost someone in a fire – or was she playing a different game now? Marmion stared at her, but Fay was looking from Bill to Judith, and there was nothing to detect in her expression except that flat smile again.

Whatever it was, Marmion decided suddenly that she'd had enough. She put her hand to her mouth as though to stifle a yawn, then stood up.

'Won't you have another drink?' Fay asked, but Marmion shook her head.

'No,' she said. 'But it's been a lovely day. Thank you.'

Crossing the garden in the almost-dark a few moments later, Marmion stopped for a moment, in the same place she'd stood that morning, to look out across the valley. The sky above the fells was violet-coloured – a transient, volatile shade like the inside of a flower or a shell. Even as she watched it changed, deepening and darkening towards night. If she had left five minutes earlier or five minutes later, she thought, she would have missed this moment, this particular, fleeting colour. She looked up at the stars, laid out in brilliant contrast across the wide stretch of the horizon, and then she heard footsteps behind her and turned to see Bill approaching.

'For I will consider thy heavens: the moon and the stars, which thou hast ordained,' he said.

Marmion smiled, thinking that she was more grateful than she could say for Bill.

'Look.' She pointed at the Pole Star, hanging poised above the summit of Helvellyn, and then at the clear outline of the Plough.

'Don't you find them scary?' he asked.

'Who?'

'The stars. Doesn't the thought of them frighten you? Such an expanse of empty space.'

'Would you rather be confined in a smaller space?' Marmion asked.

'Such an expanse of time, then. Compared to our lifespan.'

'Man that is born of a woman hath but a short time to live,' quoted Marmion, the Purcell setting they had sung this evening blooming in her head once more. 'At least if he's Henry Purcell he's got something to leave behind.'

'If he's not, he'd better make the most of the time he's got,' said Bill, slipping a hand around her waist.

Marmion quivered. 'That sounds eminently sensible.'

'Do you really . . .' Bill hesitated.

'What?'

'Nothing.'

His arm was around her still, the feel of his body familiar and comforting. 'Tell me,' she said. 'Even if it is nothing.'

She felt a little sigh on her neck. 'I was just thinking about . . . the God thing.'

'The God thing?' Marmion smiled.

'God seeing every secret thing,' Bill said. 'Don't you find that scary too?'

'No. Why should I? And why should you? We're not doing anything God wouldn't like, I'm sure of that.'

She turned then, and kissed him sweetly, lingeringly, before taking his hand and leading him into the cabin.

When it came to it, the question of sex with Bill hadn't been difficult to settle. Marmion had never been enjoined to chastity, simply to prudence and respect, for herself and others. What had been surprising wasn't that she found herself taking off her clothes so willingly that first time, but the delight it brought her. She hadn't expected that her enjoyment of other sensory pleasures would be matched, even exceeded, by touch, nor that Bill, whose experience was barely greater than hers, would be such a perfect partner in her exploration of the joys of the flesh.

She couldn't see Bill now as she had at the beginning, when she was first falling in love with him. When she looked at him now she felt his hands on her body, and a shivering awareness of all those intricacies of fleshly gratification that she couldn't put into words but longed for as soon as she thought of them. Guilt wasn't a Quaker sentiment – the idea was more to avoid it through care and principle – but even if it had been, Marmion couldn't possibly have attached it to sex, which seemed to her a God-given wonder.

Their room was barely large enough for the double bed that was squeezed into it, and the choreography of undressing and seduction was awkward, accompanied by muffled laughter and occasional yelps. But encountering each other at unexpected angles, being pressed hip to hip in the doorway, added to the anticipation of what was to come rather than undermining it. When they were finally on the bed, Bill ran his hand down the length of Marmion's body. Down in the village, the church clock chimed midnight, and the yearning ache in her belly seemed to resonate with the sound and the vivid awareness of her happiness.

September 2015
Bill

'Have you checked the traffic?' asked Isabel. 'Won't the M6 be awful on a Friday afternoon?'

Bill looked back at the house, a lingering glance, as though they were going away for a long time. He ran a checklist in his mind: doors, windows, alarm, timer lights.

'I suppose there really isn't any other route,' Isabel persisted.

'I checked just now,' Bill said. 'It looked pretty clear. We can keep an eye, on the TomTom.'

They didn't usually talk like this, he thought. They were both speaking for the sake of it, not letting there be silence. He hoped things would settle down once they were under way: he didn't think he could bear this for three hours, plus whatever bonus the Friday traffic added.

'Got everything?' he asked, and Isabel managed a smile.

'Are you sure you want me to come?' she asked.

'Why wouldn't I?'

The smile turned into something more complicated. 'They're your friends. I thought you might . . .'

'I haven't seen them for twenty years,' Bill said. 'Of course I want you to come.' But she knew he didn't, of course. Just as he knew she didn't want to be left behind. That hardly scratched the surface of the situation, actually, but even so the rational part of his brain recognised the advantage of having Isabel there. Something about camouflage; about proving he was who he said he was these days. Something about ensuring civility, or whatever they were going to need to get through the weekend.

'Come on,' he said. 'Let's get going. The traffic will only get worse.'

They lived outside Shrewsbury, in a village with a number of old and beautiful houses and a number of not-so-old and not-so-beautiful houses. Theirs was one of the latter, but it was Edwardian rather than 1970s, plain and four-square, with more bedrooms than they needed and less garden than Isabel would have liked. It had appealed, ten years ago, largely because it had seemed like a lot of house for the money, and they could afford to buy it without a crippling mortgage. They'd been hoping to have children then, to fill the bedrooms and make the less appealing aspects less important. As the prospect of children dwindled, they thought about moving – into the middle of Shrewsbury, perhaps – but for a while superstition prevented them, and then inertia took over. Instead they made other, more tentative, changes. The conservatory, the Aga; this year the new car. Bill wasn't sure why it made him feel edgy to think about the costs and the benefits now, when the money was long gone. The Midlander's natural thrift, he supposed, perhaps exaggerated by his illness. Although some people became less circumspect after an episode like that: some people threw caution to the wind once they'd got a whiff of mortality.

He smiled at Isabel now, as they joined a light stream of traffic heading east on the M54. It was a clear afternoon, and the wooded slopes of the Wrekin stood out sharply in the middle distance.

'Where is it exactly, the house?' Isabel had got the map book out.

'Griseley,' he said. 'Near the bottom of Ullswater.'

Out of the corner of his eye he watched her finger tracing the lines of roads and fells.

'There,' she said. 'Gosh, it looks like the middle of nowhere.'

'There's a pub and a church and a shop,' said Bill. 'A shop that sells everything. Or there used to be.' It would all have changed, he told himself. It would look very different to how he remembered. Not that he remembered much: he'd worked at that. Only oddments remained, things he hadn't erased because he hadn't thought of them for years. The cuckoo clock in the hall that had a mind of its own, and those bloody awful parlour games.

Isabel said nothing for several minutes. She was a sensible person, Bill thought, and sensitive in a way that wasn't wholly self-centred. Those were among the things that had appealed to him about her, and he'd been grateful for them over the years, especially during the protracted saga of not-having-children, and then his being ill. He hadn't married her for the right reasons, and the wrong reasons hadn't transmogrified over time into better ones: he hadn't managed, as he'd hoped, to cultivate ardour, although she'd never had cause to doubt his fidelity. But she knew there was something more to this weekend, to the reconvening of his Cambridge friends, than he'd told her. She held out until they were approaching Wolverhampton, and then she said: 'So this woman, the one who's left the house to you. Did she teach you at St Anne's?'

'No.' Bill hesitated. 'She was connected to the college,' he said, 'and she took an interest in the chapel choir, particularly the five of us in my year. She used to invite us to her house, take us to concerts, things like that. And at the end of our last term we went to stay at her cottage in the Lake District.'

'This cottage.'

'Yes.' He waited, and so did Isabel. 'I hadn't seen her for years,' he said. 'I didn't stay in touch.'

'So why did she leave the house to you?'

'Not just to me,' said Bill. 'To all of us. I have no idea. I expect the solicitor will explain.'

Isabel nodded. They were between motorways now, passing the turnings to Coven and Brewood, territory familiar from years ago, when he was growing up on the outskirts of Birmingham. It was odd, Bill thought, that life could land you up so close to where you'd started.

Isabel's fears about the Friday traffic proved unfounded. There were plenty of cars on the road but no accidents, no roadworks, and they kept moving steadily northwards. By six o'clock they were turning off the M6 on the South Lakes exit.

Isabel had dozed off somewhere around Charnock Richard, and Bill handled the car gently, glad not to have to talk during this last stretch. The past was seeping inexorably into his mind now, and a churn of anticipation filled his belly. It wasn't just Fay he hadn't seen for years. Guiltily, in quiet moments at work, he'd googled them all: it was easy enough to track people down these days.

Stephen Evans was a common name, but Bill was pretty sure he'd found the right one. A rather slight Internet footprint, but Bill suspected that was deliberate, and that it concealed a substantial life. Nothing on Facebook or LinkedIn, but a thread drawing together various mentions of his name: the Arabic connection was a clue, and the patronage of a charity that cared for adults with severe disabilities. Bill had been pleased with himself for remembering Stephen's brother, the other adopted son who had cerebral palsy. Stephen's interests seemed to span both business and academic life: boards of directors, honorary degrees, the text of an occasional lecture. A good deal of money, Bill thought. A lot of influence, certainly. No mention of a family, even a wife, but that might be a deliberate smokescreen. Bill tried to imagine Stephen's wife and came up with someone blonde and glossy, expensively dressed.

Judith had been easy to find, her face gazing out – as his did – from her professional website. Her chambers specialised in criminal law and she did a lot of legal aid work. There was a streaking of grey in Judith's hair, but she'd changed remarkably little. That smile, that confidence, he remembered all too well. Truth to tell, he'd googled

Judith before, more than once over the last . . . well, since Google had been around to make it easy to find your old friends. To stalk them; that was what it was called. He'd watched her not looking any older as the photographs changed and she advanced steadily in the particular corner of the law she'd chosen. Judith was on Facebook, but her profile was private, and he didn't dare make contact directly. But there'd been an exchange of emails over the last few weeks. Careful, guarded group emails, about the practicalities. He'd read Judith's messages over and over again, hearing her voice, and trying out different inflections, different emphases. Eventually he'd deleted them, frightened of giving himself away.

They were through Windermere now, on the road that led up to the Kirkstone Pass. Bill didn't remember which way they'd come last time. Fay had driven, although Judith had had a car in Cambridge that last year, in contravention of university regulations. She'd kept it at Fay's house, Bill remembered. It was odd what stayed with you and what didn't. Tiny details lodged vividly – a gooseberry fool they'd eaten one evening in the garden on Clarendon Way – while whole swathes had fallen away. It had been a Golf, Judith's car. An old blue Golf, a shade that would be called teal now. Not so much a sign of wealth as an assertion of independence.

Cressida had been easy to find too. She'd done exactly what she'd intended: she held a university lectureship in the English Faculty, and was a fellow of St Anne's. He'd found a picture of her on the college website, a slightly blurry photo that seemed, oddly, to have been taken on a beach. He wasn't sure he'd have recognised her. Her hair was short, her face thinner, and she looked very serious – as befitted an academic, but not one photographed on a beach. She'd always been serious, though. Bill remembered her wearing the frilly white blouse she used to sing in, explaining some point of pronunciation. Did she have a husband, a family? It was odd knowing about the professional lives of all these other people, his old friends, but nothing about their personal lives. Their emails had avoided that territory.

Isabel was still asleep, her head tipped to one side and her mouth slightly open. Her face looked less lined than it did when she was awake, but there was a hint of dissatisfaction in her expression that she tried hard to hide, most of the time. Well, she had as much reason as most people to be dissatisfied, he thought.

The view from the car windows was getting exciting now, glimpses of fells appearing between the trees. As they passed through Troutbeck, the world opened up suddenly, and he slowed, dazed by the drama of the landscape and the sudden explosion of memory.

June 1995

Marmion

'I never thought I could eat so much in a single weekend,' said Cressida. 'We'd have to climb a thousand fells to make up for it.'

She was sprawled – a rather un-Cressida-like pose – on a rug Fay had produced from one of the knapsacks.

'I'd almost be prepared to climb that hill again for another brownie,' said Judith. Cressida leant across and passed her one, and Judith feigned hesitation before taking it. 'Too good for words,' she said. 'Really too good.'

Fay was sitting upright at the edge of the rug, and the others were scattered across the grass or perched on the flattish boulders that ringed the level space they'd chosen for the picnic. There was a view of the lake far below, with a steamer meandering across it, and closer at hand a stream to paddle in, if they felt like it, after lunch. Which Marmion thought she would, in due course, but just now sitting back to back with Bill on a ledge of stone was much too nice for her to consider moving.

'This is lovely,' she said, to no one in particular, and Fay smiled approvingly.

'I'm glad,' she said. 'I hoped you'd like it here. I'm glad you could all come up before you leave St Anne's.'

'I'm not leaving,' said Cressida. 'If my results are OK, I'm definitely staying on.'

'To do a PhD?' asked Fay.

Cressida nodded as well as she could, propped on one elbow. 'MPhil to start with, then a PhD, I hope.'

'What about the rest of you?' Fay asked. 'I know Marmion and Bill are going to the Guildhall to sing.'

'Bar school for me,' said Judith. 'Another year of hard slog.'

'And you, Stephen?'

Stephen hadn't stirred from his supine position, but he opened his eyes now and turned his head towards them. None of them knew what Stephen's plans were, Marmion realised.

'I'm going abroad,' he said. 'I'm going to learn Arabic in Dubai.'

'Are you really?' Everyone was looking at him: Judith spoke for all of them. 'You're an international man of mystery, Stephen.'

Stephen raised an eyebrow. 'I always was a linguist,' he said.

He had indeed started out reading modern languages, before switching to social and political science – to avoid going abroad for a year, Marmion had thought at the time. It struck her now that it was rather presumptuous to assume that staying in synch with the rest of them mattered enough to make Stephen change course.

'And after that?' Fay asked. 'Where will you all be in ten years' time?'

Marmion was suddenly acutely aware of Bill's back behind her. She couldn't tell whether the stiffening she could feel was in his muscles or hers.

'Still in Cambridge, I hope,' said Cressida. 'Enjoying glowing reviews of my definitive work on Southey. Teaching tiresome undergraduates.'

'Working my way up the criminal bar,' said Judith. 'If all goes well.'

'I think you'll end up in Parliament,' said Cressida. 'You've got all the right credentials.'

'Except a passing interest in politics,' said Judith. 'Stephen's your man for that. Do you know Stephen has read the complete works of Karl Marx?'

'Not for fun,' said Stephen.

'Stephen's going to run the United Nations,' said Bill.

Stephen shut his eyes as the sun came out from behind a cloud. 'Only if I can do it from here,' he said. 'I don't ever want to leave this spot.'

Fay turned to look at him now, her face glowing. How touching, Marmion thought: she badly wants us to like it here. That's what it's been about, the fussing over food and making sure we go on the right walks and all that.

'You'll go far, Stephen,' Fay said. 'I'm sure of that.'

'Won't we all?' asked Judith – and then there was a sudden silence. Judith had hit the wrong note, producing her would-be barrister tone in the middle of a conversation that had been too gentle and ambling for it, but that wasn't it, Marmion thought. It was as though they believed Fay had some power to see the future and were waiting for her to pronounce. For a few seconds everything froze, Marmion's heart beating too fast for comfort. When Stephen started speaking she felt a rush of gratitude to him.

'You will, Judith,' he said. 'I'm in no doubt about the illustrious career of Judith Malik, QC. And so will Professor Benham, world expert on Romantic poetry. And Marmion and Bill will be on stage together at La Scala.'

Marmion laughed, doubly grateful to him now for managing a sentence which linked her to Bill while sidestepping the question of whether they would be together, ten years hence, in any other sense. Half of her wished someone would say something about a string of little Marmions and Bills waiting in the dressing room, and half of her dreaded being put on the spot like that. Bill being put on the spot, that is: she certainly wouldn't have any hesitation. So then . . .

She collected herself. Bad, bad, to let her hopes run away with her, and silly to worry about Bill, when he'd given her no cause. She leant her head back now and rested it on his shoulder, to show she was at ease. There. Perfection. Bliss.

*

It surprised Stephen to hear himself speaking with such conviction about Dubai. He'd left for Cumbria uncertain about the offer he'd just accepted, but somehow, without him noticing, the last few days had cemented things in his mind. Suddenly he could see the future quite clearly: he could see Dubai as the first of a string of beacons stretching away across a landscape that was entirely his to explore and to conquer.

But the other thing he'd said was true too – that just now he could imagine abandoning that plan and staying here. Here in Cumbria, and among his friends. He wasn't sure how those two things fitted together, the looking forward and the looking back, but . . . maybe it was partly that he could afford to feel nostalgic, now that things were settled. He could let himself feel how much these last three years had meant. The music, and the friendships: all of it so unlike what he'd imagined.

Before he went to university he'd never come across the sacred music they sang in chapel. It was chance that led him to audition for the choir: the boy in the room next door, a second-year choral scholar, had heard him singing in the shower and told him there was a vacancy for a bass, if he was interested. If Stephen had known more about it, he might have laughed off the suggestion. He'd had no musical training, and the standard was very high – but he was cheerfully ignorant of that, and in any case the technicalities of acquiring a new skill had never daunted him. He was a linguist, and what was music but another language to learn?

Except that it had turned out to be more than that. It had been, analysed objectively, a transformative experience – but there was nothing objective about the way it had taken hold of him, the way it made him feel his heart was beating properly for the first time and filled his mind with echoes of meaning and possibility and yearning. He wasn't the same kind of person as Bill, or even Marmion, but for the last three years he'd become one of them.

Stephen wasn't much given to spontaneous emotion, but a surge of affection rose inside him now. Idly (although his thoughts were never entirely idle) he pursued it, wondering what it meant, and whether it might illuminate his strange ambivalence about the past and the future. St Anne's and the choir and these friendships had given him a platform to jump off from, he thought. Crossing the globe, starting a new life in the Middle East, felt possible because he'd done something almost as extraordinary already, and he was grateful for that. Certainly that was part of what he felt: part of the rush of contentment and regret that swirled in his chest, infused with the smell of warm grass and the distant calls of lambs.

But it was also, he thought, that the whole experience of Cambridge had coalesced this weekend, distilled to a kind of pure essence that could never be matched or followed – so that at the very moment when he understood how much he'd liked it, being part of the choir and this little group, he knew the time had come to leave them behind.

*

'Anyone fancy a paddle?' asked Judith. 'Or are we going on?'

She looked at Fay, but Fay shook her head. 'Whatever you like,' she said. 'On or back or stay here.'

Marmion shut her eyes. Her bottom ached from sitting so long on the cold stone, but nothing would induce her to move until Bill did. She heard Judith persuading Cressida to come and paddle with her, and Fay questioning Stephen about his plans, and she imagined the two of them – her and Bill – floating upwards, in the heat of the afternoon, like the couple in that Chagall painting, deep into the blue sky with a goat or something playing the cello.

It felt, she thought, as though something important was passing between them: the summed-up memory of the last few days, and the last few years. Singing and cycling and lectures and late nights and love. Definitely love, rising through her mind now on a faint thread of birdsong. Not a blackbird this time, but the tiny speck of a skylark, clear and sweet and effusive. Her mind followed it, shifting through shades of green and blue and golden yellow into a future where things were different, indefinably different but always the same, a landscape seen from above, from a soaring height among the birds and the sun . . .

And then it seemed to her that she'd been asleep, and that years might have passed, and she opened her eyes in a rush and saw the others packing up the picnic.

'Come on, old thing,' said Bill. 'Time to get going.'

September 2015
Cressida

Mary-Lou was still standing on the doorstep: her face appeared again, looking doubtfully at her sister-in-law, when Cressida slammed the car boot down.

'Sure you know the way?' she asked.

'Yes,' said Cressida. 'Thank you.'

Staying the night with her eldest brother and his wife had been a mistake, she admitted. Apart from the irritation of being treated like a decrepit aunt when she was exactly the same age as Mary-Lou, she could ill afford the time. Quite honestly, this weekend couldn't have come at a worse moment, with the book still not finished and the deadline receding behind her. She smiled in a way she knew would look tetchy. 'Thank you for having me,' she said.

'It was great to see you,' said Mary-Lou, the remains of her New York accent clearly discernible beneath the overlay of smart Cheshire housewife. 'I'm so glad it worked out.'

It was a mystery to Cressida that Mary-Lou was so content in this prosperous backwater where Nicholas's work had landed them ten years before, but contentment seemed to be bred into her, along with the production of fine strapping sons. Four of them, all being educated at boarding school. Cressida couldn't begin to compute the expense.

Mary-Lou waved as the car turned noisily on the gravel, and Cressida felt a guilty sense of relief. She had tried hard to like her sisters-in-law. She'd looked forward to forming an alliance with them against the masculine hegemony of the family, in which her mother had always been a kind of totem, the ornamental figurehead of the good ship Benham, rather than a balancing power. But the three of them – recruited from the far corners of the globe, so that one might have expected more variety – had, it seemed to Cressida, simply absorbed her brothers' points of view, rather than moderating their outlook in any way. Certainly their outlook on Cressida, who found it considerably more galling to be patronised by her sisters-in-law than her brothers, whose teasing was at least rooted in a well-concealed, but equally well-understood, respect for her brain.

Mary-Lou meant well, Cressida thought now, as she turned onto the main road, but the polite questions about her work enraged her; the implication that it was an eccentric hobby on a par with Mary-Lou's charitable activities. It made Cressida feel that her life was a flimsy thing, her successes ephemeral curiosities. And it was worse just now, with the book at such a delicate stage. She had night-mares in which she hunted desperately for the lost thread of it, a glinting silver thing that was snatched away whenever she spotted it. Ridiculous, of course, when she had so many reams of notes, but it was always like this near the end. The finished article seemed more and more unattainable the closer you got, the passion and energy that had launched it fading memories.

Would she be able to recover them? she wondered. Would they rise again, bringing to light a new seam of work to carry her through the next few years? Sometimes she thought a career in academia was the very worst thing for anyone who really cared about literature. She was like someone intent on revealing the sleight of hand behind a magician's act, destroying the magic for the sake of advancing an obscure vein of knowledge. Was it Billy Collins who wrote about critics bludgeoning poetry to death? He certainly knew a thing or two.

She stopped for petrol before the motorway, then slid carefully back into her seat, adjusting the lie of her new dress to prevent the seat belt crushing the expensive fabric. She'd put it on this morning so Mary-Lou could have the benefit of it too, but she should have guessed it would crease the moment she got into the car. It was absurd to have spent so much time and money on her wardrobe for this weekend, but she'd been determined to look her best: not a frumpy forty-something academic but a successful woman whose appearance spoke of a rich and vibrant life. At least as rich and vibrant as theirs.

Judith hadn't married or had children; she'd discovered that with a bit of devious sleuthing. She didn't know about the others, but it was Judith she compared herself to. She wondered whether Judith had wanted children; how things had unfolded for her. A shadow of guilt still lurked in Cressida's mind – but it wasn't for her to feel guilty, she told herself. Certainly not about Judith. And Judith, surely, had picked herself up and got on with her life without a backward glance. Cressida clicked on the CD player, and the car filled with the reassuring voluptuousness of Strauss's *Four Last Songs*.

When Michael had finally slipped out of her grasp last year – and she could admit now that that was how it had been – she had wasted six months feeling sorry for herself, and furious with herself, and cursing men to hell. What amazed her, looking back on the seventeen years she had spent with him, was how consistently and how sustainedly she had deceived herself. About his attractions, she meant, as well as his intentions.

He'd been reasonably prepossessing at thirty-nine, when she'd first met him, recently returned from a stint at Harvard – and it was partly his influence that had got her a junior research fellowship, or so he'd led her to believe. It was easy to explain how she'd fallen into an affair with him then, flattered at being a desirable alternative to his beautiful, boring wife: even the challenge to her own morality, the flagrant disregard for her principles, had been part of the deliciously self-torturing cocktail. It was easy to see why she'd hung on to a no-strings, open-secret relationship while she was battling her way up through the groves of misogyny that were the Cambridge English Faculty. But why he still had such a firm hold on her when her career was established, and his once-audacious critical perspective was being laughed at, was inexplicable. Sometime between point A and point B she could have, should have, looked at him with open eyes and seen that he'd become a canker. A man approaching sixty with three grown-up children and a wife who was still beautiful and serene while his childless mistress began to fade towards middle age.

Even now she could taste the bile – these last few months especially, after that far-fetched episode in May Week had nearly unseated her again – but she was all right, she told herself. She mustn't flatter Michael with any more of her time or thought, especially not this weekend. She mustn't dwell on the past in any of its incarnations, in fact. And she wouldn't think about the book, either, for the next forty-eight hours. The university press could wait that long. She drummed her fingers on the steering wheel in a tattoo of determination.

She stopped, as she'd planned, at Blackwell, an early-twentieth-century villa overlooking Lake Windermere. The visit did much to restore her peace of mind: the house itself, white and many-gabled, with a grey slate roof and phenomenal views, the interior's Arts and Crafts treasures and the tea room's home-made scones – even the shop, full of things Cressida would have liked to buy. All of it fed an inner spring of aesthetic pleasure that made her feel she could face the weekend with reasonable equanimity.

She got back into the car as the light started to fade. Good: she'd be at High Scarp by seven, as she'd planned. Everything was under control. She drove through Windermere and past Troutbeck church, remembering its wonderful Pre-Raphaelite window – and then she rounded the corner and saw a car in the middle of the road.

'Shit!'

She braked hard, but the Corsa skidded to a halt just too late to avoid a slow-motion collision.

'Shit!' she said again, more vehemently. What the hell was someone doing stopping in the middle of a country road? How on earth was she supposed to see them in time?

A man was getting out of the other car now, a tall man who still had some of the lankiness of youth, although his hair was almost entirely white. Cressida stared, her heart beating furiously, the shock of the collision compounded by other emotions she didn't have time to resist. Of course it made sense for him to be on the same road, but . . . It wasn't just seeing him, she thought, but seeing him so different and at the same time instantly recognisable.

He was gesturing now, trying to explain why he'd stopped. Looking straight at her, but quite clearly not recognising her. Cressida felt a jolt of offence. Well, women did change more, of course. She'd cut her hair shorter, tried to keep the same colour, but perhaps . . . She undid her seat belt, clicked open the car door and climbed out into the road. The man's expression didn't change. Fury and disappointment welled up before she could stop them.

'Bloody hell, Stephen,' she said. 'What on earth are you doing?'

He stared at her: a pleasing transformation.

'Cressida?' he said. 'My goodness. I wouldn't have . . . You don't look old enough.'

Cressida considered this for a moment, wavering between anger and mollification. It was clearly a lie, but she had to give him credit for quick thinking.

'Balls,' she said. 'But I'm glad to have run into you first. Literally.'

'I'm sorry,' Stephen said. 'There were sheep in the road. I'll pay for any damage.'

'It doesn't look as though there is any, luckily.' His car, she noticed now, was a Jaguar. It would have been a bad start to have smashed up the back of it.

Stephen smiled. 'It's good to see you, Cressida,' he said. 'You look terrific.'

'I don't,' she said, glancing down at the floral linen she could see now was ludicrous for a weekend in the Lake District. 'I look ancient and exhausted, but I'm glad to see you too. It's been much too long.'

She came forward and let him hug her – an awkward business, but they managed it with some dignity. For a fraction of a second Cressida shut her eyes, imagining them both young again; remembering the tender, painful saga of yearning and hope and disillusionment. But she wasn't young any more. Surely there were advantages to that.

'We ought to move,' Stephen said, 'or someone else will come round that corner and run into us. Are you OK to drive?'

'Of course I am.'

'I'll see you there, then.'

Damn, Cressida thought, as she got back into her car. Damn, damn, damn. There'd been something horribly like amusement in his face before he turned away, as though she really hadn't changed at all since she was a precocious undergraduate. All that time on the motorway: she could have dreamt up some amusing entrées, some clever, self-deprecating one-liners. What was the use of a first-rate mind if she had nothing to say for herself? Damn and blast.

For a few minutes she kept close behind the elegant rear of the Jaguar, but as they climbed towards the Kirkstone Pass, she slowed. There was too little time left, now, to prepare herself, and she'd only just understood how much she needed to prepare. And then, as she reached the top of the pass, there was Nag's Pike in plain view, and the past laid out before her.

Part II

June 1995

Cressida

It was the concert, Cressida thought, that had whipped her emotions to such a pitch that she'd felt, for the first time, that it might be possible to act on them – but it was the walk the next day, picnicking above the lake and talking about the future in that delicious, indolent way as they all lay about on the mossy turf, that had stirred her courage. It had occurred to her then that the test she faced was about more than Stephen. It was all bound up with the way she thought about things, and the way she might live: with the great disjunction between mind and body. Between art and reality. As she'd shut her eyes and felt the sun on her hair and the flutter of a breeze on her face, it had seemed suddenly overwhelmingly important to act on her desires – to take responsibility for making sure the things that mattered to her came to something.

That evening there was a service of compline at nine thirty, just as the sun was setting. The church was filled with candles, and a draught of incense added to the enchantment of the ritual. *Keep me as the apple of an eye*, they sang, with a wonderful medieval curlicue on the last word. *Hide me under the shadow of thy wings*. They knelt and stood and sat together, candlelight trembling on their faces, then emerged to the pale dazzle of stars above the dark valley. As they walked back up the hill everyone was unusually quiet, and Cressida had a sense that something had altered – not just between her and Stephen, but for all of them.

'Drink?' asked Fay, when they got home.

She looked tired, Cressida thought; she wouldn't want the evening to drag on too long. Cressida was glad of that. She could feel a restlessness in the air that seemed, again, to extend to the others too, although her head was so full of Stephen, of the portents laid out for them, that it was hard to see anything else clearly. She took a glass of whisky and felt it burn a path down inside her. From her tongue to her heart, she thought. From her heart to her tongue. She chose a space next to Stephen on the sofa, and their weight tipped them towards each other on the ancient springs, but she held herself upright, her body taut with anticipation.

Everyone was in bed before midnight. Cressida listened to the sound of footsteps passing to and from the bathroom, the opening and shutting of doors and the flux of water in the pipes. Her window was open, and she could hear an owl at the bottom of the garden and an occasional sharp crack that might be a fox or a badger in the undergrowth. At last the human sounds stopped, and she found she was holding her breath, lying so still that she wondered whether her limbs would move when she asked them to. She must go now, before Stephen fell asleep. Just another second to recall the warmth of his body beside her on the sofa, and the way he'd smiled at her across the church. Just another second to summon the last drop of fire from the whisky.

Stephen's room was opposite hers. Cressida's heart jumped as she nudged the door ajar. No light; no sound. God, what was she doing? The words she'd prepared drained away. Then there was a rustle of sheets, and Stephen was looking at her.

'Cressida?'

'It's such a beautiful night,' she said. 'I couldn't sleep.'

He sat up. She couldn't read his expression in the dark. Oh God, oh God. Apologies were mustering now, but before she could speak again he was pushing back the covers.

'Shall we go for a walk?' he suggested. 'Up to the cave? We could take the rest of the whisky.'

It was warmer than Cressida had expected, and lighter, too. A quarter-moon had risen high above the fells, and the night was clear and still. As they climbed, sheep raised their heads to stare at them. At one point Cressida stumbled, and Stephen caught her arm to steady her.

'All right?' he asked, and she nodded, willing him not to let go. But the path was too narrow to walk side by side, and after a moment he dropped back behind her.

Fay had brought them up to the cave on the first day – the dragon's cave, she'd called it. Ull the dragon, after whom Ullswater had been named. Marmion had repeated the story to the couple who ran the village shop, asking if they sold postcards with Ull on them, and they'd looked mystified – then Fay had laughed and said it wasn't a proper legend, just a story her father had told her when she was little. Marmion had looked crestfallen, and Cressida had bought her some Kendal mint cake, glad it wasn't her who'd asked the question.

Tonight they heard the rush of water first. A little stream ran down the fell and disappeared into the mouth of the cave, its splash and tumble echoing back up to the surface. Stephen and Cressida stood before it, the darkness inside seeming to gather up the night and offer it back to them with the damp chill of its rocky walls.

'Careful,' Stephen said, as Cressida took a step closer. 'It's very slippery. Shall we go on up to the bench?'

'No.' It wasn't far, the Victorian bench perched on a rise from which – at least during the day – the lake could be seen in one direction and the village in the other, but it wasn't the climb that put Cressida off. The bench was too public, she thought; too formal. 'No, let's . . . Up there, look. We can sit there.'

They scrambled up to a rocky ledge, sheltered by a tree whose branches thrust out from the ground below, offering a handhold as they climbed.

'Happy?' asked Stephen, when they had both made it. He took off his jacket and spread it on the ground, and at that moment the reality of their being alone together, being out on the fell at night, struck Cressida with a giddying mix of pleasure and agitation. There must be a line of Wordsworth, she thought – but for once poetry was out of reach. Stephen set the whisky bottle down, and Cressida handed him the glasses she'd brought from the house. She couldn't let herself speak yet.

'Cheers,' Stephen said, as he poured them each a shot. 'You're very quiet.'

'Just . . .' began Cressida. She shook her head and smiled, then took a sip of whisky. 'It's lovely up here, isn't it? I mean – having it all to ourselves.' A little pitch of daring; another sip of whisky.

'It's beautiful,' Stephen agreed. 'This is a nice thing to do. I'm glad you came and found me.'

'I am too,' Cressida said. 'Not that . . . It wasn't exactly chance that I picked you.'

She risked a glance at his face then, but he was staring out across the valley. There were barely any lights visible, just the glint of starlight in the beck, and the altered shapes of the fells. She edged a little closer to him, and – primed by the whisky – leant her head on his shoulder.

'Cold?' he asked.

'A bit.'

'Here.' He lifted his arm and put it around her shoulder, and Cressida shut her eyes, feeling the pressure of his fingers through her sleeve, the slight movement of his chest as he breathed. She could smell the waterfall, its astringent, peppery sweetness rising from the cave as the stream plummeted down, down towards it. Oh, the agony of wanting to prolong this moment, but also to move on from it – the terrible difficulty of knowing whether, when, how. She didn't dare to move, to say anything, but how could she tell what he was thinking, whether he was waiting for a sign? How could she know whether she risked gambling away this state of anguished contentment?

And so they sat, drinking their whisky, gazing out at the shadowy landscape. As the silence drew out, Cressida was more and more certain of its significance. Surely Stephen, too, felt the pressure of it building up, the terrible urge and reluctance to defuse it? And if he didn't, was that because he was oblivious, or because he too was weighing the seconds, the minutes, and wondering what they meant?

At last she could bear it no longer.

'Are you OK?' she asked – hoping, hoping to ease her way into his uncertainty and discomfiture; to make him tell her how things might be even better. But his reply thwarted that hope.

'Fine,' he said. 'What about you? Ready to go back?'

'Not quite,' she said. But the magic had gone now. It felt, suddenly, a little foolish to be sitting out here in the middle of the night, drinking Fay's whisky. As if they were stand-ins, she thought, taking the place of the real actors on a film set whose romantic setting she could see now was contrived and clichéd: the moonlit night, the plash of the stream, the brooding fells. For another minute she sat, and then she drew her feet towards her and stood up.

'That was really nice,' Stephen said, his voice gentler than usual, as though he could sense her disappointment.

'Yes.' Cressida shivered a little, and busied herself brushing strands of moss off her legs. It was better to know, she told herself. Better to have had this half-hour than not. But she couldn't deceive herself that easily.

It seemed to take longer to get back to the house, even though they were heading downhill now. Cressida kept her eyes down, watching her footing, anxious that Stephen shouldn't have to help her again, and as if sensing this, he stayed a little further behind this time. When they reached the gate at the bottom of the hill, she was almost relieved that the adventure was over. Stephen walked beside her up the drive, and there was a moment of shared sensibility, a glimmer of humour, as they trod gently over the gravel to avoid being heard.

The kitchen felt warm and close, still filled with the smell of last night's supper. Stephen shut the door behind them, and then he stopped, just inside the room. A second passed, then two, then three. Cressida could feel hope building up again, and she couldn't bear it.

'Well, goodnight,' she said. 'Thank you for coming with me.'

'Cressida,' he said – and then his hands were on her face, and before she had time to think he was kissing her, and she felt everything melt and fuse inside her, delight and disbelief and a great surge of desire.

They went to his room, since hers was directly below Fay's – the murmured exchange a further source of exaltation to Cressida, confirming their intentions, their consciousness of what was happening. She could taste his mouth still, whisky and salt, as they shut the door, and then they were kissing again – oh, the extraordinary joy of it, after all this time – and she was nudging him backwards towards the bed, her hands lifting the back of his shirt and travelling up his spine while his held her, chastely, by the shoulders.

'We can,' she whispered. 'I want to . . .' He was so thin; she traced the line of his shoulder blades with her fingers, desperate to comfort him, to feed him. He seemed to hesitate, but she was sure of herself now. She lifted his shirt over his head, then pulled off her T-shirt, and – with a flush of reckless lust – dropped her hands to unbutton his fly.

She'd had sex before, but only once, very drunk, with a rugby player who had known exactly what he was doing. It occurred to her now that Stephen was a virgin; that her little portion of experience would have to do for both of them. She was grateful for the whisky, and for the fact that they hadn't had more. It made things both better and worse that they knew each other so well: the fumbling, the awkwardness, wasn't something they could pretend not to notice. But nature, surely, and the momentum of the night . . . and she wanted it so badly, the intensity and intimacy she had dreamt about in the church that morning as the sunlight was coloured and shaped by the stained glass. And he was – thank God – he was ready for her; she could feel his penis now, pressing against her fingers as she sought it out, and the little groan of release as he let her take it.

The roughness of it took her by surprise. She had imagined him tentative, courteous, but tears rose, shockingly, in her eyes as he drove himself into her, and for a few minutes she could think of nothing but wishing for it to be over. And then it was, and as he slumped down on her chest the tears trickled down towards her temples until she wiped them crossly away, feeling naïve and idiotic. It was no surprise, she told herself, that the first time, or even the second ... It might be the end of the twentieth century, but the sophistication of their understanding was no substitute for experience. What mattered was that they had done it; that they had wanted to.

Even so, she couldn't stop another wash of tears. The sharp pain between her legs had spread to her back, a kind of numbing ache that made her feel compromised, almost abused, although of course if anyone had pushed things forward, it was her. She heard her brothers' voices now in her head, the casual way they talked about women when they didn't think she was listening, and she wondered whether it was her fault that it hadn't been nicer; whether she had hastened things on until he couldn't help but force himself into her and keep going, going until he had finished. Perhaps she had spoiled it for him, too.

For as long as she could bear she lay still, and then she braced her back, hoping she could ease her hips into a more comfortable position without seeming to reject Stephen. But even that tiny movement stirred him, and she couldn't withhold a murmur of relief as he slid off her. His head was close to hers still, and she adjusted her position as discreetly, as unfussily, as she could manage. His eyes were open, watching her, and she was terrified now that he would guess how much it had hurt, how much it had disappointed her. She lifted a hand to stroke his cheek.

'That was lovely,' she said.

'Good.' He sighed; perhaps with relief, Cressida thought. She felt a gush of pity, then, at the thought that he'd been worried. It mattered to men as well as women – perhaps more to men – that they were good at sex. He looked different, she thought, a kind of sadness about him, and she wanted to ease it away.

'Unexpected and lovely,' she said next, so that he wouldn't suspect that this was why she'd come to his room, all those hours ago.

He made a little noise – of contentment, she hoped – and moved his hand to pat her arm, and then he shut his eyes. It must be very late, Cressida thought, perhaps three or four by now, but she didn't feel sleepy. A sense of elation was creeping cautiously into her mind, like a car being reversed into a narrow parking space, but she still felt too numb to enjoy it, too jangled and confused. She wanted to stay here, with Stephen's warm flesh to remind her what had happened, but she wanted to be on her own, too, to digest it.

For a little while longer she lay beside him, feeling the dampness between her legs seeping inexorably out, and then there was a horrifying moment when she wondered whether there was blood as well as semen down there, and she clenched herself tight and whispered, 'Stephen, I'm going to go now.'

His eyes opened for a moment, and there was a glimpse, then, of the Stephen she knew; the one who had put his jacket on the ground so she could sit on it and caught her arm when she'd tripped.

'All right,' he said.

'I'll see you in the morning,' Cressida said. She hesitated a moment, and then she leant across to kiss him before slipping carefully out of the side of the bed.

As she made her way upstairs towards the bathroom, a sound from behind Judith's door made her freeze in horror. Had she . . . had they been overheard? she wondered. Did Judith know . . .? The sound came again – a sort of giggle, deep and luxurious, followed by a murmuring and a sigh of pleasure. Cressida stood, motionless and disbelieving. *My God, Judith,* she heard, *oh my God.* Bill's voice, muffled but unmistakable. Bill in Judith's room, and the two of them . . . *Oh please*, Judith was saying. *Oh yes please.*

Cressida turned abruptly into the bathroom and pulled the door shut behind her, trembling with mortification and disgust. How dare they? How could they, with Marmion, guileless Marmion, almost within earshot?

But there was more to her distress than that. There was a shameful, humiliating sense of envy. How could it – why should it – be so different for them?

June 1995
Judith

'My God, you're beautiful,' he said. His voice was gentle, the Midlands lilt more a colour than an edge, close up. His face was softened, too, by the almost-darkness, the shadowing of night that made them both mysterious. 'You're like a painting. Like a mermaid.'

'Luring sailors to their death.' Judith smiled, and before he could kiss her again she pulled back a little, stealing a moment to look at him, to try to take in what was happening. There was a throb in her head which must be the sound of her heart, loosed from its tethers and galloping, galloping.

His fingers were tracing a question mark along her flank. Judith shivered.

'You're not so bad yourself,' she said. 'Not quite a mermaid, but . . .'

She had never identified his smell before, but she recognised it now: an intense draught of musk and loam, kindling something surely too pleasurable to be guilt. She shut her eyes, deliciously conscious of the heaviness of his body and the strangeness of it; the strangeness of feeling, in this moment, that every exchange of glances, every shared joke or accidental touch of hand on sleeve over the last three years had fused into something coherent and substantial. Every fleeting scent of him, too: she realised now that she had always been aware of that, a powerful, primitive signal that had made her by turns restless or irritable or inexplicably happy when she caught a drift of it. Ever since that first day, she thought. All that time she'd known all this, at some level.

'You're so different,' he said. 'I can't . . .'

'Different – from Marmion?'

'Oh, Marmion . . . Please don't . . .'

The thrill of transgression pulsed through her skin.

'I won't,' she said. Won't think of that; won't mention it. This isn't really happening, after all. It's a fantasy, an impossibility. His hands all over her, making something new of her, drawing out desires and delights she'd never imagined. She could feel the dull ache of suspense between her thighs again now, the delicious anticipation. She slipped her hand down his belly, its sinuous assurance making her shudder.

'More?' she asked. 'Are you . . .?'

'Oh God,' he said. 'Oh yes. Oh, Judith . . .'

The chiming of the cuckoo clock hovered at first on the fringe of her hearing, like a jokey sound effect. She lay very still, her brain operating in slow motion.

'Is that that bloody clock?' Bill sank down on her chest as though in despair, although she knew there was none of that in him. 'God, that's some timing.'

Judith snickered, luxuriating in the immediacy that made anything beyond the two of them feel hazy and unreal. She could hear his breath in her hair, rapid and gratified. But the cuckoo chirped on, blithely insistent; and with each stroke it twitched them both a little further out of their reverie. At last she heard it whirr and wheeze, settling itself to wait out another hour.

'It can't be five o'clock yet,' Bill said.

Judith glanced at the bedside table. 'It is.'

She knew as she said it that she was ending the enchantment, and feeling Bill's body tense against hers she regretted it sharply.

'Oh fuck,' he said. 'Oh God, Judith, I'm sorry, but I'm going to have to go. I can't . . . I have no idea . . .'

'No idea of what?' Her voice sounded calm, almost steely, and she wondered a little at it. Some other part of her must be speaking, she thought. The elements of her had melted apart; she could hardly tell who she was just now. 'No idea how this happened, or how you're going to explain it to Marmion?'

'I'm such a shit,' he said. 'You must think I'm . . .'

'You didn't exactly blunder in here and take advantage of me.'

'No,' he said, his voice softening again.

He'd come inside to fetch a glass of water, and she'd been woken by the creak of the back door, or perhaps by something else – an owl; she'd heard owls here. They'd passed in the narrow corridor, footsteps muffled by Fay's thick rugs, sleep-soft bodies brushing up against each other. That was all; that was all it took. The safety of the night and its anonymity, removing their consciousness of identities and rights and the proper order of things.

'Feel free to, though.' She smiled, reaching a hand to smooth his hair down. This was a different mode, more familiar to her, trading tenderness for provocation. Oh, it was delicious trying out his responses, feeling him scrambling to find himself again, and her echo, her imprint resonating through him. 'Feel free to take advantage of me any time you like.'

'Oh Judith,' he said again. 'Oh fucking hell, what am I going to do?'

'That depends,' she said. 'For now that depends on whether Marmion is awake when you get back. On whether she suspects anything.'

'I can't not tell her.' He rolled away now and sat up, his body very white in the faint light from the uncurtained window.

'Of course you can. For the moment. It's not as though we . . .'

He swung back to look at her, his expression stricken, and Judith's heart lurched. My God, she thought, he really – but the rest of the sentence eluded her; the rest of the expression of surprise or pleasure or dismay. Bill lifted a hand to cradle her face, and she nestled into it for a moment, brushing her lips against his thumb.

'We'll talk,' he said. 'Tomorrow. We'll find a moment. I can't really think now, except that – I'm glad, whatever happens.'

'I am too,' Judith said. It wasn't much to acknowledge, but the honesty of it felt like something weighty passing between them.

'It feels like . . .' Bill faltered, and she shook her head fleetingly to shush him.

'Go,' she said. 'Don't say anything else.'

When the door had shut behind him, Judith could feel the silence trembling around her. She tried out, for a moment, the theory that she'd invented what had just happened, or merely wished it, but she knew it was too outlandish a tale for that. Too outlandish to have happened in any realm except blatant reality.

She lay on her back, imagining Bill's footsteps re-crossing the dew-laden garden. Now that he was gone, and all she was left with were impressions – the pressure of his hip bone here, the tickling of his murmured voice there – the other reality of him came back into her mind: the Bill she'd known for three years, whom she'd watched becoming steadily more inseparable from Marmion. The Bill who sang like a young Pavarotti and spoke like the Birmingham lad he was, whose cheery assurance hid a strain of doubt and hunger she recognised instinctively.

Two things surprised her, as the grey dawn sidled over the mountains and into the room: that she'd held out for so long, and that it all seemed so simple now. She'd kept telling herself he wasn't her type, but it was like the jigsaw piece you'd never have selected for a crucial place until you tried it and saw how perfectly, how unexpectedly it completed the picture.

But, she thought. But. It might seem obvious to her – and perhaps to Bill, too – that his romance with Marmion was a sweet, childish insignificance, but to Marmion . . . Marmion *was* a sweet child; that was the difficulty. She'd fallen in love with the first man she'd met, Judith thought, as though she'd been programmed to do it: as though she'd been fed a *Midsummer Night's Dream* love potion before she arrived in Cambridge.

Marmion's good-heartedness had been their moral compass these last three years. Judith doubted whether they could have been as close, the rest of them, without her. She admired Marmion – loved her, even – would certainly never wish to hurt her, but . . . It must be a cliché to imagine oneself in the grip of an inevitable power. There was no moral right on her side; even in the heading aftermath of passion Judith knew that. There was merely selfishness, and a brazen conviction she hardly believed in herself. She imagined Bill's dalliance with Marmion as the launching craft fuelled to lift a spaceship out of the earth's atmosphere before it burned away; and her own, their own, as the real thing, the rocket soaring up and out towards the moon and the stars and the sun.

But who was to say what this was, what it meant, after one illicit encounter? Perhaps, Judith thought, they should stop before Marmion found out – but she couldn't bear that. She couldn't manage the sacrifice, and the self-control. Oh God, oh God; what on earth were they going to do?

June 1995

Marmion

Fay drove up a track that passed through a farmyard before pulling up on the grassy verge before a gate.

'We can't get any further by car,' she said.

'Is that where we're going?' Marmion asked, as they looked up at the slope rising steeply in front of them. The now-familiar horse's-head summit was hidden from view, but a long stretch of footpath was visible, leading up to an angular ridge. This was clearly an expedition of a different order to the walks Fay had taken them on over the weekend. But everyone had been so strange this morning, so unexpectedly crabby, despite yesterday ending so happily with compline and then whisky by the fire, that she'd been secretly pleased when Fay suggested this outing. Last night's service had marked the end of the music festival, and they were due to return to Cambridge today, but another dose of fresh air before they left was a good thing, Marmion thought. In any case, there hadn't been much choice. 'We always climb Nag's Pike with new visitors,' Fay had said at breakfast, as though surprised that they hadn't grasped this fact already. 'You've had a few warm-ups: you'll be fine.'

'That's the direct route,' Fay said now. She smiled suddenly, as though amused by the stony faces around her. 'The gentler approach takes a bit longer, but we've got all day. Who wants first go as water carrier?'

She was wearing leather walking boots that looked as though they'd climbed every fell on the map, and the knapsack she held out now had the same venerable appearance. It wouldn't be engineered for comfort, Marmion thought. She was relieved when Stephen took it.

'Onwards, then.' Fay pushed open the gate and struck off across the field. 'Last one through shut the gate.'

Despite the warmth of the last week, the ground was far from dry, and little squelching noises accompanied every step. Fay was the only one of them with proper walking boots, and as she led the straggling line across the first field, Marmion thought that this hearty fell-walking side of her was another surprise. She'd imagined the Lake poets were more Fay's scene than Wainwright.

It was a hot day, but to Marmion's relief a little cooling breeze followed them along the edge of the valley. They were in an elongated basin, the shapes of the fells as beautiful and evocative as the lines of some modern sculpture. You thought of dinosaurs swooping down glacial valleys, Marmion thought, or Roman soldiers marching through on their way to Scotland. You thought of all the generations of people who had walked through here, and felt a bit embarrassed at your own feebleness.

'All right?' asked Stephen, who was keeping pace with her.

'Yes. Lovely, isn't it?'

Stephen nodded. His features had a determined set this morning; Marmion suspected her own looked rather similar.

After fifteen minutes they reached a stile. Bill, who'd seen her coming, had stopped to wait on the other side.

'OK?' he said, offering a hand as she climbed over.

'I'm fine.' Marmion paused so she could hold onto his hand a little longer. She'd felt once or twice this weekend that Bill had something on his mind (which was hardly surprising – they all had plenty on their minds at the moment, didn't they?), but in between times he'd been more than usually attentive, and she thought now that it was typical of him to want to make up for those moments of distraction.

'Enjoying yourself?' he asked.

Marmion pulled a face. She'd have liked to say something more, but words didn't always come to her when she wanted them. Instead she jumped down and, bending quickly, plucked a sprig of heather from beside the path and threaded it into a buttonhole on Bill's jacket.

*

Bill had been desperate all morning for an opportunity to talk to Judith. People often separated into twos and threes on a walk like this, he'd told himself; you could easily conduct a private conversation in plain view. But it proved harder than he'd hoped to get her alone, and as they climbed steadily up the side of the valley he was plagued not just by impatience and longing, but by doubt. He wasn't much of a prize, after all. Judith's boyfriends were invariably more glamorous than anyone in the choir: sulky English students with angular haircuts, or aristocrats wearing *Socialist Worker* badges. But surely he couldn't have imagined the way she'd looked at him last night; the way she'd spoken. Oh, that voice, laughing and mocking and drawing him in, all at the same time . . .

'Penny for your thoughts,' Judith said behind him – and his head was so full of her voice already that for a moment he thought he'd conjured the words himself.

He didn't dare turn; didn't look back over his shoulder.

'Marmion's keeping Stephen company,' she said. 'Or perhaps the other way round.'

'Ah.'

She laughed. 'I thought you might have a bit more to say than that.'

'I do.' He half stopped then, panic-stricken. 'I do. I just . . . I don't know where to start.'

'OK,' Judith said. 'Well, so we could start with *that was nice, but it was a bad idea*, or –'

'No,' said Bill. 'No, of course it wasn't a bad idea. It was – I can't believe my luck.'

'I can't either,' said Judith, and his heart tipped and tumbled in relief. 'I can't believe we're going to be that lucky, I mean. Given the circumstances.'

'What do you mean?' He wanted very badly to touch her: it was no good leaving this to words, he thought. 'Judith, I . . . We're only twenty-one. I'm not married to her.'

'I know.'

'I'll talk to her,' he said. 'I'll explain. It's a natural break.'

He could drop out of the course at the Guildhall, he was thinking. He needn't see Marmion. She needn't see him.

'Not now,' said Judith. 'Let's just . . .' She put a hand on his arm, the kind of gesture that might mean anything from a distance, and he felt a shiver run through his body.

They had come to a stile, and Judith was over it before the warmth of her fingers had left him. Bill glanced away for a moment to recover his composure, and there was Marmion, only twenty yards behind. Her face was flushed – but with effort, he thought, after a wild moment of fear, not with distress.

'Are you OK?' he asked, as she approached.

She smiled. 'I'm fine.'

Bill's eyes rested on her for a moment – a moment in which the courage to speak, to say *there's something I need to tell you* almost came to him – and then Marmion was over the stile and bending to pick something up, and smiling again as she tucked a piece of heather into his buttonhole. Gypsy luck, he thought. There'd been women who came to the door every year when he was little, proffering good fortune for 50p. His mother – hard-nosed in so many other respects – had never turned them away. Fat lot of good it had done her. Bill clenched his teeth as he set off again.

Fay had taken a different angle after the stile, moving more steeply uphill. The grass was rougher and sparser now, and the shimmer of a beck caught the light, spreading carelessly across the ground as it coursed downwards.

A little way ahead, Judith paused.

'I'm not sure there's a path here,' she said. 'It's very boggy.'

'Gracious.' Marmion stopped too. 'It really is a bit . . .'

Cressida grinned suddenly. 'You're all going too slowly,' she said. 'Bogs are like custard: if you run across them, they don't give way.'

She threw herself abruptly forward then, lifting her arms wide and careering off across the field like a little girl, her long hair flying behind her.

'I've never run through custard, to be honest,' said Bill – but before he knew what was happening they were all racing along in a gaggle of arms and legs, caught up in the surprise of the moment, splashing through the marshy ground and emerging on the other side wet and muddy and elated. Cressida flopped down breathlessly on a tree root, and the rest joined her.

Judith's hair was tangled, her face full of light. 'Oh, that was so much fun!' she said, grabbing Stephen's arm. 'See what we missed, growing up in the city.'

Bill felt a terrible clutch in his belly: he wanted to make her feel like that, he thought. What could beat the thrill of bringing Judith alive, banishing that formidable poise and making her forget herself? He shut his eyes, struggling with vertiginous shifts between euphoria and despair.

Marmion had turned to admire the view. 'I can see why you've brought us here,' she said, beaming at Fay.

'Not yet you can't,' said Fay. 'We've hardly started.' She pointed towards the summit of the fell. 'Up there, the view really is worth seeing.'

There was a moment of silence, broken only by a faint sound of panting. Bill glanced at his watch. Fay looked as tired as anyone, he thought; strain showed in her face as her rousing words died away. The thought of being back in Cambridge caught at him suddenly: things would feel different there, he thought. Everything would fall into place.

'Perhaps we shouldn't go all the way up,' he said in his most reasonable voice, the one he used when someone was drunk and needed to be steered home. 'If we're leaving this evening, and everyone needs to pack . . .'

Fay looked straight at him, and her expression was horribly intransigent.

'Nonsense,' she said. 'What's the rush? There's plenty of time for packing. You've got the rest of your lives for things like that.'

*

There was a dramatic change in the terrain after the stream. The boggy lowlands gave way to a craggy moorland landscape, strewn with boulders ranging in size from small pebbles to massy lumps that might almost, Marmion thought, be fossilised whales left behind by the retreating glaciers. There was still no sign of a path, but Fay continued without hesitation, veering further to the right again so they were climbing even more steeply.

For a long while no one said anything. Marmion remembered the whispers of apprehension she'd felt earlier in the weekend and wondered whether there had been something in the air all along; something that should have made them wary. Had anyone else felt it? Bill, perhaps, with that preoccupied air? Judith was as lively as ever, but Stephen had seemed guarded this morning, and Cressida too, until that moment crossing the bog when she'd suddenly come back to life. Marmion wished she could say something, ask someone, but it was hard to catch anyone's eye – and in any case, she was too short of breath for conversation. This was the kind of hill, she thought, that made you believe in gravity.

After another half-hour, Fay halted in front of a fence.

'Right,' she said. 'This is irritating. There should be a stile here, but they seem to think we can get through this.'

Barbed wire was strung tightly between metal stakes in a line that ran as far as they could see in both directions. It was hard to imagine how there could ever have been a stile here. Sheep's wool lay in snow-like tufts along the four strands of wire.

'Anyone got any wire-cutters?' asked Bill, his good humour almost convincing.

Fay said nothing – as if this was a challenge they had to rise to themselves, Marmion thought. But her silence was almost scarier than her bossiness.

'If this is really the only way,' said Judith, 'we'd better try to widen the gap.'

Bill and Stephen moved forward obediently, taking hold of the lower two strands and yanking them firmly apart.

'OK,' said Judith. 'Cressy? You're the smallest.'

Cressida didn't look keen, but she crouched down and put a hand gingerly on the bottom wire.

'Hang on,' said Judith. She gathered up Cressy's hair, holding it in a tight bundle near her neck. 'Try now,' she said, and Cressida scrambled and slithered through the fence with a suppressed squawk as some part of her caught on the wire, then a smile of triumph when she stood up on the far side.

'Brava!' said Fay. 'See?'

That was all very well, Marmion thought, but she was a lot bigger than Cressy. Judith was wriggling through the fence now, managing it with a grace that reminded Marmion of a gymnast.

'Marmion?' said Bill.

She looked at him, and he looked back. She really didn't want to do this; really didn't want to be put through the humiliation.

'Let me get your hair,' said Judith, and as Marmion leant down she reached through the fence and twisted her hair – thicker and curlier than Cressy's – into a skein to keep it away from the barbs.

Bill and Stephen gave an extra tug on the wire, allowing her another inch or two, and Marmion edged her right shoulder through. Then she thought: perhaps head first would be better. Before she could think again she let go of the wire and fed both hands through the gap. She was on all fours now, straddling the wire with her midriff. She must look ridiculous, she thought, but this was no time for self-consciousness. Carefully, she placed her left foot on the wire. If she rested it there, adding to the pressure on the lower strand, perhaps she could get the other foot through more easily. But when she lifted her right foot the wire wobbled dangerously. She gave a kind of kick and projected herself forward, landing in a heap on the other side. At least she'd done it, she thought, wrestling her way back onto her feet, but then she noticed the rivulets of blood on her calf, beading up from deep scratches, and she felt her eyes filling with tears. Were they going to have to go back down the same way? she wondered. Was this really supposed to be fun?

Judith put an arm around her.

'OK?' she asked, and Marmion nodded.

'Bit scratched,' she said.

'Full marks for artistic impression,' Judith said.

Behind her, Fay was slithering through the fence now. Marmion held Judith fiercely for a moment.

The men scrambled through next; within a few moments they had arrived on the other side.

'Reporting for duty, Commandant,' said Stephen.

'Well done, all,' said Fay. 'They do like to put a little adversity in our way.'

She seemed to have forgotten, Marmion thought with a flash of exasperation, that all this had been her idea. She was the benign hostess again, the helpful guide.

'Anyone want some water?' Fay asked.

'Ah, is that what I've been carrying all this time?' asked Stephen. 'Be my guest; drink some of my ballast.'

'It's not far now,' said Fay. 'We rejoin the main path over there, and it's a shortish climb to the top.'

The others seemed re-energised by the halt; they set off at a brisker pace, but Marmion began to fall behind. She could feel her morale slipping, her heartbeat thumping, her legs aching. She kept her eyes on the path, taking one step at a time, trying not to feel too daunted by the distance she still had to cover.

*

The barbed wire was almost the last straw for Bill. The sight of Marmion, undignified and bleeding, and Judith kneeling beside her, offering a tissue and consoling words; of Fay looking at them all in that odd, discomfiting way. Even Cressida had glared at him when he'd attempted a we're-all-in-this-together smile, as though it was his fault Marmion had been injured, or that they hadn't stood up to Fay.

He strode off before the others had finished drinking from the water bottles Stephen produced from his backpack. It was hopeless, he thought. He remembered Judith saying, *that was nice, but it was a bad idea*, and then *not now, let's just* . . . Putting her hand on his arm as though she had no idea what effect that would have on him, and then laughing in that wonderful, windswept way when they'd come through the bog, clutching Stephen's arm, not his. How could he have thought she was interested in him? He just wanted to get this bloody awful walk over with now, this whole trip.

He hardly knew what to feel when he realised Judith was behind him. He heard her footsteps, her breathing, a little exclamation as she missed her footing. He quickened his pace, and she kept up with him. Once he glanced over his shoulder, and he could see the others were some way behind by now, but still he kept going, and so did she. Neither of them spoke: it was as if they were both intent on making a clean getaway. His heart beat faster and faster from excitement and anticipation and dread. Had he been wrong, then? Could she really . . .?

After another few minutes, he risked a halt. They had just come round a sharp corner; the others were nowhere to be seen. Judith was beside him in a second, cocking her head slightly to smile at him, breathing heavily from the climb.

'God, Judith,' he said. 'Oh God . . .' and he pulled her towards him on the narrow path and kissed her with all the suppressed vehemence and ache of his heart and his head and his limbs. No more words; just their bodies pressing and twisting against each other and the world dropping away at their feet, the steel-thin air and the beat of the sun. This was escape and sublimation: this was the answer to his dreams. He held her tight, Judith the burning flame, the source of all joy.

But then there were footsteps, voices, too close, and a sharp exclamation – Fay's voice, then Stephen's – and Judith jerked away from him.

And after that it wasn't the world at their feet but something giving way beneath them, a lurching and clutching and a frantic tumble, and Judith was falling, falling, her body slithering and somersaulting over the rocks, and he was screaming into the emptiness – 'Oh my God, Judith!' – and hearing the echo of his voice from miles and miles away.

*

Cressida had stopped on the path just ahead of Marmion.

'Look!' she said.

Marmion lifted her eyes and felt her spirits fly. They could see for miles now, right down the valley and into the next one. Ullswater lay far below, an elongated silvery S shape like a mirror carefully cut to fit between the fells.

'Oh, goodness,' she said, and Cressida smiled at her pleasure.

'How's the leg?' she asked.

'Fine. A souvenir.'

'It can't be far now. We're so high up already.'

'Let's hope.'

'We'll look back on this and be pleased,' Cressida said. 'I'm sure we will.'

But just then, a little way off, they heard a scream, a scrabble of rocks, and a voice shouting.

'Judith! Oh my God, Judith!'

Marmion's heart curdled. Bill's voice. Judith falling.

She and Cressida rushed on up the path. As they came round the next corner, the scene was laid out for them, their friends arranged like a stick-figure diagram describing an accident unfolding. Judith was out of sight, but Bill was slithering down the slope, Stephen close behind. A little way above them Fay stood stock still, looking down. Cressida veered off from the path, and Marmion forced herself to follow. Her legs were numb with fear and exhaustion, hardly capable of moving.

Judith was lying spread-eagled among a slide of rocks. She was very still, and one leg was bent at a terrible angle. Marmion couldn't tell whether she had shouted before – couldn't remember any sounds at all since that first cry of Bill's – but now she heard her voice as part of a sudden cacophony.

Oh God . . . leg must be broken . . . unconscious . . . what should we . . .

Then the cacophony seemed to fade again, exactly as if someone had turned a dial, and above it Cressida's voice rose shrilly, almost in triumph: 'I knew it. I knew something was going on.'

The fells, the aching muscles, everything extraneous about the scene was suddenly shrouded by a kind of mist. What Marmion could see was Judith lying on the ground, her dark hair scattered like an aureole and a piece of heather clutched in her hand. She could see Bill kneeling beside her, his face racked with despair – and Fay standing over them now, looking with terrible compassion towards Marmion.

Bill

2008

Bill has a recurring dream that he is standing beside his own grave. The grave always looks the same, a plain stone with his name carved on it but nothing else: no dates, no consoling line of scripture. William Matthew Devenish.

Although the grave is a constant, and there's that odd sense of recognition that alerts you to the return of a dream you know, the circumstances change – the location and the storyline and the dramatis personae. Sometimes it's set on a clifftop, sometimes deep in the woods, sometimes in a country churchyard at the height of summer. Sometimes Bill is trying to get everyone to come and look at something, and doesn't realise until the last minute that it's his grave – although there's always, then, that sneaking feeling that he ought to have known, must have remembered where he was going. Sometimes he's busy with something – reading a book, or laying out a picnic – and the grave just happens to be nearby, as though it's always there, always in the background, so that he'd glimpse it if he happened to turn his head in the right direction.

It was a while before Marmion first appeared in the dream, and when she did – when she does – she's always happy to see him. He remembers her warmth, her openness; it's a wonderful relief to see her. Tonight she had a baby in her arms, and she wanted to show it to him, wanted him to hold it. When he wakes up, he can still feel the weight of it in his arms.

It's very dark in the bedroom: the dream must have woken him hours before the alarm. He's cross with himself – he'd have liked to stay longer, holding the baby. He hardly saw its face. But then he understands that something else has roused him. The bed is soaked, as though someone's poured a jug of warm water over him. Isabel is fast asleep, curled on her side of the bed. He can feel his bladder, uncomfortably full, so he knows it's not that, at least. When he stands up, he realises that even his hair is wet. He shivers, and stumbles through to the bathroom. As he fumbles with the opening of his pyjamas, he feels something in his groin: something like a small marble, just under his skin.

The news is as good as it can be: it's Hodgkin's lymphoma, the highly treatable kind. Given his age and stage, there's an eighty-five per cent five-year survival rate. It's a sign of how his perspective has changed in the last week that a fifteen per cent chance of dying seems like good news.

They'd been just about to embark on their last cycle of IVF, he and Isabel. They've been paying for the treatment themselves, laying out a small fortune in pursuit of parenthood. Isabel is a few years older than him, approaching forty, and at her age, they both know, the chances are slim – not far off his fifteen per cent, in fact – but fifteen is a lot more than nothing. On both counts, fifteen is a lot more than nothing. At least they don't have to pay for his treatment, he thinks, but he doesn't say that to Isabel. Instead, he takes her out to dinner, the night before his first dose of chemotherapy, and apologises. He can't get the image of Marmion's baby, the dream baby, out of his head while he's speaking. Maybe Isabel can see it too, glimpse some trace of it in his eyes, because she looks horrified.

'You don't have to apologise,' she says. 'What do you have to apologise for?'

'I've let you down,' he says. 'It might have been our turn to be lucky. We'll never know now.'

'For God's sake,' she says. 'Do you think I'd rather have a baby, or keep you?'

He's surprised by this: the question hadn't occurred to him, but if it had, he'd have guessed it would be a pretty close call. He ought to feel touched, but instead he's slightly alarmed.

'Well,' he says, 'I rather hoped you'd be able to have both.'

'We can adopt,' she says. She looks pretty tonight, her face flushed in a way that suits her, but she's wearing a dress that doesn't. A sort of tawny colour, with a pattern of leaves. Bill isn't sure they'll be allowed to adopt – not until he's in the clear, and by then they might be too old – but he nods and smiles, feeling an unexpected tenderness for her. It's the dress, he thinks, that makes him feel protective. It's the wrong colour for her; it looks as though she's borrowed it from someone else, having admired it on them. Poor Isabel, ending up with all the wrong things, making all those well-meaning decisions that turn out to be so misguided. She shouldn't have turned down the ENO chorus a few years back. That might have been a launch pad for her, even if it meant living apart for a while. The bookings for local choral societies, the bit of teaching in a local school, are less than she deserves. Even the hobbies she takes up don't seem to stick: watercolours one term, quilting the next.

'What are you going to eat?' he asks. He's not hungry, but he scans the menu in search of something he could manage. Soup, perhaps. A cliché of the sick.

The treatment isn't as bad as he expected. It's a very individual thing, the oncologist tells him: some people tolerate it better than others. He's off work for a few weeks, and the weather is good (it's May, but a balmy sort of May), so he takes himself out for walks.

Everyone reminded him, when they moved back up here, how beautiful Shropshire was. They quoted Housman, and he thought of Vaughan Williams. He imagined walking a lot, looking down from Wenlock Edge and scaling the Wrekin, but somehow that hasn't happened. Isabel likes Attingham Park, the three-mile circuit of the deer park and picking blackberries or elderflower along the riverbank, and they haven't ventured much further. He can't think, now, what they have filled their weekends with all these years, but there never seems to be time for a proper walk, the kind that gets you miles from anywhere so that the world looks different, less safe, more filled with possibility.

He has to be careful, of course; he doesn't want to exhaust himself while his body's fighting this thing, but he feels sure that the air over the hills is good for him. Isabel doesn't come with him the first time, and he doesn't press her after that. He's happy striding alone across the top of the Long Mynd, like the great broad back of a whale, or following the stream up through Carding Mill Valley. Sometimes he has conversations with Isabel in his head while he walks, and he can't help feeling they go better without her there.

One morning, though, his father drives out from Birmingham to join him. They meet in Ironbridge and follow a circular trail through Jackfield and Broseley and Coalbrookdale. Remnants of the Industrial Revolution are everywhere in this part of the Severn Valley, a story of progress and misery for humankind preserved now in a group of museums and in factories converted to luxury flats. His father scrupulously avoids any discussion of the cancer and talks instead about Bill's nieces, who are fourteen now and no less worrying to their grandparents than they were during those anxious weeks they spent in the Special Care Baby Unit.

'They're nice girls,' he says. 'Get either of them on their own and they're nice girls, but the arguments . . .'

Bill nods. He's a little out of breath, but he doesn't want to confess that to his father. This outing is meant to reassure him.

'You wouldn't believe what they find to fight about,' his father continues. 'Clothes, CDs, I don't know. If they spent half that time on their school work . . .' He glances at Bill. 'We never thought they'd stay all this time. Not that we don't love having them, but it's hard on your mother, having a house full of teenagers again.'

Bill considers this. He hardly knows anything about Mia or Grace. He's always told himself it's difficult for Isabel, being faced with the evidence of Mandy's immoderate fertility, but he knows that's not the only reason he's detached himself from his family. He's on the point of saying something bland and sympathetic when his father stops suddenly.

'There,' he says, pointing. Below them there's a view of the gorge, the curve of the Severn flanked by thickly wooded slopes and the famous iron bridge spanning it. The little town clusters on the far side, prettily haphazard and thronged, these days, with tea rooms and gift shops rather than workers' cottages.

'Beautiful,' says Bill. It is an arresting panorama, the bridge at the centre of it almost too delicate, too decorative, to be a symbol of industrial might – but he's not sure whether that's what his father sees. It seems to him suddenly that the story of this place, its brave hopes and past glories, the quenching of its furnaces and prettification of its history, is too poignant for them both.

'You know there's another bridge beneath the river,' his father says. 'The other half of the circle.'

'Really?'

'The gorge is narrowing,' his father says. 'The bridge was being squeezed from each side. So back in the seventies they built a matching arch, upside down, to strengthen it.'

'Huh.'

'You wouldn't guess, would you?' His father shoots him a smile. 'You'd never know it took all that labour to keep it in one piece.'

There are some blessings over the next few months. Bill makes good progress, his cancer maintaining an orderly retreat. He can tell, every time he sees the doctors, what a relief it is for them to have a patient they can give good news to. When he goes back to work, the senior partner calls him into his office and says encouraging things about his career. And Isabel has a lucky break: a last-minute call to step in as soprano soloist in a Haydn Mass at the Proms, and on the back of that a couple more bookings for gigs in London of a higher calibre than she's had lately. As Christmas approaches, Bill tells himself that they've turned a corner. He comes out of work one evening into the winter darkness and smells smoke and pine needles on the cold air. Shrewsbury looks pretty with its streets lit up, and a faint draught of carol singing filters down the hill.

On a whim, he turns left towards the town centre rather than right into the office car park, following the direction of the music – which leads him, as he expects, to the shop just off the market square that sells CDs and art materials as well as books. He doesn't think they have any CDs of Christmas carols at home. Perhaps the shop will sell him some decorations too, something newer and shinier than the plastic wreath and sagging paper stars they hang up every year. He imagines adorning the house, filling it with music for Isabel's return. Perhaps he could cook something that would smell warm and festive, gingerbread or mulled wine or mince pies.

Then just as he turns into the shop, a new track starts. A solo voice this time, rather than a choir, singing one of the movements from Britten's 'Ceremony of Carols'. It's unmistakably a female voice, not a boy treble, but even so it's a pure, clear sound.

> *That yongë child when it gan weep*
> *With song she lulled him asleep*
> *That was so sweet a melody*
> *It passèd alle minstrelsy.*

He hasn't dreamt of Marmion since the summer, but now he sees again the image of her holding the baby, her face alight with pleasure. The baby has her hair, a shimmer of dark copper over its soft head.

But the voice, he thinks; that isn't Marmion's voice, it's Judith's.

He turns on his heel and hurries back down the hill, hot with confusion and desire. Judith hasn't entered his dreams for years. He's thought of her, though – of course he's thought of her. Judith whose voice was the sweetest, for all her fieriness. Judith whose eyes flashed a witty retort faster than her tongue. Judith naked in his room, bold and slender as a sunflower.

His hands are trembling as he pulls out of the car park and follows the familiar route out of town. The winding streets give way to the tangle of dual carriageways that surround Shrewsbury, and then the flash of street lights ceases and he's on a country lane, heading deep into the countryside towards their village. He must be mistaken, he tells himself. That can't be the recording they made at St Anne's – oh, fifteen years ago. Surely like the dreams, like the night sweats, there's a twist there he's been taken in by, a hole in the sequence of assumptions. It's all in his mind, he tells himself; but he knows that's the problem.

The house is in darkness when he arrives. Isabel isn't due back yet; that's why he thought of . . . That image of stars and carols and gingerbread seems a million miles away. All he can see now is the awkward, over-large house, its blank windows reproachful. Some of the bedrooms have started to smell like the unused rooms in old people's houses, with that slight sighing shift of sequestered air when you open the door on them. Bill wonders how they could ever have imagined this house full of children.

He's still sitting in the drive when another set of headlights looms round the corner and swings off the road to park beside him. He hears the crunch and slam of the car door, and then Isabel's footsteps. She's almost at the front door when she stops. Turning his head, he sees her looking straight at him.

'Bill?'

She comes back towards the car and opens the driver's door.

'My God, you gave me a fright. What are you doing there?'

'I've just got back,' he lies. 'Just a few moments ago. I was thinking something through.'

She smiles. 'A work thing? Forget about it now. Come inside: it's cold out here.'

'OK.'

She turns, and goes on ahead of him into the house. He watches the downstairs windows lighting up, one by one, some shining bright white and some paler and yellowish with light that percolates through from other rooms. He sees Isabel coming towards the sitting room window to pull the curtains across, and then silhouetted in the kitchen window, filling the kettle at the sink.

So what is he going to do? he wonders. Leave Isabel to fill the whole house by herself? For what – the stab of an old wound? The weariness of surviving disaster?

He climbs out of the car and follows his wife into the house. For a fleeting moment he savours the surprise of seeing the interior afresh, as though he's been away for a long time. But almost before he can grasp at the feeling, and the insight it brings, everything settles back into its usual form. From the kitchen doorway he can hear the hiss of the kettle and the hum of the oven, the clatter of crockery as Isabel delves into the cupboard. When she sees him, she straightens up and comes towards him.

'My poor Bill,' she says. Her tone is unfamiliar, as though whatever he has been through has communicated itself to her, but she doesn't look frightened. She puts her arms around him and pulls him in close. He can smell the cold air still in her hair, and a trace of her perfume.

'I'm all right,' he says. 'I'm all right.'

Part III

September 2015
Bill

High Scarp was both as Bill remembered it and not. The approach, up a steep and rather narrow track, called up at once the memory of that first arrival, and the grey stone walls and white window frames were just as he would have described them. But the architecture looked different, somehow; the way it fitted into the hillside. Certainly some of the trees had grown: the house was more overshadowed now, half buried in a canopy of branches.

'Wow,' said Isabel, as he turned off the engine. 'It's bigger than I imagined. Look at all that garden.'

The garden surrounded the house, most of it on a slope, with areas of lawn fringed with rhododendrons and dotted with fruit trees. It looked less well-kempt than Bill remembered. That would be an expense, he thought. There would be lots of expenses. Might the others agree to let it out for part of the year, or would that have been prohibited by Fay?

'Let's find the key,' he said. 'It's supposed to be in a safe round the side.'

He hadn't anticipated that they would be the first to arrive, but he was glad they were. He found the safe without difficulty, entered the code they'd been given, and took out the keys – not the big old-fashioned one he remembered, but a modern pair for a five-lever mortise and a Yale.

'Are the others bringing their spouses?' Isabel asked.

'I don't know.' Bill opened the door into the kitchen: entirely unchanged, he noted, with a mixture of relief and misgiving. 'I don't know if they have spouses.'

103

Isabel considered this for a moment, hanging back in a way that caused Bill a flare of impatience.

'Did you think I might be the only one? Is that why you –'

'Why I what?' Bill turned to face her. She looked anxious now; that wasn't a good sign. 'Darling,' he said, 'I'm afraid I didn't think about it that hard. You seemed keen to come, so . . .'

He was spared the rest of this circumlocution of the truth by the sound of a car straining up the track. Isabel raised her eyebrows, and Bill took a step towards the door. The car stopped outside the gate: he heard doors slamming and the sound of voices. Perhaps another spouse after all. Then the car began wheezily backing down the hill, and after a moment someone came through the gate, carrying a suitcase. Judith. Of course it would have to be Judith. He watched her approach across the gravel, judging the moment for his greeting, and then, on a whim, launched himself through the front door.

'Well, well,' he said, 'Judith Malik, as I live and breathe.'

'Bill,' she said. Her smile was just the same: jaunty, considering, fearless. She looked a bit older in the flesh than she had in those website photos, but otherwise . . .

'This is Isabel,' said Bill. 'My wife, Isabel Crookham.'

Isabel didn't move. She was standing behind Bill now, in the doorway. They were all stuck, Bill thought, just for a moment, like chess pieces arranged so that none of them could move without peril.

'Oh, well, I know Isabel, of course,' Judith said. 'Though you won't recognise me.' She smiled again, and Bill felt Isabel stiffen. 'Bach Choir,' said Judith. 'You sang the soprano solos in the *Messiah* with us, a couple of Christmases ago. You were wonderful.'

'Oh!' said Isabel. 'That's right, I did. I'm sorry, I don't remember . . .'

'I didn't realise Bill had married a celebrity,' said Judith.

She picked up her case, which had been set down on the gravel, and Bill and Isabel moved aside.

'Hardly a celebrity,' Isabel was saying, and Bill felt a dart of pity for her. He could tell that Judith had finished with her, having delivered her compliment – and having won Isabel over more effectively than she could have imagined. It was more than a couple of Christmases ago, that Bach Choir gig, and there hadn't been as much work recently, certainly not in London.

But he felt a dart of feeling for Judith, too. Not quite pity; it had never been possible to pity Judith, and he was already certain it still wasn't. But Judith had been at least as good a singer as Isabel, once upon a time. Somehow her being in the Bach Choir made him feel that things hadn't worked out quite as he'd imagined, or as she might have hoped – but that was ridiculous, he told himself. Judith radiated purposefulness and prosperity. She would despise his blundering sympathy. He flushed, sharply conscious of the hazards ahead; the ease with which he might be tripped up.

'This kitchen looks exactly the same, doesn't it?' Judith said now. 'What about the rest of the house?'

'We'd only got this far,' Bill said. 'Should we wait for the others, or . . .?'

But Judith was already moving on. They followed her, Isabel just ahead of him. The living room was through the door on the left, Bill remembered, the bedrooms off to the right. Two on this floor, and at the end of the corridor a staircase led down to a couple more, cut into the hillside. He felt suddenly queasy, as though everything that had happened here was plainly visible still, the imprint of it left behind among the furniture and the whitewashed walls.

Judith put her suitcase down in the biggest bedroom, the one that had been Fay's, and went to look out of the window.

'Gorgeous view,' she said. 'I remember that well.'

Even from the doorway Bill could see the still-familiar sweep of fells, with Nag's Pike in the middle of it – but Judith had turned away again now, having given the panorama barely more than a moment's attention. She didn't bring her case with her when she left the room. Bill made a little noise, a sort of throat-clearing, and Isabel frowned at him.

'Oh, and the living room!' Judith said, doubling back the other way. 'Goodness, do you remember that game we played – the sound-effects game?'

Bill shook his head.

'You did a bird,' Judith said. 'Can you still do that? Birdsong?'

'I don't think so. I haven't tried for years.'

'I bet you can,' Judith said. She stopped in the middle of the room, silhouetted against the window which filled the whole of the opposite wall, and looked straight at him for the first time. 'Is this going to be fun, do you think? I was absolutely dreading it.'

Bill stared at her. The mixture of frankness and dissimulation was devastating. It seemed to him that she was playing a role, saying things simply to make the position she'd taken convincing to herself.

'It's been a long time,' he said, as easily as he could manage. 'I suppose . . .'

But Judith had turned to inspect the ancient sofas, the fireplace, the Heaton Cooper print of Derwentwater that hung above it.

'What do you make of it?' she asked. 'Fay leaving us this place? Does it make any sense to you?'

'Well,' Bill began. 'From a legal point of view, it's clear that she . . .'

Judith was a lawyer too, he remembered.

'I've been wondering whether there was something odd about the whole set-up, back in the day,' Judith said.

There it was again: plunging in head first to show there was nothing to worry about, and making it impossible, then, to edge towards things with any sincerity.

'What do you mean?' he asked.

Judith made a dismissive gesture. 'You were too wrapped up in Marmion to notice.'

Bill blushed deep scarlet. Jesus, he thought, the woman was lethal. Isabel was looking at Judith, not at him, thank God.

'What was she like?' Isabel asked – and then, after a tiny hesitation, 'Fay, I mean?'

Judith cast a glance at her, then sat down in the middle of the smaller sofa. He'd forgotten that, Bill thought: that ballet dancer grace, revealed when you least expected it. That pleating movement just then. Nothing like the way she spoke: or perhaps it was. Economical, elegant.

'I think she saw herself as a cross between a godmother and an older sister,' Judith said. 'Much older. Though in fact she probably wasn't a lot older then than we are now. Do you realise that?' She looked at Bill: another frank, nothing-to-hide look. He moved towards the armchair nearest the door, but didn't sit down. Isabel was hovering, agonised, beside Judith's sofa.

'We met her at a reception in the Master's Lodge in our first term,' Judith went on. 'She found out it was Stephen's birthday the following week, and she invited us to dinner.'

Bill had forgotten all that. If he really tried, he could summon a memory of the dark green walls of the Master's drawing room.

'Gosh,' said Isabel – although the story was hardly remarkable, repeated in this way. Perhaps that was Judith's point.

'I think it must have been a whim,' Judith said. 'I think she must have done it from time to time, with students, but she took to us. We were entertaining, I suppose.'

'Were we?' Bill asked.

'We were a troupe,' Judith said. 'An amusing act. Though whether we would have been, quite so much, without Fay, I don't know. She chiselled us off from the rest of the choir. Made us into a sort of semichorus, you could say. Bill might disagree.'

Bill looked from Judith to Isabel. The oddness of the situation made him feel a little dizzy. These two people – women – here together, and the others who weren't. Like mixing flavours that didn't go; that emphasised what was missing.

'I'm going to make tea,' he said. 'Anyone want a cup?'

'Is someone bringing food?' Judith asked.

'There's the pub,' Bill said. That would be a blessing: getting away from High Scarp to more neutral territory. He felt his spirits lift, just a tiny bit.

But the fridge in the kitchen was full. Milk, bread, bacon, sausages. Exactly the same food as twenty years ago, he could swear. Surely this wasn't the Penrith solicitor acting on his own initiative? Fay, then, from beyond the grave? What else, he wondered, a little horrified now, had she prescribed for the weekend?

'No need for the pub,' he called, his voice jaunty now in the same way as Judith's. 'Someone's been shopping for us.'

June 1995
Judith

'I don't know how you could,' said Cressida.

She and Stephen were sitting on either side of Judith's hospital bed. The late-afternoon sun threw a triangle of light across one corner of the cramped room, making the rest of it look dim and rather desolate. Judith's head ached abominably, but she'd refused the last round of painkillers because they made her feel so groggy.

'Cressida . . .' said Stephen, but Cressida ignored him.

'I really don't,' she said. 'Right under Marmion's nose. How could you imagine she wouldn't find out?'

'She's got concussion, Cressida,' said Stephen. 'This isn't the time or the place.'

'I might not get another chance.' Cressida's face was rigid with determination. 'I can't say this with Marmion in the room.'

'Is she likely to visit me?' asked Judith. Her head throbbed with every word, but it pleased her to be able to speak; to be able to understand what was being said and respond to it, even if the exchange was unpleasant.

'Of course she's visited you,' said Cressida. She seemed unimpressed with Judith's accomplishment in contributing to the dialogue. 'She was here most of yesterday evening.'

Judith took this in. Every thought hurt too, as though her brain was working on some backup system involving cogs and pulleys that jolted distressingly among the bruised tissue in her head. The facts – those Cressida was referring to, and others connected to them – were surprisingly clear, as though they had been lying in wait while she swam in and out of consciousness, up and down from vivid, violent dreams. She had fallen, while they were climbing Nag's Pike with Fay; that was why she was here. She'd hit her head on a stone, and Bill had rushed to her side, and his distress had revealed their treachery to Marmion. Marmion was distraught, and Cressida, it seemed, was angry. Judith had lain here now for . . . Actually, she had no idea about that. Was it one day, or two, or more?

'How long have I been here?' she asked.

'Only since yesterday,' said Stephen. 'You've been pretty out of it, though. Do you remember what happened?'

'I'm not sure what I remember, and what I remember being told.' The images in her mind – the mountain, the blue sky, people screaming silently – seemed to have arrived pre-packaged: it was as if someone had stocked the shelves of her memory with merchandise more brightly coloured than she would have selected for herself.

'Do you remember the helicopter?' Stephen asked.

'No.'

Cressida made a cross sound, as if she was being deliberately flouted. 'Judith,' she said, 'I'm sorry if I'm being bossy, but this has got to stop.'

'This?' Judith rolled her head with an effort to face Cressida's side of the bed. It would be easier if she and Stephen sat next to each other. Cressida had the sun behind her, too: there was a dazzle around her head like a vindictive halo.

'Whatever you want to call it. Your thing with Bill.'

Judith shut her eyes. She could feel things slipping away from her, not making sense any more.

'I'm very sleepy,' she said.

'That's convenient,' said Cressida.

'For heaven's sake leave it now,' said Stephen. 'Let her be. It's not the time or the place.' And Judith knew she'd heard those words before, so that it must be a dream. She let herself sink, sink, blissfully sink, until the room, the voices, had faded from view.

June 1995
Cressida

'Stephen.' Cressida shut the door of Judith's room behind her and hurried after him. 'Stephen, wait.'

Ahead of her, Stephen halted. It was ridiculous, Cressida thought, that there hadn't been a single moment until now when they could talk. Every time she'd thought she might be left alone with him these last couple of days, something had prevented it. And of course everyone was worried about Judith, and about Marmion too, so that it seemed selfish to be thinking about what had happened the other night. But Cressida was worried that if she didn't say something, it would soon be as if it had never happened. She could already feel the memory of the waterfall, the whisky, the wonderful moment in the kitchen when he'd kissed her becoming hazy and uncertain, eclipsed by the bigger drama of Judith's fall and Marmion's betrayal.

'Stephen, I know ...' she began. She could see reluctance in his face, even distaste for what she might be about to say, but she held fast to her courage. 'It's just – I don't know when there might be another chance to talk.'

'No.' He looked embarrassed now, and Cressida felt a rush of hope. Perhaps he thought he'd taken advantage of her. Perhaps he'd been dreading this conversation because he felt guilty.

'It was lovely,' she said. 'The other night. It was really lovely. I know – there's so much else to think about now, but I didn't want you to think ...'

They were still several feet apart, Cressida clutching her bag in front of her and Stephen standing with his hands hanging down uselessly beside him. The light in the corridor was dim, giving the pale green paint a murky, stagnant feel.

'Cressida,' he said, 'I don't –'

'I know it's not the moment,' Cressida said. 'With Judith and Marmion and everything. But I just wanted . . .' She gazed at him hopefully. 'Perhaps when we're back in Cambridge, or –'

'Excuse me.' An orderly came round the corner, pushing a wheel-chair containing a very old man, and Stephen moved back into a doorway to let them pass. The old man looked at Cressida with red, heavy-lidded eyes, and she smiled, suppressing a stab of impatience. As they rolled away up the corridor she looked at Stephen again. She wouldn't say anything more, she thought. She always said too much. She would wait for him now, leave the ball in his court.

Stephen wasn't looking at her. His face didn't move, but she assumed he was thinking, gathering himself.

'It's not fair to blame Judith,' he said eventually.

Cressida stared. 'What do you mean?'

'It's not fair to lay into her when she's so ill. It's not reasonable to judge her.'

'I'm only thinking of Marmion,' Cressida said. 'I'm not making a moral judgement.'

'It sounded like a moral judgement.'

'I'm sorry,' she said. 'I didn't mean . . .'

Stephen didn't reply. A frown had settled on his face now. Cressida felt numb: this didn't make any sense, she thought. They were friends, she and Judith. They all were. You could say things like that to friends, surely. You could tell them what you thought.

'I didn't mean to offend you,' she said. 'I didn't mean to seem small-minded.'

Still he wouldn't look at her, and she felt the beginnings of desperation now. That lovely evening, she thought: the way everything had come together at last – and then the sex had been more complicated than she'd expected, but that made it even more important that they didn't let things drift. She was painfully conscious of their inexperience, of the things stacked against them – even more, now, with all that had happened in the last couple of days.

She wished suddenly, vehemently, that she could take back what she'd said to Judith. She couldn't bear Stephen to think badly of her, as though she'd revealed her true colours in that self-righteous outburst. The worst thing was that he was right, in a way: it was a moral judgement, or at least . . . She remembered that moment, standing outside Judith's bedroom door at High Scarp: the murmurings of pleasure, the gurgling laughter, the unthinking rapture. All of it so different from what she and Stephen had managed; so effortlessly free from guilt or inhibition or clumsiness.

She felt tears rising now. She couldn't bear that one occasion to be all there was. She especially couldn't bear it if it was her envy and disappointment that ruined everything. It was all so confusing – and this was a terrible place to have this conversation, in this dingy hospital corridor. Why had she been in such a rush?

'I'm sorry,' she said again. 'This was the wrong moment. Can we . . .'

'We need to go, anyway,' Stephen said. 'Fay will be waiting in the car.'

'Of course.'

She was on the point of apologising again, but she stopped herself. It wasn't all her fault, she thought. He ought to say something too; he ought to make some effort. As they reached the front of the hospital he held the door open for her. There was just a moment, then, when their eyes met, and what she saw in his gave Cressida a doubtful sort of hope. Not anger, she thought. Not warmth, either, but a vulnerability, an uncertainty, that seemed, just then, to match hers. Patience, she told herself. Patience, and a long view. Although if he was really going to Dubai in the autumn, there wasn't much time left for that.

September 2015
Stephen

The last fifteen minutes were spectacularly beautiful: the Kirkstone Pass, the descent into the valley, the patterning of sheep on the fells. Stephen drove slowly. Seeing Cressida – meeting her in that almost comically dramatic way in the middle of nowhere – had caught him off guard, sharpening his recollection of that long-ago weekend.

He hadn't been back to the Lake District since 1995, but he remembered, now, how powerfully this landscape had gripped him that summer. He remembered lying on a grassy plateau far above the lake one afternoon, while the others chattered and laughed and speculated about the future, toying with the idea of staying here, finding casual work as a waiter or a farmhand.

The one thing none of them could have imagined during that sunny picnic, he thought, was that they would be meeting here again in 2015, having not seen or spoken to each other for two decades. He'd been separated from them all within a few months, of course, by geography. Geography and a general inclination – no, be honest: a specific inclination – to steer clear. What about the others? What had they been doing all this time?

As the car rolled smoothly through the village, he forced himself to acknowledge both the flush of nostalgia and the itch and prickle of the things none of them would want to talk about this weekend. But amidst the challenge and complexity of his life there was very little that engaged his emotions, he thought: it would do him no harm to embroil himself in what was to come. After all, he had less cause than the others to feel agitated about 1995. Less to reproach himself for, at least, although he couldn't claim complete indifference. Of course he couldn't claim that, even after all this time.

RACHEL CROWTHER

There was only one car in the drive, a four-by-four of the kind lots of people drove these days. Which of the others was most likely to have a vehicle like that? Stephen wondered. He could hear Cressida's car straining up the hill behind him now, and he waited until she had pulled in beside him before he got out.

And then the front door opened and there were three people standing on the threshold. Good Lord, a trick of the mind: his old friends aged and repackaged and assembled in one place again. That must be Bill, that man with a beard. And Judith, unmistakable. But who . . .? His heart did a brief flip, and then he quelled it. Bill's wife, he thought.

'Hello!' Bill held out a hand to shake Stephen's, withdrew it, then tried again, laughing. 'I don't know what to do,' he said. 'Let's shake hands. It's good to see you.'

'Good to see you too, Bill,' said Stephen.

'This is Isabel, my wife,' said Bill. 'And my goodness, Cressida!'

'We should let poor Cressida sit down,' Stephen said. 'She's had a shock. I had to stop for some sheep, and she came round the corner and ran into me.'

'I'm all right,' Cressida said. 'Don't fuss.' But she looked pleased, the lines on her forehead (the watermark of loneliness, Stephen thought, in a flight of fancy that took him by surprise) eased for a moment. It had never taken much, he remembered, to cheer Cressida up. He felt a momentary disquiet then, recalling that ill-judged, long-submerged encounter that had been part of the muddle and misadventure of their last stay here. Part, surely, of the things not to be talked about.

They followed each other into the house. So far, so civilised, Stephen thought. In the big sitting room, he halted: the sun was beginning to set across the valley, bathing the room in pinkish light. It was this room he remembered best, and he felt a strange quiver of sentiment as he looked around at the furniture, the pictures, the William Morris curtains.

116

'That smell,' he said. 'I remember that smell. What is it?'

'Ash,' said Cressida, 'from the fire. And old carpets.'

'Books,' said Bill. 'And a whiff of polish.'

Judith laughed. 'God, this is like one of Fay's games,' she said. 'Please let's not have any of those this weekend.'

There was silence for a moment, as though the thread of conversation was too fragile to be tweaked so briskly. Cressida was looking straight at Judith, her expression unreadable. Bill's eyes were firmly on his wife. Stephen was on the point of asking about bedrooms when Isabel spoke instead.

'Is this everyone?' she asked.

'Yes,' said Judith, a note of decision, almost of defiance, in her voice. 'This is everyone.' She looked at Stephen. 'Bill found some food in the fridge. Shall we do something about supper?'

The kitchen was too small for five people. Bill hovered in the doorway for a few moments, then seized on the idea of making a fire, and Cressida announced that she was going to have a bath, if they could do without her. That left Stephen with Judith and Isabel. Glancing from one to the other, he deduced that Judith had no wish to demonstrate domestic proficiency, and that Isabel (dark and plump and rather sweet) was reticent about putting herself forward. Stephen remembered cooking breakfast in this kitchen, but more fortifying was another memory: threadbare meals cooked on a faltering Calor stove in a remote Nigerian village. That was only a few years after the High Scarp weekend, he thought, wondering at the odd way life laid itself out in your memory, but it reminded him that he was an adult, and competent.

'Sausages and mash?' he said. 'And we could make a fruit salad. What d'you think?'

This, he thought, was like one of the reality TV shows he found bizarrely fascinating after so many years away from the UK. *Come*

Dine with Me meets *Wife Swap*, perhaps. Bill passed to and fro a couple of times, fetching wood and kindling and searching for matches, while conversation among the cooks flitted between safe topics such as the optimal blend of fruit for the salad, the bluntness of the knives, and how long it had taken them all to get here. Isabel might not be aware of the danger zones, Stephen thought, but her presence somehow made it easier to skirt around them.

'Is Cressida OK?' Judith asked, after a little while. 'It wasn't serious, I take it, your prang?'

'No,' said Stephen. 'No damage done, I don't think.'

'Good.' Judith went on chopping apples. Silence spooled out for a time. Bill reappeared, his hands covered in soot.

'Roaring blaze,' he reported. 'Not the easiest chimney, but it's drawing nicely now.'

He was looking at Judith, Stephen noticed. His expression was hard to decipher, but the steadiness of his gaze spoke for itself. Or did it? He wanted to know what she was thinking, certainly. Perhaps Judith was conscious of his eyes on her too, because she put down her knife and said, 'I need a drink. Did our fairy godmother leave a bottle of wine in the fridge?'

'I'm afraid not,' said Bill, but Stephen had remembered something.

'There used to be a whole cellarful downstairs,' he said. 'Shall we go and look?'

'Let's.' Judith swept up her hair from her shoulders, as though to twist it into a plait, then let it drop again. 'God, that's an exciting thought. Do you think the wine has all been left to us too?'

'Don't get ahead of yourself,' said Stephen. 'There may not be any.'

Isabel tipped her pile of fruit into the bowl and turned to smile at her husband.

'All done,' she said. 'I thought I'd pick some flowers for the table. Come with me?'

The light had gone in the cellar – a half-finished room built into the hillside behind the two downstairs bedrooms – but even so it was obvious that plenty of wine remained in the racks around the walls.

'This is a turn-up,' said Judith. 'We can get absolutely rat-arsed.'

'Not me,' said Stephen, 'but I shall watch your progress with interest.'

'You're not teetotal, are you?'

'Not quite. Just out of the habit.'

'I hope you haven't turned boring on me,' Judith said. 'I was relying on you to get me through this.'

Stephen studied her face for a moment. Not entirely fine, he thought. Not as fine as she looked at first sight.

'I was relying on you to unravel the legal knots for us,' he said.

'Bill's your man for that. Not my area.'

Stephen pulled a bottle out of the nearest rack. 1989 claret: goodness. Perhaps they shouldn't drink that. 'What is your area?' he asked.

'Defending thugs,' said Judith. 'AKA the poor and dispossessed. Not usually thugs, actually. Women, immigrants. Discrimination. Human rights.'

'Interesting.'

'Didn't you look us all up?'

'I didn't, actually.'

'Very honourable.' Judith grinned. 'Have you found anything decent?'

'I hardly know where to start. You pick something.'

Judith pulled out one bottle and then another, making little staccato comments. After a moment she held one out to him.

'Beaujolais,' she said. 'Might be a bit over the hill; we'd be doing everyone a favour by drinking it up. How many do you think? Three?'

Stephen took two bottles from her and moved back towards the door. It was rather gloomy down here, and he felt a sudden qualm about allowing himself to be aligned too closely with Judith. That would be easy to do, he thought, but not the right way to go about things.

'Promise me one thing,' she said. 'No games. I meant it.'

Stephen nodded. 'Sure,' he said. But he wondered, as they climbed the stairs again, whether she meant exactly the opposite.

September 2015

Cressida

Cressida had been relieved to escape the enforced camaraderie of the cooking party, but when she emerged after her bath she felt – and how common this feeling had been in her life, she thought – that she'd missed out on some crucial moment of bonding. The others were sitting around the fire, and there was a jollity about the scene that made her quail a little. They had all made more progress than she had, she thought, over the last two hours – and the last two decades, she felt sure. Grown into different people, with more dimensions than they'd had before. She'd simply become more settled as a stereotype: no longer the quaintly entertaining would-be bluestocking, but the real thing.

She hesitated in the doorway, waiting for one of them to notice her, to welcome her into the circle, but no one did. Marmion would have been the one to do it, she thought, with a twinge of sensibility. But she mustn't allow herself to confuse compassion for Marmion with self-pity.

'Hello,' she said, mustering her best High Table smile. 'How pretty those flowers are.'

'That was Isabel,' said Judith. 'Stephen and I picked wine instead. Have a glass – I should think you need it, after being run over by that outrageous car.'

For a moment Cressida was heartened: Judith might have mellowed, she thought. Then she saw Judith grin at Stephen, and she understood. Bill was off limits; he'd brought his wife. That only left Stephen, and although Judith wouldn't have given Stephen a second look when they were all young . . . Damn it, she thought. Nothing had changed. Not a bloody thing.

'Come and sit down,' said Bill, indicating the space next to him on the sofa. 'Supper's all ready, but we thought . . .'

'Keep up the High Scarp traditions,' Cressida said, accepting a glass of wine.

'Ha!' said Judith. 'I'd forgotten that was one of them. Drinks before dinner. God almighty.'

'What do you mean?' Isabel asked. There was a brief silence then – long enough for Cressida to feel a little sorry for Isabel. She had an air of competence, the plucky sort rather than the effortless sort, but she certainly wasn't any match for Judith. But Judith smiled sweetly.

'There were lots of rules and regulations, the last time we came,' she said. 'There was something of the control freak about Fay.'

Cressida was on the point of protesting, but she stopped herself. Dangerous, she thought, to assert any kind of moral superiority. Quite apart from the bellyful of hypocrisy she'd had to swallow over the last couple of decades, she was at enough of a disadvantage already this weekend.

'Did you stay in touch with Fay, Cressida?' Stephen asked. 'Back in Cambridge?'

'Not for long. She moved, soon after – not long after we graduated.'

'Moved away from Cambridge?' Bill looked surprised. 'That house seemed so much of a piece with her. All those books and records – and do you remember the roses? Fay pruning the roses?'

'The house is still there,' said Cressida. She cycled past it sometimes, slowing to look across the front garden. There were prams and scooters in the porch these days, and Fay's rose bushes had all gone.

'Where did she move to?' asked Stephen.

'I don't know.' Cressida hesitated: she'd hoped to leave all this rather hazier. 'She just . . . There was a 'sold' sign up one day, and she'd gone.'

'She can't have been living up here,' said Judith. 'No Wi-Fi, same old television. You couldn't live in a house for twenty years without . . . But perhaps Fay could.'

She ended on a reflective rather than a sarcastic note, as if realising that another satirical remark about their benefactress might be ill-judged. But she was right, Cressida thought, that nothing had changed in the house. Imperial Leather soap in the bathrooms, lapsang souchong tea in the kitchen. The same curtains, the same bedclothes, the same towels, like a trick of the memory.

'Maybe she went abroad,' said Stephen. 'Italy, perhaps. Wasn't there somewhere near Rome she used to stay?'

'She was keen on Italian food, I remember,' Judith said. 'All that risotto.'

Cressida remembered lamb chops at Fay's house, lots of red meat of the kind people didn't eat any more, but she didn't say so.

'And awful liqueurs,' said Judith, as though she couldn't stop herself; couldn't help the note of parody in her voice. 'Chartreuse: do you remember drinking chartreuse? Or absinthe. That was even worse.'

It was Judith, Cressida thought, who'd said she didn't want to play games. They were all silent now, not meeting each other's eyes. It was a relief when Bill stirred.

'I don't know about the rest of you,' he said, 'but I'm hungry. Shall we eat?'

Isabel was on her feet first. 'It's all ready,' she said, and then she blushed, as though she'd claimed too much credit for herself. 'Many hands, light work.'

'Does anyone have a theory,' Judith asked, when the fruit salad had been distributed and the small talk about jobs and parents and holidays had begun to fizzle out, 'about why we get the house?'

'It's odd she didn't have anyone else to leave it to,' Bill said. 'I'd imagined her taking on another group of choral scholars after we left, but . . .'

'She left Cambridge, as I said.' Cressida reached for her wine glass: she rarely drank red, but a glass or two had felt necessary this evening, and there was no white on offer.

She didn't much want to talk about Fay, for reasons she knew were shabby. It was partly a general squeamishness about the past – about their past – but she was also reluctant to admit how quickly her efforts to stay in touch had foundered, back in 1995. At the time she'd felt both culpable and aggrieved about Fay's disappearance. It was ridiculous to imagine that Fay might have left Cambridge to avoid her, but even so it had seemed to underline all that had been lost that summer. It had made her feel she had no talent for holding onto anything she cared about. She could have made more effort, she acknowledged now – asking the college if they had a forwarding address, for example – but she'd been out of love with St Anne's that autumn; she'd kept away as much as she could. She couldn't be blamed for that, surely?

'I assume it's a token of affection,' she said now – but she wished the phrase unsaid as soon as it was spoken. Affection was too dangerous a word for this evening.

'It does rather seem to underline our importance to her,' said Stephen, 'but then we don't know how much else she had to leave. High Scarp might have been an afterthought, almost, in her will.'

'You mean she bequeathed it to us on a whim?' said Bill.

'Possibly. She was pleased that we liked the place, wasn't she? That we enjoyed ourselves here.'

'And what else do you think she's going to require of us?' Judith demanded, a slight roughness of tone revealing a chink in her sangfroid. 'Apart from charades and absinthe, of course.'

Isabel looked at her, wide-eyed. Cressida was struck suddenly by her resemblance to Marmion. Seeing her beside Bill, and the way she kept looking at him . . . Did they have children? she wondered. There'd been no mention of them. For some reason that thought didn't make her feel any better. Nor did the way Bill's eyes kept flicking past Judith without settling.

'Speaking of absinthe,' said Stephen, 'I seem to remember a little cupboard – yes, look, over there by the fireplace. Would anyone like a whisky, if there is any?'

As Bill leapt to his feet and Judith shook her head and poured the last of the wine into her glass, Cressida felt an unexpected prick of sadness. They hardly knew each other, she thought. Somehow she'd imagined them picking up exactly where they'd left off, and although she'd dreaded the thought of that, it was worse to discover that all that history, that intense undergraduate friendship, was more an obstruction than a way in. It might, she thought, be a very long weekend.

June 1995
Bill

The morning light cut through the faded curtains with the steadfast beat of a summer day set fair for sunshine. Bill's head throbbed with a pain that was equally steadfast but strangely hard to locate: the sound of it pulsing and racketing seemed to echo around him like a siren, as though everyone for miles around must be able to hear it too and trace it back to his shame and distress.

Shutting his eyes again, he examined his state of mind cautiously. The things he ought to feel and the things he did feel had a way of flitting from one camp to another which made it hard to take an inventory. Shame and distress, yes: but was it shame for what he'd done, or what he wanted to do now – or even what he absolutely didn't want to do? And distress distributed in the wrong proportions between Judith and Marmion and himself.

He groaned, hiding his face in the pillow. Stephen had offered Marmion his room last night and Bill had been grateful, more than grateful, hoping it would be easier to face Marmion in the morning. He knew now that that had been a vain hope – but he also knew that he couldn't put it off any longer.

Marmion was alone in the sitting room when he appeared. She didn't seem surprised to see him, but neither did she meet his eyes. She was sitting by the fireplace with a cup of tea.

'Hello,' he said.

'Good morning.' She picked up her teacup – an ordinary gesture, but it wrenched at his conscience that she should feel in need of that kind of cover. 'There's a pot in the kitchen if you want some.'

Bill could have done with a cup of tea, but he knew he couldn't leave the room again. He stood looking at her, wondering what to say.

126

'How are you?' he asked at last.

'I'm OK,' Marmion said. 'Better than Judith, I expect.' She hesitated, still not looking at him. 'What's going on, Bill?'

Bill came closer, perching on the arm of the chair opposite her. A mistake: too deliberately temporary, as though he might flit off at any moment. Marmion was looking down at her hands now, waiting for an answer.

'That's not entirely clear,' he said eventually.

'Certainly not to me,' Marmion said.

'No.' Bloody hell, this was impossible. It was no use trying to be reasonable, no way to explain in terms she'd understand. Everywhere he looked there were clichés. 'Marmion, I . . . it isn't quite how it looks.'

'What does it look like, would you say?' He had never heard her voice so crisp. His spirits rallied a little in the face of her self-possession.

'I suppose it looks as though Judith and I have been having a – fling,' he said. 'In fact we –'

'I'm not really interested in the details,' Marmion said. 'In fact, I'm not sure I want to know any of them. I'm more concerned about the – about your feelings, Bill.'

'Yes.' He moved down into the seat of the armchair. Better, he thought: more steady and responsible. But might it look as though he was edging towards staying put; staying with her?

'I don't know if this will make any sense to you,' he said, 'but my feelings for you are – they haven't changed, but it's as though the world has changed around them. I can't – that's the only way I can explain it.'

'You make me sound like a soft toy,' Marmion said. There was a wobble in her voice that ought to have called up pity and protection, but instead it irritated him. *Don't be silly*, he wanted to say – but wasn't that exactly how it was? He'd outgrown her; outgrown their romance. He couldn't have anticipated that, but it had happened.

'Marmion,' he began, and at the same time she said, 'And I suppose Judith is in love with you?'

'I don't know,' Bill said. He could see that in Marmion's eyes, being betrayed for anything less than insurmountable passion made things worse, but he couldn't bring himself to make any claim for Judith's feelings – or even his own. 'It was . . . Hardly anything has happened,' he said. Not that that was strictly true. 'It's – it was – just beginning.'

'But the world has changed already,' Marmion said. 'The world has changed around me.'

'I'm sorry.'

The words sounded cheap and inadequate. Bill looked at her, wondering what more he could say, what balm or rationalisation or defence he could offer, but there was nothing.

'Well,' Marmion said eventually, 'I'm going for a walk. I'll see you later.'

There was no one else in the house, Bill discovered, and Fay's car had gone too. Perhaps she'd taken Stephen and Cressida back to the hospital.

Replaying his encounter with Marmion as he made himself toast and coffee, he was less and less certain how he'd left things; what she had understood. *I'll see you later.* Was she expecting to pick up the conversation when she got back, then? He really couldn't bear that idea. He took his breakfast over to the cabin, grateful to have that refuge – but as soon as he came through the door, Marmion's belongings confronted him. Her concert dress hung from a hook, black and shiny like a skin shed by a selkie.

Bill sank down on the bed, paralysed by a sense of self-loathing that felt both deserved and disproportionate. God, this was a nightmare. But wasn't it just the sort of thing that was bound to happen to him, this fatal mixture of minor transgression and bad luck? Wasn't it exactly what a Devenish should expect? His family had always been at the mercy of fortune, from Birmingham's decline sending the hotel steadily downmarket to Mandy's pregnancy – another perfectly ordinary event whose consequences had been dismayingly, unluckily worse than anyone could have expected. He imagined Fate laughing at his cheerful hope of escaping his birthright. He wasn't like Judith: she was in charge of her own destiny. That was part of her allure, that sense that he could catch hold of her coat-tails and fly far, far away from the constraints and expectations of the world. But there was a reason why the Devenishes were downtrodden and moth-eaten and defeated by life; why they were so wary of risk and hubris.

The windows of the cabin were small, and set high in the wall. Through them Bill could see the sky, a blank, bland blue today. Was he going to give in, then? Abandon the unattainable prize and settle for a life of safety and decency? He thought of his grandfathers, the hard-working owners of two modest businesses. He thought of his father, who had encouraged his music-making and watched with pride and apprehension as Bill made his way to Cambridge on a choral scholarship. It wasn't a mire he'd scrambled out of, and he hadn't done it single-handedly, but . . . He'd begun to believe his life would be different from theirs, Bill thought. And – dammit – maybe it still would. Wallowing in gloom and self-pity wasn't the response of a survivor: of someone worthy of Judith. No, he mustn't give in. If he could get through the next few days, the next few weeks, surely things would come out all right.

He stirred himself then. Packing his clothes hastily into his duffle bag, he left it just inside the door, so he'd be ready to leave as soon as Fay said the word. As he crossed the garden again, he heard a car turning into the drive. Slipping into the sitting room, he took a book from the shelf and settled into an armchair, as though he had been sitting there peacefully all morning.

June 1995
Judith

When Judith woke again, the conversation with Cressida and Stephen had been filed among the other garish, distorted memories in her head. The hospital room was empty and the window was black, although a low light had been left on beside her bed. A tray of food had been left for her too – an unappealing-looking sandwich, covered in cling film, and a bowl of what might be soup or some indeterminate dessert. Judith was hungry, but the effort of reaching over for the food didn't seem worth it. She might go back to sleep, she thought – but while she waited to see whether that would happen, she took the packaged memories in her mind down from their shelves one by one and examined them again.

She had fallen, on a walk, and banged her head. Bill had rushed to her side (that phrase seemed settled; it was part of the story). Marmion had realised something was going on between Bill and Judith. Even so, she'd come to visit Judith in hospital, where the helicopter had brought her. Cressida was angry with Judith and Bill. Stephen was angry with Cressida. And Bill: had Bill been to see her?

Judith felt a pang of queasiness. Perhaps she should eat the sandwich. Perhaps she should call a nurse. There was a red button she could press: somehow she knew that. If Marmion had visited her, perhaps she wasn't as angry as Cressida thought. Marmion was good at forgiving people. Perhaps it would turn out to be a good thing, this fall and Marmion finding out. Judith closed her eyes again, pleased with that resolution. It was night-time, she thought; she ought to sleep.

In the morning the world was back to normal, and the dream sequence of the last few days had faded to ordinary workaday colours. The room was full of people, but Judith didn't recognise any of them. A woman in a white coat smiled.

'Ah, good: you're awake. How are you feeling?'

'Better,' said Judith. That seemed safe, and she thought it was true.

'Can we have a look at you?' the woman asked. The badge on her coat informed Judith that she was Dr Elizabeth Harrison.

Judith tried to nod, but it was a false economy, more painful than speech. 'Yes,' she said.

Dr Harrison stepped back, and a younger woman came forward, someone not much older than Judith. Her badge said *Miss R. Budd, Medical Student.*

'I'm going to shine a light in your eyes,' she said.

Judith heard a clucking sound, and the young woman halted and turned.

'Well, no; carry on now you've started. Do the neurological examination first.'

Dr Harrison smiled reassuringly at Judith over the student's head, and a bright light, horribly painful, pulsed into her eyes.

The next ten minutes reminded Judith of a dog being taught to do tricks – follow a finger with your eyes, jerk your leg when your knee is tapped – and like a dog being trained, she was required to repeat her performance several times for the benefit of the whole group of medical students. In the course of all this she discovered that her leg had a metal plate in it and that she had a considerable amount of what the students referred to as cerebral contusion, but that none of them, to their evident disappointment, could find anything wrong with her brain.

At the end of it all Dr Harrison sat down on the chair next to the bed, as though recalling her bedside manner at the last minute.

'How are you feeling in yourself?' she asked.

'My head hurts,' said Judith.

The doctor smiled. 'We can give you something for that. Is there someone to look after you?'

'Where?'

'At home. When we let you go.'

131

It occurred to Judith then that she had no idea where she was, in which hospital or which town, but she thought that if she asked now they might think twice about releasing her, and she didn't want to stay in this room any longer than she had to.

'My parents are both doctors,' she said. Perhaps she should have produced this fact earlier: it might have saved her from the medical students.

'Excellent. Are they here?'

'They're in Bristol,' said Judith, but then – and this made her realise that she wasn't quite better yet, that things weren't quite back to normal – the door opened and there was her mother, taking in the pack of students with a swift glance.

September 2015
Judith

Judith was regretting staking a claim to Fay's bedroom earlier in the evening. She'd wanted to avoid the room she'd had last time, for reasons that were at once obvious and strangely obscure, but she didn't even like this room very much, now she was in it. The scent of possession hung over it, the accretion of decades of occupation. She recognised Fay's hairbrush lying on the dressing table, and the well-dubbined walking boots in the bottom of the wardrobe. Everything was neat and recently dusted, but even so the place felt musty, stagnant, forgotten. As though it knew Fay was dead, Judith thought. As thought it knew they were interlopers, their occupation of the house unwarranted.

Damn, damn, damn. She could tell she wouldn't sleep well, and that tomorrow would be worse than this evening. Why had she come? There was no explanation apart from greed (and she had, frankly, no great interest in owning a share of this place) and prurient curiosity about how her once-upon-a-time friends had fared in life. The same, presumably, was true for them. Cressida, poor thing, was clearly eager to show off her academic standing and to conceal her disappointment with life. It was a shame, Judith thought, that Cressida was less happy and less likeable than she'd been twenty years ago. Her erudition, which had always been curiously charming, had multiplied into something ungainly.

Stephen: that was more mysterious. What could possibly be in this for Stephen? It was obvious, for all his lack of ostentation, that he was as rich as Croesus. It wasn't so much his possessions as his manner, the casual presumption that things were possible. Judith had had enough

133

rich clients over the years to recognise the signs. Could he really be interested in rekindling old acquaintance?

Then there was Bill.

Judith had convinced herself, really convinced herself, that there would be no difficulty about Bill. What could be more settled, more boringly steady, than a provincial solicitor? Probate and conveyancing, perhaps a hand in local politics or civic committees. And his bringing his wife meant either that he wanted her here or that she wished it, both of which constituted a solid safeguard. Judith had been sure Bill would be keen to stay at arm's length, and equally sure that there would be no hint, on her side, of whatever feelings youthful fervour had conjured up two decades ago. She'd found his photograph on his firm's website: hair more sandy than ginger now, and an expected fullness in the face; a rather foolish half-smile, half hidden by that unflattering beard. Surely not even a desire to prove that she hadn't lost her touch could tempt her, she'd thought.

But it had never been easy to account for Bill's attraction, and he had aged better than his photograph suggested. He was the kind of man in whom at forty you could still clearly see the twenty-year-old, just as at twenty there had been a lingering boyishness about him. He still had that way of smiling that suggested a great fount of exuberance ready to burst forth; that unexpected softness in his eyes.

Putting Bill's face deliberately out of her mind, Judith moved over to the window. The night was clear, the fells just discernible in the moonlight. She wasn't good at stars, but there was the Plough, set out like a diagram in a child's book, and a sprinkle that might be Cassiopeia. It was odd to think that neither the sky nor the disposition of the landscape had altered since they were last here. Odd, too, that the passing of two decades had made so little impact on the house. Perhaps it simply hadn't been used that much, Judith thought – but neglect tended to show. Oh yes, neglect took its toll all right.

With a little snort of self-deprecation, she kicked off her shoes. Her overnight bag sat on a ladder-back chair beneath the window, and she took out her nightdress – a full-length cotton one she hadn't worn for years – and sponge bag.

Tucked up at last beneath blankets and counterpane, she felt unexpectedly sleepy, despite the hardness of the mattress and the creaks and whispers of the house. Owls, she remembered. Were there still owls up here?

She was woken, though, by a different kind of bird call – an abrasive hoot, repeated several times and then falling silent. Judith lay still, waiting to see whether it would begin again. She'd only half heard it, drifting up from sleep: perhaps she'd dreamt it? And then she remembered. The cuckoo clock. Fay's damned cuckoo clock, its utterances provokingly irregular and piercingly intrusive. Why, sod it, had it chosen to chirrup its greeting to the household now? She reached for her phone and checked the time: 4.02. Damn and blast: she'd never get back to sleep now. These hours of the night were distressingly familiar, with or without cuckoo clocks to rouse her. Insomnia, she'd read, was a growing plague among women in their forties, but it was no consolation to feel herself part of the zeitgeist.

After a few moments she climbed out of bed. The house was completely dark, but she was sure, as soon as she opened her door, that someone else was up. Any one of the others, woken by the wretched clock. Should she retreat until the coast was clear? No, that was ridiculous.

She passed the bathroom door and went on towards the kitchen, and just as she reached it someone came out of the sitting room. Bill.

'The cuckoo clock,' he said. His smile was at once embarrassed and amused, the flick of his eyebrows adding a nuance Judith recognised with a little shock.

135

'Do you think Fay planned it?' she asked, half speaking and half mouthing the words.

'I wouldn't put it past her.' He looked at her appraisingly. Judith could almost hear the phrases being shaped and rejected in his head.

She shivered. 'Is the fire still going?'

'We could revive it.'

She gave a little nod, and he turned back into the sitting room. The door was heavy; it swung shut behind them with a gentle clunk. Bill knelt in front of the fireplace, adding kindling and balancing a larger log on top. When he pulled back, there was a leap of flame. Should she turn on a lamp? Judith wondered. If she did, the light filtering out into the garden might be visible from the bedrooms. She hesitated for a moment, then sat down in one of the armchairs that flanked the hearth.

'That's good,' said Bill. He kept looking at the fire as he sat down in the other armchair, as though installing himself as guardian of the grate; as though placing himself opposite Judith was the last thing on his mind.

For a few moments the silence reshaped itself around them, offering both protection and possibility. Judith felt strangely relaxed now. They couldn't have planned this, and she certainly wouldn't have willed it, but it felt like a – well, a not unhappy chance. An observance, perhaps, or an acknowledgement, or . . .

'I never stopped loving you, you know,' Bill said.

The words seemed to land dead, without reverberation. Had he actually spoken them? Judith kept her eyes on the hearth, watching the flutter of flame about the dark logs, her heart thudding.

'I never stopped loving you,' Bill said again, as though he wasn't sure, either, whether he'd spoken aloud.

For the first time, Judith looked directly at him. In the glow from the fire his hair looked redder, his face more sculpted, and his eyes were bright with reflected light.

'That's –' she began.

'I know you didn't,' he said. 'I mean, you did. Stop. I just wanted you to know. For the record.'

For the record? For the charge list inscribed on her conscience, did he mean? No: something gentler than that; something more devastating.

'I'm sorry,' she said – another phrase that could be interpreted dozens of different ways, and none of them accurate. 'I mean – God, I don't know. Look at us: we're forty-one.'

He frowned. His face, his expression, was strange to her, but . . . For goodness' sake, she mustn't think like this. Of all the things that should be left to lie, this was surely the most dangerous. Maybe it was a good thing to have raised the ghost, but only to banish it again. Like an immunisation, testing each other with a tiny dose of reminiscence. But still she didn't move, and nor did he. She could feel the years shimmering between them, the billions of miles starlight had travelled in that time, piercing the sky to reach High Scarp night after night.

'I feel as though life's going by and I'm hardly even looking,' Bill said.

'Looking for what?'

He shook his head. 'Not for anything in particular. Just – I feel as though I haven't dared to look up for twenty years. I had . . . I was ill, a few years ago, and it . . . Maybe it should have changed my perspective more than it did.'

She could see alarm in his face now, as though he was afraid he'd said too much.

'Bill,' she said, 'I know I'm the reckless one, but really, what could we possibly . . .?'

Surely not a clandestine fling, under the nose of his wife. Too ungainly; too tainted with history; too thoroughly pointless. And certainly nothing more. Even if . . . There were too many gaps, Judith thought, in their knowledge of each other. He would never make sense of what she'd become. Imagine her as his second string, he as her third. The thought made her smile, and at the sight of it the cloud cleared from his face.

'Don't say anything now,' he said. 'Just sit here for a little while. I just want to look at you.'

Oh, bloody hell, Judith thought. The terrible truth was that her blood was stirring too, seductive poison spreading through her limbs, her chest, the pit of her belly. For a moment it almost seemed to her that the world might be simple again; as simple as it had seemed on that night twenty years ago. For a moment her scruples felt inexplicable, anachronistic – and then abruptly clear again.

This was madness: a pathetic yearning for lost youth, for a story that hadn't been true even then. And even if she could admit that there had been moments of regret, over the years – even if they could possibly have done things differently, back then – they weren't the same people any more. Everything had changed.

'Are you married?' Bill asked. 'Or . . . spoken for? I should have –'

'No.'

The inflection of her answer caught his attention: the ironic slant she couldn't help putting on it. She wasn't ashamed of the choices she'd made, but she hated the thought of explaining herself to Bill, and she could see him speculating about her reticence now, wondering if and why she was concealing a lover. Would he interpret that in his favour, she wondered, or the opposite? Neither alternative was bearable.

'I need some more sleep,' she said, getting to her feet. 'Perhaps we could kill that clock, now it's ours.'

Still she hesitated, though, and he stared at her as she stood irresolute on the hearthrug.

'Yes,' he said eventually. 'I expect we could.'

The Bill she knew had retreated again, Judith thought. That was for the best, certainly for the best. But even so, she could feel disappointment trailing like a soft veil behind her as she crossed the room and made her way back along the corridor.

September 2015
Bill

The bedroom was very dark when Bill returned. He could just make out Isabel's head on the pillow, and its stillness and the faint whistle of her breath elicited a dart of relief. He stood for a moment beside the bed, not so much looking down at his wife as looking in on himself. Back across the blurred sweep of the years to another moment – not in this room, thank God, although the congruence was powerful enough without that detail.

Carefully, but not too carefully – it would be worse if Isabel were to wake and detect uncharacteristic stealth – he climbed back under the covers and lay flat, thinking.

Marmion had looked so peaceful that night – that early morning – when he'd come back to bed. The contentment in her sleeping face had raised a kind of futile rage in him, and then a surge of guilt and self-disgust. He had crossed the garden, he remembered, full of exaltation, marvelling at the delicacy of the world as dawn shimmered over the fells and mist melted from the grass, certain that he had found in Judith an answer he hadn't been seeking, an insight he hadn't known he lacked. What he'd felt for Marmion had been real enough, but he'd realised that night that it was more like a foreshadowing of love. Like make-believe, almost: a child's game in which adult emotions were acted out with earnest conviction. He'd felt pity for Marmion, and tenderness, and at that moment a determination that he would deal gently and honestly with her, as she deserved. That was what he was most ashamed of: his failure to live up to that promise. Her heart had been broken not just by his betrayal, but by his dishonesty; his lack of courage.

It was a deep irony, he acknowledged, that it was Marmion, rather than Isabel, to whom his thoughts had turned tonight. Marmion who was beyond any hurt or mitigation, rather than Isabel who was his wife, and who was sleeping beside him now as peacefully as Marmion had been twenty years ago, even if hers was a sleep induced by sedatives rather than blameless happiness. Isabel who still seemed, after all this time, an almost accidental consort.

His marriage was a strange thing. It was, he thought, a cloak of many colours, offering each of them a kind of protection that was expedient rather than embracing. He had never dared analyse it as a whole: it was safer to consider it piecemeal, reserving his gaze to details of fabric or workmanship. There was, for example, that particular combination of vulnerability and self-reliance he'd seen in Isabel's face when they first met. Marmion's view of the world had been all of a piece, he thought now, and finding a flaw in one part had undermined her belief and pleasure in the whole. And despite her buoyancy and firm foundations, it had turned out that she needed Bill more, far more, than he'd realised. Isabel, by contrast, wore her neediness on the surface, underpinned by a core of hard realism. Bill had detected that at once, and he had often had cause to be grateful for it. That hard core had been enough for them both, at times. He thought now of their first outing together – you could hardly call it a date, when he'd been stretched tight between grief and guilt and a choking desire for Judith.

'I could do with a drink,' Isabel had said, at the end of one of those bewildering days at the Guildhall, before he'd abandoned the singing course and found his way to the College of Law. 'You look as though you could too.'

That had settled something between them: an alliance built on separate need, jointly solved. Was need something you solved? Bill wondered now. Certainly that had always seemed the right verb for them. For him, anyway, cast violently back on his own resources and the doleful consolation of his family that autumn. It had been another five years before they'd got married, but although he'd imagined, along the way, that he had a free choice in the matter, when it finally happened he'd seen that it had been inevitable from the start: that he needed Isabel's grit as much as she needed, wanted, a husband.

Then there was the question of the stitching of this peculiar garment: the question of love, or what stood in for it in their marriage. He'd assumed, hoped, that love would develop over time, but the moment he'd imagined like a homecoming had never arrived. Other feelings, certainly – gratitude, responsibility, affection, pity – a changing panorama over the years. Enough to weave their lives together, but not to give them the sense of shared purpose he saw in other couples. Always, at the back of his mind, there had been Judith.

Bill was conscious of a growing ache in his shoulder from lying stiffly at the edge of a bed hardly big enough for two people, but he didn't dare move for fear of waking Isabel. It was a luxury to have this time to think: to savour that encounter by the fire, and to set it in context.

It would have been quite possible, he thought, to find that his feelings for Judith were more myth than reality after all this time. But he'd felt her power over him as soon as she'd arrived this afternoon – and he'd been terrified by it, at first. It wasn't so much a feeling as a physical reaction, as though every cell in his body was programmed to respond to her. That shining hair; that voice tinged always with some extra colour of amusement or deprecation. And if certain qualities in her had been desiccated by the passage of years – that brash, spiky manner that had lost the bounce and resilience of youth – wasn't that proof that she needed him: that she needed to be fully loved?

It seemed to him now that he'd been like a man living out a prison sentence these last twenty years. He had accepted that he deserved to suffer, and he'd been grateful for the lenient terms he'd been permitted. But all along there had been the expectation of release, once his dues were paid. And now, surely, was the time. Thank God there were no children to consider. And he'd endured the lymphoma: didn't that in itself qualify him for parole? Judith's qualms did her credit, but he'd seen something else in her eyes this evening, something he was sure he

142

hadn't mistaken. Gazing at her for the first time in two decades, he'd felt a great swelling of anticipatory joy, and with it a sort of wonder that he'd spent so many years only half alive.

But in the wake of this wave of confidence, he felt doubt creeping into his mind now. Had he been too hasty this evening; too naive? Judith had turned him down, turned him away, three times now. Had he misunderstood her motives each time? Was he playing with fire, risking more suffering than he could survive?

Lying in the dark beside his wife, Bill called up with an effort the passion and frustration and heartache of twenty years before. He'd always believed Fate had conspired against the two of them. If he'd blamed Judith at all, it had been for a failure of will, a laudable but excessive susceptibility to guilt. Had he been wrong? Had the circumstances been a convenient cover for her indifference?

No; he wouldn't believe that. He'd been competent, back then, to judge her feelings. Each of them, he thought now, had faced a battle against predestination: he tainted by the passivity of his family, the timidity and disappointment that had kept them on the back foot all their lives, and she so caught up in the narrative of her own self-determination that she hadn't been able to carry him, and the burdens of complication and guilt, with her.

Was that right? And if it was, could they overcome all those barriers now?

June 1995
Cressida

Cressida found Marmion outside, wandering among the shrubs and fruit bushes in the lower end of the garden.

'I haven't been down here before,' Marmion said, as she approached. 'Look at all this fruit. These gooseberries are almost ripe.'

Cressida could see at a glance that the gooseberries were still small and hard, nowhere near ready to pick. 'So they are,' she said. 'Almost. Next week, maybe.'

Marmion cupped a little bunch of gooseberries in her palm, their pale veins tender and vulnerable. She didn't look at Cressida. 'I saw Fay down here, a few days ago,' she said. 'Maybe she was hoping they were ready.'

'They might do for jam now,' Cressida said. 'I suppose you could try. But . . . I came to tell you Fay's going to drive us back to Cambridge this afternoon.' She hesitated. 'Judith's parents are taking her home.'

'I see.' Marmion plucked a gooseberry off the bush and bit into it, then pulled a face. 'You're right. Not ripe yet.'

'They're very sour even when they are ripe,' said Cressida, with an effort at cheerfulness. 'You have to add masses of sugar. We have a whole thicket of gooseberry bushes at home.'

'Really?'

'Maybe . . .' An idea had occurred to Cressida, and she held it up to the light for a moment, wondering how to broach it. She could tell Marmion wasn't really interested in the gooseberries, or in her, or in anything very much, just now. But nothing ventured, she told herself. 'Maybe you could come and stay with me for a while, over the summer?' she said.

There was a bulge of tears beneath Marmion's eyes now. 'That's very kind of you,' she said. 'I don't have any plans, except for camping in the Isle of Wight. We always go to the same place. I'm rather dreading it this year.'

'Come and stay with me instead, then. Come to Burcombe.' Cressida felt a rush of enthusiasm, both for her beneficence and for the prospect of Marmion's company. She could see them both lying in the garden, going for walks, holing up in the attic. If this was a Jane Austen novel, Marmion's broken heart would be mended by one of Cressida's brothers, but she couldn't quite . . . Tim was all right, though. Marmion would be good for him. 'Please do,' she said.

'Maybe I will.'

But Marmion's eyes had dropped again, and Cressida felt a flutter of defeat. Marmion had borne her wounds, she thought, without drama, but without false bravery – and Cressida was trying to do the same; to accustom herself to disappointment. She was increasingly sure that her forwardness, her indelicacy, had been too much for Stephen. She'd as good as forced him into having sex, and the pressure of the moment had made him rough and hasty and left him embarrassed. And then she'd grated on his nerves by criticising Judith – making, she thought now, some kind of implicit judgement about their rightness as well as Judith and Bill's wrongness, as though she felt certain of her position, not just on the moral spectrum but with Stephen. Although the irony was that it was uncertainty that had made her sound so shrill and censorious. Uncertainty and inadequacy and envy – all things to feel ashamed of. In any case, there'd been no more conversations with Stephen, and she was beginning to see that there wouldn't be, now. What Judith and Bill had done had tarnished all of them, she thought, but she only seemed to have it in her to make things worse.

Marmion plucked another gooseberry and pressed it gently between her finger and thumb.

'Did I ever tell you that I'd auditioned for the Juilliard?' she said.

'No.' Cressida frowned as the words sank in. Marmion was supposed to be going to the Guildhall, along with Bill. 'The Juilliard in New York?'

'They offered me a scholarship. I haven't given them an answer yet. I never really meant to go, but now I wonder – I can't think why I auditioned unless I had some idea I might need . . .'

Marmion turned towards another bush, a kind Cressida didn't recognise, covered with pink powder-puff blossom. Cressida watched her picking the flowers delicately, deliberately, as though she was selecting them for some special purpose. She wondered whether she was supposed to encourage Marmion about the Juilliard, or perhaps discourage her. Could she really want to run as far away as New York? But inviting Marmion to stay had disheartened her. She had no idea what Marmion wanted, she thought, and she had nothing to offer her anyway.

'Not to rush you,' she said, 'but I think Fay would like to get on the road quite soon.'

As Cressida walked back up towards the house, she saw Fay standing on the terrace.

'Have you been inspecting the fruit?' she asked.

'Marmion was down there,' said Cressida. 'She was hoping the gooseberries were ripe.'

'They're like bullets still, I'm afraid,' Fay said. 'We could have made a fool, otherwise.'

Cressida climbed the last steps and stood next to Fay, looking out at the view. It was very hot today; the swathes of heather and bracken on the fells seemed to blur and shimmer in the glare of the sun. 'Will you be back up later in the summer?' she asked. 'You'll have quite a harvest in a few weeks.'

But Fay's smile had vanished: as though she'd remembered some-thing, Cressida thought. Remembered that they'd disappointed her, perhaps. She felt another little plunge of defeat.

In most important respects Fay had been staunch since the accident – rushing down the mountain at high speed, with Cressida stumbling behind, to find a farm cottage with a telephone; driving them all down to Lancaster to visit Judith in hospital; dealing with the doctors and with Judith's parents. She'd been the capable, responsible adult that the rest of them weren't, yet. But back at High Scarp she'd spent a lot of time in her room, claiming tiredness or a headache. There had been no more effortlessly produced meals, no more group activities. She must be upset about Judith's accident, Cressida had thought; she must feel responsible for what had hap-pened. But there'd been no sign of self-reproach in her manner, when they saw her. If anything she seemed to blame them: to blame Judith herself, or Bill, or perhaps all of them. Not that she'd said anything explicit. It was just the way she looked at them, as though she hardly noticed them any more; as though she couldn't be both-ered with them. But then, when Cressida had got used to this new distant mode, the old Fay would suddenly appear again, as she had just now. Just for a few minutes, anyway.

Cressida waited for a moment longer, then she turned towards the house. She could hardly blame Fay if she'd had enough of them all – but it had been her idea, she thought crossly. The whole trip had been Fay's idea, and climbing Nag's Pike, too. But shame pressed at her again as that thought took shape in her head. They all needed to get away, that was all. Away from here, and from each other.

'I'll go and pack,' she said. 'I've told Marmion we're leaving.'

In the sitting room, she found Bill deep in an armchair.

'Hello,' he said, shutting his book hurriedly, as if he'd been discov-ered in some misdemeanour.

Cressida felt a prick of impatience. Bill had done his best to hide, these last couple of days. He'd hovered in the background, betraying his presence with a sort of buzzing of nervous energy. She wondered what he'd said to Marmion; whether they'd talked at all.

'We're leaving soon,' she said. 'Are you ready?'

'Leaving for where?'

'Cambridge. Fay wants to get home.'

'Fay was in here a moment ago,' Bill said. 'She didn't say anything.'

Cressida gave a little shrug. 'Perhaps she didn't see you.'

Marmion sat in the front: that seemed to be agreed without discussion. Cressida hung back while the others got in, and allowed Bill to move over to the middle of the back seat to give her a space by the window. No one made any comment about any of this, and Cressida felt a little ridiculous. It came from having brothers, she thought: it had always taken careful scheming to avoid the short straw in every aspect of family life. And the drive was going to be ghastly enough without being wedged between two men, especially when one of them was Stephen.

On the way up, even more pressed for space with four of them in the back, they'd talked and played games and listened to a quiz show on the radio. But as they drove back down the valley today, passing the turning to Nag's Pike, there was silence in the car. The silence continued until they were almost at Windermere, when Fay suddenly stopped the car and sat forward, one hand braced on her forehead. There was a rustle of expectation – all of them anticipating a speech of some kind, Cressida thought, perhaps even an ultimatum – but then after a few moments Fay simply put the car back into gear and drove on. They all stared straight ahead, not daring to exchange glances.

When they reached the motorway, Fay opened the glove compartment and handed a box set of tapes to Marmion. A moment later, the overture to *Tristan und Isolde* filled the car. Perhaps it was intended, Cressida thought, to put their emotional dramas into perspective. Certainly it would be more than enough to last them all the way home.

June 1995
Bill

Bill spent most of the first day back in Cambridge in bed with a hangover – the result of a pub crawl the night before with a group he'd played football with in his first year, whom he'd run into by chance on his way out for a walk. He was out of practice at the footballers' drinking games, but the rapid descent into oblivion had been a welcome escape, and his shambolic state next morning an equally welcome excuse to hole up in his room.

By six o'clock, though, he needed to get out. He hadn't eaten all day, and he knew he couldn't hide away forever. He pulled on his clothes and clattered loudly down the stairs, as though hoping that anyone lurking nearby, anyone he didn't want to see, might be scared off like pigeons by the noise. And then, emerging from the shadows at the bottom of the staircase, he stopped, startled. A sheet of black cloud hung low over the college, and beneath it the slanting evening sun poured through the archway and spilled over the parapet, filling the court with a surreal intensity of light and colouring its mild sandstone a violent apricot. Bill stared. It was as though he'd stepped into a film set: as though, while he lurked in the fug of his room, a transformation had been wrought in the world. Beneath that lowering sky, life had been compressed, intensified, sharpened.

'Amazing, isn't it?' said a voice behind him.

Cressida, of all people. For another moment Bill stood, feeling the melodrama of the scene slipping, altering.

'Hello,' he said. 'What have you been up to?'

'I walked to Grantchester,' Cressida said. 'I went for lunch at the Rupert Brooke.'

'How was that?'

'Rather boring on my own. Everyone seems to have vanished.'

Cressida kicked at something, a tiny pebble lodged among the cobbles. 'What are you doing?'

'Nothing.' Bill stared at the ground for a second or two, watching the pebble skitter and settle. 'D'you fancy a drink?'

Bill was sure Cressida was no keener to spend time with him than he was with her, but neither of them could escape now. He hoped the drink could be kept short, and that they could talk about something safe. The Tory leadership election, perhaps. Cressida was sure to have a view about John Major's resignation. Were the Benhams Eurosceptics? he wondered. He could see them as Redwood supporters.

'How about the Fort St George?' he said, as they passed the porters' lodge. Of all the pubs he could think of, that had the fewest associations.

'Horrible food,' said Cressida, 'but never mind. I had a pie at lunchtime. I don't need to eat again.'

They crossed the market square and made for Midsummer Common, the sky still hanging heavy above them and the streets filled with the treacle thickness of the evening sunlight.

'Is it going to rain, do you think?' Cressida asked.

'I can't tell. It feels as though something's going to happen. A storm, maybe.'

'Not before we get back, I hope.'

'We don't have to be long,' Bill said, but he regretted the words as soon as they were spoken. Like giving away his final chance, he thought. Like Orpheus, unable to resist looking back.

'I know I shouldn't say this,' Cressida said, when they'd found a table. 'I know I shouldn't say anything at all, but I'm going to. I can't not.'

Bill forced a smile. He almost felt he hated Cressida, just now. 'Say whatever you like,' he said.

But for a moment she didn't speak again, and when she did, it was with a question rather than a statement.

'What are you planning to do?' she asked.

'In general,' Bill said, 'or . . .?'

Cressida sipped crossly at her glass of cider.

'About Judith,' she said. 'About Marmion.'

No messing around then, Bill thought. And what sodding business was it of hers, anyway?

'I haven't given it much thought,' he said.

'Come off it, Bill.' Cressida scowled at him. Her expression – petulant, impatient, disapproving – was unfamiliar, but somehow characteristic, even so. 'Have you talked to Marmion?'

'When?'

'At all. Since Nag's Pike.'

'Yes.'

He certainly wasn't going to repeat that short, painful exchange for Cressida's benefit. But her directness was better, he thought, than skirting around the subject with meaningful glances.

'She's gone home,' Cressida said. 'Did you know that?'

'Yes,' Bill lied. This information came as a relief, though.

'Maybe you should go and see her.'

'Judith?'

'Marmion.' Cressida frowned again; or perhaps the frown had never gone away. 'Don't you feel you owe her that? She trusted you, Bill. She loves you. Don't you feel you ought to –'

The sentence might have trailed away anyway, but Bill never found out, because at that moment there was a tremendous crash, as though that great weight of sky had simply fallen down upon them, and a dazzle of lightning so bright that it lit up the dingy windows of the pub and made the electricity flicker in awe.

'Fucking hell.' Bill's heart thumped. He'd been frightened of thunder as a child, and even now it seemed to him momentous – Zeus, straddling those dark clouds and hurling a missile down at him. Raining fire and brimstone, storm and tempest upon the ungodly.

'You were right,' said Cressida.

Another thunderclap broke over their heads almost before the last one had faded away, followed by a great rolling, rumbling roar. Bill leapt to his feet. It felt like a warning sign, he thought, a call to arms.

'Come on,' he said. 'Let's go.'

'You're not going out in this?' Cressida said, half laughing. 'You'll get struck by lightning.'

Bill hesitated, looking down at her.

'I need to get back.' His voice was half-drowned by another explosion of thunder. 'I could call you a taxi.'

Cressida stared at him as though she hardly knew him. 'Don't bother,' she said. 'I'll stay here. I'm in no rush.'

I'm being a cad, Bill thought. His father's word, and he could hear his father speaking it. Frustration boiled inside him again, self-hate doing battle with an irresistible tide of self-determination. It wasn't Cressida's fault, but she represented everything he couldn't bear, all the forces of moderation and mediocrity that wanted to drag him down. He had to let himself be caught up by the moment, by the storm: he had to seize the wonderful, fantastical possibility of being.

He took a ten-pound note out of his wallet, the last cash he had on him.

'Here,' he said. 'For the drinks. Or a taxi. I'm sorry.'

He could feel Cressida watching him as he crossed the room, expecting him at any moment to turn round, but he didn't. As he reached the door and flung it open the summer rain enveloped him, an immeasurable consolation.

June 1995

Stephen

Stephen cycled across Coe Fen in a blaze of sunshine. It was a relief to be back in Cambridge, after the weekend from hell at High Scarp. He'd come out of it less scathed than the rest of them: poor Marmion broken-hearted, Judith broken-boned, Bill consumed by guilt and Cressida by – well, in the end by a righteous indignation that mostly seemed to be directed at other people, thank goodness. But even so, he'd been very glad to return to normality. Not that this no-man's-land week before graduation felt very normal, with Cambridge blinking and dusting itself off in the unaccustomed sunshine that had followed that dramatic storm the other night, and tourists outnumbering students ten to one.

And not that Stephen was looking back, either. He'd spent the last few days holed up in the Oriental Studies department, getting a head start on Arabic in the language labs and reading voraciously about history, politics, religion – anything that would help him get his bearings when he landed in the Gulf. He'd always been happiest when he had an objective, and Dubai was firmly in his sights now.

But tonight he was going home to Surbiton. He'd promised his parents he'd be there for a night or two before driving back up with them for graduation day. It was a big deal for them, coming all this way, and bringing Robert – and Stephen going to the Middle East was a big deal too. He could see them watching him, the baby cuckoo preparing to leave the nest, and he hated himself for his impatience to be away. Although his father worked at Gatwick and watched people coming and going every day, streaming in and out of the country, round and round the globe, they had never been further than Bournemouth, fearful of taking Robert and his wheelchair on an aeroplane and scandalised by the idea of leaving him behind. Perhaps they blamed themselves, Stephen thought, for his wanderlust. Perhaps they thought a few well-chosen package holidays might have stopped him dreaming about the rest of the world.

He'd do his best by them this summer, he told himself. They'd have him for ten weeks, including a fortnight in the familiar hotel in Bournemouth with its invaluable ramps and lifts and its sympathetic staff. There was time enough to placate and reassure, and to practise his Arabic calligraphy too. He loved his parents and his brother, but there was no point denying the itch he felt – that he'd felt ever since he could remember. His excitement about this adventure, just like his excitement about going to Cambridge three years ago, was partly about that yearning, that needling curiosity. Not about his birth parents – he certainly didn't expect to find them in Dubai – but about himself. About what he could do, what he could be, how far he could go. It wasn't just the beguiling terrain of the future he was so impatient to discover, it was himself as well. More of himself than he'd found in Cambridge.

But he reminded himself as he crossed the swathe of meadow that, just as he was grateful to his parents, he was grateful to this place too, and to the people he'd known here. That thought had come to him very clearly on that afternoon when they'd lain on the grass above Ullswater, and he was pleased he'd been able to feel it, absorb it properly, before everything had gone so wrong – Judith's accident, and Marmion's misery, and before that his own ill-judged encounter with Cressida. He still couldn't quite understand how that had happened; how he'd been beguiled by the moonlight and by Cressida's breathless expectation. He knew it was shameful, but a little bit of him was relieved that the Nag's Pike saga had made it easier to shrug Cressida off. In fact, although it was a pity things had ended on a bad note, he couldn't help feeling that the trip to Cumbria had drawn a rather convenient line under the choir clan. To everything a season: it was good to move on with fewer regrets, fewer ties.

Even so, as he cycled under Fen Causeway something nagged at him.

It seemed to him suddenly that he had failed – they had all failed – to see the High Scarp episode from Fay's point of view. She might have been overbearing at times, and perhaps less fun and easy-going than usual, but they had taken her hospitality and her protection for granted, and the payback had been . . . Looking back, he could see that she'd borne it with characteristic fortitude – the emotional upset and the practical consequences; all that driving up and down to Lancaster – but that she'd been irritated, or disappointed, or perhaps both. There'd been a kind of aloofness about her in those last few days. A sense of strain, too, which was hardly surprising.

He ought to make his peace with her, Stephen thought. More than that: establish some sort of basis for keeping in touch, on different terms to the old ones. He liked that idea. There was more to know about Fay, he thought, than they'd ever bothered to find out. She was an interesting woman, and she'd always been interested in him, too: not so much more than the others that the distinction was obvious, but he'd noticed the way she addressed a question to him, sometimes, or that her gaze rested on him when he spoke. And who knew what insights she might have that could be helpful to him? What connections, even? Pedalling across Lammas Land now towards Barton Road, he was pleased by the thought that his altruism, his desire to make amends, might play to his own advantage.

The roses in the front garden were in full bloom, a bravura display of red and pink. Stephen left his bike round the side and rang the bell, and after a minute or two Fay opened the door. His first impression was that she wasn't very pleased to see him, but it was gone before his good spirits had a chance to waver.

'Come in,' she said, and he followed her through to the sitting room, where the French windows stood open. The room felt rather chilly, even though the garden was bathed in sunshine. 'Would you like tea?'

It was only two o'clock; Stephen felt another twinge of embarrassment.

'I really came . . .' he began – but then he couldn't think what he'd come for; what he'd imagined. 'A cup of tea would be nice,' he said, 'if you're not busy. Shall I – can I give you a hand?'

'I can manage a cup of tea,' Fay said. Her tone of voice was hard to place, neither playful nor offended. She left the room again, and Stephen stood looking about him, feeling the self-assurance that had carried him here dissipating. He'd been in this room many times before, but never alone, and he had the sense now that its contents – the rather elaborate chairs, the glazed bookcase, the grand piano – were inspecting him, just as much as he was inspecting them. With a show of insouciance he moved over to the mantelpiece and picked up a photograph of a small girl – presumably Fay – wearing a dress with a tight bodice and full skirt, standing between her parents in a garden. Could that be High Scarp? Stephen wondered. Was that the blurred outline of Nag's Pike in the background? He put the photograph down again and picked up another that had been tucked behind it. This must be Fay again, but . . .

Stephen stared. The young woman in the photograph was holding a baby. Holding it in the way a mother would, with a rather anxious smile. She was wearing a pale summer dress and standing in front of a house Stephen didn't recognise, with a lot of windows and a tarmac drive. The baby looked, to his inexpert eye, very young, still swaddled in a shawl. Could it be a sister's? A friend's? No; he felt sure it was Fay's.

He heard a clink of china just then, and he shoved the photograph back and moved quickly away to the French windows.

'Doesn't the garden look splendid?' Fay said, carrying a tea tray into the room. 'I'm glad you've come to see it in its prime.'

He turned to see her smiling, any reserve in her manner gone. It was almost as though she was the one compensating for the embarrassment of his trespass. Stephen smiled back, wishing he could recover his geniality.

'Let's take it outside,' Fay said. 'I hope you like digestives. I haven't got anything more exciting.'

On the train down to London, Stephen brooded. His conversation with Fay had been filled with misunderstandings and disjunctions, and that was because of the photograph, he knew; because he was flustered to have discovered a secret Fay clearly had no intention of sharing. Was it a secret, though? The photograph was there on the mantelpiece, even if it was hidden behind another one. But if Fay had a child – a grown-up child by now – why had she never mentioned it? A child she'd lost contact with, perhaps living abroad? Or a child who had died: that would account for her affection for them all, and would add a certain poignancy to the situation, but . . .

No, there was more than that swilling around in his subconscious. One photograph of a mother and baby outside a house that had a faintly institutional look. No sign of the father in the photo; no hint, ever, in the time they had known her, of a marriage, let alone motherhood.

Might she, then, have put the baby up for adoption? Might she . . . She knew when his birthday was, Stephen remembered: that was the first time she'd asked them to dinner. Could it have been that unexpected coincidence that had prompted her to invite them? And then, when she found out about his background, the startling suspicion that it was more than coincidence?

Could that be why she'd taken such an interest, made such an effort with them all? Could it even – possibly, extraordinarily – be true?

Stephen

1999

England has changed in the four years he's been gone. Stephen is surprised how strange it feels: the food in supermarkets, the advertising on billboards; the ubiquity of English in print, while other tongues weave around it in the air, and the way people move, gesture, respond to each other. There are some things, of course, that are indisputably new – buildings that have gone up or come down since he left; a political shift with the arrival of New Labour. Perhaps it's simply that the unfamiliar throws the familiar into vivid, almost exaggerated relief: a recipe for the strange, doubtful nostalgia he feels every time he ventures out.

Today, leaving the motorway for smaller roads that run through countryside still lush despite the warmth of July, he is in a version of England even a City boy recognises by instinct: the modest hills and valleys of Gloucestershire, where small villages punctuate the politely graded greens of copse and grass and hedgerow. Has he missed this country? he wonders. If not London, then the ready access to pleasant, fertile countryside? It's hard to say. It feels as though the person who left England is not the same as the one who has come back. Perhaps that's the answer.

So what kind of person has he become, then? He is . . . well, he's becoming a force to be reckoned with in a world few of his Cambridge contemporaries know about: the mysterious meeting place of high finance and cutting-edge technology. He's becoming an expert on knowledge, and the future, and the future of knowledge: he knows what it is that you'll need to be an expert in, to thrive in the decades to come. Since he graduated he has picked up a passable fluency in five languages, including several that are supposed to take years of study:

163

Arabic, Japanese, Mandarin. Sight-reading psalm chants hardly even registers on the scale of challenges faced, or skills acquired.

And now it's Wagner he's planning to conquer, he thinks, as a tractor pulls out of a gateway in front of him and he applies the brakes with a quick glance at the clock. One of the great cultural phenomena of the Western world, which people seem either to love or to hate. Stephen's responses to things tend to be more measured, but he's keeping an open mind. The opportunity came out of the blue: the last three-quarters of the Ring Cycle, spread over a week, at an opera festival two hours from London. Just a single ticket, I'm afraid, Riordan Cartwright said. My wife hates Wagner. The first night was marvellous, but I've got to be in Sydney this weekend; you know how it is. Fine, Stephen said. Why not? He's on holiday, after all, and the operas are on alternate nights. He tells himself that if there had been two tickets he'd have tried to persuade his mother to come with him, but the truth is that the single ticket is what really sold the idea to him. Three days on his own, doing something that he'll probably never do again. Driving through the English countryside to listen to music the Nazis held dear.

This morning, while his mother read the newspaper (it pleases him that she sits and reads these days: he remembers her always on the move), he digested the synopsis from the programme Riordan gave him, so he knows what to expect. Valkyries and giants, warriors and gods and star-crossed lovers. He's packed a picnic so that he can pass the long interval as he's supposed to, and he's ironed a dress shirt and unshrouded the dinner jacket he hasn't worn since he graduated. Riordan's directions prove a little sketchy, so he almost misses the turning, but here he is, bumping across a field and then joining a steady trickle of people emerging from Porsches and Bentleys and battered Land Rovers, tramping in their finery towards a collection of tents grouped around an elegant Cotswold house. Stephen leaves his picnic hamper under a tree at the edge of the garden and follows the crowd into a tent, where he purchases a glass of champagne.

The opera house itself is in a converted barn. It's one of several Glyndebourne lookalikes that have sprung up recently. This one specialises in Wagner, which it regards itself as perfectly entitled to stage without the resources of Bayreuth or the Met. The reviews Stephen's read allude to the distinctive identity of Micklethorpe's supporters, but he's in no position to judge whether this audience is different from the ones who flock to see Mozart or Puccini at other opera festivals. One or two people smile as though they recognise him, and he responds with a little nod. Some of the men, he notices, have opted for more eccentric versions of evening dress than the penguin suit: there are several velvet jackets, a couple of kilts, one or two in somewhat ostentatious clerical dress. Perhaps he might chance a hakama and montsuki one night, or even a thawb and bisht. Either would be cooler than a dinner jacket, although none of the men here are dressed in lighter garments than his. What strange people the English are, he thinks. How odd that he should feel less at ease here than he does in Damascus or Mumbai.

But as soon as the performance begins, he knows that he was right to come, and that he won't regret the time or the money or the mild discomfort of the experience. He'd expected to have to work hard to engage with the music and to bear the sheer length and scale of it, but instead he is instantly drawn into the fantasy world it conjures. The German presents no problem for him, of course, and the acting is good, the characters convincingly passionate. There's even a moment when he laughs out loud, as Brünnhilde promises Siegmund the services of a harem of wish-maidens in Valhalla. The interval arrives sooner than he anticipated, and he thinks with pleasure of eating his picnic in the last of the evening sun.

But he's not allowed to get to it just yet. As the lights go up, the woman on his left, a slight, sixty-something grande dame in yellow silk, turns to him with an irresistible air of authority.

'Wagner is not a laughing matter,' she says.

'I beg your pardon?'

Her voice is slightly nasal, but perfectly audible. 'Wagner is not a laughing matter,' she repeats. 'If you want to laugh, young man, go home.'

Stephen is astonished.

'Madam,' he protests, 'I laughed at one line.'

'At one of the most exquisite moments in opera,' she says. 'You are amongst those who take Wagner seriously: you may not come here and laugh at it.'

It occurs to Stephen to say that since he has bought a ticket he may do what he bloody well likes; or even that he has spent the last few years in countries where civil liberties are less assured, but in England, as far as he knows, there is not yet a proscription on mirth; but he doesn't much like confrontation. Besides, there is another hour and a half to go, and he rather fears that he may have to sit next to this terror not just for the rest of the evening, but for the rest of the cycle.

'I beg your pardon,' he says again. He doesn't smile, reckoning that any further sign of levity would go amiss. He glances beyond her, noting a distinguished English gent and a girl close to his age, wearing a white dress and, at present, an expression like thunder.

'Hmmph,' says the woman. She gets to her feet, and her family do the same. Stephen waits until they have exited at the end of the row before he follows: to his relief, his neighbour on the right has gone out the other way.

It would be possible to feel deflated by this encounter, but Stephen isn't easily deflated. Instead he stores it away as part of the cultural experience of the evening, and seeks out his picnic, grateful that no one else has chosen a spot close to his.

He's pouring coffee from an old thermos when he spots the girl in white, walking along the line of trees towards him. Going back to the car for something, he assumes, but as she gets closer he realises that she has come to look for him. She stops a few feet away, as though uncertain of her reception.

'I'm sorry about Mummy,' she says. 'She's extremely rude. She doesn't care what she says to anyone.'

Her voice is quite different from her mother's, low-pitched and pleasant.

'That's nice of you,' Stephen says. 'Don't worry; I'll live to fight another day.'

'I suggested that I change seats with her, but she wasn't keen. She thinks you'd be a bad influence, I'm afraid.'

'She's quite right, of course.' Stephen smiles. 'Do you want some coffee?'

She shakes her head, then seems to think about sitting down, but doesn't. 'I'm Suky,' she says. 'Astonishingly enough not a Wagnerian name.'

'Stephen,' he says. 'Have the rest of your family got Wagnerian names?'

'There's only me. I'm sure if I was a boy they'd have called me Tristan or Siegfried, but even they couldn't quite stomach Brünnhilde, thank God.'

'That would have been quite something in the primary school playground.'

She laughs. 'Actually, it wouldn't have been that odd at my school.'

A little way off, a handbell rings, signalling the end of the interval. Stephen spots the teenage boy whose job it is to summon them back to the auditorium wending his way towards them; a dark-haired boy in a dinner jacket that's rather too large for him.

'Back to the fray,' says Suky. 'Are you here of your own accord? I suppose you must be, if you're on your own. Mummy ought to be impressed by that.'

'I bought the tickets from a friend,' says Stephen. 'He had to fly to Australia at short notice.'

'The fat man who was here on Wednesday?'

'Yes.' Stephen grins. Riordan Cartwright, global mogul, reduced with the same efficiency Suky's mother employed on him. The fat man who was here on Wednesday; the young man who laughs at Wagner.

Suky doesn't quite walk beside him; she stays half a step ahead and a couple of feet to the left. Even so, her mother spots her in his company and glares.

'Hello again,' says Stephen. 'I suppose we ought to be introduced, if we're going to be neighbours for the rest of the week. I'm Stephen Evans.'

'Lucy Atkins,' says Suky's mother, with a mixture of ice and graciousness-designed-to-instruct. 'This is my husband, Peter. Lord Justice Atkins.'

Stephen hears Suky stifling a snort of laughter.

Stephen is determined to devote the whole of Saturday to his mother. Janet Evans has put a brave face on widowhood: Kenneth was almost ten years older than her, so it was always on the cards that he'd pre-decease her, even if neither of them anticipated that he'd barely reach retirement age. A year on, her routine continues much the same as always. She's still child-minding, her house filled from Monday to Friday with a gaggle of tiny children who adore her, their hours occupied with a familiar routine of walks to the park, painting at the kitchen table and playing in the sandpit in the garden.

She has put less of a brave face on the departure of her sons – Stephen to the far corners of the world, as she puts it, and Robert to a residential community where he can have some independence and be properly looked after. Stephen has seen for himself that it's a wonderful place, the best possible solution for Robert, and he's already started to donate a regular sum to the charity that runs it. But he can also see that it's been a terrible blow to his mother, however tough the burden of caring for Robert had become.

As he lies awake in his old room on Saturday morning, he looks around at the boyish clutter that still fills the shelves. It seems no time at all since he was dependent on parents he assumed to be ageless and invulnerable, and now he's his mother's mainstay. He's used to responsibility – he has more on his shoulders already, in some ways, than either of his parents ever did – but this duty of care feels unexpectedly weighty. Emotional responsibility rather than financial, he thinks; and a responsibility conferred by birth rather than by choice. Except, of course, that his has nothing to do with birth.

That thought causes another tug on his conscience – and on his heart. He never wondered, as a child, what might have happened to him if his parents hadn't adopted him, but he thinks about that now, and about how much there is that he and his mother have never discussed. He sees her in his mind's eye as a woman who has always been grateful for what she's had, but he wonders whether she is essentially unrequited by life. Has he – have he and Robert – been enough recompense for her infertility? Has losing Robert revived the pain of those early years of childlessness? None of this, he knows, could ever be discussed, but it seems to him that he ought to consider questions like these if he's to look after her properly.

He throws off the duvet and pulls on a T-shirt and a pair of shorts, thinking that he'll go down and make his mother a cup of tea, as his father did every morning. He treads carefully, avoiding the step that creaks, wondering whether there's time to nip out to the bakery down the road. He remembers their bread, so soft and dense and delicious that he used to eat a whole loaf in a sitting sometimes. But as he reaches the front door he hears his mother's voice from the kitchen.

'Stephen?'

'Mum.' He turns sharply. 'I thought I'd beaten you downstairs. I was going to go and buy things for breakfast.'

'That's a nice thought,' she says, 'but there's no need. Everything's ready.'

169

Coming into the kitchen, he sees that the table is laid: cereal, jam, toast rack, eggs ready on the side. His mother is in her dressing gown, not out of laziness, he knows, but because they always used to make a special occasion of Saturday breakfast in pyjamas. He glances down at his own clothes and smiles.

'Sorry,' he says. 'I don't have any pyjamas. I don't usually wear them these days.'

'We must get you some,' she says. 'You'll need them when you've got children. I can tell you'll be one of those modern fathers who gets up in the night when they wake, won't you?'

Stephen laughs, and his mother shoots a glance at him.

'I'm jumping the gun. I know I shouldn't.'

She passes the teapot, and he pours himself a cup. It's plain from the way her words slipped out that she has given a good deal of thought to the matter, even if he hasn't. And of course, he thinks, grandchildren are what she wants; what he owes her, even. Grandchildren perhaps settled nearby, if he really must keep flying off around the world. He feels a clutch of dread that takes him by surprise. A half-remembered phrase from English A level flits into his mind: something about a man with a fortune being in want of a wife. He doesn't exactly have a fortune yet, but he has plenty to support a family, and he's attractive to women, he knows that. But things aren't that simple for him. Oh, they're not: and how can he begin to explain that to his mother?

'So,' he says, 'what kind of wife would you recommend for me, Mum?'

She looks hurt. 'Don't make fun of me, Stephen.'

'I wasn't.' He leans across the table and puts a hand over hers. 'I don't get much chance to meet people, you know. Not socially. And you're the expert on marriage.'

She colours slightly. 'Do you want cereal?' she asks. 'Or straight on to toast?'

'I'll have some Grape Nuts,' he says. He's never seen Grape Nuts anywhere else in the world, but they're here every time he comes home.

They spend the day in what Stephen hopes is exactly the way his mother would choose. Since she defers to him at every turn it's hard to be sure, but she's always had a way of turning things to her way of thinking. *Oh, but I thought you wanted to check that tyre first*, she'll say, or *There's really no need to go all that way on my account.*

The bathroom cabinet is falling off the wall, so he takes her to Habitat, where she objects to the price of a new one, but only in principle, it seems; they choose a sleek stainless-steel version with a mirrored door. Stephen finds his father's tools and puts it up – an achievement which gives him a sense of pride he can't confess to his mother, in case she realises how hopeless he really is as a handyman – and then he drives them round the M25 to visit Robert.

It's almost an hour and a half each way in the car: a serious undertaking for his mother on her own, Stephen thinks, as they spin along the motorway. She's never liked driving long distances, and he can tell from the set of her face that she's thinking about what it's like to make this journey alone.

'It's quite a way,' he says.

'There's a train,' his mother replies, 'but it takes a long time. You have to go across London.'

'We could always get someone to drive you,' he says, and she turns a horrified face towards him.

'You mean a taxi? All that way? It would cost hundreds of pounds, Stephen.'

'That doesn't matter,' he says, but he can see that it does; that she's offended by the profligacy of this suggestion. He can hear an echo of an accusation, in the silence that follows, that he's trying to buy his way out of his obligations. He feels a flash of irritation that briefly eclipses his guilt.

'Look at the fields,' his mother says. 'You'd never guess it had been so dry.'

On Sunday afternoon, Stephen prepares to leave for Micklethorpe with mixed feelings. He hates to leave his mother alone on a Sunday, and the prospect of another evening alongside the Atkins family is not very enticing, even if they parted on polite terms at the end of Friday's performance.

But his mother urges him away: there's plenty on the television on Sunday evenings, she tells him, and she knows he won't enjoy that as much as 'your opera'. And once the decision is made, Stephen feels a flutter of excitement. He considers for a moment the possibility of donning some fancier form of dress, then settles for digging out the lime-green and yellow St Anne's College bow tie he used to wear to sing close harmony. He grins at himself in the mirror as he ties it: a little more subtle than that Lord Justice business, he thinks, but he suspects it won't go unnoticed.

And it doesn't.

'St Anne's,' says the judge, as they take their seats. 'When were you there?'

'I graduated four years ago,' says Stephen.

'Ha. Sing there?'

'In the chapel choir? Yes.' Stephen smiles, marvelling at the ease of it. Like turning a key in a well-oiled lock, he thinks.

'See, Lucy?' Lucy hasn't been listening: her eagle eye has been caught, perhaps, by another infraction. 'St Anne's choral scholar.'

'Really?'

She is in grey satin this evening, pinched in at the waist. Suky is wearing a black dress with lace at the front, more risqué than last time. Stephen wonders if it's for his benefit, then catches her eye and decides it is. He's flattered: she's one of those English roses who has a little too much of the golden retriever about her, but she's unquestionably pretty.

There are two intervals this evening: the first is for tea, a fifteen-minute break after Act One, with the long picnic interval following an hour later. Stephen's hungry by then, having resisted the cake on offer earlier. He's on his feet before the Atkins clan, and he's taken aback when Lucy turns to him.

'Would you care to bring your picnic to join us, Mr Evans?' she says. 'We have a table in the patrons' tent.'

The Atkinses' picnic is not as elaborate as some Stephen has seen, but it certainly represents due diligence. What Lucy Atkins evidently considers the minimum number of elements necessary to a proper Micklethorpe picnic have been packed in Tupperware containers of various sizes and then fitted inside a wicker hamper with the precision of a mathematical puzzle. A great deal of time is spent locating the requisite boxes, decanting their contents into dishes, serving them up, and then repacking the remains into the boxes and the dirty plates and cutlery into a plastic bag that has been brought for the purpose. Less time is spent on eating the food. By the time this rigmarole has been completed three or four times (smoked salmon on crustless brown bread; a pale-looking quiche and several salads; strawberries and cream; cheese and crackers), Stephen has long since finished his egg sandwiches and slice of fruit cake.

The advantage of all this, however, is that he has plenty of time to observe the Atkinses, while they are unable to devote much energy to interrogating him. Sir Peter (Stephen has done his research: he doesn't intend to be caught out on a point of etiquette) limits his conversation to well-chosen compliments on each course and observations about the orchestral playing and the clemency of the weather. Lady Atkins dispenses food with determined efficiency, clucking from time to time as though an anonymous minion has interfered in some way with her arrangements. Suky has evidently learned strategy at her father's knee and she too says little, but she offers Stephen a smile from time to time.

'Coffee?' says Lucy, at last. The question includes Stephen. Glory be, he thinks. Nary a strawberry, but perhaps an After Eight, if he's lucky.

'So you were at Cambridge,' Suky says, as though an unseen signal has indicated that more general conversation may begin. 'Did you love it? I applied, but I didn't really have a hope.'

Stephen considers this. Did he love it?

'It feels rather a long time ago already,' he says. 'A different life.'

'What do you do now?' Suky asks.

'Just at the moment I'm based in Riyadh,' he says. 'I'm home on leave for a couple of weeks.'

'Oil?' asks Sir Peter.

'In a manner of speaking.' Stephen smiles. 'Not much happens in Riyadh that isn't connected with oil, although that's starting to change.'

There's a small silence after this statement, but then Suky smiles at him.

'I'd love to go to the Middle East,' she says.

'Whatever for?' asks her mother. 'No place for a young woman.'

Stephen sees a retort on Suky's lips, a *how would you know*, and he feels a dart of admiration. He's torn between waiting to see if it emerges and offering a comment of his own, and meanwhile the moment passes and Lady Atkins's remark is allowed to stand. Prudence, he thinks, wins the day.

'What do you do?' he asks Suky instead, and she blushes a little, as though she's not used to being regarded as an adult.

'Oh, I've only just finished university,' she says. 'I'm not sure what you do with a maths degree. Teach, maybe.'

'Corporate finance,' says Stephen. 'The banks need good people, and a maths degree is the right entrée. I could give you a few names.'

Another silence: he's gone too far, Stephen thinks. It's not for him to offer connections. But Sir Peter nods.

'That's a good thought,' he says. 'Worth looking into.'

They are spared further conversation by the boy with the handbell, coming into the marquee to signal the end of the interval. The same boy as the other night, in the too-large dinner jacket. Stephen watches him for a moment, then turns his eyes away, back to Suky.

'Thank you,' he says. 'It's been a pleasure.' He glances round, wondering if he should offer to help, but the Atkinses' picnic has vanished without trace into the wicker basket.

Driving down to Micklethorpe again on Tuesday night, Stephen examines his heart with unaccustomed candour. He has fallen in love with Wagner, he acknowledges, but as the Gloucestershire countryside unfolds, he admits that part of the glow of anticipation he feels is for Suky rather than *Götterdämmerung*.

His mother's words about marriage have kept coming back to him these last few days. Is it for that reason that he feels a glimmer of interest in Suky? No: there's something about her – several things, in fact – that intrigue him. Attract him, even. On the face of it, she's the last kind of woman he'd expect to have anything in common with – a scion of the upper middle classes, brought up in a large house in Hampstead, conventionally beautiful in a way that will set and harden into a version of her mother. But then there's that gentle voice with its infusion of irony; the fact that she studied maths rather than art history, and that she is neither cowed by her mother nor obdurately rebellious. She strikes him as a misfit, someone who has her eye on a different kind of life from the one mapped out for her. No one has mapped out Stephen's life, and she might enjoy the freedom that brings.

And Suky has skills he doesn't have: she's good at people, he thinks. She would open doors, smooth paths, fill evenings. And she seems to find him worth bothering with. If he's learned one thing over the last few years, it's never to let an opportunity pass without proper consideration.

He is aware, though, that other factors are at play, and as the car winds once more through the country lanes, he reviews them dispassionately. As dispassionately as he can, anyway. There's his mother's desperate hope of grandchildren. There's a desire – not to join Suky's family, not that at all, but to find out what might by created by combining her genes, her upbringing, with his. This is tricky ground – on several counts it's tricky ground – but for Stephen, who has never dwelt among his kith and kin, the idea of establishing himself as a patriarch, of founding his own family, is powerful.

And then, of course, there's the tempting prospect of rising to the challenge of Lucy Atkins's opposition – because Stephen is under no illusion that her invitation on Sunday evening was prompted by anything other than a good general's instinct to keep the enemy under surveillance. He may have made her smile, even nod in agreement once or twice, but she has found out quite enough about him to decide that he can never be more than a curiosity to the Atkins family. Her husband is an affable chap – it's Lucy rather than him who would be a real terror on the Queen's Bench, Stephen thinks – but his views on the matter are unlikely to make any impression. His views on any matter, in fact, are rapidly corrected by his wife.

'Which recording of *The Ring* do you prefer?' Stephen asks, as they take their seats for Act One that evening. It's a mischievous ploy: he knows they won't be able to resist the question, but can't possibly answer it satisfactorily in the few minutes before the curtain goes up.

'It's hard to beat Karl Böhm's Bayreuth recording from the late sixties,' begins Sir Peter.

'Nonsense.' His wife smiles crisply as she cuts across him. 'You simply have a weakness for Birgit Nilsson. Fürtwangler's RAI recording is a much better option. And the Goodall recording in English is excellent too, for a newcomer. Rita Hunter at the peak of her powers.'

'Stephen speaks fluent German, Mummy,' says Suky.

'Flagstad, actually, is my favourite Brünnhilde,' says Sir Peter. Stephen catches a smile that has a hint of the conspiratorial about it. Perhaps this is one advantage of Wagner: a licence to nurture passion for women other than your wife. Stephen can't see anyone burning with ardour for the Finnish soprano singing Brünnhilde this week, who is constructed on an uncompromisingly Wagnerian scale, but he can imagine soothing his soul with her recordings on the many nights he spends in hotel rooms around the globe. He's glad to have established that she has plenty to sing tonight, and he settles back in his seat to enjoy it.

'Joining us again?' Sir Peter leans past his wife to catch Stephen's attention as the curtain comes down for the long interval.

Ah, he's cannier than he looks, Stephen thinks. Years of practice, no doubt, in managing his way silkily around Lucy's authority. She can hardly countermand a public invitation.

'I'd be delighted,' he says.

Suky's smile, behind her mother's head, is radiant. Stephen feels his heart falter in a way that he tells himself represents the awakening of love.

Later – much later – Stephen looks back on that evening without regret. On its sequelae, too. He succeeded in freeing Suky from her mother, for one thing. He gave his own mother, who was diagnosed with lung cancer two weeks before the wedding, a daughter-in-law. In the game of Twister that his life has come to resemble, placing his right hand in the circle labelled 'marriage' for a few rounds has done him no harm. And he understood afterwards, if he didn't before, that he will never dwell among his kith and kin.

Part IV

Part IV

September 2015

Stephen

Stephen was awake early. He'd long since given up wondering which time zone his body thought it was in, or contemplating remedies for its confusion. He'd never needed much sleep, and he needed less and less as the years passed. And there was still something exciting to him about waking before it was light: it reminded him of childhood Christmases, of the pleasure of a day not yet begun.

Pulling on a T-shirt and jogging pants, he padded up the corridor past the bedrooms in which the others still slept. In the sitting room he was surprised to find the fire burning vigorously, a large log barely half-consumed. Someone else was up then, or had been not long ago. An insomniac rather than an early riser, perhaps. He imagined each of them claiming their quarter of the night, their stake in the house. For a moment he considered settling by the fire with a book, but the thought of tasting the fells before sunrise was too tempting. He'd come close to trouble sometimes, slipping out of hotels in unfamiliar cities to roam the streets in the small hours, but he wasn't likely to encounter anything more dangerous than sheep here. The thought filled him with a strange elation: he was so rarely away from civilisation.

He remembered the path that started just below the house, one fork leading round to the waterfall cave and the other tracking up the side of the fell towards a small tarn. He'd go that way, he thought. He remembered looking down on High Scarp from above, a little way along: a useful view of a property you were about to inherit.

The moon had been bright at midnight, but it wasn't visible now, and the dawn was only a water stain in the cleft of the valley. But the ground seemed to give off its own faint light, just enough to

181

follow your footsteps, and Stephen barely stumbled as he climbed the stony track.

The unease he'd felt the previous evening was ebbing away now. He thought back to the conversation over dinner, the disquieting alternation of assertiveness and self-deprecation, formality and familiarity. 'Cambridge has changed beyond all recognition,' Cressida had said at one point, claiming a particular position as gatekeeper, and Judith had laughed a little unkindly and said, 'I expect there's a Costa in King's Chapel now, eh?' And then Bill's exaggerated bonhomie as he said, 'It's a toss-up some days whether I feel sorrier for my clients or myself.' His wife sitting silently, her eyes moving from one face to another, and finally asking, in the middle of a hiatus, 'What exactly is it you do, Stephen?' 'Oh, this and that,' he'd said; 'most of it very dull.' They would think he was a spy, he thought now, with a glimmer of amusement. Although they'd all been inclined to reticence, or at least been selective about what they revealed. And they had connived, between them, to keep the conversation away from Marmion. Or so it had seemed to him: each of them aware of her name hovering in the air, and willing someone else to speak it first.

Two hours was all they had managed, anyway, before they'd agreed to call it a night. It had been almost eleven by then, and they'd all had a long day, a long journey, but even so Stephen had felt a pinch of disappointment that they weren't sitting up late over whisky and firelight. A pinch of disappointment that emanated, perhaps, from some shared sensibility which they hadn't quite managed to reinhabit.

If Fay had hoped to reunite them in spirit as well as body then she might be disappointed, he thought now, scrambling over a steeper, rougher part of the track, as a sheep shambled hastily away. He'd cavilled at Judith's tone last night, but she was right that Fay had liked to be in charge. Mostly – perhaps entirely – in a benevolent way. She'd been a kind of fairy godmother, and fair enough if it had been on her terms. He realised now that they'd taken her patronage very much for granted. They'd shared a youthful arrogance, an assumption that it was perfectly natural for an older woman to take such an interest in them. Towards the end he'd had his own theory, of course, about her motives – a theory that had thrust itself back into his mind when the solicitor's letter had arrived a few weeks ago. There must be some explanation, after all, both for Fay's kindness to them twenty years ago and for her bequest. Presumably the lawyer would bring answers, later today – not just to that question, but perhaps to others too.

Stephen halted for a moment at a fork in the path and looked up: the sky was perceptibly lighter already. The day would come quickly now. Below him, the landscape was taking shape, the curve of river and road in the valley bottom overlaid still with the sepia tint of night, but no longer lost in shadow. The tarn must be further than he remembered. Perhaps it was time to turn back, so that he'd be there when the day began at High Scarp. They may not owe each other anything, but it might be as well for them all to stick together, this weekend.

As he made his way back down the hill, Stephen pondered this thought. It was almost as though he kept catching himself in double-think; in recovering hopes he hardly knew he had. Part of him could see quite clearly that the five of them had been united, twenty years ago, by a general compatibility which had been fostered and cemented by circumstances. By Cambridge and music, and by Fay. And it was only because of Fay, of course, that they were together again. But now he felt a prick of shame at the cool rationality of this analysis. He was wary, still, of his motives, and of the risk of self-deception – but however complicated things had become, it was certainly true that they had owed each other something once, and that wasn't something you could ignore.

Reaching the gate at the bottom of the hill, he ran his hand along the smooth surface of the wood – the very same wood, no doubt, that he had touched, that they had all touched, twenty years before. Beside the fence, heard rather than seen, ran the narrow ghyll that dipped underground a few yards on, and overhead the branches of a sycamore sighed and whispered. It wasn't true that he cared nothing for the others, Stephen admitted. He'd used that defence twenty years ago, flying away to his new life across the globe, and it hadn't been true then either. He wasn't used to thinking about other people in this way, but the feeling, though uncomfortable, wasn't entirely unwelcome.

There was still no sign of life when he re-entered the kitchen, but the clock above the door stood at ten past seven. He'd been out for longer than he'd realised. He made a cup of tea and took it through to the sitting room, where the fire was in need of reviving now. He raked the embers and added another log, then sank down in one of the sagging armchairs. Most of the furniture needed to be thrown out, he thought. The beds were execrable. The dining chairs could be reupholstered, but most of the rest was well past its sell-by date. An expression of his mother's – not that she had thrown out a piece of furniture in her life, not even when he'd urged her to let him provide more comfortable sofas, or a new kitchen. Stephen felt a perverse pride in such thrift, but even so he would do his best, he thought, to persuade the others to dispose of the contents of High Scarp.

He heard a noise in the kitchen then, and a moment later the door opened.

'Hello,' said Judith. 'How long have you been up?'

'I'm an early bird,' Stephen said. His mother again, ever eager to approve of his habits. 'I've been for a walk. Up the fell.'

'Earned your breakfast, then.'

Judith glanced towards the window: Stephen had the impression she was weighing up something she might say to him.

'Even if it's not your speciality, you must know a bit about the legal side of this,' he ventured.

'A bit,' said Judith. She didn't turn round at once: she made a show of flicking through a book she'd picked up, before shutting it and sliding it back into the shelf. 'Not the detail, of course, but the general set-up. It's called a condition precedent.'

'Requiring us all to come up here this weekend to meet the lawyer?'

'And whatever else is specified.'

'Such as?'

Judith made an impatient gesture, then countered it with a quick smile. She looked tense, Stephen thought. Not because of this conversation, he guessed. He remembered that log, burning brightly at five o'clock this morning.

'Your guess is as good as mine,' she said. 'Practically anything's possible.'

'Charades, perhaps, as you said last night. Either in the literal sense or the figurative.'

Judith pulled a face. 'It's very odd being back here,' she said. 'I found some old Scrabble scores in a drawer. Marmion's name there among ours. It's almost as though we've never left. As though Fay's still here, calling the shots.'

'Let's hope for moderation, then.'

'Indeed.'

Looking at Judith now, at her forced smile and the shadows under her eyes, Stephen had a sudden memory of their graduation day: of Bill standing a little apart from the throng and watching Judith, still in her wheelchair, laugh with false bravado at something someone had said. He'd wondered then what would come of that liaison. He'd wondered whether Bill and Judith were a better match than Bill and Marmion; imagined Judith awakening something more compelling in Bill. Was that fanciful? He'd certainly thought Bill might amount to more than a small-town solicitor – a fine thing to be if it made you happy, of course, but it didn't seem to him that Bill was happy.

But perhaps Marmion's virtue was what Bill had needed, Stephen thought now. Perhaps it was her loss, rather than his failure to secure Judith, that had been the tragedy of his life. He'd certainly chosen a version of Marmion to marry. Had Judith noticed that? Had Bill, even? He felt a wave of pity, then, for Isabel, but also for Bill and for Judith. They'd been unlucky, he thought. Very unlucky.

Judith was looking directly at him now, her gaze steady.

'I'm sure Bill knows more about conditions precedent than I do,' she said, giving the words a little more weight than they required, as if to conceal another conversation they might have been having. 'There's a chance we could set aside the will and arrange things differently – but that depends on how the rest of the estate is disposed.'

'Meaning . . .?'

A quick shake of the head. 'Let's cross that bridge when we come to it.' Judith yawned ostentatiously. 'God, I'd forgotten how awful the beds are here.'

'I was thinking that might be our first act. Replacing them.'

'Unless it's prohibited, of course, by St Fay.'

Stephen cocked his head and smiled at her. That was better: a glimpse of the old Judith. 'Lucky we've got two lawyers among our number to help us find a way round any difficulties.'

'Or ensure the finer points are observed.' Judith grinned too, then turned her head sharply as a door opened somewhere in the house.

Stephen stood up. 'Shower for me, I think. Best foot forward for the solicitor. Then bacon and eggs?'

'Sure.' Judith got up too, as though she was anxious not to be left alone in the room. 'What time is the wretched man –'

But before she could finish the sentence, Isabel appeared in the doorway. She looked younger this morning, Stephen thought, her cheeks flushed with sleep like a child's.

'Good morning.' Isabel's eyes took in Stephen, then Judith, and Stephen felt Judith stiffen. Curious, he thought. He wondered whether Isabel knew what had happened between Bill and Judith that calamitous summer. And whether he was right about that burning log, too.

'I thought I was first up,' Isabel said. 'Bill's still fast asleep. I thought I'd make breakfast for everyone.'

Judith's hesitation was almost imperceptible.

'I'll help,' she said.

He ought to stay too, Stephen thought, but instead he found himself moving towards the door. After all, it was better to pretend to ignorance.

'I'm going to have a shower,' he said. 'I won't be long.'

June 1995
Judith

Back in Bristol, Judith submitted to a swaddle of fond parental care while the country submitted to a heatwave. The cast on her leg was horribly uncomfortable in this weather. Her nights were still filled with overwrought dreams, and she spent her days lying on a sofa, or on a sunbed in a shady corner of the garden, reading Mills and Boon novels and drinking chocolate milkshakes, dozing in front of daytime TV and waiting for news from High Scarp, or Cambridge, or wherever her friends had dispersed to.

She'd assumed she'd go back to St Anne's for graduation, but the more she thought about this plan the more doubts she had. The ceremony itself meant something to her, but that wasn't really the point: for the five of them not to graduate together when they'd shared so much these last three years was a shame. The last week shouldn't be allowed to overshadow everything else. But then . . . That conversation in her hospital room still haunted her. Did the others all hate her now? What had they said to Bill, and what had he said to Marmion?

Oh, that thought tumbled her heart. But even so, even so, the strangest thing was that in this tangled web of emotion and conjecture, she could hardly identify her feelings for Bill. Was this, as she'd imagined in those few heady days at High Scarp, a grand passion – the love of a lifetime – so that long, long in the future the wrinkle of this summer, the curious detail of swapping partners within their little group of friends, would be recalled with mild ironic chagrin? Or was it a mad fling they'd soon regret, so that Marmion's happiness had been ruined for nothing?

Judith turned restlessly, painfully, on the sofa, her cotton skirt sticking to her skin and the hated plaster cast weighing her down. She longed for Bill, dreaded seeing him, wondered why he didn't come. She read obsessively, distractedly, fretfully, living other lives while hers quivered nerveless in the summer heat.

And then, one afternoon, the doorbell rang. Her parents were both at work, and Judith took a long time to answer the door, struggling through the house on her crutches.

'Hello,' said Bill, when she opened it. 'Thank goodness. I was beginning to think this might be a wild goose chase.'

'Bill,' she said.

He'd never been to her house before, but he was the sort of person, she understood, who had no difficulty with maps and timetables. Judith felt her limbs dissolve with the shock of realising that he wasn't an abstract concept but a man of particularities, of flesh and imperfection, just now a little travel-rumpled and conspicuously anxious. And that no reasoning, no rationalising could account for the fact that she loved him.

'I would have rung,' he said, 'but your number's ex-directory.'

A stream of questions presented themselves: how did he have her address and not her phone number? What had prompted him to come now, today? She gazed at him, counting the days that had passed, wondering what had been happening to him.

'Shall I come in?'

He followed her through the house to the terrace, where swallows circled over the suburban gardens.

'How have you been?' he asked, as she lowered herself onto her steamer chair and heaved her leg up.

'OK,' she said. 'Bored and hot. Reading trashy novels.'

'Ah.'

'The last one was about a ship's captain who falls in love with a flame-haired stowaway.' She looked at him, wondering what all these words were for, how soon they could get past them.

'There was a redhead on the train,' said Bill. 'And a rather smelly man with a dog, which the guard didn't take kindly to.' He stopped, and reached a hand tentatively towards her. 'I've missed you,' he said. 'It seems much longer than five days. Cambridge felt very odd without you.'

'Have you been back there?'

He nodded. There was a pause, across which neither of them could offer a bridge. His hand hovered, still, an inch or two from her knee. The smell of honeysuckle and jasmine – an Indian smell, her father called it – suffused the still air, and Judith felt as though she was holding her breath, stretching out a single moment into something that might, if she willed it hard enough, last for ever – the moment before they had to ask each other the questions that waited for them.

'Tea?' she offered.

'No,' said Bill.

'Wine, then? Beer? We might have beer.'

'To be honest, Judith . . .'

His hand flitted up to her cheek, to her neck, to her shoulder. She watched his face soften and yield, and she felt herself giving way too, and then his mouth against hers and all defences gone. The throb in her leg seemed to swell and spread to fill her whole body with an intensity of feeling in which pleasure and pain were no longer different things but a great conflagration of guilt and desire and sharp, stinging happiness.

'The bloody cast,' she said, somewhere in the depths of his embrace. 'I can't move. We can't . . .'

'I'll carry you,' he said.

She started to object, but then he was kissing her again, and she shut her eyes tight against the glare of the sun as he lifted her awkwardly in his arms, kicking over a glass from beside her chair that rolled away and smashed on the steps. No matter, she thought.

Nothing mattered. Nothing but this moment, this banishing of words. This was what her life had been building towards: this was the beginning of everything.

'Tell me what's been happening,' she said.

He didn't answer at once. His eyes were shut; her fingers trailed over his chest as though to smooth something away. Somewhere nearby a lawnmower started up, breaking the hushed silence the heat had laid over the drowsy suburb.

'They took you to Lancaster,' he said eventually.

Judith nodded: she hadn't expected him to start there, but it was fine; anything was fine. All she really wanted was to hear his voice, to let him tell her things. Bill lifted himself onto one elbow so that she could see his face, and she felt a quiver run through her, an aftershock of contentment and agitation.

'Stephen went with you in the helicopter.' He hesitated. 'It was terrible on that mountain, Judith. We didn't know how badly hurt you were, and Marmion . . .'

'I gathered.'

'She was – very restrained. But everyone could see that you and I . . .'

Judith nodded. 'I remember Cressida, in the hospital,' she said.

'Yes.' His lips tightened for a moment. 'She's been back in Cambridge.'

'And Marmion?'

'Marmion went home,' Bill said.

He tried to smile at her, but his face seemed to resist it.

She wondered suddenly how long he would stay. Did he plan to go back to Cambridge tonight, or to Birmingham? Panic filled her: her parents would be home soon, and if he left then . . . Foolish, foolish, to let the afternoon slip away. Foolish to want to know what had been said, or what the others thought, when he was here with her, when they could be . . .

She tried to move, to shift her body a little closer towards him. Perhaps it was the wrenching pain in her leg, or the flat way the sun caught his face just then, or the abrupt silencing of the lawnmower, leaving a weight of expectation in the air. But quite suddenly, quite unexpectedly, came a shift of perspective. Quite suddenly it was as if they had been wallowing here in these rumpled sheets for weeks; as if they had walked deliberately and consciously into a cheap betrayal of wives and husbands and children. As if they had misconstrued everything. She remembered that first rehearsal in the chapel three years ago; the first time she'd met Bill. Some instinct had warned her off then, and she'd forgotten it, ignored it. Or had that just been fear – of the strength of her feelings, and perhaps of his?

How could she know?

'Bill,' she said, 'I'm not sure . . .'

'Not sure of what?'

He looked surprised by her tone of voice but not worried, not at all worried yet.

'This. Us. I'm not sure we should be doing this.'

'What do you mean?' he said. 'I love you, Judith. Everything will be all right.'

His face looked strange now, at once wary and unguarded. Judith was conscious of her power to hurt them both, and she could feel conflicting urges doing battle inside her: to twist the cord further or to release it, laughing off this flutter of doubt and letting it drift away through the open window. Which way did her true, brave, noble feelings lie? There seemed to be nothing but mush in her head.

'I don't know what to think,' she said.

'Don't think.' His voice wavered a little. 'You've been through an awful lot, Judith. Maybe I shouldn't have come, just yet. Maybe it was the wrong thing to do.'

'No,' she said. 'No, it wasn't.'

'Has Cressida been in touch with you?' he asked. 'Is that what it is? Or – Marmion?'

'No,' said Judith. 'No one. Just you. Just today.'

'So what can possibly be wrong?' He smiled then, lifting his hand to stroke her hair. 'Please don't worry. I'll take care of everything.'

'What "everything"?' Judith shut her eyes: she felt a little sick now.

'Marmion. Cressida. Whatever it is you're worried about.'

'It's not them.' Judith couldn't help herself: the words just came. 'It's us. I don't think we should be doing this. It feels all wrong.'

He said nothing for a moment. She could see she'd wounded him, and part of her was glad. Part of her wanted to drive him away, even though she knew that would hurt her as much as Bill.

'Perhaps we need a little more time,' he said eventually. He was scrabbling for a foothold, Judith thought, trying to prevent things slipping any further.

'When's graduation?' she asked.

'Thursday.'

'I'll come,' Judith said. 'My parents will bring me, and we can all be together. Then I think we shouldn't see each other.'

He was trembling – or was that the heat, shimmering like a mirage over them both?

'You can't mean that,' he said. 'You can't just dismiss me like a –'

'Like a what?' She was a little bit mad, she could tell that, and part of her was terrified now, but another part was very calm, watching things unfold from somewhere outside her spinning head. 'Like a what, Bill?'

'I thought you felt something for me,' he said. 'I thought we were both . . .'

And then it was as if a balloon deflated abruptly inside her. The pain in her leg was almost unbearable; she didn't want to talk, to think, any more.

'I don't know,' she said. 'You said it yourself: we need some time.'

'How long?' he asked. How much time?

She shook her head. 'It's not a – quarantine. Not a prescription. Just . . .' He was still looking at her, and the expression in his eyes almost made her relent. But she was right; she was sure she was right. Reason came flooding in now to justify her. If their feelings were real, they would last. If they tried to make a go of it now, with all the complications of the last few weeks stacked against them, they might never know for sure. 'Three months,' she said. 'The end of the summer. If you still . . . We'll know what it means, then.'

August 1995
Stephen

Stephen wasn't entirely sure that this meeting was a good idea, but he made his way to the Northern Line platform at Waterloo buoyed up by a sense of purpose. It was weeks, now, since any of them had seen each other, and he'd kept thinking he ought to do this. Not quite restitution, but . . . Well, anyway, he would see what came of it. Three stops later he bounded up the escalator, and when he came through the ticket barrier and out into Oxford Street, Marmion was already waiting.

'Hello,' he said. 'Sorry I'm late.'

'You're not. I'm early. I'm always either early or late. It's very nice to see you, Stephen. It's very nice of you to suggest this.'

She still looked as drawn and as enervated as she had in those last few days at High Scarp. His father had looked like that after his heart surgery last year, Stephen thought, but he'd bounced back since then. He looked better than ever, now.

'I thought we'd go to Pizza Express,' he said. 'Is that OK?'

When they were sitting down, Stephen smiled across the table. 'You look very well. Have you been away?'

'I'm afraid I don't really, but I have been away. A couple of weeks on the beach.'

'Where?'

'The Isle of Wight. But it felt like the South of France, this year. We got through gallons of suncream.'

'Snap. We've just got back from Bournemouth.'

They looked at each other for a few moments, then dropped their eyes at the same moment to the menu. He had nothing to feel guilty about, Stephen reminded himself. Nothing except a temptation to brush her under the carpet along with the rest of them, and he was here, wasn't he, resisting that?

'What do you fancy?' he asked.

'I always have the Veneziana. Ever since –'

She stopped. Their first tour with the choir had been to Venice, two summers ago. Stephen remembered Marmion and Bill hand in hand, leaning over the side of a vaporetto, the sun catching their faces as it sank towards the lagoon.

'I'll have the same,' he said. He turned to summon the waiter.

When they'd placed their order, Stephen sat back in his chair. The truth was that he had absolutely no idea what to say. Were High Scarp and Cambridge and the others all off limits? Music, then? Her family?

'What are your plans for the rest of the summer?' he asked.

'I've got a job,' Marmion said. 'In a bookshop, covering someone's maternity leave.'

'That's good.'

'I quite enjoy it,' Marmion said. 'I think they thought – Cambridge graduate, must know about books. I haven't confessed that I'm practically illiterate.'

Stephen could see from her face how much the effort at joviality was costing her. 'I've got a job too,' he said. 'At Gatwick.'

'With your father?'

'Not working with him, but he suggested it. I'm driving a shuttle bus.'

'Really?'

'To and from the long-stay car parks,' Stephen said. 'Not very exciting, but the pay's reasonable. I need to save up for Dubai.'

'Of course.' There was a moment of silence, and then she said: 'What does your father do there? I've never asked.'

'He's in charge of one of the baggage-handling teams,' Stephen said. 'It's not . . . It's quite a responsible job, really.'

'Of course. I can imagine you have to be . . .' Marmion foundered. Her parents weren't grand, Stephen thought, in the way Cressida's were: they were freelance-musicians-turned-teachers. In any case,

Marmion was the last person to look down on anyone. But he could see she was distressed that no ready compliment came to hand. It was as if the bountiful spring of love and goodwill inside her had dwindled over the course of this hot summer; as if she was having to pump up supplies by hand.

Their pizzas arrived just then, and with relief they concentrated on eating. Stephen had never had a Veneziana before: its combination of sultanas and capers and pine kernels was rather surprising. Arabic influences, he thought. But North African, presumably, rather than Middle Eastern. As in the Moor of Venice.

'This is good,' he said.

Marmion seemed less enthusiastic: she picked half-heartedly at her pizza. The Grand Canal was too much in her mind, Stephen thought. Poor Marmion. Neither of them, it seemed, could think of anything else to say, and as the silence lengthened, desperation drove out of him something he hadn't meant to mention to anyone.

'I went to see Fay, a few weeks ago,' he said. 'Before I left Cambridge. I thought I'd . . . Well, anyway, a strange thing happened.'

Marmion looked wary. Was this dangerous too? Stephen wondered. But he pressed on.

'I saw some photographs,' he said. 'They were on the mantelpiece in the sitting room, but I'd never noticed them before. One of Fay as a little girl, and one of her with a baby.'

'Really?' This was less a question than a polite acknowledgement, but Stephen was happy to take any cue.

'It looked like her baby,' he said. 'At least – she looked like a mother, the way she was holding it.'

'Really?' A different tone this time; a spark of interest. 'Do you think she had a child, then? What can have happened to it?'

Her eyes filled, perturbingly, with tears. Stephen hadn't meant to say any more – certainly not to divulge his fantastical theory – but he couldn't bear Marmion to weep over the death of a baby.

'I wondered if she'd put it up for adoption,' he said. 'I don't know why: just that she's asked me, a couple of times, about my parents – my adoption – and I wondered at the time whether she might know someone who . . . Anyway, there it is.'

'You didn't ask her?' Marmion said.

'Certainly not.' He could imagine Marmion questioning Fay, though, in her artless way. 'Don't say anything,' he pleaded. 'Don't mention it to her, will you?'

'Of course not. What a funny thing, though. Goodness, Stephen!' She stared at him suddenly, her eyes wide. 'How silly of me not to see what you meant. Do you think you might have been her baby?'

'Well,' Stephen blushed. 'I did actually wonder . . . Do you remember, the first time we met Fay, she picked up on the fact that my birthday was coming up? I wondered –'

'Maybe you have the same birthday as her baby? Oh, Stephen . . .'

'It's pure speculation,' Stephen said, wary again now. 'It might be someone else's baby in the photograph, or her child might just be living somewhere far away. We never knew very much about Fay, did we? About her private life?'

'Don't you want to find out?' Marmion asked. 'Have you ever tried to find your birth mother?'

'No.'

She looked at him for a moment.

'You're a good son,' she said. 'To your adoptive parents, I mean. You love them.'

'Yes,' Stephen said.

It was more complicated than that, much more complicated, but he wasn't going to explain, not even to take Marmion's mind off her woes. He did love his parents, of course. But this possibility, this wild possibility, had niggled at him for the last few weeks. His mother must be musical, he'd always thought. And Fay was tall. He'd stared in the mirror every night lately, wondering if he could recognise Fay's eyes, or her nose, in his own features. But he couldn't tell Marmion any of that.

'Do you fancy going to the British Museum after lunch?' he asked instead. 'I feel I ought to make the most of London, before I leave.'

'Me too.' Marmion fixed him then with a brighter, a more purposeful expression. 'I'm going abroad too. I wanted to tell you. I'm going to New York. To the Juilliard, to study singing.'

'Really?' That was a big step, he thought. A long way to go to be away from Bill. 'That's terrific,' he said. 'Really terrific.'

'I hope so,' Marmion said.

Stephen looked at her, taking in the doubt, the hope, the bravery.

'I'm very pleased, Marmion,' he said – and then, after a little hesitation, 'I felt very sorry for you, up at High Scarp. You deserve to be happy again. I hope you will be.'

October 1995

Cressida

It had been strange coming back to Cambridge alone, and with the different perspective her new status gave her. St Anne's graduate hostels were on Madingley Road, a fair way from the college, and in the first few days Cressida felt as though her map of Cambridge had been flipped over as she cycled to the University Library and the Sidgwick site from what had always been the far side.

The change was welcome, though. High Scarp had undone the blandishments of nostalgia, and she worked hard at making a new life for herself. She bought a standard lamp and a swivel chair for her room, befriended the Chinese economist and the German engineer who lived on her floor. She ignored the old haunts and found new ones – a coffee shop on Bridge Street that had opened over the summer, and the Grad Pad in Granta Place, where the view of punts stacked by the bridge below gave her a pleasing sense of elevation.

It was impossible not to think occasionally about the others, but the only person she'd heard from was Marmion. When she'd arrived back in Cambridge there'd been a postcard from Marmion, explaining that she'd decided to accept the Juilliard scholarship and give up her place at the Guildhall. Cressida could hear Marmion's voice as she read it, striving for common sense and for candour. The picture on the front was of John Keats listening to a nightingale on Hampstead Heath: she could hardly bear to think about the care with which it had been chosen.

So Marmion was off to America, and Stephen to the Persian Gulf, and she didn't expect to see either of them again before they left. Judith and Bill would both be in London, but Cressida suspected that neither of them would come back to Cambridge any time soon. Perhaps after all this was the safest place to escape the past.

One person who kept drifting into her mind, though, was Fay. They'd all parted awkwardly, but before that, beyond that, were all the happy times they'd had together. She and Fay could go on being friends, surely. Fay might think it was odd if she didn't get in touch, in fact. Newnham wasn't part of her daily orbit, but one afternoon when she left the library she turned right rather than left, and ten minutes later she was at Fay's front gate. The house looked exactly as it always had – like a dress rediscovered at the back of your wardrobe, Cressida thought, more familiar than you can credit. She parked her bike at the side and rang the bell.

For a long time nothing happened. Fay's car was there, but there was no sign of life inside. On the point of turning away, Cressida rang again, and this time there was a sound from deep in the house. It was Fay who opened the door, but she didn't look like the Fay Cressida knew. Shrouded in shawls, her hair was unbrushed and an odd smell hung about her. Camphor, perhaps. Something chemical and old-fashioned.

'I'm so sorry,' Cressida said. 'You're ill. I shouldn't have kept ringing. Shall I . . . I'll come back, shall I, when you're better?' She hesitated. 'I'm back at St Anne's, in one of the graduate hostels.' Another pause, more alarming than the first. 'Is there anything I can do? Anything I can get you? I could go to the chemist, if you like, or –'

'No,' said Fay. She looked as though she was attempting a smile – or was she? It was hard to tell. She must be drugged up, Cressida thought, on some powerful painkillers, or one of those flu remedies that make you drowsy and a little high.

'Are you sure?' Cressida lingered for a few more seconds, but Fay didn't speak again. She didn't shut the door, though; she just stood, looking at Cressida as though waiting for something. 'Go back to bed,' Cressida said. 'You look terrible. It must be a really nasty bug.' Still Fay didn't move. 'Go back to bed,' Cressida said again, in the cheery, bossy sort of voice Fay herself might have used in these circumstances. 'Get some rest. I'll come back another day. Get well soon.'

In the end she almost pushed Fay back inside the house, caught between a desire to be useful and embarrassment – both at her ill-timed intrusion and at the oddness of Fay's demeanour. She recalled the abrupt shifts of mood in those final days at High Scarp; the sudden stop in the road on the way home. Had Fay been ill then? Perhaps even . . . going mad? Was she . . . But then she checked herself. Too much time alone this last fortnight had given her a taste for melodrama. She'd make a joke of it, next time she saw Fay: *You gave me quite a scare, last week. You looked like death, you poor thing.*

Even so, as she cycled back up Queen's Road, Cressida felt the taint of the encounter clinging to her, a faint nagging voice accusing her of getting things wrong once again. She began to think up treats for herself – a pizza, a film, a cocktail in the chic new bar up Castle Hill. It was Saturday evening: she deserved some fun.

There was a phone in the hostel's entrance hall that took incoming calls, and as Cressida came in she saw a note propped against it with her name on the front in large letters. Before she could pick it up, Gerhardt, the engineering student, appeared on the landing above her.

'Your friend Bill called,' he said, consternation thickening his accent. 'You need to call him, straight away. I am afraid that it is bad news.'

October 1995
Judith

They met in a pub in London; nowhere they'd ever been before. Judith wasn't sure who'd suggested it, nor exactly how the news had spread: she hadn't spoken to Bill for months, not since the end of June, the awful formality of their farewells on graduation day. It was Cressida who'd called her, last night, and since then Judith had sat in her bedroom, paralysed with dread and disbelief.

They were all there when she arrived, sitting in the furthest corner behind a small pub table. The first thing that struck Judith was that someone was missing – and then she felt a drenching, deafening flood of realisation. Those words, that voice down the phone, made suddenly true: *Marmion's dead.*

'Hello,' said Stephen, and Judith made some kind of movement with her face – a slight pursing of her lips that was nowhere close to a smile.

They all looked smaller and paler than when she'd last seen them, diminished partly by the Sunday-afternoon dinginess of the pub and partly, she surmised, by shock. None of them had drinks: she wondered whether she should offer to buy some, then thought better of it.

'Have a seat,' said Cressida, pushing a chair out, and Judith took it. It was only a few weeks since her cast had come off, but she knew that wasn't why her legs felt unsteady. She still hadn't made eye contact with Bill, but when she looked up she caught his gaze, and she was sure she felt the others' eyes on them. Christ, she thought, could they not deal with one thing at a time? Could they not all be in this together, just for the moment?

'Is anyone going to have a drink?' she asked, at exactly the same moment Stephen said, 'Shall I get a round, now we're all here?'

Even that tiny social stumble seemed to floor them. She and Stephen stared at each other for a moment, and then Judith said, 'Let's both go. What does everyone want?'

At the bar, Stephen put a hand on hers, the gesture of a doctor or a priest, and Judith thought she had never been so grateful for an act of kindness in her life. Her hands shook a little as she picked up Cressida's gin and her glass of wine. She'd have liked to say something to Stephen, but it felt wrong to speak to him alone: too risky, somehow.

'Cheers,' said Cressida, when they'd sat down again. 'What are you supposed to say? Long life.' Her face folded, and then she recovered herself and gave Judith a thin smile. To reassure her that nothing would be said, Judith thought, no repetition of her accusations earlier in the summer. Judith felt a flash of relief, and then of shame. None of that mattered the tiniest bit compared to the horror of an aeroplane falling from the sky. She felt herself trembling again.

'They're saying it was a terrorist attack,' Stephen said. 'No one seems to know who.'

'Does that make it better or worse?' Cressida's voice, Judith thought, was shriller than she intended. 'I can't see that it makes any difference how it happened.'

'It might to her parents,' Judith said. She meant the suddenness of it, the difficulty of believing in a death on the other side of the world that left no trace apart from what could be salvaged laboriously from the sea. But that wasn't the only difficulty, of course. 'Quakers and terrorism don't . . .' she began.

They all looked at Bill then, realising that he must have spoken to Marmion's parents; that he might still be Marmion's boyfriend, in their eyes. How much would she have told them, Judith wondered, about what had happened at High Scarp?

She met Bill's gaze again, and seeing the anguish in his face, pity shot through her – another emotion that felt not quite pure enough for the due process of mourning. None of them had said how dreadful it was, how shocking and sad and barbarously unexpected, and she felt that in other circumstances, in simpler circumstances, they would have done. But how could she know that? How could any of them know anything, faced with this devastating transformation? They were lost without Marmion, she realised. Marmion would have known so much better than the rest of them what to think and say and feel.

Bill cleared his throat.

'The funeral is on Friday,' he said. 'At the Quaker meeting house in Camden.'

'Do they want us to sing?' Cressida asked.

Bill shook his head. 'There's no order of service,' he said. 'No – well, it's just silence, unless people want to – are moved to – speak, or anything.'

'Christ,' said Cressida, and then she blushed. 'I mean – not even a service to hang on to.' She looked at Judith. 'Whatever you think of the words.'

Death ought to unite, Judith thought, but instead it divides.

'It's such a terrible shock,' Stephen said then: winding the conversation back to where it should have started, Judith thought.

'Yes,' she said. 'It's impossible to believe she'll never be here again.'

Bill nodded. 'I really can't take it in.'

Each of them, Judith thought, taking a turn now on the tightrope, saying something obvious and foolish so that it would have been said.

'It's not just . . .' Stephen began. 'It's such a freakish thing to happen to someone you know, isn't it? Being blown out of the sky. That's what makes it so hard to accept.'

Judith glanced at Cressida, waiting for her to add her phrase, to seal the circle, but there were tears streaming down Cressida's face. And then Judith realised that she was crying too, almost without feeling anything – as though what she felt was too enormous to be either eased or exacerbated by weeping. Stephen had put an arm around Cressida's shoulders, and Judith wished he'd do the same for her. Every bit of this was intolerable, she thought; every aspect of it. She didn't think she could bear to stay much longer, though God knew what she'd do when they parted.

'But we're all invited, are we?' Stephen asked. 'To the funeral?'

'Yes, of course,' said Bill. 'They want – the Hayters are very keen that all her friends should be there. It's on Regent's Park Road. At three o'clock.'

Cressida dabbed her eyes on her sleeve and nodded – as though a time and a place was something to hang on to, Judith thought, even if there were no funeral sentences in prospect. Stephen pulled a handkerchief out of his pocket and handed it to her. Judith felt a rush of affection for them all, and then – quite unexpectedly – its opposite. Almost an electric shock, warning her off. A thought came to her suddenly: that she didn't see how their friendship could survive this.

The week that followed felt both preternaturally ordinary and dizzyingly unreal, almost as if Judith herself had died, and had been transported to a realm where everything looked deceptively normal, but nothing was the same any more. She did her best to stay away from the television and the newspapers, but the air crash was a national *cause célèbre* and the topic of conversations all around her, between strangers and fellow students and talking heads on the radio. Among the dead was a pair of newborn twins who became the totems of the tragedy, their pictures everywhere and their names on everyone's lips. Judith never heard Marmion mentioned, but she kept expecting it, and the strangeness of that, of knowing she might hear her name at any moment but would never see her again, was hard to endure.

She kept coming back to what Stephen had said in the pub about the freakishness of it. Of all the people to be blown up by terrorists,

Marmion was the very last you would imagine: too ordinary, too solid – too good. It made no sense for her to be a scapegoat for the shadowy extremist cell that had at last claimed responsibility for the attack. And it made no sense that their little drama at High Scarp was somehow connected to an act of global terrorism; that the two had become part of the same tragedy. It made that scene on the side of Nag's Pike seem absurdly trivial, but at the same time distorted it, magnified it, as if it were the beat of the butterfly's wing that had reverberated across mountains and oceans and galvanised evil into being.

It was impossible not to think about it every minute, every hour, but even so the days rolled on, one after another, taking them steadily further away from Marmion. Judith had started at bar school, and the routine of lectures and seminars and reading provided some distraction. She didn't make contact with any of the others again, and although she wondered how they were and what they were doing, none of them seemed quite real to Judith during those few days. It was as though the realm they had all occupied together no longer existed and they were fading like ghosts, leaving behind the kind of sketchy recollection you might retain after years, rather than days, apart.

But Marmion remained clear and vivid in her mind's eye. Not the Marmion who had died so publicly, so dramatically, but the Marmion who had been alive until a few days ago. Little video reels of memory were triggered by the least thing, or by nothing at all: Marmion's laugh, Marmion's smile, Marmion's pronouncements – sometimes over-simple, but often cutting to the heart of the matter. Marmion's voice; that glorious contralto. How could they possibly have sung at her funeral without her?

On the bus on Tuesday evening, Judith caught a glimpse of someone who might, just for a second, have been Marmion, and before she understood what was happening she was on her feet, calling out. The woman turned – a woman in her mid-thirties, nothing like Marmion – and Judith was choked with embarrassment.

'I'm sorry,' she said. 'I thought you were someone else.'

The woman smiled – she wasn't English, Judith thought, or at least she didn't reply to this garbled apology – and Judith sat down again, her heart racing.

She could hardly bear the elation of that split second when she'd believed that there had been a horrible mistake, and that Marmion wasn't dead after all. Not just joy that she was alive, but relief that she hadn't killed her.

Until that moment, Judith hadn't allowed herself to articulate that thought. Surprise and wild hope had sprung it from a locked vault somewhere in her mind, but now it was out, there was no escaping it. She sat on the bus, numb with grief and remorse. This was the crux: she hadn't just betrayed Marmion and made her miserable, she had caused her death. She and Bill. If Marmion hadn't found out about them – if there had been nothing to find out – she would have gone to the Guildhall with Bill, as she'd planned. She wouldn't have accepted the offer from the Juilliard, she wouldn't have been on that aeroplane to New York, and she wouldn't have died.

The counterarguments were ready and waiting in Judith's mind too, as though her subconscious had been wrangling with itself all this time. But they made no difference: Judith knew that as soon as they began to plead their case. No, she couldn't be blamed for the actions of terrorists; no, she wasn't unique, at twenty-one, in sleeping with her friend's boyfriend. But she was still culpable. She was still stifled by a guilt that even she – quick-footed, quick-witted, quick-tongued Judith – could see no prospect of escaping.

No one else was in when she got back to the flat in Bayswater. Her new flatmates had jobs, and they often went drinking after work. When Judith had told them about Marmion's death they'd suggested she join them, but she hadn't. It suited her that their lives barely intersected.

The phone rang while she was hanging up her coat. Judith picked it up without thinking.

'Is that Judith?'

Bill's voice: her heart clanged so loudly she was sure he must be able to hear it, but an invisible hand around her throat made it impossible to speak.

'Judith? Can you hear me? Is Judith there?'

She put the phone down. It rang again a few seconds later, and she left it for five or six rings, then lifted the receiver and pressed it down again to end the call.

That afternoon in Bristol seemed aeons ago, but it was only three months. The time they had allotted themselves then was up: it had been up almost exactly the day Marmion died. Judith had no idea whether that . . . adjournment – was that the right word? – made things better or worse. It shouldn't, surely couldn't, make any difference now, against such a monstrous backdrop, but it did. Her own actions mattered; her own motivations.

The compulsive logic that had driven her to reject Bill had fallen away rapidly after graduation day, and since then her feelings had veered between violent extremes. At times her self-denial had seemed almost romantic: she'd imagined herself as Scarlett O'Hara, waiting out the war, hoping she and Bill would be joyfully reunited in the end. But the cool pragmatism of the plan had appealed to her too, and that was more alarming: the thought that she could so calmly submit their desire for each other to some kind of gamble. Rolling the dice again, instead of collecting her winnings. And of course there had been moments, many moments, when she'd longed to turn up on Bill's doorstep, as he'd turned up on hers that day, and tumble him into bed. She longed for it now, even, when she knew that the bet was over and the dice had fallen against her; when touching Bill would surely call down a lightning bolt of retribution on them both.

No, there was no way back now; no answering of his calls. All she wished – all there was, hopelessly, to wish for – was that it had made a difference to Marmion. But seeing them hold back from the passion that had ruined her own hopes could only have made things worse for Marmion. If their feelings for each other were so easily contained, how much did that diminish Bill's for her?

Judith

2010

Midnight. The window is open onto the warm night and city sounds drift up from the street below: the shouting and laughter and honking of horns sound closer than they are, a reassuring backdrop for someone used to urban life. Judith lies very still. The sheets are slightly damp and haphazardly strewn across her. It feels like lying under leaves, pungently evocative of reckless pleasure and its clammy aftermath. Bloody hell, she thinks – but the quiver of disbelief isn't entirely unpleasant. It shifts, like a colour-change bulb, between dismay and jubilation and hilarity, softened by darkness and wine and by the strangeness of her surroundings.

One version of the story, she thinks, reads like the opening of a romcom: meet a man you vaguely know on a plane and end up in bed with him in a Paris hotel. It's the variations on the theme that make or break the plot, though. A man you know because he was once a client. Not so long ago, in fact. A man you defended on a charge of sexual assault, going against your principles because you believed his story, not the intern's, and because his wife was a feisty, admirable person and she believed him too. A man whose parting shot, after the trial, left you wondering whether you'd both been wrong.

Thinking about what she has just done with this man, what extraordinary and unexpected things, it's all Judith can do not to squeeze herself tight around the lingering trace of it, as though to keep hold of it, keep it to herself. Keep it, certainly, from the wife and the intern, and from the judge and jury, although they're beside the point now. The logic of the world is a peculiar thing, she thinks. The order of things. The shifting of contexts.

It wouldn't have happened if she'd had someone with her on this trip – the trip she won in a raffle promoted by the senior clerk in chambers last Christmas. She'd have liked to bring her mother, but she is too poorly at the moment, between cycles of chemo, to manage a city break. Other women, Judith knows, would have a string of friends they could ask, but somehow none of the women she counts as friends quite fitted the bill. Not close enough, not fun enough, not free enough. And it's out of the question for Arvind, of course. For a risqué arrangement their relationship is remarkably low on risk: Arvind will never be seen with her in the outside world, never anywhere but her flat.

Over the years Judith has met dozens of men, plenty of them good-looking and interesting and available, and she considers again now, lying awake in a Paris hotel room, the perversity of falling for Arvind, back when he was a pupil and she was a very junior tenant, and then sticking with the limited, limiting pleasures he has brought her. He was already married then, to a pretty girl who is happy, despite her English upbringing, to play the good Indian wife to her barrister husband, and who has produced two little girls whose photographs Arvind keeps in his wallet. No: there will never be a weekend in Paris with Arvind, and she knows, in some corner of her mind, that it was that knowledge which drove her into the liaison; which has kept it alive.

Should she be grateful that the way was open, is always open, for encounters like this one with Jonty Scott? She hardly knows. The Judith who asks questions like that is a different Judith to the one who answers them.

Down below she hears voices raised: a Saturday-night rabble on their way home from a bar, or perhaps on their way to another. Judith listens idly, trying to fit a storyline to the soundtrack. How many people? Arguing or just teasing? Who has a beef with whom? She can't make out the words being hurled about, but she can imagine some of them: perhaps the phrase she heard on the Métro earlier, delivered with fine invective by a young Parisienne into her mobile phone. *Putain de merde, mais qu'est-ce que t'as foutu?* Judith's French is rusty, but it used to be good enough to swear with gusto. Rolling the phrase around in her head, enjoying the feel of it, it occurs to her that she has no call to swear like that in any language these days. Her life, for all its unconventionality, has become sedate. For a moment self-pity flushes through her, but then there's a scream down below, cutting across the rest of the noise: an ululating scream that starts at full volume and doesn't let up.

Judith freezes, listening intently now. Sooner than she would have thought possible a siren accelerates up the narrow street and comes to a halt just outside the hotel, and then there are more voices, raised and urgent, before the siren resumes, tearing away again. After that there's a quiet that feels more unnatural, more alarming than the noise that still echoes in her ears.

My God, Judith thinks, is someone dead? Was it a dereliction of responsibility to lie motionless while someone was killed twenty metres below – to lie here and have no certain idea what was happening? There would have been nothing she could do, she tells herself; there are plenty of other windows to provide witnesses. But even so she feels a waft of guilt, and doubt catches at the tangle of feelings about her own little adventure – which suddenly seems both more serious and less; something happening at one remove, like the incident in the street, or an anecdote being told years later. And where does it end, the anecdote, she wonders? What's the punchline?

Nothing breaks the silence now, and Judith can feel her grasp on the night start to loosen, and a gust of wind lifting her out of herself, filling the space where she's been with white noise. Not yet, she thinks, as the world throbs and blurs and fades. I can't go to sleep when someone has just died: or did I dream that? She scrabbles for a handhold, something to help her cling on to consciousness. Not yet: I need to know how it ends first.

Since her mother fell ill, Judith has found herself looking at things differently. Not just the things you might expect – mortality, loyalty, suffering – but other things too. In fact, principally herself: in the last few months she has often come face to face with the present-day Judith with a jolt of surprise, as though she has aged ten or twenty years in a flash, instead of inching forward year by year. This isn't what's supposed to happen when one of the people you love most in the world is critically ill, but it has hit Judith with slam-dunk inevitability: a sudden clarity of self-awareness.

She isn't middle-aged yet – thirty-seven is surely not middle-aged, in this century – but she's not young any more, and the feisty, clever, confident Judith who set out into the world at eighteen hasn't yet solidified into any of the final adult forms she might have taken. She hasn't made the transition from promise to proof – and the more she thinks about it, the less sure she is about how far she's travelled along that road. Of course it's hard, as a barrister, to know whether she's on the right track, edging gradually towards silk, but it's not just her career that suffers this sudden lurch of perspective. She's always known she won't have children with Arvind, but she finds now that she's been assuming she still has a free choice about motherhood, and when she faces that assumption squarely she can see that it's flawed. Nothing's certain. Nothing's certain at all. Standing beside her mother's bed as she drifted in and out of consciousness after her first operation, it occurred to her that life might consist of the steady erosion of certainties, rather than the cementing of them.

She and her mother have always been close. Perhaps it's no surprise that she should falter too, when her mother does. There are phrases for this, clichés: the foundations of her life are being rocked. Judith imagines, though, a kaleidoscope being shaken, the recognisable pattern of the world metamorphosing before her eyes as it did once before. She can see all at once how fast the decades pass, the acceleration towards forty and fifty and sixty, her life a whirligig spinning out of control.

And it's not just the passage of time that troubles her, the slip and slide of possibility. She's always imagined that her exotic ancestry distinguished her from the general run of people, setting her on a particular, privileged trajectory through life. She must, surely, have a more complex, more nuanced perspective than her peers, her insights infused with that rich brew of genes and her judgements shaped by the heady atmosphere of enquiry and tolerance in which she grew up. But in those long nights of introspection, while her mother underwent tests and more tests and started on treatments that frightened even her, Judith began to suspect that she should have taken less for granted than other people, not more: that navigating a life without the conventional struts of culture and religion, the reassurance of tradition and convention, requires greater clarity of purpose than she has brought to bear on hers. It occurred to her that the most distinctive thing about her is that she's an only child, clever but spoilt, with an only child's belief that she'll get what she wants from life – but she hardly knows, still, what it is she wants. And meanwhile she's getting too old to be spoilt, and her body has more than a trace of the soft doughnut flesh of her Pakistani grandmother these days, a little less of the sharp, calligraphic angles of her elegant Jewish mother.

You look tired, her mother said, next time she visited. You look worse than me, Judith: you should have a holiday. Judith smiled and shook her head – but when the raffle prize fell into her lap, she booked the flights before she could change her mind.

The hotel curtains are thin, and the coffee-coloured fabric does no more than add an earthy tone to the early-morning light. For a second – not even a second – Judith thinks the man beside her might be someone else, but he's not.

This is the wrong light to see Jonty Scott in, she thinks. Although it's difficult to know what the right light would be; whether any light could make him look less like a thug. A hard bastard, he called himself at some point last night, although that was meant to be ironic, self-deprecatory. Or so Judith thought at the time: it's not easy to imagine irony or self-deprecation playing any part in Jonty when you see him asleep. If there's any gentleness in the man, it's not in his body, the heavy torso filling three quarters of the bed and the ugly face that looks pugnacious even in repose. It's the kind of face some women swoon over, but not Judith, until now. Judith has always preferred her men smooth-skinned and boyish.

As she looks at Jonty he stirs, cocks open an eye. She doesn't move, doesn't smile; waits to see what he makes of his situation.

'Morning, gorgeous,' he says. The estuary colour comes and goes, she's noticed. Not much of him is susceptible to disguises, but in that respect at least he's a chameleon. 'Been awake long?'

'No.' She yawns – not deliberately, but she realises too late that it looks like an attempt at verisimilitude.

'Sleep OK?'

'Apart from the murder below the window in the small hours.'

He raises an eyebrow. 'Really?'

'That's what it sounded like. Police sirens and lots of screaming.'

He grins. 'Sleep of the just, for me,' he says. 'What's the time?'

'Ten thirty.' He must be in Paris on business: has he got meetings this morning? she wonders. But his face doesn't change.

'Don't suppose they run to room service here. Shall we go out for breakfast?'

Despite herself, Judith feels a frisson of pleasure. Even if it's just breakfast, that's more dignified than parting at her bedroom door. On impulse, she leans forward and kisses him quickly on the lips before she slides out of bed and into the bathroom.

One thing in Jonty's favour: he has plenty of money. Two things, in fact: he has plenty of money and he knows how to spend it. The place he takes Judith to for breakfast is sumptuous, with Moorish tiles and plants everywhere, orchids and aspidistras and cacti studded with jewel-like flowers. The food looks sensational too. Scrutinising the menu, Judith feels suddenly ravenous.

'Anything catch your eye?' Jonty asks.

'Everything,' says Judith.

He lifts an eyebrow as the waiter approaches, and orders, in heavily accented but confident French, two *petits déjeuners gastronomiques* – enough food for a day or two, Judith thinks. Perhaps they can sit here all day and eat it. The thought makes her smile, and Jonty smiles too.

The cold light of morning, Judith thinks, ought to make her consider his wife, but she suspects Jonty's wife would be unsurprised to see him here with her. She might even be seen in a place like this herself, with a man who isn't her husband. This is the way they do things, Judith thinks: she won't be the first or the last. That thought is reassuring, but it also needles her into exerting herself. She's noticed other women clocking Jonty, and she likes the thought that he's a prize, even if he's not her kind of prize. She wants to be sure she can keep his attention as long as she wants it: that when there's dismissing to be done, she's the one doing it.

Contrary to conventional wisdom, Judith has found that what men like best is not to be asked about themselves (especially when there's a risk of saying things they might regret) but to be entertained. As the first selection of delicacies is set before them – pastries *sucré* and *salé*, fruit juice in thin goblets, smoked salmon wound in spirals on Melba toast – she assembles a series of anecdotes to amuse him. Being locked into Notre-Dame after a VIP visit when she was here, five years ago, for a conference. The school French trip in the fifth form, when two teachers had an ill-concealed affair under the scandalised eyes of their charges. Her mother's French penfriend who still keeps in touch, from the château in the Tarn where she lives with her fourth husband.

Jonty eats more than her, listening while she talks, but from time to time (she doesn't want to give the impression that she's working too hard: the effusion must seem spontaneous) she pauses to give her full attention to the food.

'Good, eh?' He watches her hesitate between a tiny *pain au chocolat* and a *chausson aux pommes*. 'Have them both. They're only small.'

'You'll make me fat.'

'You could stand to be a little fatter. It suits you.' And then, before she can launch again into the amusing saga of the penfriend and her marital adventures, he says, 'I hope we can see each other in London, Judith. If you do that sort of thing.'

The news of her mother is mixed. She's been entered in a clinical trial, double blind, but she's pretty sure from the side effects that she's getting the new experimental drug.

'Is that a good thing?' Judith asks, on the phone.

'It is if the phase one results are borne out.'

'But it's making you feel worse than the other one would?'

'Who's to say worse.'

Judith says nothing for a moment. She could go down this weekend, she thinks, but . . .

'You had a good time in Paris, anyway?'

'Very good.'

'Did you meet a glamorous Frenchman?'

'No.' Judith hesitates. 'An Englishman, actually.'

'Married?' her mother asks – and then, without waiting for an answer, 'Of course he's married. All the good ones are married.'

Judith smiles. It's a joke between them, the Jewish-mother act. It's supposed to cheer her up. But what really cheers her up is being reminded of her mother's uncanny intuition, where Judith is concerned. Abigail Malik, mother and clairvoyant.

'Married and a former client,' she says. 'Very bad idea.'

'You don't want me to get better, Judith,' says her mother.

'Of course I don't. I'm coming down this weekend to make sure you're not getting better.'

'Don't do that. I'll be growly this weekend. See your man, if he's got time for you.' There's a cough at the end of the phone – probably nothing, Judith thinks, probably just a cough, but even so she feels a clutch in her chest. 'Does this mean you're getting rid of the other one?' Abi asks.

'I'm planning on assembling a whole football team, actually,' says Judith. 'But not this weekend. This weekend I'm coming to visit you, growly or not.'

There's a brief silence. 'Your father's coming on Sunday,' says her mother. 'Do you want to see him?'

This was the deal when her parents split up: Judith was on her mother's side. No matter that they were both at pains to explain that it was a joint decision. Sharing herself between them was too difficult for Judith, and since her father's adultery had triggered the separation, the choice was straightforward. The irony of her harsh judgement of her father didn't escape her, but her own behaviour, she tells herself, hasn't undermined a marriage. If anything, it's helped Arvind's marriage, offering him something he needs and demanding precious little in return.

But her ostracism of her father has caused some difficulties. Judith doesn't do things by halves, and they are both too proud to offer olive branches. I see him, her mother says, from time to time. If I'm friends with him, why can't you be? They have met occasionally – at her mother's sixtieth birthday party, a cousin's wedding, an uncle's funeral. Never, since the divorce, *à trois*.

On Friday, during a tedious day in court, Judith wonders about the weekend: about how she will find her mother, what they will do. It would be nice to take her out, she thinks, but nowhere too strenuous, and nowhere with crowds, either. Her mother has explained the risk of infection. If they stay at home all weekend, will there be enough to say?

But of course her mother has a plan. Why did Judith imagine it would be down to her to organise the entertainment?

'I thought we'd go to Wildwood tomorrow,' she says, that evening. 'A friend of Drusilla's is exhibiting at the moment. I liked her work when I last saw it.'

'Great,' says Judith. 'How's Drusilla?'

'Doing better than me,' says Abi.

Wildwood is a farm on the way to the Quantocks which has nurtured artists rather than cattle for the last forty years – a favourite haunt of Judith's mother, run by an old friend of hers. The thought of it makes Judith unexpectedly happy. It's the kind of place, she thinks, where things never change, and no one seems to get any older.

'It's good of you to come, Judith,' Abi says. 'I know you have better things to do.'

'Never,' says Judith. Now she thinks she might cry, and where would that get them? 'What did you teach me? Nothing is more important than looking after your mother.'

Abi laughs, and there's that wheeze that turns into a cough again. 'It's nothing,' she says, hearing Judith cluck. 'It's a cough. Don't make that sound.'

They get up late on Saturday morning. Her mother looks better, Judith thinks, a little more colour in her cheeks. She's never been good at breakfast, though: together they pick at a slice or two of toast and drink the herbal tea which seems to have replaced the rooibos in Abi's kitchen.

Looking out of the window, Judith notices that her mother's Mondeo isn't in the drive.

'Where's the car?' she asks.

'At the garage,' says Abi. 'Being patched up, just like me. We can take the little black car.'

'*My* little black car?' asks Judith. 'The old Fiesta? I had no idea you still had it. You don't keep it taxed, do you?'

'Just recently,' Abi says. 'They gave it the once-over. I thought I might sell it. Or, you know – if I needed someone to run an errand, it might . . .'

She shrugs. Judith stares at her for a moment, recognising with a chill her mother's first admission of vulnerability. She wants to ask why the errand-runner couldn't drive the Mondeo – why they wouldn't have a car of their own – but she understands that it's a need for safety nets, for security – and besides, who is she to argue, when she's not here to run errands?

'Well,' she says, 'this'll be a trip down memory lane, then.'

The car is parked in the garage beside the house. It looks, Judith thinks, like a tin box – and when they open the door, she wonders what her mother can be thinking.

'It stinks,' she says, as she slides reluctantly into the passenger seat. (Abi, it seems, is determined to drive.) 'It smells as though something's died in here.' And then she catches herself, and the last word is almost lost in a kind of hiccup.

Her mother pats her hand. 'You don't have to mind what you say,' she says. 'They're familiar, those words. I've used them my whole life.'

Judith blushes then, like a child reprimanded for swearing. While her mother starts the ignition, she wonders whether she means that the vocabulary of illness and death is familiar to her as a doctor, or simply as a human being. Is that one of the things that happens when you get cancer: that part of your language is withdrawn by well-meaning friends and relations, just when you need it?

As they head out of the city, Judith rolls her window down and the smell is diluted by a rush of cold air.

'Too much?' she asks, and her mother shakes her head.

'It goes well, doesn't it?' she says. 'The car?'

Judith smiles. She wonders how much it cost to get the Fiesta back on the road, and how much it's worth. But that's not the point, she knows. It's the same satisfaction as finding an old coat that's survived the moths and come back into fashion; finding that you're still here to enjoy it.

'Are you doing any singing at the moment?' Abi asks, a little later.

'Not really. Just the Bach Choir.'

'There must be other groups you could join. Smaller groups.'

Better groups, her mother means. She knows Judith finds it frustrating being in such a big chorus; that it's a step down from the glory days of the chapel choir. Judith ran into Deep Patel at the Coliseum a few weeks ago – he runs a semi-professional chamber choir these days, alongside his other jobs, conducting and playing and teaching. *Come and sing for me,* he said. *We could do with another sop in the Leighton Singers. There're a few faces you'd recognise.* Judith smiled, as though she was really too busy for all that. She'd heard the Leighton Singers on Radio 3 the week before. She didn't tell him she wouldn't dare audition for him.

'They're all too good or too bad,' she says now. 'I wouldn't get into the ones I'd like to join.'

'You have too low an estimation of yourself, Judith,' says her mother.

Judith laughs out loud. 'Only you could possibly think that about me,' she says. 'Only my mother.'

'Only your mother could know it's true,' Abi says.

Judith doesn't reply. After a moment her mother glances at her. 'You were so talented, always,' she says. 'All that music.'

They both know that isn't what she meant, just now: that she had shimmied in a blink from singing to men; to marriage, specifically. Among many things on which they disagree – often with relish – it is the only topic that hurts them both.

'You're always so busy, I know,' Abi says now. 'I suppose they ask too much, those choirs.'

This is a peace offering; it wrenches at Judith's heart. It's not that her mother doesn't have the strength to argue, she knows, but that she doesn't want to waste precious time on it. Or perhaps, even worse, that she's given up hope: not just of a wedding, but of recalibrating Judith's life.

'I should look around,' Judith says, trying to keep her voice steady. It's important to sustain the charade, she thinks. Who knows where they might end up otherwise. 'You're right: it would be good to do some more singing.'

Her mother brightens. 'You'll find there are opportunities,' she says.

Abi herself has never cared for music. She encouraged her daughter to practise – drove her to it, in fact – because she saw it as an accomplishment, a garnish, and because people said Judith was good, and she believed you should make the most of your talents. Her own passion is for art. If she hadn't been a doctor, Abi might well have been a painter. The house is filled with her canvases: the early watercolours and the tentative oils, the bright post-divorce acrylics. Looking at the row of defiant nudes along the landing last night, Judith wondered what the chemotherapy series would look like. Whether her mother would ever dare to solicit her own show at Wildwood.

Drusilla comes out to greet them, her welcome conveying the delight of a surprise as well as the satisfaction of a pleasure regularly renewed. Judith thinks, not for the first time, that they could hardly be more different, these two women of the same age and the same upbringing. Drusilla is as broad and unruly as her mother is neat and trim; her greying hair blooms around a tie-dyed bandanna.

'Do you want tea?' she asks. 'Do you want tomatoes? I have a glut.'

'I want to see the paintings,' says Abi. 'First I want to see the paintings, and then we'll drink some tea.'

Some of the paintings are huge and some much smaller. Abi moves at once towards the far wall, where a gigantic triptych hangs against the bare stone. Judith drifts from one picture to another, half an eye on her mother, and comes to a halt in front of an unframed canvas about a metre square. The label beside it says *Continuum III*. It looks like a close-up of the sea on a stormy day, overlaid with a loose filigree of copper wires. She stares at it, self-conscious, as she always is when faced with art in the presence of her mother. The painting is restful, she decides. That's what she'll say if she's asked for an opinion.

'I like this one best too,' Abi says, joining her. 'The bigger ones aren't as successful, are they?'

She puts a hand on Judith's shoulder, and Judith feels a charge of comfort and consolation course through her. She remembers her mother taking her hand as they walked to school when she was five, hugging her when a teenage romance floundered. She'll buy the painting for her, she thinks. Secretly, before they leave: a memento of the day.

On Sunday morning she makes up her mind about her father's visit.

'I'm going to head back this morning,' she says. 'You'll have company today, and I've got lots to do.'

That's true, anyway. She's got a case starting on Monday morning, the kind of case that might advance her a little along that arduous path to silk, if she does well enough. But her mother's not deceived.

'Next time, maybe,' she says, her eyes resting on Judith's face.

'Sure,' says Judith. 'Next time.'

She leaves a card propped up in her room with the receipt for the painting inside. She hopes her mother will find it before her father arrives.

On the way back to London she gazes out of the train window at the rush of the countryside. Perhaps this is how artists look at the world, she thinks: seeing it as it comes at them, not leaping always to what they know is there. A phantasmagorical swirl of green rather than a pattern of trees and fields. And then, with a sudden fanfare of conviction, she decides that this week – this evening, even – she will break off her twelve-year-old arrangement with Arvind, and her one-week-old fling with Jonty. Perhaps she'll even screw up her courage and audition for the Leighton Singers. *A few faces you'd recognise*, she hears Deep saying again. Not, of course ... But who knows? Who knows what Fate might deliver, if she dares to take the first step? She feels a thrill of excitement, of resolution, of ambition. Jumping off the train at Paddington, she jogs along the platform towards the Tube, as though the rest of her life is waiting impatiently.

When she gets back to her flat the landline's ringing, and she can see the answerphone light flashing. She lifts the receiver, blissfully ignorant.

'Judith?' Her father's voice. 'Judith darling, I've been trying to get hold of you. I'm very sorry; I've got some bad news to tell you.'

Her mother is dead. Judith listens to the medical detail without hearing it; hearing only that it was a freak occurrence, perhaps a complication of the experimental drug. Out of the blue, her father says, with his characteristic habit of using stock phrases in a way that jars a little. 'She wouldn't have felt a thing, not for more than a second.'

'You can't know that,' Judith says. It's the first time she's managed to speak – the first thing she's said to her father for months. She's understood already that he wasn't there; that he arrived to find Abi crumpled in the hall.

'The cancer was worse than she admitted, Judith,' her father says now. 'I'm not saying she would have chosen this outcome, but it isn't the worst way to go.'

Judith shuts her eyes. None of it makes any sense: it's only a few hours since she was pouring tea for her mother. She knows it's not her fault, that there was probably nothing she could have done even if she'd been there, but even so those optimistic plans she made on the train feel shameful now. She's filled with hubris, with the enormity of wanting more for herself, a fresh start, a clean slate, when her mother . . .

Her father goes on talking for a while, and then his voice falters.

'Shall I phone back later, Judith?' he asks.

She wishes he wouldn't keep using her name.

'OK,' she says. They will have to talk, of course. And she'll have to go back to Bristol at once: her mother would want the proper Jewish rites, secular though she was in life, and her father can't be trusted with those. She thinks how odd it is to feel indispensable to her mother now, when it's too late. And that the one person she needs to talk to, who would understand, will never be available to her again.

She sits down, then, on the corner of the sofa. The one person . . . Terrible, terrible, she thinks, for her thoughts to fly so swiftly to someone else; to another source of succour, so long ignored. The shame and the hubris come flooding back – and although she can hear her mother's voice behind them, scoffing at her overwrought scruples, she shakes her head, willing herself to resist. She should, she must, bear this alone. What would she say, anyway? What could she say, even if . . .

But she can't help it. Before she can think any more, she grabs her laptop, googles *phone book*, types in the name and location.

There's only one result: W Devenish, Middle House, Emscott, Shrewsbury. It's three o'clock on a Sunday afternoon: perhaps he'll be out. That thought tightens her resolve. If she rings and he's out, she tells herself, she won't call again. She has just enough self-possession to dial 141 before the number, and then it's ringing, ringing, and she's imagining the house, Middle House, and Bill in the garden, perhaps, or sitting with a newspaper –

'Hello?'

Judith freezes. A woman's voice.

'Hello?' it says again.

'I'm sorry,' Judith says. 'I think I have the wrong number.'

'Who are you after?' She sounds friendly, efficient.

Judith wants to put the phone down now, but something forces her on.

'Bill Devenish,' she says, 'But –'

'No, this is the right number.' Judith can hear the quick smile, the chair being pushed back. 'Hang on – he's just here.'

But Judith's thumb has found the hang-up button now. As she sits with the phone in her hand, the dead silence around her, she can hear the woman's voice still in her head: *Someone for you, Bill, but we were cut off. I expect she'll try again.* Funny: she'd never imagined a wife for him. So he's settled down, moved on. She'd never anticipated that.

Part V

September 2015
Judith

When the sitting room door had shut behind Stephen, Judith and Isabel looked at each other. She should have moved more quickly, Judith thought, claiming she too needed a shower, following Stephen down the corridor – but somehow she'd known, when Isabel came into the room, that she was going to stay. Not exactly as a penance, because there was really no reason to feel guilty about last night's encounter by the fire. Nothing had happened. Nothing except words. And none of it was her fault. She'd done nothing to encourage Bill, and she certainly hadn't seen his declaration coming: she might have imagined a frisson of nostalgic suggestion this weekend, but not . . .

Isabel's face gave nothing away, but some instinct told Judith that she knew something had changed; something was up. Had she heard Bill coming back to bed? Had he explained himself, made excuses, talked in his sleep? All these years she'd lived with the possibility of facing Arvind's wife, she thought, or Jonty's. There was less basis for jealousy in this case, but the stakes were higher, even so. She could admit that: the stakes had always been higher with Bill. And her sang-froid about Isabel – about her existence and her presence this weekend and her position vis-à-vis Judith herself – was less secure this morning.

'We seem to be the catering team,' she said.

'Yes.' Isabel gave a quick smile. 'I don't mind. I'm happy to be useful.'

Perhaps she was wrong, Judith thought. There was no wariness in Isabel's manner. 'Shall we check out the provisions, then? Stephen fancied bacon and eggs.'

There was plenty of bacon in the fridge, but no eggs. Odd, Judith thought.

'That's a shame,' said Isabel. 'Could we get some in the village?'

It was ten to eight: the shop would probably open any minute. But Judith hesitated. Her mind felt disconcertingly maladroit this morning, struggling to settle on the right course.

'It's worth a try,' she said.

She'd imagined them walking down the hill, but as they came out of the house Isabel clicked the remote to unlock her car, and Judith was relieved, then, at the thought that the expedition would be shorter.

Isabel backed gingerly out of the drive.

'Steep,' she said, and Judith nodded.

They passed a couple of walkers, backpacked and booted, heading for the fell. Judith looked up through the windscreen: the sky was very grey, but the clouds were high still. She heard Fay's voice suddenly: *Rain's always round the corner, up here.* Not that it had been, that summer. She remembered day after day of sunshine.

The village shop was open, but there were no eggs.

'They'll be here in half an hour,' the woman said. 'I'm sorry: we sold out last night, and we're waiting for a delivery.'

'Never mind,' Judith said. 'We can do without.'

'There's a lady down the road who sells them at her gate,' the shopkeeper said. 'It's only a mile or so – sharp left after the National Trust car park.'

'Thank you,' said Isabel. 'We'll try that. Thank you very much.'

This had been a mistake, Judith thought, as Isabel started the engine again. She'd thought – some rash part of her had thought – it might be a way to normalise things. She and Isabel hanging out, as her father would say, with his careful embracing of colloquialism. Well, if they were on a quest now, she'd better make what she could of it. Get on the front foot.

'How did you and Bill meet?' she asked.

'At the Guildhall,' Isabel said. 'The Guildhall School of Music, on the postgraduate performance course. Bill moved to law college after a few weeks, but we met before he left.'

Judith was silenced. At the Guildhall in 1995? The very month that Marmion died? God almighty: he hadn't wasted much time. She'd imagined this marriage as a fallback, something Bill had settled for, perhaps years later. But if . . . It must, then, have been a grand passion. Grand enough to wipe out not just Marmion, but her. Although Bill's words last night . . .

'We didn't get married for a few years,' Isabel said. Had she inferred anything from Judith's silence? It was impossible to say. 'Bill was . . . Well, it was just after – Marmion died.'

'Yes,' said Judith. And then, with a dose of spite that was directed partly at herself: 'Do you have children?'

'We tried,' Isabel said. 'Five cycles of IVF. But then after Bill – you know he had cancer?'

'No.' *I was ill*, she heard Bill saying. *Maybe it should have changed my perspective more than it did.*

'He doesn't talk about it much,' Isabel said, and for some reason those words caused Judith a stab of pain. Because they spoke for Isabel's knowledge of him, or for what Bill had been through? Judith couldn't tell.

To her relief, Isabel braked abruptly just then, pointing at a National Trust sign. 'Look – this must be the turning.'

There was no gate at the roadside, but they turned onto a track which led sharply uphill, doubling back on itself as it climbed into the woods.

'Is this the right place?' Isabel asked. 'Did you see a sign? "Fresh Eggs", or anything?'

'No,' said Judith. 'God – are we OK?' There was a grating sound, a sudden lurch.

'It's very slippery,' said Isabel. 'I'm not sure this is right.'

'Stop, then. Let's go back.'

Isabel put the handbrake on. It was surprisingly dark; the trees hung over the track, enclosing them in a fairy-tale wood. Up ahead there was the suggestion of a house now – a building, at least – and Judith could hear a dog barking.

'I'll have to reverse,' Isabel said. 'I don't fancy trying to turn: it looks very soft at the sides.'

She looked calm and capable. Judith imagined her ministering, soothing, coping, when Bill was ill, and she felt a flash of jealousy. But if it was domesticity he'd been after . . .

She remembered that time she'd rung their house, the day her mother had died. The shock of hearing Isabel's voice, and the sense, afterwards, that she'd given herself away, after years of restraint. Could Isabel have guessed who it was? Had she even known Judith existed? She certainly hadn't shown any sign of recognition when they'd been introduced the night before. No, Judith had the advantage there. She'd found out, after that phone call, who Isabel was; she'd been prepared to meet her. She allowed herself a flicker of satisfaction about that.

The car began to edge backwards, slowly and steadily – and then there was another lurch, a skid, a slide, and Isabel slammed the brakes on.

'Damn,' she said. 'Hold tight.'

She turned the steering wheel, put the car back into first gear and let off the handbrake, but when she tried to pull forward again, the wheels spun.

'Damn,' she said again. 'I think we're stuck.'

Damn was about right, Judith thought. Damn the bloody eggs.

'I'll get out,' she said. 'Hang on a moment, and I'll see if I can do anything.'

The back of the car had skewed off the track. It was hanging over a shallow ditch, the rear wheels sunk into the mud. Marvellous, Judith thought. Bloody marvellous. It was only a quarter past eight in the morning, and she was stuck in a bog with Bill's wife. It was cold in the depths of the wood, and they were probably trespassing.

Isabel put her head out of the window.

'Shall I ring Bill?' she called. 'Shall I ring the house?'

'No,' said Judith. 'Not yet.' The other side of the track was much drier: they should have kept over to the left. They should have looked, before they started reversing. But there were some fallen branches she could put under the tyres, and a few large stones that could brace the car from behind. Then if she pushed, and Isabel drove . . . She started gathering sticks and forcing them into the mud, making a grid for the tyres to grip. It might work, she thought, she might be able to get them out, and she felt a flare of pleasure at her resourcefulness.

After a few minutes, Isabel got out of the car.

'What are you doing? Can I help?'

Judith halted. She was sweating and grimy by now, a long scratch on her arm.

'I was going to – see those stones there? I was going to put them behind the wheels.'

Isabel stood for a moment, hands on hips.

'I think it might be better to ring for help,' she said. 'What if the car rolls further backwards?'

Judith frowned. 'It won't be able to if we wedge those boulders behind it.'

Isabel prodded the ground with her foot. 'It's very soft,' she said, a dubious look on her face, but after a moment she shrugged. 'OK,' she said. 'Let's have a go.'

They worked in silence then, lugging sticks and stones, placing them around both rear wheels. They heard the dog barking again, and a man's voice shouting in the distance. After a few more minutes Judith stopped to survey their progress.

'I think that's enough,' she said. 'Let's try. You drive and I'll push.'

Isabel opened her mouth to object again, but Judith was already leaning against the boot, testing her footing. Isabel climbed back into the driving seat.

'Ready?' Judith called, and as the engine revved she leant her whole weight against the back of the car. 'Come on, you bugger,' she muttered. 'Just –'

And then she leapt backwards to avoid the splatter of mud as the car jolted forward, mounting the mat of branches and heaving itself back onto the track.

'Hurrah!' Judith brushed herself down, grinning, as Isabel drove a few yards up the hill then halted again. 'OK,' she called. 'Back down again, and keep to the left this time. Slowly, slowly.'

There was a deep gash across the green of the verge and a litter of sticks and stones, all of it looking conspicuously intrusive. If there was a house further up, if the man with the dog came down this way, it would be obvious someone had been here. Judith kicked some of the branches out of the way, then turned her attention to Isabel, reversing cautiously down the hill.

A few minutes later they were on the main road again, heading back towards High Scarp. Beside them, the lake gleamed in the early sunshine, an expanse of quicksilver between the mountains.

Judith had expected some bright chat, or perhaps philosophical reflection – some means, at least, of establishing a joint view of the expedition which they could offer the rest of the group when they returned – but there was complete silence in the car. The escapade in the wood seemed to have set them back, if anything. Perhaps they were both waiting for the other to speak, to set the tone, to decide who owed whom an apology or a vote of thanks. Or perhaps, Judith thought, they had both realised they had nothing, absolutely nothing, to say to each other.

What did Isabel and Bill talk about? she wondered. She imagined for a moment their twenty years of conversations – trivia and endearments, arguments and in-jokes – as a great stack of paper, a whole room full of marriage-talk in toppling piles, proof of staying power and of the sheer weight of time. But in her mind's eye the paper was all blank. She must be wrong, of course, but she couldn't imagine a single thing they might say to each other, even in the context of cancer and fertility treatment. The things she could deduce about Isabel – her pragmatism, her caution, her sheer ordinariness – gave her no clues. Was she satisfied by life? Was she certain of Bill's affections?

But then it struck Judith that those sheets of paper weren't blank at all, just written in invisible ink, never to be read by anyone else. And it struck her, too, that Isabel loved Bill in the same straightforward, candid way that Marmion had. Perhaps the reason she couldn't figure Isabel out was because she wasn't Marmion. She wasn't Marmion twenty years on, in the way they were all themselves twenty years on, but she was in Marmion's role, she even looked a little like Marmion, and . . . But that was ridiculous, Judith told herself. She'd never have called Marmion pragmatic or cautious or ordinary. She wasn't even sure, now, that that description could be applied to Isabel. She was a singer, a musician; she was Bill's wife.

Those words still brought Judith up short. She didn't envy Isabel, she told herself, nor pity her. It was more complicated than that. It was as if Isabel's existence, the existence of the world she had occupied these last fifteen or twenty years, had thrown Judith's world off kilter. As though she'd been looking at life from the wrong angle all this time.

As they got closer to home, Judith felt suddenly gloomy. This outing had boxed her in, she thought, to a way of acting, a way of thinking, that she hadn't wanted to settle for, or . . . No, it was too obscure to pin down. She wished she hadn't gone, that was all.

It was only when they turned up the drive to High Scarp that she realised they'd forgotten the eggs. All that trouble, and they'd come home without them.

October 1995
Bill

Bill's self-possession held until the day before the funeral. His emotions were too immense, too overwhelming even to know what they were: they bore down on him like an avalanche, smothering any glimmer of normality. But on the outside he managed a reasonable semblance of composure. He got himself to the Guildhall every day and went through the motions of meeting his tutors and fellow students. He restricted himself to ringing Judith once a day at the flat, and – after the first couple of times – putting down the phone without leaving a message. He answered his mother's calls, doing his best to allay her concern for his well-being and to ignore the hint of censure in her voice.

Early on Thursday morning he woke to hear the phone ringing, and he rolled out of bed to answer it.

'Is that Bill?' said the voice at the other end, and he felt a drenching chill. Marmion's mother sounded startlingly, dismayingly like her daughter.

'Yes,' he managed, after a moment. 'Hello, Mrs Hayter.'

'How are you, Bill?'

'Well,' he said. The word was intended to temporise, but, to his confusion, it seemed to be taken as an assurance.

'Good. I'm glad. Bill, would you come and have supper with us this evening? We'd like to have you with us, as part of the family.'

Bill's hand tightened on the telephone. 'This evening? I'm not . . . Yes, of course I can.'

'I'm so glad. We'd like that very much. Come at six.'

As he stumbled back to bed, Bill wondered whether it was possible for shock to feel so much like a physical illness: whether the symptoms of flu or pneumonia or some sinister tropical fever were common in the bereaved and the guilty. He pulled the sleeping bag over his head to block out the light, but the smell of the ancient nylon was unbearable.

He was staying, while he looked for somewhere permanent to live, with a friend of a friend in a shabby flat in Leyton. The room was scattered with discarded glasses and half-full ashtrays: he had hardly registered its squalor before. The heathen are sunk down in the pit that they made, he thought. He was seeing the room now through Marmion's eyes, he realised – or through her parents' – in comparison to their wholesome, homely house, where the only things out of place were books, the only excesses those of artistic feeling. Must he really go there tonight? Why had he not had the presence of mind to devise an excuse, or the courage to offer it? How would he find clean clothes, let alone prepare his mind, his conscience for the Hayters?

Marmion's family lived in a modest terraced house in Crouch End, twenty minutes' walk from the tube station. When Bill had visited with Marmion he had been charmed by the way so many people fitted into so small a space without any appearance of discomfort, but as soon as the door opened this evening it seemed to him that their collective grief was too great to be contained by the unassuming white stucco: that pain and sorrow and disbelief seeped out from the scuffed skirting boards and the scrubbed floors.

'How nice of you to come, Bill,' said Mrs Hayter. 'I know you'd rather be with your friends, but it's a great kindness.'

'Not at all.' Bill tried to smile. 'It's . . .' Not a pleasure; that was the wrong thing to say. There was no right thing. Nothing to be said at all.

He was being shown into the little front room where all the musical instruments were kept, including the grand piano that filled half the floor. With a shock Bill recognised Marmion's violin case, lying along the front of a shelf. And then he saw, with a greater shock, the photographs of Marmion that sat on every surface, some in frames and others propped against books or candlesticks. Marmion as a baby, her dark curls and bright eyes unmistakable; Marmion as a little girl, plump in a primary school pinafore; Marmion as a teenager, shielding her eyes on a beach; Marmion on graduation day, only three months ago. That photograph had been in the newspaper a few days before: seeing it now, here, closed some kind of circle, as if there had been, all this time, a loophole lying open in his mind. Bill gave a little yelp, then tried to cover it by clearing his throat. Mrs Hayter didn't seem to have noticed.

'I wanted to talk to you, Bill, just for a few moments,' she said, settling herself in one of the narrow easy chairs that sat between the bookshelves and the tiny hearth.

'Of course.' Bill squeezed himself into another of the chairs. It bemused him that the solid Hayters managed with such flimsy furniture.

'I know that you quarrelled, you and Marmion,' said her mother, without further preamble.

Bill looked up sharply. He hadn't expected this: hadn't prepared himself, he realised, for any specific conversation at all. He'd imagined an evening of platitudes and painful companionability.

'I know that's why she decided to go to New York,' Mrs Hayter went on. 'I'm sure you blame yourself, Bill. I wanted to tell you that you mustn't.'

Bill said nothing. He tried to keep his eyes on Mrs Hayter's face, its expression as calm now as if she were explaining that he wasn't responsible for the falling of rain or the coming of night, but his gaze slipped ineluctably, shamingly, down to the floor.

'Young people do quarrel, Bill,' Mrs Hayter said. 'You made her very happy; remember that. It isn't right to lie about our feelings. Nor is it right to assume responsibility for events beyond our control.'

Bill looked up at her again. He'd assumed that she had only a partial understanding of the situation, which would have made her forgiveness excruciating. But he wondered now whether she knew more about what had happened this summer than he'd imagined. For a moment he wanted desperately to ask, to explain, to beg for full and proper absolution, but he couldn't. He couldn't because despite his affection and pity for this woman – despite his affection and pity for her dead daughter – what possessed him, filling his mind with a throb and beat beside which everything else was reduced to a whisper, was Judith. Even here among all the photographs of Marmion, in the house where she had grown up, he couldn't stop thinking about how badly he wanted to see Judith. He wanted to throw himself on her mercy, to lose himself in her and obliterate his shame.

Flushing deeply, he stood up.

'That's very kind of you,' he said, hating the unsteadiness of his voice, and the way it would sound to Marmion's mother. 'More than kind. When you have so much to . . .'

'Come and eat now,' she said. She didn't look at him again. Perhaps she had exhausted her self-control, he thought, or perhaps at last she had detected his perfidy.

By the time he left, Bill felt ragged with exhaustion and self-hatred. The Hayters had eaten, as they usually did, in silence, but this evening the silence had been punctuated with remembrances of Marmion, each of them offered as a gift to the others around the table but reaching Bill as a reproach. With a false show of reticence and of deferral to family custom, he had avoided the shy glances of the younger Hayters and the more candid gaze of Pip, the eldest. He felt like a stain on this blameless family; the ruin of them all. As soon as he decently could he escaped, promising to see them at the meeting house tomorrow, promising to keep in touch. It seemed impossible now that he had ever, as her mother claimed, made Marmion happy. He was a villain from a morality tale; an evil wizard dressed up as a handsome prince.

October 1995

Cressida

The Friends Meeting House in Regent's Park Road was among the oldest in London, Cressida had discovered, a demure but distinguished neighbour to the Nash terraces that flanked the park. Inside it was plain, light-filled, high-ceilinged, with unostentatious white panelling and long windows set high in the walls. The doors to the main meeting room were open, but a lot of people were milling about in the outer room, where a large book lay open on a table.

The murmur of voices was subdued, but even so the atmosphere wasn't what she'd expected. The marking of death in silence had conjured something brutally austere in her mind, but it was clear as soon as she walked in that this would not be an occasion without comfort – and paradoxically that realisation, the recognition of the warmth that could both temper and intensify grief, undid the control she'd managed to sustain all the way here on the Tube. Standing just inside the door, she felt tears sliding down her cheeks.

'Cressida?' said a voice, half familiar. 'It is Cressida, isn't it?'

She turned to see Marmion's mother, tall, staunch, providential – and so like Marmion that Cressida was shocked out of her tears.

'Yes,' she said. 'I'm so sorry, Mrs Hayter. We're all completely devastated.'

Mrs Hayter put a hand on her shoulder. 'It's very good to see you, Cressida,' she said. 'We shall need Marmion's friends. There's a book – we'd like a record of who was here. Do sign it, won't you?'

'Of course,' said Cressida. Across the room she could see Marmion's little sisters, Becky and Maggie, and her brother Pip, smiling and shaking hands. The wrench of loss tore at her chest again; the multiplicity of grief. How much they must feel it, she thought, this close-knit family.

Mrs Hayter pulled her suddenly into an embrace, then released her with a tiny collecting sigh.

'Do go in, when you're ready,' she said. 'Whenever you're ready.'

Ready, Cressida thought. What an extraordinary thought: that she might be ready to say goodbye to Marmion; that her family might. That they should all congregate here so calmly, spend an hour together and go away having passed some kind of watershed. It struck her then that among the layers of sorrow was one that arose from her certainty that she could never feel as much for the death of one of her brothers as the Hayters, for all their Quakerly restraint, could feel for Marmion.

She had imagined the St Anne's quartet gathering beforehand, sitting together, but none of them had been in touch since that meeting in the pub, so things had been left to chance, and it seemed that chance had no desire to throw them together. It was ten to three, and Cressida couldn't see any of them. People were moving through to the meeting room now, leaving space for latecomers in the outer room, and Cressida followed the tide. Never mind the group, she thought. The group was no more, anyway: if Nag's Pike hadn't undone it, Marmion's death certainly had. And perhaps their grief for Marmion was nobler for not being pooled.

She stopped briefly on the threshold. Sunlight fell across the wide room, glancing off a large framed picture of Marmion propped on an easel at the front. Cressida felt her pulse throb: it was a recent photograph, so lifelike that the shock of recognition crowded out, for a moment, the realisation that it stood in the place where the coffin might have been. Of course there couldn't be a coffin, she told herself, but its absence was somehow more appalling than its presence would have been. Her mind skittered over news reports and police procedurals, wondering whether Marmion had been found, whatever was left of her – but no, she wouldn't think about that, about any of that. It was too much to cope with. She took a deep breath, steadying herself, and looked about her for a place to sit. Her eye fell on a man in a suit sitting alone near the end of a row, with a spare seat beside him. As she made her way towards him, he turned slightly, and with a start she realised who it was.

'Stephen!' Her voice was louder than she intended; she blushed, even though there seemed to be no rule of silence in place yet. Oh, she was pleased to see him. Stephen, of all of them.

'Hello,' he said.

'You look . . . The suit, Stephen! And you've had your hair cut.'

'I'm flying to Dubai in three days.'

'Oh . . .' Cressida was embarrassed by the anguish in her voice. Of course he was going; of course there was no reason for him to change his plans. 'I can't bear the thought of you flying,' she said, scrambling to recover herself. 'I mean, after . . .'

He smiled, and tilted his head to one side in the way he did that meant *oh well* or *so be it*.

'I'll be all right,' he said. 'What about you? How are you?'

'I'm fine,' Cressida said – although at that moment she felt utterly bereft. She knew Stephen had always planned to go abroad; she knew none of this was her fault. But she couldn't help feeling that what she'd done and said had made it impossible for those who were left to recover any part of what they'd lost. She couldn't help feeling that if Stephen thought better of her . . .

'I've got a tiny flat in the graduate block on Madingley Road,' she said, collecting herself as best she could. 'It's very quiet. There's a garden at the back.'

'Good,' said Stephen. 'I can picture you there, cooking up soup when you get back from the library.'

Cressida's mouth trembled. 'I can't,' she said. And it was true: the prospect of it all, the excitement of settling into her new life, had evaporated in the last week.

Just then they were aware of quiet falling over the room. Marmion's family were moving up the aisle, making their way to the front. Marmion's father, tall and spare, stood facing them all. For a few moments he said nothing, and then, in a voice that betrayed no sense of hurry, no sense of heaviness, he welcomed everyone, thanked them for coming and invited them to join in remembering and giving thanks for their wonderful daughter Marmion, taken from them so suddenly and loved by so many.

He was about to sit down when he stopped, smiled almost to himself, then went on in a slightly different tone of voice.

'Those of you with a literary bent will be aware that Marmion is an odd name for a Quaker child – that it's the title of an epic poem about the Battle of Flodden, and that its eponymous hero was a famous reprobate. I should perhaps explain that Marmion was named after her great-grandmother, whose parents had certainly never read Walter Scott.' A faint ripple of amusement went round the room.

'However,' Mr Hayter continued, 'however. Scott has provided us, in Marmion's name, with some lines that seem too apt to pass over as we consider how to comfort each other.' He unfolded a piece of paper, glanced at it, then hesitated again before he went on.

'*O! many a shaft, at random sent, Finds mark the archer little meant; And many a word, at random spoken, May soothe or wound a heart that's broken.*'

There was silence now; a listening, thinking silence Cressida had rarely encountered before.

'*And come he slow, or come he fast, It is but death who comes at last,*' Mr Hayter read. '*But search the land of living men, Where wilt thou find their like again?*'

He cleared his throat. 'There are no words I can speak that will honour Marmion fittingly, but I hope you will find the words – the thoughts – to do so, and will feel free to share them with us.'

As Mr Hayter took his seat, tears brimmed again in Cressida's eyes. With a quick sidewards glance, Stephen passed her a handkerchief – a proper cotton handkerchief, properly ironed. Pressing it to her face, she breathed in the smell of starch and soap powder, a smell she had never associated with Stephen but which seemed suddenly absolutely his, redolent of the broad tracts of his life she knew nothing about. What on earth did his parents think – his mother who ironed his handkerchiefs – about him moving from Surbiton to Dubai?

After a while the tiny shifts of breath and cloth that filled the room and the distant accidents of sound from outside fell away, leaving only the white space and the silent hum of thought almost palpable around them, gathering like cloud or candyfloss or the invisible spinning of hundreds of silkworms. What Cressida could hear in the centre of it was music: Marmion's voice joining with theirs to sing Bruckner's *Locus iste*. In the silence she followed the motet quite clearly: the soprano line soaring to its climax for the second time, floating through the pianissimo echo, then dropping towards the delicious hanging discords where the two top lines leant on each other, drawing apart step by chromatic step before the final, gentle resolution. She heard Marmion's wonderfully resonant low Bs, dipping down towards the tenor part before rising towards the soprano line again; saw the radiant intensity on her face as they heard the final chord echo above them.

It was almost inconceivable that it was only a matter of weeks since they had sung that piece together in the little church in Griseley. *Locus iste a Deo facto est:* this place was made by God. That place had felt as though it was made by God, that stone church in its idyllic valley, but the snake, Cressida thought, had been among them all the time.

She heard a rustle of movement then and she realised that someone was sitting down, having stood up to speak. Had she been so lost in recollection, in Bruckner, that she hadn't heard what was said? Bewildered, she glanced at Stephen, wondering what she'd missed, but his face betrayed nothing. Cressida's heart thumped a little, but in a moment the silence had settled around them again and her agitation was stilled. Other people spoke after that: sometimes beginning

246

timidly, they each said poignant, graceful things about Marmion, and Cressida wished she had the courage and the eloquence to add her contribution – but what she most wanted to say didn't bear public examination. It seemed to Cressida that the purpose of this occasion for her – perhaps for all of them – was to recover, as best they could, the joyful Marmion, the serene Marmion, the person she would surely, eventually, have been again.

And then, before she would have thought it possible, the hour was over. Everyone was shifting and coughing and whispering, and the silk net was lifting, melting back into the air. Stephen stood up, and Cressida followed suit. Across the room she spotted Judith, incongruous in severe black, and at the same time Stephen said, 'There's Bill.'

So they were all here, after all. And there were others from the choir too, from the years above and below: there was Deep Patel and Lawrence Watts and a couple of other dons Cressida recognised. Within the crush of people drinking tea and eating cake in the adjacent hall afterwards, the St Anne's cohort clustered together, those who'd known Marmion less well diluting the fraught intensity of the inner circle. No sign of Fay, though. It wasn't usually hard to pick her out in a crowd. She must still be ill, Cressida thought – and then, with a jolt of guilt, it occurred to her that perhaps no one had told Fay that Marmion was dead.

'What a turnout!' said Lawrence, catching Cressida's eye. 'Terrible shame, though. Terrible waste.'

Cressida managed a thin smile. She would have liked to punch him, but he was doing his best; they were all doing their best.

'Have you had a good summer otherwise?' Lawrence blundered on. 'Been away at all?'

'Not really,' said Cressida.

'And you're back in Cambridge, I gather. If you ever want to sing with us . . .'

Cressida made an indeterminate gesture. Never, she thought. She didn't want anything to do with St Anne's, with the choir, ever again. 'Excuse me, I'm sorry, but I . . .'

Slipping past him, she put her cup down on the edge of a table. Enough, she thought. This meant nothing, this part of the proceedings: watering the hordes, her mother would call it. She felt a sudden need for her mother, for the abstracted certainty of her world view and the reassuring chill of the house. Perhaps she would go back to Burcombe tonight. Perhaps she could slip away now without saying any good-byes. Stephen was the only one she . . . But Stephen would understand. Or perhaps not. Perhaps he wouldn't even notice.

September 2015
Cressida

Everyone else was up by the time Cressida emerged from her room on Saturday morning. She'd slept soundly: a pleasant surprise, because she disliked strange beds, but she always brought her own pillow when she went away, and she'd packed earplugs too on this occasion. Not that there was much ambient noise up here, apart from the odd owl or fox, but she'd remembered how the sound of voices carried in this house, and she'd suspected – rightly – that others might be awake before her.

Pulling on her clothes (another dress bought for the occasion, a grey linen shift which felt both uncomfortable and inappropriate now), she could hear a buzz of conversation along the corridor and was irritated to find herself rushing. She was curious, of course, to see how things would evolve this morning, and to know whether the atmosphere would feel easier or more claustrophobic now the first encounter was behind them. But there was also an echo of a sense she'd often had twenty years ago, and had recalled clearly last night: the suspicion that she was missing out on something. You could say, she thought with a stab of self-destructive pleasure, that that was the story of her life.

Those few glorious weeks earlier in the summer when she'd believed that if she wished hard enough for something she could have it seemed like a fantasy now. That wasn't how it was for her. It never had been. All the things she'd achieved – a place at Cambridge, an academic career – had turned out to be the wrong things, hollow or flawed or simply narrowing her life into a channel that had become more and more limiting. Even the men: most of all the men, she corrected herself. Michael had spread like a fungus through two decades of her life, while the others hadn't even put down the slenderest of roots.

But then there was ... She stopped, catching sight of her face in the mirror and seeing fleetingly, disarmingly, a glimpse of the Cressida who'd been here before, all that time ago: a Cressida who'd been, she could see now, more sure of herself than she was now.

But then there was Stephen.

That was so long ago, she told herself, so very long ago, and she had failed to make anything of it then. There was no reason to think ... But he was divorced; he was more than eligible. There was a hard edge to his life, of course, a slightly chilly competence to replace the awkwardness of the undergraduate, and he moved in such different circles to her. But even so, she thought. Even so it had been clear to her almost at once, when he stepped out of the car on that empty stretch of road last night, that he was still the same man. She'd recognised that stimulating, unsettling hunger; the unexpected flare of his smile. As she shut her bedroom door behind her she allowed a flutter of fancy to tease her mind. Who knew, she thought. Who ever knew what might happen when you weren't expecting it?

The other four were sitting around the table, and a place had been set for Cressida at the far end. Cereal and toast were laid out – and behind them all, the valley was illuminated by autumn sunshine.

'Oh my goodness,' she said. 'I'd forgotten that view.'

'How did you sleep, Cressida?' Bill's voice was very earnest. 'We were all saying how terrible the beds are.'

'Very well, thank you.' Cressida slid onto the chair that Stephen pulled out for her and helped herself to a cup of tea from the pot. 'I must have been lucky with my bed.' The others seemed to have run out of things to say: four pairs of eyes watched as she buttered a piece of toast. She opened her mouth to make some remark about feeding time at the zoo, then thought better of it. It was very strange, all this. Very different from how they might have imagined a gathering of their forty-year-old selves. How wonderful it would be to open the door onto one of those carefree mornings in 1995 and see them all, just for a moment, as they'd been then. Just as she'd seen herself in the mirror a moment ago, her lines and shadows erased, and the future still full of promise.

It was somehow no surprise that it was Stephen who broke the silence in the end.

'The solicitor's not due until noon,' he said. 'Does anyone fancy a walk before that?'

'I do,' said Cressida.

'Me too.' Isabel looked towards the window. 'Which of these mountains did you climb when you were here before?' she asked. 'They look so enticing, don't they? I'd love to go up that one that looks like a horse.'

There was a different kind of silence then. No one looked at Isabel, nor at each other.

'I'm not sure there's time for that,' Stephen said eventually.

Cressida glanced at Isabel, wondering how much she'd registered. Bill looked ragged this morning. She felt a little sorry for Isabel, for them both, but impatient too: Bill had had plenty of time to explain things to her. But even so, someone had to rescue them.

'Why don't we walk down to the village?' she said. 'I'd like to see the church again, and it's a decent walk if we go the long way.'

The little procession started out half an hour later, covering its awkwardness with a flurry of small talk that dwindled gradually into an unsettled sort of silence. But something odd happened as they made their way along the side of the fell. Happened, at least, in Cressida's head, although the strange thing was that she had a powerful sense of thoughts, sensations, impressions infusing simultaneously into all their minds, almost as though some collective consciousness had taken them over. As though each of them had succumbed to that momentary longing she'd felt at the breakfast table, and been reeled back twenty years to the time when they'd shared so many of the same preoccupations that they could almost read each other's thoughts.

The landscape – the then-and-now landscape – seemed to play a part in this sleight of mind too. Every detail of rock and bracken and turf felt charged with significance, reminding them of what they'd forgotten; of all that they had failed, or refused, to see. A Wordsworthian feeling, Cressida thought. She grasped for the lines, lodged somewhere inside her. *For I have learned / To look on nature, not as in the hour / Of thoughtless youth, but hearing oftentimes / The still, sad music of humanity.* That was Tintern Abbey, not the Lake District, but it was apt; it was what she felt.

The others were strung in single file along the path, Judith just ahead of her, then Stephen, then Bill, and Isabel out in front, as though – no, this was fanciful – but yes, as though the magnetic pull that prevented the four of them drawing too far apart had no hold on Isabel.

And then Cressida felt among them, more powerfully than a single imagination could possibly conjure her, the presence of Marmion. She remembered suddenly the irresistible impression she'd had in the middle of Marmion's funeral that she was there, her voice clearly audible in that deep, still silence. Had that been delusion, or memory, or wishful thinking? Was that what this was too: a fervent wish for them all to think of Marmion, as they traversed the dale from High Scarp to the church once more, and so to invoke her in their midst?

She hadn't thought about Marmion for a long time; not properly. What had persisted, she admitted, were her own feelings. If Marmion had come into her mind, it had been to allow herself a moment of bittersweet nostalgia, a fleeting comparison between her own flawed, partial life and Marmion's unfulfilled promise. *And yet a Spirit still, and bright / With something of an angel light.*

Oh, but death, Cressida thought: one should not forget death. She had felt sharply at the time the irrevocable alteration that the awareness of mortality had brought. Almost a contagion: a stain on the living that could never be expunged. A boy at her primary school had died at eight or nine from a rare kind of cancer, and that had been shocking, but the death of a child had the chancy, fictional feel of something that couldn't possibly happen to you. But the death of a friend on the brink of adulthood was different; perhaps the most devastating kind of loss. Just as they were all poised to take wing, she thought – a terrible metaphor to apply to Marmion's death.

But it was clear to her now, as they approached the little bridge that crossed the beck, that she had allowed Marmion's death to blur into something else, over the years: to become a curious, sad chapter in the narrative of her own life. She had never quite believed that Marmion was gone for ever. She had lost the others too; they had been no less absent, these last two decades, and she could see now that she'd imagined Marmion removed, like them, to some distant place from which she might eventually be recovered. Reaching the steps that led up to the bridge, Cressida stopped, dizzied by insight. She must have swayed, because suddenly Stephen was beside her, grasping her arm.

'Whoa – are you all right?' he asked.

'Yes,' said Cressida. 'Yes, I'm fine. I'm – I was thinking about Marmion.'

'So was I.' His hand gripped her more tightly for a moment. 'It's hard to believe it's so long,' he said. 'Twenty years since she was here.'

Cressida nodded. She didn't trust herself to say anything more – not because she was afraid of being overcome by emotion, but because she was afraid of seeming sentimental in front of Stephen. She was afraid of her reflections being diminished by exposure to the light.

'Do you want to sit down for a moment?' he asked.

'No, no. We're nearly there.' The church tower was hidden just now behind a cluster of pine trees, but it wasn't far. In a moment they would be able to see it. 'I was quoting Wordsworth to myself,' she said, suddenly bolder. 'It's funny you should have been thinking about Marmion too: I had a kind of feeling we all were. *A motion and a spirit, that impels all thinking things . . .*'

'*. . . o'er them sweeps plastic and vast, one intellectual breeze,*' said Stephen.

'Absolutely,' said Cressida. 'Very impressive. That's Coleridge, of course, but . . .'

'My father loved Coleridge,' said Stephen. 'He'd studied him at school. He liked the idea that I was swept up in an intellectual breeze, I think. He used to quote that line at me when I came home for the holidays. Slightly missing the point – but who am I to interpret Coleridge to the doyenne of lit crit?'

Cressida was conscious that she was blushing. This was Stephen who never used to speak about his family; who had seemed, last night, reluctant to speak about anything at all. This surpassed her hopes. Guiltily, she felt Marmion slip a degree or two out of focus.

'Do you read much, these days?' she asked.

'Not much. Airport thrillers, I confess. A lot of board papers. But occasionally poetry. I –' Stephen lifted an arm to say *after you*, and Cressida stepped onto the footbridge. 'I look at reviews, from time to time, and I buy the odd volume on Amazon, but I'm afraid I don't often read them. They sit in a bookshelf giving a false impression of erudition.'

'One day, maybe,' said Cressida. She couldn't see his face now, nor he hers, and she was glad of it. She felt more moved by this confession than she could explain. Not just the purchase of the poetry books, but the failure to read them: it spoke to her somehow of an unfulfilled need.

'Maybe,' he agreed. 'I know it's ridiculous to imagine that they somehow percolate into my brain from the shelf. No, not just maybe: I hereby resolve to read a little poetry every night.'

Cressida didn't reply. She could tell from his tone of voice that he meant to be gallant, and it spoiled things a little. She'd preferred him being honest: she felt shut out again now. But there had been that moment; she wouldn't forget that. *One intellectual breeze*, just for a minute or two. That glimpse of . . . And then she blushed again. What on earth did she know of Stephen's needs? He lived a life that was entirely alien to her, and he had enough money, surely, to satisfy every conceivable whim – but that was a horrible thing to think. If she meant to punish herself, she should do it without besmirching him.

The church was just as she remembered. The colours of the stained glass weren't at their most brilliant this morning, but even so Jesus's halo shone over the crowd gathered to hear him preach beside the brook, over the sheep herded by a pair of crouching collies (had she forgotten that detail, or not seen it before?), over the smooth surface of the lake into which the faithful had waded in readiness for baptism.

'I remember the acoustic in here,' Bill said.

Shutting her eyes, Cressida could almost hear Marmion's voice, speaking rather than singing, intoning the words of the evening collect. Marmion had found the Anglican liturgy curious, but she'd loved that collect, Cressida remembered. *Lighten our darkness*: a proper Quaker sentiment. And most apt just now. She had a powerful sense, in the dimness, that they were waiting, all of them, for a shaft of light. Perhaps that was, like her Wordsworthian vision in the dale earlier, mere whimsy, but looking around at their faces – altered, guarded, expectant – she could see in each the need for illumination. For elucidation. All those light-filled words, exposing their separate shadows.

Meanwhile, no one had answered Bill. He had led them back to 1995, Cressida realised. They were all there, caught up in it again.

'Do you remember that extraordinary farmers' choir?' Judith said at last. 'Agricultural close harmony? God, how we laughed.'

Her words seemed both to tap into the poignancy of the moment and to downplay it; a skill she'd always had. But laughter, Cressida thought, was almost the most painful thing to remember. Marmion's infectious smothered mirth as the barbershop group had mangled its *hey nonny no*'s.

'And my boob in that Stanford motet,' said Stephen. 'That was quite a moment.'

'It's funny, isn't it,' said Cressida, her voice sounding as brittle as ash, 'that we're so adept at ignoring mortality. We act as though life is solid and permanent, but in fact . . . The rented world, that's what we live in. Marmion's no different from us, she just died sooner.'

For a moment she could hear her words hanging in the air, and then she felt Stephen's hand on her arm for the second time that morning. 'Steady on, Cressy,' Judith was saying, and Bill was observing that she looked pale, wondering whether she was all right, urging her to sit. Their voices sounded hazy. Cressida felt herself dissolving, and the faces around her swimming, blurring. And then she heard Stephen's voice, clear and present: 'Heavens, it's a quarter to twelve: shall I run back and get the car?'

October 1995
Stephen

All morning Stephen dithered. His suitcase was packed; his farewell meal was prepared. They had taken Robert for a walk in the park, called on the Andrews next door, traced the likely route of the aeroplane on his father's old globe that still showed the USSR and Rhodesia and even Ceylon, and whose faded colours and obsolete boundaries filled Stephen with a turbulent, impatient desire to spin the past out of sight and fly, fly away into the future. Fretfully he wandered the house, staring at the carefully ordered shelves of the bedroom that seemed to him already like a museum, and pondering the decision he'd been circling for days.

And then, at last, he made up his mind.

'I need to go to Cambridge this afternoon,' he said, as his mother began heating soup for lunch.

'Cambridge?' She looked dismayed. 'It's your last day, Stephen.'

'It won't be the whole day,' Stephen said. 'Just a few errands.'

His mother smiled sadly, stroking his hair the way she used to when he was small, and Stephen felt a tug of affection and an opposing tug of irritation.

'I'll be as quick as I can,' he said. 'I'll be back by teatime, I promise.'

Two hours later he was walking down Fay's road, turning in at her gate. It felt odd not to have a bike to lean against the fence. He rang the bell and waited. The roses were all finished, except for one late climber still flowering on the front of the house: Stephen could just smell its scent, hanging on the still autumn air. After a few minutes he rang again, and then he wondered if she might be in the garden. The gate at the side was rarely locked, he remembered.

'Fay?' he called, pushing it open. 'It's Stephen.'

There was no answer. Stephen scanned the shrubberies, then stood in the middle of the lawn, looking up at the blank windows of the house. She must be out, maybe even away. He couldn't believe now that he'd come all this way without checking she'd be here. Was he a complete idiot to have cooked up this outlandish story on the strength of one photograph? Fay might never have had a baby, and if she had, there was really nothing to suggest she'd given it up for adoption. Certainly nothing to suggest that it was his own story he'd stumbled upon. What had he been thinking – Stephen the rational, the careful, the clear-headed?

But still he hesitated, standing in the middle of this familiar, pretty garden. He couldn't be sure, that was the trouble. He couldn't be sure about any of it: even whether Fay hadn't wondered, these last three years, if Stephen was her son. He knew birth mothers couldn't search for their children, that they had to wait to be sought out. Fay had been so kind to them all, and who knew what she'd hoped for? He'd come because he owed it to her to find out, to set things straight.

Except that he couldn't, because Fay wasn't here, and he was flying to Dubai tomorrow.

He shut the gate behind him and walked slowly away. Frustration flared inside him again before being replaced by a different, a more complicated emotion. Perhaps Fay wasn't out, but hiding inside the house. Had she realised he'd seen the photograph, and guessed that he'd stumbled on the truth? Perhaps his deductions were accurate, but not his assumption that she wanted to know, and to claim him back. After all, she could have said something at any time over the last three years: she could have dropped a hint that would have alerted him. If any part of his theory was right, then Fay had deliberately said nothing. For her own protection, or perhaps for his – for some complicated reason he couldn't fathom – she had chosen to let things lie. And so must he, now.

Home, then, he thought, numb with confusion and – though he resisted it fiercely – distress. He could be back by five if he left now; his mother would be pleased. His mother, who had taken him in and loved him and made of him everything in her power. How could he forget what he owed her, with all this wild speculation about Fay? How could he be so stupid and selfish, so greedy for more than the generous lot he'd been given? He should get back as fast as he could now, and put all this behind him.

But as he walked back along Barton Road, he remembered Cressida. He hadn't seen her leaving Marmion's funeral, hadn't had a chance to say goodbye. Perhaps today's journey wouldn't be totally wasted if he could find her now. He'd been glad, afterwards, that he'd made the effort to see Marmion earlier in the summer: even if that colourless lunch hadn't been much of a comfort to her, it had been the right thing to do. It mattered how you said goodbye, he told himself, for lots of reasons. It mattered how you left things. He should tidy up his loose ends as well as he could. He should take his leave in such a way that he left as little as possible of himself behind.

October 1995
Cressida

The surprise of finding Stephen on her doorstep was almost unwelcome. Certainly the emotion that hit her when she opened the door was so intense that it felt more like anguish than pleasure.

'Hello,' he said. 'I had to come up to Cambridge today, and I thought – well, your description of your tiny flat was intriguing. I thought I'd come and see how you were settling in.'

'You're lucky I'm here,' said Cressida. She only meant to stall for time, but the words sounded dismayingly sharp. It was Sunday afternoon: he must be leaving tomorrow. Her mind reeled with the enormity of his coming to see her; with the need to avoid reading too much into it, or allowing it to flatter her out of her carefully constructed equanimity. 'Do you want to come up?' she asked. 'Or . . .'

She couldn't ask him how long he was staying. The impropriety of that question had been drummed into her as a child, and today the answer, whatever it was, would be too painful to bear.

'This is nice,' Stephen said, when they reached her rooms. 'So you're on the next rung of the ladder now. How does that feel?'

'Not as glamorous as what you're doing.'

Cressida tweaked distractedly at her skirt. It felt uncomfortable talking about the future, about life going on, when Marmion . . . It was only because he was going abroad that he'd come at all, she reminded herself. Only because it was a one-off; because he wouldn't have to see her again. For a moment she felt breathless with desolation.

'Have you seen Fay?' Stephen asked, as they walked along the Backs half an hour later.

'She's had flu,' Cressida said. 'I called in last week.'

'I suppose that's why she didn't come to the funeral.'

'Probably.'

'I went to the house earlier,' Stephen said, 'but she wasn't there.'

'Maybe she's gone away to convalesce.' Cressida looked away, resisting a pang of jealousy. He'd been to see Fay first; perhaps he'd only come to find her because Fay hadn't been in.

'Maybe.'

The remains of a bird lay just off the path, a scattering of feathers among the first drift of sycamore leaves. Death was everywhere, Cressida thought. Things falling out of the sky. She wished Stephen hadn't come: it wasn't fair, stirring things up like this.

'How do your parents feel about you going so far away?' she asked.

'Nervous.' He looked sideways at her. 'But they wouldn't stand in my way.'

'Of course not. No parent would.' Hers might, though, she thought. They assumed she was staying in Cambridge to prolong her hunt for a husband, and they wouldn't have thought Dubai at all suitable for that pursuit.

They didn't speak for a while then. It saddened Cressida that there was so little to say, and it made her defiant, too. She had suffered, she would continue to suffer, as much as anyone, she thought.

'I know you thought I was wrong to criticise Bill and Judith,' she said, in a little rush. 'I know you all thought that. And I know you think I'm congratulating myself on being proved right, but I'm not.'

'Congratulating yourself?' Stephen turned, horrified. 'How could I possibly . . . Do you really imagine that's what I think?'

'I only meant . . .' Cressida's voice was sulky, now, with embarrassment. 'I misspoke. I only meant that you might think I was – that I might be . . .' She blushed in confusion.

'Cressida.' Stephen stopped; for a moment she thought he was going to take her in his arms. 'I'm sure no one thinks that,' he said. Cressida could feel tears collecting in her eyes now. She would have liked his voice to be gentler, at least. 'Something like this – you can't think about what came before. It's been a huge shock for all of us, but we have to . . .'

For several moments Cressida waited, but the sentence wasn't finished. *We have to stick together*, she imagined him saying. *We have to go on somehow.* Or might he have come up with something more profound? She would have loved to know what he really thought, but that wasn't Stephen's way, especially not now. He was too wary of her, and of the situation.

In the gentle autumn light she saw with sudden clarity how ridiculous she'd made herself. At every step she'd got things wrong. She had no hope with Stephen, and she had no one to blame but herself.

'What time's your train?' she asked: decorum seemed redundant now, and so was self-preservation.

Stephen looked at his watch, making a brief show of indecision. 'I really ought to get the 4.17,' he said. 'My mother – it's my last night at home. She's cooked a chicken.'

'Of course.' Cressida forced a smile. 'I'll walk part of the way with you. I wouldn't mind a bit more air.'

After that neither of them spoke very much, and things felt easier. The sun shone weakly, as though applauding their effort at civility, and once or twice a gaggle of students passed, chattering excitedly, barely noticing Cressida and Stephen stepping off the path to avoid them.

'It's Freshers' Week,' Cressida said. It was impossible to believe that so little time had passed since she and Stephen and Judith and Bill and Marmion had been among a crowd like that. Impossible to believe that they were invisible now, lost in the undertow as a new wave broke over them.

September 2015
Judith

Judith had found herself being driven back to High Scarp with Stephen and Cressida, after Cressida's strange turn in the church. That was certainly better than walking up the hill with Bill and Isabel, but even so, she felt uncomfortably as though she was caught between two couples. Not that poor Cressy was ever going to secure more of Stephen's attention than she had right now. She could see Stephen felt he was doing the right thing, appointing himself as Cressida's protector, but she could also see that it was useful to him to have a role to play, a disguise to prevent them seeing too much of the real Stephen, whoever he was. And she could see, too, that Cressida, for all her critical-analytical skills, hadn't got any better at reading men: that even at forty-one she couldn't distinguish romantic gestures from good manners.

Perhaps, she thought, as Stephen's expensive car climbed the rutted track to High Scarp, the same was true of her, but in reverse. She'd tried to pretend this morning – especially after the outing with Isabel – that the fireside interlude had been a dream, or at least a transport of folly. But it hung there still like a dust storm she might step into at any moment; a tiny tornado that could lift her up and out of the realm of sense.

She'd been conscious of Bill watching her all the time they were walking, and as the rawness of his feelings came back into focus, the insight she'd had into his marriage earlier on – that complicated sense of constraint and exclusion and incomprehension it evoked – had shifted. Surely, surely it hadn't been a grand passion but a desperate leap into the unknown? And although something of that hour with Isabel still lingered, Judith was aware that her scruples, stout as they'd proved last night, were not inviolable.

She understood, too, that this was a different, a more serious business than her carefully managed alliances with Jonty or Arvind. It would never be possible to have half-measures with Bill: if she once succumbed, she couldn't control what would happen, couldn't keep herself in reserve, and that frightened her, just as it had twenty years ago. And she knew, just as she had twenty years ago, that it was the same for him – that she would be offering him something marvellous and dangerous, and that he would accept it without hesitation. The thought of kindling the spark of hope she had seen in his eyes last night both thrilled and terrified her.

She stared out of the car window at the green sweep of the valley, dotted with trees edging towards their autumnal bronze. She could see now, down the long corridor of hindsight, that her rejection of Bill on that stiflingly hot afternoon in Bristol twenty years ago had been the result not just of weariness and guilt but of resentment. Resentment, she understood suddenly, of his coming later than she'd hoped, at a moment of his choosing, as though his passion could be calibrated by the days allowed to pass before he came to claim her. They'd had a shot at something marvellous and dangerous back then: at a flawless, limitless kind of love that was almost impossible to imagine after the fervour and idealism of youth have passed. She hadn't been able to bear the corruption of it, Judith thought now. Guilt they might have borne – guilt could sharpen and season passion – but not the dulling effect of compromise. Even now she could understand that.

After two decades in which she'd barely allowed herself a taste of love, the remembrance of what they had almost had, she and Bill, was still hoarded away, treasured, like a glimpse of immortality. For years she had barely admitted its existence, but she allowed herself, now, to think about what had happened that summer; to consider how one step had followed another, and where it had led them.

Perhaps that first rejection had been headstrong and perverse: but had it, she wondered, made any difference in the long run? Had there been any way for them to escape the trap Fate had set for them? After Marmion died it had been impossible to turn things round, to say yes to Bill instead of no, but suppose they had spent the summer together, feasting on forbidden fruits: wouldn't the moral heft weighing against them have been even greater, when that aeroplane was shot out of the sky? Perhaps if Marmion hadn't died – but that line of thought led nowhere but to misery and self-destruction.

No: the devastating thing was the way the succession of circumstances had made things seem related when they weren't. The way an event of no real significance which had passed for a calamity within their small protected circle had been magnified by Marmion's death – by the manner of Marmion's death – into something of real tragic proportions. That was what had made their position irretrievable.

But there was, now, another conundrum. Were the questions, the obstacles, the same now, or entirely different? Bill was married, of course, and besides that . . . Oh, it would be simpler, Judith thought, so much simpler, if it were a question of weighing up rationally what might be gained and what might be lost, but it was never like that; never a logical decision. One never really believed, in the moment of leaping off the cliff, that the bungee rope would hold: it was always an act of utter recklessness, and this time the recklessness was almost impossible to construe.

She sighed. Perhaps the best safeguard was that Bill had played his cards so early. Bill never did have much subtlety, she told herself, gathering her self-possession around her again, and the bluntness of other people's emotions had always bored her. She turned that phrase over in her head: it had a hollow core, she knew, but the words had a comforting ring even so. They had the familiar tonality of the stream of consciousness that had kept her safe these last twenty years.

'Here we are,' said Stephen, as the car came to a halt. 'Goodness, and not a moment too soon, by the look of it.'

Looking out of the car window, Judith could see a man coming up the lower path towards the front door – a man immensely tall and strikingly good-looking. Could that really be Fay's lawyer?

'Hello,' she said, as she stepped out onto the gravel. 'You must be Giles Unwin.'

There were two memories from her childhood that returned at moments Judith least expected. One had taken place, she assumed, in the garden of her parents' house in that leafy Bristol suburb, when she was perhaps two or three: a hot day with the sprinkler playing, and a small girl with a black plastic bucket on her head teetering about in a dizzy sort of dance, laughing and laughing. The girl must be her, but the strange thing was that she could see her antics, in her mind's eye, as though she'd been watching. But she could also feel the pain of laughing so much that her chest hurt, and the pain of knowing that she had to keep laughing, keep swaying, keep her head hidden in the bucket, even though she was frightened about how it might end. It could almost have been a dream, except that she had a photograph that confirmed the truth of it: a faded colour photograph of herself as a small girl wearing a dress with a garish 1970s floral print, playing in a sprinkler with a bucket of water lying nearby. Had she poured the water over herself, or over someone else, before she'd put the bucket on her head? And how *had* it ended? Had someone rescued her, or had she toppled over and dislodged the bucket herself? How had she ended up, in some corner of her mind, playing out that afternoon on a never-ending loop?

The other memory was less remote, although the self that occupied it was almost as indistinct. Her parents had taken her to Cambridge, when she was fourteen, to show her around. They'd insisted that it was simply a nostalgic trip for them, since they'd first met at Addenbrooke's Hospital, on the outskirts of the city, but Judith had known that they meant her to fall in love with the place, and she'd resisted with every ounce of her considerable will. This was a stage when she couldn't be bothered with school; couldn't be bothered with anything much; and her parents – each of them diligent, self-motivated, ambitious, despite their proudly professed nonconformism – had been worried about her. They'd thought that if she found something to set her heart on, she might see the point of school work. They must have dragged her round some of the colleges, but Judith had no recollection of that, beyond the vaguest impression of pinkish stone turrets and a garden glimpsed through an archway.

No, what stood out, what recurred, was one moment. They must have given up on the sightseeing and set out to walk to Grantchester for lunch, and the meadow had been so thick with buttercups that if you half shut your eyes they blurred and fused until it looked as though someone had broken a giant egg yolk over the ground, and the sky was the darkest, heaviest slate grey, lit from beneath by shafts of sunshine that made magic with that great rich spread of colour. And then the rain had come down suddenly, furiously, noisily, but only for a few minutes, only for the count of fifty; and when it stopped, the light had changed and the spell had been broken.

Her parents had never mentioned any of it afterwards: not the buttercups, nor the light, nor the sudden rain. Had they meant it to be something she could have for herself, or had they simply not noticed the wonder of it? Judith had never known. She had never seen Grantchester Meadow like that again either, never even particularly noticed buttercups growing on it, but the memory had never faded. It had become a lodestone, a mirage, to flicker in her mind through the years of adolescence that followed. Perhaps it still was: a piece of magic never recovered, just like the bucket day. An instant in the past where a part of her had been stranded all this time, waiting for life to begin again.

It seemed to Judith just now – now that she could look back not just on childhood and adolescence but on a suddenly surprising stretch of life – that there might have been other pieces of magic offered to her, at different times, that she had failed to recognise: visions of the world that might have transformed her if she had allowed them to. Why should that thought occur just now, greeting Fay McArthur's solicitor on the doorstep of High Scarp, waiting to be told how and why this house had been left to her and her former friends? Was it because he looked, this man, more like a magician than a solicitor, his bulky briefcase surely capacious enough to hold white rabbits and quantities of red silk rather than simply wills and codicils? Because he had come to open a door onto the past as well as the future, to invite them to reconsider what they had held to be true – and perhaps to offer them the chance to start again from the beginning?

The visitor didn't reply at once to Judith's greeting, except to extend his hand for a formal handshake, and Judith studied his face for a moment, searching it for clues. The others were watching him too – Bill and Isabel had just come up the path, and Cressida, poor sappy Cressida, was standing very close to Stephen without quite daring to touch him again. All of them gathered, hopeful and wary, ready to face what was coming.

The law allowed Fay plenty of scope, Judith thought, to test them, enlighten them, perplex or offend or distress them. What might she have required of them all? What did her knowledge of Fay suggest? She remembered Fay's generosity, but also her insistence on tradition; her strange combination of imperiousness and spontaneity.

What she hadn't taken into account was Fay's love of games, but the tall stranger's opening words brought that characteristic sharply back into focus, proving her first instinct about him more accurate than she would have credited.

'I'm afraid I am merely a messenger from Mr Unwin,' he said. 'Mr Unwin will be here at noon tomorrow. I am bidden to request your patience for a further twenty-four hours.'

Cressida

2014

Cressida looks at her watch, then out of the window of the University Library, and swears under her breath. She has never lost the habit of swearing, nor the habit of concealing it. Most of the time, at least. Lately she has heard herself swear aloud once or twice, and has noted it as an indication of something, a sign she ought not to ignore.

Outside the window, rain falls steadily on the patch of grass between the library and King's College Choir School: falls vertically, so that it barely spatters the panes and can be perceived only with an adjustment of the eye similar to that needed to recognise the seethe of ants beneath a tracery of grass.

'Damn,' Cressida thinks, or says. Damn the rain, and the bike waiting for her outside. Damn Cambridge, where it's always raining unless it's too cold for rain, and where cycling is the expected mode of transport even for a middle-aged woman of some standing in the university. Many of her colleagues have viewed the recent revival of enthusiasm for the bike's health-giving, eco-sustaining virtues with the smug complacency of lifelong devotees, but not Cressida. The bike reminds her of – connects her to – her years as an undergraduate, and then as a graduate student, a junior research fellow, a newly minted university lecturer. It makes the decades in Cambridge run together into a single continuous line, and it makes her wonder what it has all meant.

She wonders now, looking out at the rain, in which of those phases she felt most easy about the place, and herself. When she was young she'd understood, as most others didn't, that undergraduates weren't

271

important; a necessary evil passing through in three-year waves, barely ruffling the surface of the institution. But now she looks at them, riding around the cycle-friendly city with all the grace and confidence of youth, and wishes she could be back among them. At least then, she thinks, with another smothered curse, she might still have chosen a different path, one that led her away from the rain-drenched fens and the gathering knowledge that she will never really count for anything here; that hardly anyone ever makes a mark on the university.

She gathers her papers with a swift sifting movement and closes the books that lie open in front of her. Enough for today. The rain won't let up, not until much later, and she's in no mood to spend the evening in the library. Besides, Wednesday is a Michael evening, and although he has never been tied to anything as tedious as a regular routine, she's sure he said something about this evening, this Wednesday. Although perhaps he said he was doing something else tonight, she thinks, as she unlocks the bike, already cold-fingered. It's September: it should be warmer. She should be further on with the work she hoped to get done over the summer. Next month the university will fill up again, and another year will begin.

Michael does come that evening, almost on the strike of the clock in the hall (her grandmother's gilt-bronze wall clock, ugly but valuable), as though he has an appointment. Cressida hasn't allowed herself to cook – hubris is a stern mistress – but she has a pizza in the fridge which could feed two, and a packet of salad she can tip into a bowl. All these things run through her head as she goes to the door: the ability to provide for him without looking as though she was counting on his presence. She feels a prick of pride at her competence at this game, and then a wave of loathing for herself and for the maze of double-bluffs and second-guesses and stifled motives. It was all very well at the beginning, she thinks, but . . . How many years has it been?

Time has deceived her, stretching itself out when she wasn't looking, foreshortening itself when she cared to glance at it. Seventeen years this autumn.

As she approaches the door she feels a disorientating lurch, as if Michael's outline, seen through the glass panel, has melted and re-formed in front of her eyes, hustled through two decades of time-lapse photography. It occurs to her, more strongly than it has done for years, that she disapproves of infidelity, and that she deplores her part in it. When she opens the door there's a flutter of reassurance, of things settling back into place, but it's short-lived. There's something in Michael's face she has never seen before; she's sure there is.

Michael is fifty-nine, and he bears the imprimatur of the academic who is oblivious to his appearance. It's a badge of honour with him, this dishevelment: the slight staleness of his clothes, the impatiently pushed-back hair which has receded obligingly beyond his reach. Cressida has tried, sometimes, to find a term for it: asceticism is one she likes, or unworldliness. She has always known that it isn't altogether unconscious, nor wholly a matter of indifference to him: now, in a moment of giddy clarity, she sees that he is as vain in his way as the next man, and that this veil of learning, of thinking, of greatness, is what he has cast out to snare her and draw her in. It's no different to a peacock's tail or a bullfrog's chant. It represents what she might want in the father of her children, the spectacular brain and single-minded purpose of a charismatic scholar.

He looks back at her from the cramped porch with a glimmer of impatience. Rain drips down his nose.

'Are we to conduct a conversation on the doorstep?' he asks.

Cressida steps back from the door without saying anything. Her mind is hurrying onwards, dragging her along in its wake. That expression she glimpsed, a moment ago. She's sure she knows what it means: that he's steeled himself to dispose of her. He's giving up his college teaching this Michaelmas; he could spend more time with her in future, but he doesn't want to. She's been a convenience, but he can sense the possibility of her becoming a nuisance. So.

There's no room for emotion: other things matter more just now. Some instinct tells her that preserving her self-respect, her pride, will send her forward from this encounter on a little wave of borrowed energy, whereas if she leaves matters to him she'll fetch up stranded on the beach while the tide creeps away.

'I haven't got any food, I'm afraid,' she says, 'but I can give you a glass of wine.'

'I'm not hungry,' he says. 'A glass of wine would do nicely.'

Is his tone any different from usual? His speech, his wit, his affection have always been dry, but now that doubt has been seeded it's hard to dispel. Especially since the doubt is about her own feelings as well as his.

Michael has always preferred white Burgundy, and there's a bottle of Puligny-Montrachet in the fridge, a gift from one of her brothers. Cressida has no idea why it's all right to field such an expensive bottle of wine but not a Waitrose pizza, but that unexpectedly capable instinct is in control still. She seizes wine glasses in one hand and the bottle in the other, stops to dig a corkscrew out of a drawer.

Michael is standing beside the piano.

'Do sit,' Cressida says, as though he's a formal visitor, not familiar with the house. She sets the wine and the glasses down on the little lacquered table they bought together at a shop in Ludlow at the end of a walking weekend a few years ago. She can smell the wine as she pours: peach and lemon, she thinks, Michael's training deeply ingrained by now. A dash of honeysuckle.

She holds a glass out, but keeps hold of it when he leans forward to take it from her.

'Michael,' she says, 'there's no easy way to say this. This is a fare-well toast.'

His reaction isn't what she expected. He sags a little, as though something that has been giving him extra padding or stiffening has been removed. The expression on his face doesn't reveal sorrow or even surprise: irritation is closer to the mark. It's almost as though he regrets the waste of a journey on a wet evening. It occurs to her that she read the signs wrongly when he arrived, that he had no intention of breaking off with her – and then she is filled with an extraordinary cacophony of feelings. Impossible, she thinks, grasping her wine glass tightly, to identify any of them accurately, but she is quite certain that nowhere among them is a morsel of doubt that she has done the right thing.

In the months that follow, that cacophony of emotions has ample opportunity to reveal itself, ingredient by ingredient. The grind of the academic year is marked out, this year, by the changing colour of Cressida's anguish: a brief flare of triumph to see out September, succeeded by fury in October, self-loathing in November, disbelief in December. The new year brings sorrow in January, and then indigna-tion in February, regret in March, anger again in April – a procession that bears no relation to any sequence of mourning she has read about, and which shows no sign, as spring approaches, of moving towards a resolution.

In fact, as time goes on, another thread is discernible, running in the wake of her feelings about Michael: she begins to suspect that very little of the blame can be placed at his door, and she begins to fear that the same failings which allowed her to devote so much of her life to him are going to keep her in thrall to this self-pitying, self-perpetuating cycle of regret and despair for ever. She never deserved better than to be Michael's half-considered mistress, she thinks, and to be left by the wayside once the modest glow of youth had passed. For the first time in years, she remembers how much she blamed herself for scuppering another chance of happiness, once before. She knows that isn't an entirely just interpretation of events, but she can't muster the energy to defend herself. She can only feel regret, and contempt for her own shortcomings. What hope is there for her if she can't drag herself out of this morass, just as she failed to salvage things twenty years ago?

And then June arrives, and with it a burst of sunshine. The change is quite sudden: the flick of a switch, banishing the chill of May and the gloom in Cressida's soul. She wakes one Saturday morning to the warmth of sunlight through her curtains and an unfamiliar feeling which she diagnoses, with surprise, as happiness.

She's not sure, at first, to what she owes this unexpected blessing. She's been spared Finals marking this year, which means the next fortnight will be unusually free. The *TLS* has invited her to review a novel which has been tipped for the Booker Prize. The irises she planted last year along her front path have started to flower. No, it's none of these, although each adds a further glow of warmth. She must have had a good dream, she thinks, and she feels a flicker of disappointment: she never remembers her dreams, especially not the good ones.

But then it comes to her. Not a dream, but her last waking thought last night, almost lost in the fringes of sleep. She wants a baby.

Cressida is forty-one. She's aware that conceiving a baby at forty-one is not as simple as it would have been at twenty-one, or even thirty-one, especially without an obvious candidate for fatherhood at hand. But the practicalities seem less important just now than the sudden, glorious discovery of maternal yearning. She feels it opening within her, a door into a realm of unexplored delights. The rest of the world seems to shrink into a meaner perspective: the same feeling she had when she was first absorbed in the pages of a book at five or six, and family life receded to an agreeably safe distance, her brothers no more than tiny caricatures in a world whose existence she could deny, after that, whenever she chose.

And what can she deny now? Oh, almost anything, she thinks, airily. Her work, or at least the tiresome aspects of it; the fretting over reputation and status. Who gives a fig what people will remember of you if you have a child to leave to the world? Who cares whether your paper is accepted, your abstract approved, if you can come home to the milky scent of a baby? Certainly men, with their uncongenial habits and displeasing smells, have had their day. Men with their arrogance and their closed minds and their certainty that age doesn't wither them: what could she possibly want from a man now, except the wherewithal to make her pregnant?

Happiness always makes her orderly: it's an instinct honed in childhood, to keep her pleasures under close control. Today, she thinks, she will have breakfast at the little table in the front garden so that she can admire her irises, and when she has read a hundred pages of the *TLS* novel she will reward herself with an hour on the Internet. There is a vitamin you're supposed to take when you're planning a pregnancy, she thinks, and certain foods to avoid. All of that must be explored. This afternoon she will read in the back garden, which faces west. It doesn't cross her mind that the sun might disappear before that.

The sun obliges, but Cressida makes slow progress with her reading. Since her scholarly edition of First World War poetry came out last year – a brief sidetrack from her pursuit of Romanticism – literary editors have taken to sending her war narratives to review. Most of them she likes well enough, but this one, an account of an African genocide written by a man who was a school teacher in a remote village until it was razed to the ground, contains the most graphic descriptions of

277

rape she has ever read, and in Cressida's view they do little to enhance
the book's literary merit. She isn't usually squeamish about violence
on the printed page, but today . . . It's almost as though she's pregnant
already, she thinks, putting the novel aside and shutting her eyes for a
moment. And why should she not bring her feminine sensibilities to
bear on this great slab of male aggression? She peeks inside the book
again: page 92. Enough for now.

Cressida's joy doesn't falter over the next few days. If sheer conviction
could make life spring into existence within her then she would have
no difficulty in conceiving, but as the days pass her mind turns, a little reluctantly, to the technicalities. She's found websites that will lead
her to donated sperm, and although the notion of syringes and clinics
horrifies her a little, she knows she'll have to get used to messiness and
indignity if she's to manage pregnancy and childbirth. It's too bad, she
thinks, that it didn't occur to her to let Michael impregnate her, the
biggest-brained bullfrog in the fens. But she doesn't want Michael's
baby. It might be a girl, and inherit his peculiar ears. Worse, it might
be a boy and inherit his peculiar ears.

Meanwhile, there are other things to distract her. It's years since
she's sampled the festivities of May Week (Michael, of course, dis-
paraged such frivolity), but she accepts an invitation to a garden
party given by the college's English students, and is more warmly
welcomed than she anticipated. One thing leads to another: 'Are you
coming to watch the Bumps, Dr Benham?' asks a first-year who has,
if his essays are anything to go by, spent considerably more time
rowing than reading this year. And yes, the sun shines again, and
it's fun to cycle to the river and to be borne along the towpath by a
crowd of bellowing, banner-waving students following the college's
First VIII. At the barbecue afterwards, a colleague she has never
exchanged more than two words with talks to her about the genocide novel – which Cressida brought with her in case of boredom,

and which he has read with, as he puts it, a human rights hat on – and as they are leaving he invites her to the Law Faculty cocktail party the next night. And so on Friday evening she finds herself searching in her wardrobe for a silk dress she bought for a cousin's wedding a couple of years before. It's prettier than she remembers, with a bold print of tiger lilies. She has no idea if it's in vogue or not, but the Cambridge Law Faculty is hardly Paris Fashion Week, and she's impressed by the sight of herself in the mirror. See, she tells herself: life has changed.

But when she arrives, her nerve fails. Among the crush of people she can see from the door there is no one she knows. Clustered in little knots, they throw back their heads and laugh, the women elegant in simpler dresses than hers. The colleague who invited her is nowhere to be seen.

It seems to her suddenly that the last week has been an absurd fantasy. This is who she is: a woman in her forties who can't manage a simple social encounter. A woman who would rather run away than accept a free glass of wine. How foolish it was to imagine that her life could still be transformed. But she makes a bargain with herself, the kind of face-saving bargain she's made more often than she'd care to admit: she'll go into the party, drink a glass of Prosecco, then pull out her mobile phone and fake an urgent call. In half an hour she'll be safely home again, and she might even finish the hateful novel tonight. With her colleague's political spin to draw on, she could manage a rather stylish review in the end.

Thus steeled, she smiles at a waiter, takes a glass, catches a glimpse of her reflection in a window and is gratified by what she sees. Her plan is almost accomplished, her exit in sight, when she spots Michael on the far side of the room. Michael, at a party? But it's definitely him – and worse, he's spotted her. Bugger and fuck: too late now to escape. Instead, she turns towards the group of people on her right and smiles broadly, as if she's been talking to them all along.

The people smile back, and Cressida feels a wave of gratitude. There are three of them: a dark-haired man, a fair-haired man, and a much younger woman, perhaps an undergraduate.

'Hello,' she says, 'I'm Cressida Benham. I'm an interloper from the English Faculty.'

'Mark Mason,' says the dark-haired man. 'This is Tilly Beeton, and Heming Erikson, who's visiting us from Trondheim.'

'Hello,' says Cressida again. Is this what people do when you barge up to them at parties, she wonders, or are the polite introductions intended sardonically? Oh well: in for a penny – she'd rather make a fool of herself with a group of strangers than let Michael see her standing by the door on her own, anyway. 'How long are you in Cambridge for?' she asks the Norwegian.

As he turns towards her, Cressida notices something about Heming Erikson. He is quite extraordinarily attractive: a Nordic god with white-blond hair and blue eyes and high cheekbones. And then she notices something else: Mark Mason has taken Tilly Beeton by the arm and is leading her off towards the bar. Cressida feels another reversal come upon her; another giddy turn in the story of the evening.

'I have been here for six months,' Heming says, in almost unaccented English. 'Sadly, I have to return to Trondheim this weekend. I have to teach on a summer school starting on Monday.'

'Just when the sun's arrived,' says Cressida. 'That's too bad.'

'It's sunny now in Trondheim,' says Heming. 'In fact, we have possibly more sunshine than you, although it's never very warm. Of course our summer days are very long. We have around twenty hours of daylight in June.'

'Gosh,' says Cressida.

A waiter passes with a bottle: Cressida accepts a refill, and motions the man towards Heming's glass. Good: they don't have to fight their way to the drinks table.

'What is your specialism?' Heming asks.

'Nineteenth-century poetry,' Cressida says. 'But my interests are fairly broad.'

She takes a large swig of wine, and Heming regards her solemnly.

'I expect you know Ibsen pretty well,' he says. 'We also had two Nobel Prize-winning authors in the twentieth century, Knut Hamsun and Sigrid Undset.'

'I'm afraid I haven't read either,' says Cressida. Her head is beginning to spin a little, either from the wine or from the peculiarity of the situation. She tries to think of other Norwegian writers she could cite, but she's stumped: Scandinavian names swim in her head, the Swedish and the Danish indistinguishable, just now, from the Norwegian or the Finnish. Jonas Lie, she thinks – she's sure he was Norwegian. But by now it would be obvious, if she mentioned his name, that it was the only one she knew. Instead she smiles.

'And what area of law are you interested in?' she asks.

It's hard to say when a definite intention to seduce him takes shape in her mind, but when it does, she's dizzied by the simple brilliance of the plan. Much better, so much better, to adopt the old-fashioned solution rather than the tawdry business of scanning catalogues of sperm donors. And seduction proves very much easier than she might have feared, even if all those glasses of Prosecco hadn't immunised her against fear. It feels a little like shoplifting, but the merchandise she's helped herself to has none of the sour taste of a stolen sherbet fountain. Oh, those years of missed opportunities, stuck with the faithless warthog . . . But perhaps the disappointing years played a part, as they do for fairy-tale princesses. She's gone from bullfrog to prince: she should have had more faith in the power of narrative. He whispers to her that she's the first Englishwoman he's slept with, and it seems churlish not to believe him.

For months afterwards, Cressida wakes from something that is not a dream, but a sleeping remembrance. She wakes flushed once again with sex and chutzpah, certain that the Norse god's sperm cannot have failed her. Sometimes it's a full minute before she remembers that it took only a week for that possibility to be washed away by the unstoppable logic of her menstrual cycle.

Part VI

September 2015

Cressida

When the man who was not Giles Unwin had gone, there was a palpable sense of deflation in the little group standing around on the drive outside High Scarp. Frustration, bewilderment and anger showed in their faces – but also wariness. They'd psyched themselves up for this moment, Cressida thought, and this latest development had undermined their defences. Was that what Fay had intended? Was it possible that this had all been planned?

Clearly Bill was wondering the same thing.

'So what's this about?' he asked. 'Is the delay accident or instruction?'

'It sounds like instruction,' said Judith, 'or there would have been an explanation. That fucking . . .' She gestured impotently after the car that was disappearing down the hill.

'Well,' said Stephen, 'there's no obligation to stay any longer, of course.'

'There is if we want the house,' Cressida said. There was that shrill tone again: the others turned towards her and she blushed crossly. But wasn't that why they were all here?

Judith looked at her, then back to Bill. 'Do we all have to stay for the conditions of the bequest to be fulfilled?'

'Certainly everyone had to come up to High Scarp,' said Bill, 'but –'

'Bloody hell,' said Judith. 'We should have questioned him. That clown.' She sighed in exasperation, before continuing in the brash, give-a-damn tone she used to flaunt sometimes in the old days. 'Does anyone actually want the house? I'd be perfectly happy never to see this place again.'

'Why don't we go and have lunch at the pub?' Stephen suggested. 'We can talk things over there.'

'It's very early for lunch,' said Bill.

His wife looked at him. 'I'm hungry,' she said. Her voice was quiet but – another curiosity, Cressida thought: Isabel was more of a force to be reckoned with than you might imagine. She hoped that was true. 'By the time we get down there and order ...' Isabel went on. 'And there's no more food here, anyway.'

'Well, that's clearly what we were meant to do, then,' said Judith. 'Good old Fay, still pulling the strings.'

'Steady on,' said Stephen. 'We're free agents. What would you like to do, Judith? A longer walk, maybe? Take a picnic and blow away the cobwebs?'

'Oh, I don't know.' Judith kicked savagely at the gravel. 'The heavens are about to open, by the look of it. I suppose we can't blame that on Fay.'

The rain started before they reached the Queen's Head: proper, no-nonsense Lake District rain, not the insidious drizzle that was Cambridge's stock-in-trade. The five of them hurried down the lane with coats pulled up over their heads. Inside, the pub was warm and rather dark. Dripping onto the bare boards and surveying the fire that blazed in the wide hearth, everyone looked a little more cheerful. Escaping the rain was a sure-fire consolation, Cressida thought. Perhaps it would even furnish them with conversation for a while.

But of course it was Fay they all wanted to talk about.

'Did anyone see a death notice?' Bill asked, when they'd retreated to a nook by the fire. 'I couldn't find one online.'

'No one to place it, perhaps,' said Stephen. 'Leaving High Scarp to us rather suggests she had no living relatives.'

'What about her other house?' Cressida asked. 'She must have been living somewhere after she left Cambridge.'

'It's possible the proceeds from that house are to be used to maintain High Scarp,' Bill said.

'In our dreams,' said Judith. She'd ordered a whisky and ginger, and it was finished already. Cressida could see her eyeing the others' glasses, wondering when it would be acceptable to buy another. 'But you're right, we've been told nothing about the rest of the estate. That's something we need to know.'

'Why?' asked Cressida. 'If we've got High Scarp, surely –'

'What Judith means,' said Bill, 'at least, I assume what she means is that if there are other legatees, that limits our flexibility. If we're the only people to benefit from the will, we can agree to set it aside, which means we can set aside any conditions it imposes.'

'I wouldn't get your hopes up,' Judith said. 'I doubt Fay would have failed to close that loophole. The vicar will have a bequest, or something.'

'The scouts,' said Bill, with a sudden grin. 'Stroppiest legatees of all time. The vicar would be a lamb by comparison. The Church is always far too accommodating for its own good.'

'God forbid,' said Judith. 'But scout camps in the garden doesn't sound much like Fay.'

This was an improvement, Cressida thought. More like the old days. Except . . . The strange thing was that she could remember so little of their conversation back then. A few in-jokes – Bill's red hair, Judith's godlessness, Cressida's smart school – and a lot of talk about music and the choir and poor clumsy Lawrence Watts, but all the detail had vanished. These days there'd be a whole trail of exchanges on Facebook and Instagram; reams of emails and text messages to document their friendship. It was as though they'd grown up in the Dark Ages – only a scattering of photographs, a couple of postcards left in the pages of a book, to show for those three years.

'We won't have to speculate for long,' said Stephen. 'All will be revealed tomorrow. But if anyone does want to throw in the towel now . . .?' He stopped, looking round the table. Directing them, Cressida thought, and the notion was, to her shame, rather pleasing. 'Otherwise, I suggest we find something to fill this wet afternoon.'

'What about Troutbeck church?' Cressida said, perhaps a little too eagerly. 'I've always wanted to see the Pre-Raphaelite windows.'

'Or Townend Farmhouse?' suggested Isabel. 'That's near Troutbeck. It's National Trust.'

Bill was scowling: not at his wife's suggestion, Cressida thought, but at the way Stephen had taken the lead. But if Stephen noticed, he ignored him.

'We could do both,' he said. 'A cultural tour: how delightful. Cressida and Isabel can be our guides.'

The rain was easing by the time they reached Troutbeck. The church, set a little above the road, was surprisingly plain inside, the stained glass window at the east end dominating the whitewashed interior.

'Are you going to tell us about it, Cressida?' asked Stephen, as they stood looking up at it. 'It's rather wonderful, I must say. I like all the greenery around their heads.'

'That's William Morris,' said Cressida. 'His workshop made the windows to Burne-Jones's design, and he's supposed to have added the leaves.' She frowned, studying the two pairs of figures flanking the Crucifixion. 'Those must be St Peter and St Paul and St John,' she said, pointing. 'And Mary, of course.'

For a few minutes they all lingered, looking at the glass, and then Judith made a little show of studying a leaflet she'd picked up on the way in. 'There's a war memorial cross in the churchyard, apparently. And notable yew trees, it says.'

Out of the corner of her eye, Cressida saw Bill taking a step towards Judith, and Stephen hesitating, then following them. She wasn't going to involve herself in that little dance, she thought.

'Some of the other windows are worth seeing, too,' she said. 'There's a Burne-Jones Ascension further down.'

Isabel was still beside her as the door closed behind the others, the sound echoing theatrically up the empty church. Cressida smiled at her, and Isabel smiled back, her face relaxing for a moment in a way that made Cressida realise how tense she'd been, perhaps for the whole weekend.

'I did a stained glass course once,' Isabel said.

'Really?'

'I went through a phase of doing courses. I decided I ought to – well, find a hobby. I don't have many artistic genes, though.' Isabel smiled again, with an inflection of self-parody Cressida found touching. 'I like the pictures at the bottom there,' she said, turning back to the window. 'Look at those lambs being blessed. And the children, on the other side.'

Isabel's eyes lingered on the image of Jesus receiving a child in his arms, and Cressida was conscious, suddenly, of a connection between them: two childless women, each of them searching, hoping – missing something, she thought. For a moment she considered sharing with Isabel what she hadn't told another soul: the story of Michael's dereliction and the Norwegian prince who'd vanished back to the fjords, and the baby that had never been. Possibly, even, the hope she'd begun to nurture, to rekindle, in another direction. But before the words came, Isabel spoke instead.

'Are you all right now?' she asked. She gave a quick, appeasing smile. 'I could see you were upset, earlier. In that other church.'

'I'm fine,' Cressida said. 'Thank you, though. It's kind of you to ask.'

Her heart was still beating fast. The moment had passed, and she wasn't sure, now, whether she was glad not to have spoken. What might it have felt like to divulge her secrets to an almost-stranger? Isabel gave another quick tweak of a smile, and Cressida could see there were things she might say too, questions she wanted to ask.

'You were fond of her, weren't you?' she said; and then, after a little stumble, 'Of Marmion?'

'Yes,' Cressida said. 'We all were. She was a very easy person to be fond of.'

'Bill never talks about her,' Isabel said. 'He's never talked about any of you, really, until this bequest came along. but I know he and Marmion . . .'

'They went out for nearly three years,' Cressida said, hating the awkwardness of the terminology, the outdated words she'd chosen. 'I expect . . . You must know what happened?'

'I know she died,' Isabel said. 'I met Bill just after that. And I know – he told me they'd split up, before she died. That made things worse for him, I think.'

'Yes.' Cressida glanced away, avoiding the look of appeal in Isabel's eyes. Did she know, suspect, about Judith?

'You were all very close, weren't you?' Isabel asked. 'Until that summer you'd all been good friends.'

'Yes,' Cressida said again. She steeled herself, searching out a version of events that would be truthful, helpful, without causing unnecessary pain. 'We'd lived in each other's pockets for three years, but we lost touch, after we graduated. Stephen went to Dubai, and the rest of us went on to other things, and – Marmion died.'

Isabel nodded. They hadn't moved away from the east window, and Cressida could feel the light from the stained glass, a greenish-yellow glow of haloes and foliage and flowing robes, falling on them both.

'I wondered . . .' Isabel began. 'I thought there might have been something else. I thought something might have happened, when you were all here before.' She swallowed. 'Something to do with Fay, maybe. The way you've all talked about her, I wondered whether . . .'

Cressida hesitated. The truth, then? Or another thread of it? *It was a strange time*, she could say. Or a direct answer to the question about Fay, describing the little shifts and alterations in her manner, the things Cressida had pondered afterwards, when Fay disappeared from view.

But she was spared the decision. Behind them, the door clunked open.

'Ah, you're still here.'

Bill came a little way down the aisle and then stopped, as if wondering what they might have been saying to each other. Almost, Cressida thought, as though the pressing presence of all they had not quite said was palpable in the air.

'We're just coming,' Isabel said. She shot a tiny glance at Cressida, a glance of complicity but also of – not quite caution, Cressida thought, nor closure, but – gratitude, possibly. She didn't deserve gratitude, though. If she'd reassured Isabel, that was more a disservice than anything else. She looked at Bill, and wished she hadn't seen the apprehension in his face.

September 2015

Bill

Standing in the low-ceilinged kitchen at Townend Farmhouse, Bill's eyes strayed from the tour guide to the other faces around him. Isabel's was rapt as she listened to the history of the farming family who'd owned this place for centuries, while Cressida maintained a discerning reserve and Judith a barely feigned interest. The barrage of facts and objects was a trial, he thought, but even so, this was a good way to spend the afternoon. Despite himself he'd rejoiced at the lawyer's stay of execution, at being given another day to work things out, and it was hard to think how else they might have passed these hours.

The guide sent them on to the next room, inviting them to examine the furniture that had been elaborately carved by a long-gone patriarch. Bill stood back to let an elderly woman pass, and then his arm brushed against Judith's in the doorway – just the lightest, the slightest of contact, but even so he felt his skin flare. Melting back through the crowd, he pressed himself against the wall, his heart beating hard. Judith was only a foot or two away, and he knew she had felt the touch too, that the thrill of it had passed between them like a match being struck. She lifted a hand to brush back a strand of hair, exposing a delicate triangle of skin above her collarbone that quivered as her pulse throbbed beneath the surface, and Bill felt something inside him tremble too. Oh, if he kept his eyes just there, just there, he thought, he could be happy forever. That small portion of her, that soft place, was enough to entrance him. If he could only – but then he felt Isabel's hand sliding into his, and it was all he could do not to flinch; almost more than he could manage to squeeze her fingers.

'Wonderful, isn't it?' Isabel said, pointing at a pair of carved feet sticking out at the bottom of a grandfather clock, and Bill smiled and felt treason course through him.

He must deal humanely with Isabel, he told himself. He mustn't let guilt and panic overtake him as they had once before. But it was hard to act rationally when he was stretched tight between craving and dread and remorse – and when he tried to think things through, he got tangled in knots. Would it be honourable, or unnecessarily cruel, to tell Isabel he was still in love with Judith before he was sure of Judith's feelings? He hadn't been as good a husband as Isabel deserved, but what she'd had all these years was worth something, and he shouldn't jeopardise that if . . . But could he really go on being that husband, if Judith wouldn't have him? Could he manage another twenty, thirty, forty years?

Every outcome seemed impossible just now, that was the trouble. He couldn't imagine his old life continuing, but he didn't dare believe in a new one. Judith's response to his declaration last night had tormented him all day, but she'd posed a question, he kept telling himself, not given a judgement. *I know I'm the reckless one, but really, what could we possibly . . .?*

It seemed to him now that the failure of will twenty years ago had been his, not Judith's. She'd rejected him, but perhaps she hadn't meant – hadn't wanted – to be taken so literally. He felt increasingly sure that she'd been testing his resolve, and that he had failed her. Had she too counted the wasted years, regretted the *folie à deux* that had allowed them to be separated all this time?

The tour guide was heading upstairs now; he'd missed the last part of her commentary.

'Thank you for bringing us here,' Stephen said to Isabel. 'It's a fascinating place.'

'I was thinking how much Marmion would have liked it,' Cressida said, with an edge of defiance in her voice. 'Not all the carving, perhaps, but the house. The family history.'

Bill's heart thumped again – but there was no need, he told himself, to feel . . . Oh, everything was such a muddle. The things he'd done wrong and the things he hadn't; the things that had turned out worse than he'd expected, worse than he deserved. Wasn't that what made him hesitate: because cause and effect had never really matched up in his life? He'd so often been outsmarted by tricksy footwork on the part of Fate, but he was no less nice, surely, than most men; no less worthy of a simple happy ending. Wasn't it time, now, to seize it?

'Which did you prefer?' Isabel asked him, as they drove home. 'Townend, or the church?'

'That window was beautiful,' Bill said, turning his attention to her with an effort. 'The Burne-Jones. But the house was interesting too.'

'I know you didn't really like it,' she said. 'I could tell you weren't enjoying it.'

'I was,' he protested. 'All that marvellous carving.'

She smiled a little sadly. 'You're a bad liar, Bill,' she said.

He glanced sideways at her. Was that true? he wondered. Did she suspect . . .? For a few moments there was silence as he cast about for a way forward. *Isabel, you know that I . . . There's something I really have to . . .* But Isabel's next words brought him up short.

'Judith seems to me rather an odd person,' she said. 'There's so much brilliance and bravado, but she's so – bad-tempered, isn't she? So cross with life. It seems a shame.'

'I'm not sure . . .' he began. Could cross and bad-tempered mean lovesick? Certainly this assessment couldn't come from a wife appraising her rival, could it, unless Isabel was cannier than he'd ever suspected?

'Cressida is nice, though,' Isabel went on. 'I like her.'

'I'm glad,' Bill said. 'She's never been an easy person to like, but . . .' Perhaps she and Isabel could support each other, he was thinking, conscious, even as the thought took shape, of its callousness. 'She's always had a soft spot for Stephen,' he said. 'I think she still does.' Cressida's eyes had hardly left Stephen all weekend, in fact. Another one of them hoping to resurrect an old passion, he thought, with a painful dart of irony.

'Stephen?' Isabel looked surprised. 'Goodness.'

Bill glanced at her, wondering what she meant – whether she might have thought Cressida held a candle for him, rather than Judith – but they were pulling into the drive at High Scarp now. Bill sat where he was for a moment after turning off the engine, but Isabel was already undoing her seat belt and opening the door.

'The others are back,' she said.

Bill followed her into the house with a gloomy feeling of déjà vu. Here they were, just like yesterday evening, the five of them assembling and –

A scream from inside the house cut abruptly across his thoughts.

'What is it?' Bill called. 'What's the matter?'

Other people were shouting too; everyone was racing towards the sitting room.

In the semi-darkness Cressida cowered. 'There's something in here,' she cried. 'It came at me when I opened the door. It hit me in the face.'

'A bird,' said Judith, and they all looked where she was pointing, above the piano. 'Don't move: you'll scare it.'

But it was too late: the bird was off again, thrashing and crashing around the room, its frantic movements making a sound like a tiny tornado. It was strangely terrifying: a blackbird, frightened out of its wits, the beat and brush of its wings flicking past one person and then another.

'Shall I open a window?' suggested Stephen. 'Would it find its way out?'

'How did it get in?' wailed Cressida.

'Down the chimney,' said Isabel. 'Probably down the chimney. It's a crow.'

'That's a bad omen, a crow in the house,' said Judith. 'It's a portent of death.'

It was impossible to tell from her tone of voice whether she was mocking them. Bill looked away; he didn't want to see what the others were thinking.

Stephen had got the window open, but the bird was at the far end of the room now, buffeting against the paintings on the wall. After another few moments it dropped, exhausted, onto the back of the sofa.

'Keep still,' Bill said, and he sidled up to the bird quietly, sideways on, then dropped his hands to cover it, closing his fingers tight around its wings. 'There. Safe now.'

The creature's heart beat furiously inside its warm little body, but it didn't struggle as he picked it up and carried it across the room. Its feathers felt soft, almost silky: it was hard to imagine it as that jagged, battering dervish that had flung itself about the room a few minutes before.

The kitchen door was still open. Standing on the step, Bill released his hands, and the bird vanished into the trees with a final fluster of wings and sharp feet.

'Well done,' said Stephen, when he returned. 'I'd forgotten you knew about birds.'

'I don't,' said Bill. 'But that wasn't a crow. Not big enough, and it had an orange beak. It was a blackbird.'

'Well, I don't know what a blackbird in the house signifies, I'm afraid,' said Judith.

Cressida looked at her with a flash of antipathy. 'In the medieval bestiary,' she said, 'the blackbird represents the temptations of the flesh.'

And then, blushing deeply, she rushed out of the room.

October 1995

Bill

The entryphone at the bottom of Judith's block was broken, and the front door had been left on the latch. Bill pushed it open and climbed the stairs, his footsteps echoing off the concrete walls.

He'd been to the Guildhall today, but only because he had nothing else to do, after the funeral on Friday and a torturous weekend at home. He couldn't see himself finishing the course, but for now he hardly cared what he did to pass the days. All he cared about – all he could think about – was Judith. They'd avoided each other at the funeral, and over the weekend he'd resisted the telephone, although he'd hardly been able to bear wondering what she might be doing or thinking. He'd felt, understood, that an interval was necessary. A watershed. But he was sure – as sure as he dared, hoped, struggled to be – that she must be expecting to see him. Perhaps not exactly now, but how was he to decide, except by testing the limits of his own patience? There was no algorithm for this situation; no established social convention.

Flat 13 was on the fourth floor. By the time he reached it, Bill was sure his intrusion must have been detected and that a caretaker or the resident vigilante would be waiting on the landing, but there was nothing except a row of shoes outside one door and a folded bicycle beside another. He knocked, and the door was answered by a short, blonde girl. Of course there were other people living here; he'd forgotten that.

'I'm sorry to disturb you,' he said. 'The buzzer's not working. Is this where Judith lives?'

The girl hesitated for a moment, then pulled the door back to let him in.

'Judith?' she called. 'Someone for you.'

Judith was wearing pyjamas made from some silky, satiny material which shimmered and swooped over her smooth curves.

'Hello,' she said. There was a shaft of irony in her voice, but not of surprise. No glimmer of a qualm, either, but Bill saw with pain how tired she looked.

It was only the third time they'd had sex: that thought flitted through Bill's mind, incongruously banal, as they lay together in the narrow single bed in blessed post-coital exhaustion. It was an extraordinary relief, he thought, half thought, for the burden of need and desire to be briefly assuaged. And Judith had been as eager and as voracious as him: they hadn't waited for a glass of wine, a cup of coffee, a decorous pause. He had kissed her on the doorstep, not caring who saw, then followed her to her room, mesmerised by the movement of her hips and the thick gleam of her hair.

It occurred to him now that Judith's scruples at the beginning of the summer had turned out to be a blessing, and their restraint these last three months a saving grace. At last something to be grateful for, he thought, and through the regret and remorse he felt a warming surge of hope. And then he lifted his hand an inch, encountering Judith's ribcage and the soft overhang of her breast, and everything else was banished.

'Judith,' he said. 'Oh, Judith, I love you.'

She kissed him gently, lightly, then more seriously. But as he shifted himself back on top of her, she said: 'You can't.'

He froze then, and she gave a little smile. 'Not that,' she said. 'I don't mean . . . but you can't love me. We can't love each other. Not now.'

'Of course we can.' He slid off her again, his erection gone, his heart beating fast. 'I know it's complicated, Judith, but there's no reason –'

'Yes, there is.' Judith lifted a hand to stroke his face. 'I'm afraid there is.'

'That's bollocks,' he said. 'It's a terrible thing, a terrible situation, and believe me I feel . . . But there's no point punishing ourselves. We can't undo what's happened.'

'No.'

He pushed himself up on one elbow, trying to see her from a different angle, to catch the meaning behind her words. What was she . . .? What did he . . .?

'I need to be with you,' he said. 'I can't manage without you. I've never been more sure about anything in my life.'

Judith didn't take her eyes off his face, but she didn't speak again. Bill gazed back at her. Her dark hair was dazzling against the white sheets and her face soft and flushed: his heart's desire, within his grasp but suddenly, bewilderingly, unattainable. Nothing had made sense, he thought, since that weekend in June. Nothing, nothing had happened as he could have expected.

And then, in the silence, he heard Marmion's mother's voice: *It isn't right to lie about our feelings.* It seemed to Bill now that he had no idea, really no idea, whether he was speaking the truth – to Judith, or to himself. Everything had seemed so clear earlier, so clearly pointing to a resolution, a consummation of desires that were burned into his flesh and his soul. But the tangle in his chest couldn't be given the names of any human emotions Mrs Hayter might recognise. It bore no relation to the sweet simplicity the world called love.

Perhaps there was no truth to tell, he thought. There was just an inverting loop of longing and guilt and self-loathing that he would never resolve, never follow through from one end to the other without finding himself on the opposite side.

September 2015
Judith

Judith was aware that she was behaving badly. There were plenty of reasons for it, plenty of excuses, but that wasn't really the point. The deferral of the lawyer's visit, the rain, the frustration of feeling helpless in this peculiar web Fay had spun – none of that was very much to the point. What was unsettling her was much closer to home.

The drama of the blackbird had at least broken the spell of forced civility and allowed them all to draw apart for a while. Isabel had seized on another lull in the rain to take Bill out for a walk, and Cressida and Stephen had gone off in his car to buy food for supper. Judith had announced her intention to have a bath, but once she'd been left alone in the house she'd found she didn't have the heart for it. High Scarp had a beautiful old-fashioned bath with claw feet and a rolled edge, the kind you could float in if you drew your knees up, and she remembered it vividly: she remembered Marmion emerging, draped in towels, from another long soak, her cheeks pink and her hair damp and tousled.

It wasn't rational to be haunted by Marmion, when Isabel was alive and present and manifestly eager to hold onto Bill, but the sense she'd had this morning of being out of kilter with Isabel's world worked both ways. In Judith's world, it was Marmion she had stolen Bill from; Marmion whose death had scuppered their hopes; Marmion whose presence in this house still complicated everything. Or was that another fluent stream of self-deception? Of course she could still conjure the love, the anger, the guilt – all the long-submerged emotions Marmion had left her with. But did they have anything to do with the present? Did she really know what she wanted now, or why she'd acted as she had twenty years ago? Perhaps she was simply seeking to excuse the decision she'd made back then – and to justify a hesitancy that might be no more than cowardice.

Out in the hall the cuckoo clock struck six. Soon they would have to gather again, and endure another evening under Fay's watchful, imagined eye. Judith moved restlessly around her room, looking but not touching, as though an alarm might trigger if she interfered with the stage set Fay had left behind. At the window she paused, glimpsing two figures who might be Bill and Isabel trailing up the path behind the house. A tremor went through her: partly a shiver of disbelief, and partly a thrill of desire.

Beneath the histrionic reversals of mood there was, she admitted, something she could no longer deny: an alteration in her feelings. Or perhaps not alteration, but – clarification. No, not even that. All she knew was that something inside was full of fire, so that any touch could ignite her skin, and when she spoke, smoke and flame poured out of her mouth.

Desire was a mysterious, an unreasonable, an excessive thing, she thought. It was impossible to account for it; to mark out its co-ordinates. But among the clutter and incident of the last twenty-four hours – that first meeting on the doorstep last night, then the uncomfortable evening and the encounter in the small hours when the bleak infinity of starlight had filled her head; the walk to the church, the sparring over legal detail, the pub lunch, the visit to Troutbeck – among it all, she could see moments of radiance: a trail of stars alight in her head now like a constellation. Bill blushing last night, just after they'd arrived, when she mentioned Marmion, and then feeling his eyes on her as she talked to Isabel, and knowing that they would be on her all weekend. His confession of love, late at night – too hasty, too direct for her at the time, but now she could see that it had been the acknowledgement of an irresistible fact. And then, at Townend, that brushing of arms in the doorway which she had known beyond all doubt he'd felt too, and Bill standing so close behind her afterwards so that she could almost feel his breath on her neck. She had never felt any of this for Arvind, nor for Jonty. She had settled for too little, her mother had always said. She had never dared to risk anything more, to raise her hopes.

She heard herself, then, searing the air with her words: *That's a bad omen, a crow in the house.* And Cressida's retort, a few moments later: *The blackbird represents the temptations of the flesh.* Oh, that little bird, held softly in his hands. That wild, terrified, flailing thing stilled, soothed, at peace. How could she not wish for that stillness for herself?

Supper that night was a subdued affair. Cressida and Stephen had bought lamb chops and a tray of sticky toffee pudding at the village shop, but their pleasure in producing a meal for everyone was muted. Judith, for one, had nothing to say for herself at all; no fire to breathe tonight.

Afterwards, the moment she had been dreading all weekend came to pass. Strangely, it was Isabel who suggested it. Did she think she was doing them all a favour, Judith wondered, or was this another calculated risk? She felt sure that Isabel had realised what she was up against. If she hadn't known before, something about today had alerted her.

'Would anyone like to do some singing?' she asked. 'I found some sheet music in the cupboard by the piano.'

'Why not?' said Stephen. 'What is there?'

This was a terrible idea, Judith thought. She had abandoned even the Bach Choir this last couple of years, and who knew whether the others still sang. She couldn't bear them to defile anything they'd sung together before. But perhaps it would be worse if they shied away from it now. Certainly if she refused to join in.

Stephen held up a madrigal book. 'Any takers?' he said. 'I know madrigals were never our strong point, but we could have a go.'

Judith couldn't tell whether his enthusiasm was genuine or not, but it seemed to convince Cressida.

'Is "The Silver Swan" in there?' she asked.

Stephen flicked to the index. 'Yes,' he said. 'Scored for SSATB too, so we can manage that, if . . .'

'I don't mind singing alto,' said Cressida.

Christ, thought Judith. Was it bravery or merely a flagrant assertion of innocence, offering to take Marmion's part – and proposing the piece that carried with it perhaps the most sentimental attachment of any in that book? Why not something about the springtime, the only pretty ringtime, rather than Gibbons's plangent, heartfelt lament? *Farewell, all joys! O Death, come close mine eyes* – could they really sing that, in the place where Marmion had sung her last, and sung no more? But the others seemed intent; even Bill was making no objection.

'OK,' she said, taking a copy from Stephen. 'OK.'

The second soprano part was too low for her, but the upper part was more exposed than she cared to attempt, and too fraught with memory.

'You can have the top line,' she said to Isabel.

They were all on their feet now, standing in a circle around the piano. Bill played the opening chord, and then suddenly they were singing. Singing different parts, with different voices than they'd had before, but even so Judith felt an irresistible pulse of joy as she reached the run of quavers that introduced the second line; felt something yield between them as she and Stephen began the third together and the overlapping threads of harmony were teased out between them; felt a deep thrill of satisfaction as they settled at last on the final chord, underpinned by Stephen's sonorous bottom F. Isabel's voice was too operatic for the floating high notes, but that was all right, that was a saving grace. So was her show of pleasure at the end, her smiles and thanks: they allowed everyone else to say nothing.

Goodness, thought Judith. My goodness, that was nice. The music, the singing of it, seemed to have swallowed up, dissolved, embraced so much. It had carried them all along so willingly on its rising lines, its swooping melody that pulled them apart and then drew them back together again. She had forgotten the joy and satisfaction of singing like this, feeling that you weren't just joining in but creating something that depended on each one of you to bring it to life. And feeling beneath, above, within the notes so much being shared, being said. Even Marmion's absence, the richness of her contralto missing from the texture, conveyed something profound and particular that it would have been almost impossible to express in words: a lingering, bittersweet melancholy that encompassed the joy of recovering something deeply important to them all. It was almost unbearable; almost more than her heart, her mind, could allow.

But for the moment it was enough to let the music speak for itself. Judith smiled, and caught Bill's eye, and he smiled too. She remembered him, then, singing the solo in 'Blue Moon', and 'Smoke Gets in Your Eyes' – oh, and so many other songs that had been at their fingertips in those days, ready to be produced at the end of an evening.

'Another?' asked Stephen, and they murmured yes, certainly, why not, and flicked on through the book recognising, remembering.

'What about "Come Gentle Swains"?' suggested Cressida. 'That's in five parts too.'

'Long live fair Oriana,' said Bill. 'Very good: I think we could manage that.'

This piece was more restrained, a delicate filigree of lace rather than the sumptuous velvet and flowing silk of 'The Silver Swan', but as it danced nimble-footed to its ringing conclusion, it too called up a recollection so deep it was almost a folk memory.

'Ridiculous music,' said Stephen when they'd finished, in the tone of voice a father might use to acknowledge his pleasure in a new baby, failing to disguise the disconcerting power of its grip on his heart. Isabel was apologising for a note that had been a little sharp; no one took any notice of her.

After that they sang 'Construe My Meaning' and 'Sing We at Pleasure' and 'All Creatures Now Are Merry-Minded', with a thrill of gratification each time that they could read their way through them with reasonable competence: with a sense that this, this was what they could do, all of them, to make sense of things. Even so, Judith was relieved that both 'Draw on, Sweet Night' and 'Sleep, Fleshly Birth', each of them poignantly melancholic, turned out to have six parts, and was happy to end on a bumptious note with 'Now is the Month of Maying'. Who would ever have imagined, she thought, as they made an exaggerated rallentando through the final chorus, that singing madrigals could give them such profound and such grateful pleasure? The idea of them all, back in 1995, spying on their future selves singing *fa la la la la* with earnest delight, almost made her laugh out loud. But the future was always mysterious; always a surprise. Perhaps, she thought, it was just as well that none of them could see further than this moment.

September 2015
Stephen

It was, again, barely dawn when Stephen woke, but it felt this morning like a different season; a different place. What light there was, creeping around the thick curtains and under the door, was bluish and cold, and as he lay half-awake in the unfamiliar bed he felt a potent sense of sadness. In his mind he replayed the memory of the evening before, the jollity of the madrigal singing, and his melancholy perplexed him at first. *Now is the month of maying,* he thought – not that it was, exactly – but despite the smiles and the pleasure of the singing, merry lads and bonny lasses they were not. He was not, anyway.

He stared at the ceiling, shadowed and sculpted by the darkness. He liked having a puzzle to mull over, and the early morning was usually a good time to worry at things that would seem less ductile later in the day. But he wasn't used to teasing out psychological puzzles. Emotional puzzles, even. The way to soften a deal or to broker a bid was his territory: how to account for a discrepancy in share price, not mood. The twisting threads of twenty years of life were more baffling than the most complex political and economic data.

He'd thought last night that singing together had been good for them, but it seemed to him now that it had opened a door that might have been better left shut. Several things had been clear, when the madrigal books had been closed at last: that Cressida was more unhappy than she cared to admit; that Judith and Bill were still tortured by guilt and uncertainty; that Isabel, for all her appearance of tranquil good sense, had been unsettled by the weekend. Or were those, each of them, simplifications too facile to have any meaning?

And what of himself? What was behind that door for him, except the realisation that his days of maying, of barley break, were behind him? The shadow of Fay, perhaps. The admission that this place and its associations had a stronger hold on him than he'd acknowledged.

He pushed back the blankets and got out of bed, then went through to the kitchen, where the rain pounded like kettledrums on the Velux window. No early walk this morning, then, unless he wanted to get soaked. Instead he made a cup of tea and took it into the sitting room. Here, too, the noise of the rain was insistent, the light tempered and qualified by the density of cloud and water. None of the peaks were visible this morning, not even Nag's Pike, but even so he had, in that moment, a powerful sense of the place: the valley, the village, the house, all so little changed, when the four of them had moved on so far. It was always odd, he thought, to find that one could so easily revisit the scenes of the past, but not the past itself: it hardly made sense that certain aspects of what one remembered were still here, while others had vanished completely. It was that conundrum that made memory so painful, he thought. The yearning, the seeking after clues and mementoes, the temptations of nostalgia – singing madrigals, visiting churches – were, in the end, the seeds of self-delusion.

He smiled then, thinking how little he'd indulged himself in this respect over the years. He'd received the St Anne's bulletins every year but had never once been to a reunion dinner, and he hadn't returned to Surbiton since his mother had died and the house had been sold. Even singing had become something to avoid, on the advice of his sub-conscious. Had he gone too far? Had prudence – at least in emotional matters – ruled his life too firmly? He'd been successful, of course, more than successful, and he'd seen plenty of life. But could he accuse himself of a lack of fulfilment? Had he become too much an island?

Not everyone was made for pair-bonding, he'd always told himself. It was absurd to judge the success of any human life in those terms, anyway – and if one did, his failure was no greater than Cressida's or Judith's, or indeed Bill's. A marriage of that kind could hardly be held up as a shining example of anything except (and now he permitted himself a rare measure of spite) the fear of being alone. No: he wasn't persuaded. His watchword, in his personal life, had always been to do no harm, and that he thought he'd managed. Suky – he had made amends with Suky; she was all right. His mother had died regretting the absence of grandchildren, but believing that cancer had snatched her away too soon to see them, and he had done all he could, everything in his power, to make her life happy and comfortable. No one else had any claim on him.

Except . . . He shook his head quickly, irritably. Clearly that subject would keep coming back today. Was it really possible that Fay had lived all these years wondering whether he was her son, waiting for him to make contact? Was it even conceivable that he was?

There was a desk in the corner of the sitting room, tucked in beside the aged sofa. He hesitated for a moment, listening for sounds elsewhere in the house, then crossed the room. The top of the desk opened flat, revealing several cubbyholes filled with pens and paper clips and stationery. The top drawer contained ancient receipts and instruction leaflets, and the one below was full of jigsaw puzzles. Stephen inspected the contents methodically, then shut the drawers again, feeling faintly ridiculous.

What had he been looking for, anyway? Surely any paperwork was more likely to have been kept in Fay's other house, wherever she'd moved when she sold the place in Newnham. And photographs . . .

He moved over to the bookcase now, looking among the battered paperbacks and crumbling hardbacks for a photo album. But there was nothing there. Out in the hall there was another bookcase, filled largely with maps and guidebooks, but that too yielded nothing. He was being foolish, Stephen told himself. He'd got caught on a current of sentiment and was allowing it to carry him to places he had no real need to visit. The tantalising shadow of the mother complex – surely he'd put all that to bed long ago?

After his mother died – his adoptive mother, the only one he'd ever known – he'd wondered whether he should try to trace his birth mother. There were some questions that still nagged at him, he'd realised: about who she was, why she'd given him up, whether she'd thought about him over the years. And if she was indeed Fay, why she had never made herself known. Questions with which he had a curious relationship, both detached and deeply intimate. He'd realised, too, that an array of answers had been waiting in the same dark corner of his mind, cooked up by his subconscious when he wasn't looking. It had been tempting to try to find out whether any of them came close to the truth, and to tackle the faint echo of guilt, the tiny hook lodged in his heart that made him wonder whether he'd been guilty, all these years, of a sin of omission towards Fay.

But he hadn't done it. He couldn't explain why, except that it had seemed the rational course for a man who was content to be who he was. But he could see now that it had been an emotional, even a romantic decision: that he had never wanted to have his fantastical theory disproved. The memory of that day when he'd come looking for Fay, on the eve of his departure for Dubai, had held him back. The memory of all those painful, squashed emotions.

And now it was quite possible that he'd know the answers to some of these questions by the end of the day, and that thought filled him with trepidation. It was the unknown, he thought: the unknown bits of himself. That and the fear – absurd now when he was an adult, a prominent man – of exposure in front of his friends; of secrets being revealed over which he had no control. But he had no choice, now. If there was anything in his theory, the lawyer was likely to reveal it. And if he didn't – then either Stephen's theory was wrong, or Fay had lived and died without divulging her suspicions, and he must forget all about them.

Suddenly there seemed a long time to wait, though, until noon. It was only eight thirty: the hours passed very slowly here, he thought, the minutes and the seconds creaking past in the seclusion of the old house. Perhaps he should cook breakfast. He had bought the ingredients yesterday at the shop, locally reared bacon and free-range eggs and other things he hadn't eaten for years: black pudding and kidneys and hash browns. From the cupboards he selected knives and pans and boards. If the others weren't up by the time it was ready, he would eat alone and leave the remains in the oven for them.

But by the time he had finished cooking, everyone had appeared. Judith was last, her hair damp from the shower. Stephen was glad, then, to have been the one to provide not just food but diversion. They lingered over the eating of his feast, glancing now and then at the rain outside but doing their best not to look too plainly at each other. Toast, jam and fruit were appended to the meal, surely not out of hunger. Afterwards, the washing-up was made into a performance too, the kitchen scrubbed clean, and Cressida even found an elderly hoover in a cupboard and pushed it half-heartedly around the sitting room and down the passage. Bill made more coffee and produced a newspaper he had bought the day before, spreading the various sections on the coffee table for the others to sample. Isabel built a fire; Judith took a book out of the bookcase and installed herself on the far side of the sitting room from Bill.

Stephen hesitated for a moment, surveying this domestic scene, for all the world like a wet Sunday morning passing peacefully in a holiday cottage in the Lake District, and admiring the concerted effort that had gone into it. There were some emails he needed to answer, but instead he took the Travel section of the paper and read an article about hotels in Venice. Venice, indeed: there seemed to be traps for the memory everywhere.

As twelve o'clock approached, the silence in the room became more determined, and the noise of the rain more insistent. Loud enough, in fact, to conceal the approach of the lawyer's car, so that the first warning they had of his arrival was a rap at the door. Each of them jumped – but it was Judith who was on her feet first, going through to answer it.

Giles Unwin was less prepossessing than his stand-in from the previous day. A small man, perhaps in his mid-fifties, with thinning hair drawn over his scalp and a Dickensian face, thick-lipped and weak-chinned. Perfect, Stephen thought, for the part he was playing. He looked round at them all when he came into the room, then put his briefcase down on the table and smiled – unctuously, Stephen thought; that was the word.

'I am sorry to have kept you in suspense,' he began. 'It was, as you may have guessed, on the instruction of our late client. That is to say – her instructions were that you should all spend the weekend here, and I was left to contrive how best to achieve that.'

For a moment self-satisfaction flickered across his cautious face – even, perhaps, a flush of excitement about this unusual commission. Then he sat down at the head of the table, leaving them to digest this speech and to decide how to arrange themselves. Judith scowled, but she kept her mouth shut, and sat down next to Stephen. Isabel, with a glance at Bill, withdrew to an armchair in the corner. Cressida hesitated for a moment.

'Would you like some coffee, Mr Unwin?' she asked.

'No, thank you.' Unwin cleared his throat: another unconvincing, actorly gesture, Stephen thought. 'If I could ask you each to identify yourselves, please? Before we begin I should like to be certain that all the legatees are present.'

With a mixture of eagerness and impatience, they gave their names and produced the passports they had been instructed to bring with them. Unwin looked at each in turn, his eyes resting for a moment on their faces as though he was mentally aligning their features with what he knew of them.

'Very good,' he said, when they were finished. 'Well, there's no need for further delay. I am here, as you are all aware, to acquaint you with

311

the contents of the last will and testament of Fay Elizabeth McArthur, made on the fifteenth of October 1995.'

'Wait,' said Cressida. 'Nineteen ninety-five? Why did she . . . Surely there must be a more recent will? Surely she must have updated it sometime between then and now?'

Giles Unwin gazed at her, unblinking.

'Oh no,' he said. 'There was no opportunity to revise the will. Fay McArthur died two days after she had signed it.'

Part VII

October 1992

Fay

Coming into the familiar room, Fay hesitated for a moment. The smell of the St Anne's Master's Lodge hadn't changed in all the time she'd known it. There was always that sweetish scent: a faint waft of decay, endlessly deferred but never conquered for good, overlaid with wood smoke and sherry and – the specifics altering with each new generation of undergraduates – a draught of cheap perfume. The boys often smelled stronger than the girls these days, she'd noticed. They dressed their hair with gel and wax: some of them did, anyway. Not so often the ones who sang in the choir.

Just ahead she recognised the new choral scholars, whom she'd identified earlier in the chapel – cassock-less now, and laughing at something one of them had said. A nice group, she thought. A very tall boy who looked as though he hadn't quite got used to his height yet, listening attentively to what was being said. A shorter, squarer, ginger-haired boy with an affable air of self-confidence. And three girls, all unalike: one blonde in what Fay recognised as the patrician style; one strikingly beautiful, perhaps with Middle Eastern blood; one plump and smiling, with a face one would instantly warm to. She took a step towards them, wondering if it would seem strange to introduce herself, but before she could do so the Master swept up to her, bearing a glass of sherry.

'Fay. I'm so glad you could come.'

'Hello, Jeremy.' Her least favourite cousin, she called him. It was only partly a joke: he was, in any case, her only cousin. 'How are you liking it here?'

Jeremy's appointment as Master of her old college had both amused and infuriated Fay. She could see that she might enjoy her association with St Anne's a little less from now on, even if she was invited more often – but she didn't mean to let Jeremy interfere with her particular pleasures. She was willing to bet that he rarely went to evensong, anyway.

'You'll have to help me decorate,' Jeremy said, with a sweep of his hand that took in red brocade and wood panelling and murky green paint. 'You know Elspeth hates that sort of thing.'

'So do I,' said Fay. He laughed, and she said: 'You don't need to bother with me, Jeremy. I know most of these people.'

'You know the Fellows better than I do, you mean.' He laughed again, joyously, to show that he didn't believe this statement for a moment. 'Say hello to Elspeth, won't you. She's over there somewhere.'

As Jeremy glided away, Fay turned to inspect one of the pictures on the wall – a Rowlandson watercolour of St Anne's that used to hang in the Combination Room rather than the Master's Lodge, she was sure – and caught a fragment of conversation from the group of choral scholars.

'You can talk, Bill,' the dark beauty was saying. 'You didn't quite seem to have that psalm under control.'

'It was pointed differently at the cathedral,' the redhead protested.

'I loved that anthem,' said the plump girl. 'I absolutely loved it.'

'You love everything, Marmion,' said the blonde. 'You . . .'

A gale of laughter from the other side of the room drowned the rest of the sentence, and Fay moved away then, before they suspected her of eavesdropping. Marmion: was that Walter Scott? An unusual name. They seemed rather charming, she thought. So young; they were all so young these days. She felt a stab of sorrow, and dispelled it firmly.

'Fay!'

She turned to see Lawrence Watts, the Director of Music.

'Hello, Lawrence. Lovely service this evening: you must be pleased.'

Lawrence gave the smile of a man who couldn't quite believe his own good fortune.

'Wonderful new recruits,' he said. 'Choral scholars. So talented. Going to make a real ... Here they are, in fact. Let me – ladies and gentlemen, can I introduce Fay McArthur?'

They turned, five open, ardent faces.

'Bill,' said Lawrence, indicating the ginger-haired boy, 'Stephen' – the taller boy – 'Judith, Marmion, Cressida' – dark, plump, fair. 'Fay is a – friend and patron of the choir.'

Fay smiled, demurring. Lawrence didn't know she was an alumna, and she was grateful for that. If he had mentioned it, the fact that she'd been in St Anne's very first intake of women in 1970, she would have felt obliged, out of fastidiousness, to say that she had never graduated – and she much preferred not to. Jeremy, she thought, might – but Jeremy wouldn't want to acknowledge her prior claim on the college. He had never quite got over the fact that he hadn't got into Cambridge at eighteen. All his success, Fay often thought, all his eminence, had been achieved on the back of that needling failure.

'It's nice to meet you,' said the girl called Marmion. 'Do you often come to evensong?'

'Once or twice a week,' said Fay. 'I only live round the corner, in Newnham. Are you all enjoying St Anne's?'

She sounded like an old fogey, she thought. A maiden aunt. But they liked being asked about themselves.

'Enormously,' said the blonde girl – Cressida, Fay repeated in her head. She had a slightly fractious look, on closer inspection, but it was overlaid with happiness at the moment. The others nodded and murmured assent.

'And have you all sung before?' Fay asked.

'Not really,' said the tall boy. Stephen. 'Bill's miles ahead of the rest of us – he was a cathedral chorister.'

'I've never sung anything like this,' said Marmion. 'But it's wonderful.'

'Well, you've made a difference to the choir already,' Fay said. 'I look forward to following your progress.'

She didn't mean to stay long; one glass of college sherry was enough. She exchanged a few words with one of the Fellows, said hello to the organ scholar and was waylaid by the librarian, who had been a couple of years below her at St Anne's, then put her glass down on the table and started towards the door. The new choral scholars were in the middle of the room still, talking ravenously, their eyes shooting from one face to another. If you were painting this scene, Fay thought, they would be at the centre of it. She imagined them captured by Titian or Raphael, their faces radiant against the well-worn background of academic life.

'They must be proud of you, your adoptive parents,' she heard Marmion say as she passed: startled, she couldn't help glancing back. 'Are they coming up for your birthday?'

'No.' It was Stephen who answered. 'No, they can't leave my brother.'

On an impulse, Fay turned again.

'Excuse me,' she said. 'Did I hear that you have a birthday coming up? I wonder . . . Sometimes I invite some of the choir for supper. Would you all like to come? One evening this week?'

'That's very kind,' said Cressida. 'I'm not sure exactly –'

'I'm sure we'd love to,' said Marmion. She looked round at the others, and there was more nodding. 'It's Wednesday, Stephen's birthday.'

'Wednesday it is,' said Fay. She took a notebook and pen out of her handbag and wrote down the address, then tore it out and handed it to Marmion. 'Can you read that? It's not far. Shall we say eight o'clock?'

It was one of the features Fay liked least in herself that shyness – a shyness she would have hated to admit to – made her manner rather stilted, but she told herself, as she walked back through the college and across the river, that they wouldn't think anything of it, that young tribe. In their eyes she was a different species from them: certainly middle-aged, perhaps even old. If they found anything odd it would be her invitation, not its formality.

She felt a little giddy at her audacity – but it was only an invitation to supper, she told herself. Part of the giddiness was due to that wash of emotion as she'd watched them, imagining them in the centre of a Cinquecento canvas: almost awe, she thought, at their youthful certainty and vibrancy and beauty, and a desire to earn herself a taste of that vicarious joy. But slowly, slowly, she warned herself, already conscious of the agony of overstepping the mark, putting them on their guard. A deal of self-restraint would be necessary. She had never been good at love affairs, she thought wryly, even when it was more an idea than a person, than people, that had captivated her. Even when it was herself she really yearned for; her younger self, glimpsed in the radiance that surrounded that quintet.

The broad sweep of grass and trees along the Backs seemed magical this evening. It was a clear night, the sky dappled with stars and a heavy three-quarter moon hanging low over the dark bulk of the University Library. Sometimes Fay thought it would have been better to sell her parents' house and move elsewhere, somewhere without associations. But the associations were more good than bad, and she'd feared that there wasn't enough within her to populate an existence elsewhere: that Cambridge was too much part of her for it to be possible to separate herself from it. Here she could be someone – not Someone with a capital S, like Jeremy, but a person who passed muster. Here her knowledge and her accomplishments and her possessions added up to just enough. There was always a balance to be struck between claiming, wanting, attempting too much for herself and too little: either could be disastrous. But on that narrow distinction, she thought now, rested the equilibrium of her life.

Turning up Barton Road, she smiled at the tone of melodrama that had crept into her internal monologue. She sounded like a crank, she thought. She wasn't a crank. Those children wouldn't think she was a crank. She felt she knew them a little already. Marmion looked to her like a saint: not a Cinquecento saint but a modern-day one, with that wonderful smile and eager kindness. And Stephen: did she mind, Fay wondered, about the adoption? No; it was . . . In any case he was younger, only a little younger, but – she wouldn't think about that, anyway. She wouldn't confuse things in that way.

Cressida, she decided, was either cleverer than she looked, cleverer than girls of that kind usually were, or not quite as clever as she hoped. Either way, she would be anxious about her degree for the next three years, poor thing. Bill, the ex-chorister, had a Midlands inflection to his voice that made him sound solidly comfortable in his own skin – which he might be, of course, although if he was a musician his psyche might not be quite so straightforward. And Judith: she seemed to Fay the most mysterious. The most dangerous, if one wished to continue being melodramatic. She would take trouble to pay attention to Judith, to get to know her properly.

Back home, she put the kettle on and sliced bread and cheese for supper. It tasted good: the same kind of Cheddar she always bought, and the end of a loaf she'd started yesterday, but the whole somehow greater than the sum of its parts. She would have to include her mood and this evening's encounters in the sum, she thought. It felt good to ride this little billow of elation. To sense the possibility of happiness – or if not quite that, then at least something more than maintaining an even keel, a steady state, although that had been enough to aim for, enough to settle for, these last few years. It was three years, now, since she was last . . . She felt safe, now, from all that: safe enough to hope for something, a little something. But she must be careful not to let her expectations build too far.

September 2015

Judith

For several seconds there was silence in the room. If the solicitor hadn't had their full attention before, Judith thought, he certainly did now.

'She died *when*?' Cressida asked, her voice almost a squawk.

'The seventeenth of October 1995,' said Giles Unwin. 'She took some trouble to . . . The terms of her will included a requirement that the news of her death be concealed, as far as possible. I can see that that endeavour was successful, at least as far as the four of you are concerned.'

'Why?' asked Bill. 'Why did she want to keep her death a secret, and delay the bequest? She must have given an explanation.'

Unwin shook his head apologetically. 'The will was drawn up and witnessed by a partner in our London office, Mr Boreham, who died some years ago.'

'She must have known she was dying,' Judith said. Her mind was fizzing with inference and memory. Fay must have been ill, that summer: had they missed the signs of it?

'And she changed the will in our favour just before she died?' Cressida asked.

'No previous wills survive,' said Unwin, 'but I understand that this was the first to name you all.'

'What about Marmion?' asked Cressida. 'Does her name – was she included too? Marmion Hayter?'

Unwin shook his head again. 'No, just the four of you.'

'Marmion was dead by the fifteenth of October,' Stephen said. He hadn't spoken before, and they all turned to look at him now as though his voice had greater authority than the rest. 'Fay must have known that Marmion was dead when she made the will. I wonder if that . . . I suppose we'll never know whether that affected her decision.'

'Are we the only legatees?' Judith asked. 'What about the rest of her estate?'

'The major part of the estate was left to the four of you,' Unwin said, 'after a bequest to St Anne's College, Cambridge.'

Of course, Judith thought. Not the scouts or the Church: St Anne's.

'And what conditions were attached?' she asked. 'I assume there was a condition precedent?'

'Indeed,' said Unwin. 'The more unusual elements of the condition precedent have already been discharged. That is to say: that the property be held in trust for twenty years, and the terms of the will not be disclosed during that period. Also that this house, High Scarp, be maintained in the same condition in the interim, and that the four legatees be required to spend a weekend in occupation before the bequest took effect.'

'And the rest of the condition precedent?' asked Bill. 'Is there more?'

Unwin turned to look at him.

'I know that you are a solicitor, Mr Devenish,' he said, 'and that Ms Malik is a barrister. You can of course read the will for yourselves.'

'For the lay people among us,' said Stephen, his voice unfamiliarly terse, 'a summary would be helpful.'

'You are required to keep the house, High Scarp, for a minimum of five years,' Unwin said. 'Ample funds are available for its upkeep. You are required to spend a weekend here, together, every year during that period. After that, you are free to dispose of the property as you wish.'

'That's all?' said Bill.

'All?' said Judith. 'It sounds . . .'

A weekend here, with Bill, with all of them, every year, she was thinking. Fay couldn't have had any idea what that would mean.

'I don't understand about the twenty years,' said Cressida, 'but otherwise it's extraordinarily generous of Fay, don't you think? Extraordinarily.'

'Is there nothing more?' Stephen asked. 'No – letter for us? No further explanation?'

'Nothing of any substance,' said Unwin. 'The rest is merely detail.'

'Lapsang souchong,' said Judith.

'I beg your pardon?'

'Maintained in the same condition down to the contents of the kitchen cupboards,' Judith said. 'The brand of soap in the bathroom.'

'Miss McArthur's wishes were closely followed.' Unwin permitted himself a self-satisfied smile.

'Clearly.' Judith felt slightly sick now. It felt very strange, all this. The terms of the will had proved unexpectedly simple, but its impact was more devastating than she could have imagined. She had no idea, no sense at all whether Fay's intentions had been benign or malevolent: after all this time it was impossible to deduce what had been in her mind, nor how she'd imagined this bequest affecting them all. And in the face of this discombobulating fact everything else felt less clear – as though her mind was a pool which had just settled, only for something large and heavy to drop into it, throwing up a swirl of weed and sediment to cloud her view again.

It seemed to her now that they had all been taken in, last night, by the madrigal singing and the current of nostalgia that had flowed through that hour. She'd been taken in, anyway: perhaps the others had kept their heads. How funny that they'd always seen her as the hard-headed one, the hard-hitting one. That thought made her smile briefly, and Bill, catching her eye across the table, began to smile too.

Oh Bill, she thought, speared by a sharp pang of desire and regret. He was right that they had passed up – that they had denied themselves – what, though? Could it ever have been an uncomplicated happiness? Was there such a thing?

She knew the compromises and concessions in the strange life she had concocted for herself did her no good. It was almost unbearably tempting to believe that she and Bill might have a second chance now of something better, but she didn't believe in happy-ever-after, or in people getting what they deserved. Not even in them getting what they hoped for, or worked for, or snatched back from the ruthless grasp of life – and she had never hoped, never worked, hard enough. The most terrifying thing was that she hardly believed in her own life any more; in the conviction she had sustained that everything was essentially all right. Or if not that, that her actions, her motives, could be traced back to a right intention.

As Giles Unwin gathered together the papers that provided the final account of Fay's life, a great depth of inconsolability yawned open inside Judith. It was as though she had imagined all this time that she was living her life as proof of something, and she had forgotten long ago what she needed to prove, or to whom. She seemed, now, to have been living utterly without point or purpose.

March 1995

Fay

'Go home and think about it,' the Consultant said. 'Don't make a decision now. Is there someone you can talk it over with?'

'Yes,' Fay said. She'd forgotten this doctor's name: that seemed a bad sign, but presumably it was shock that did that. She leant forward slightly, trying to see his name badge, but it was hidden by his lapel.

He looked at her, concerned. He was a big man: a rugby player, perhaps, in his day. She didn't like to think of those hands inside her head.

'Do you want to ask anything else now?'

'Your name,' she said. 'I've forgotten your name.'

He smiled briefly, not quite managing to conceal a flicker of something that might have been distress, but was probably impatience.

'Reynolds,' he said. 'Mr Reynolds. Jim.'

Fay nodded.

'We'll book you into my clinic on Friday,' he said. 'We can talk about it again then. OK?'

'Yes,' said Fay. But she knew already what her decision was. Not surgery. The maths didn't mean very much to her – so many per cent chance of this or that – but she had grasped the bottom line: whichever way you looked at it, the news was bad. There was little hope that an operation would improve things, and a substantial risk that it would make things worse. Surgery was what they offered because there wasn't anything else. Radiotherapy wasn't indicated, the Consultant (she'd forgotten his name again) had said, in this particular case. In the case of her particular brain tumour.

As she drove home, the world swam a little – not the world she was driving through, but the one in her head. What she'd been told seemed highly implausible, and the fact that she was being advised to do nothing about it confirmed the impression that it was something she didn't really need to think about. The headaches weren't so very bad, and now she knew there was nothing to be done about them, she could take whatever painkillers she liked. Everything would be better when she got home; when she got back to normal.

When the bell rang at eight, she was taken by surprise. On the doorstep the five of them stood, cheerful, expectant. Bill held out two bottles of wine.

'Are we early?' he asked.

'No.' She mustn't let them see that she'd forgotten they were coming. 'No, of course not. I thought we'd go out tonight. I thought I'd take you out.'

She drove them to the Chequers at Comberton. By now she felt a little shaky, but they didn't seem to notice. They were engaged in an argument, passionate but humorous, about punk rock, which they seemed to regard as a historical phenomenon. They had always been good at entertaining themselves, her little coterie. And at entertaining her, of course. They had no idea, she thought, how much difference they had made to her: that she wanted to live, now, more than she had for years. There was a strange sort of whistling in her head, like a tap running or a radio that wasn't picking up a signal, but if she focused hard on what they were saying she could ignore it. She ordered fish and chips – she hadn't had fish and chips for donkey's years – and ate the whole plateful.

'It's all right for you,' Judith was saying, the next time Fay tuned into their conversation. 'You've only got three exams, if you don't count that wishy-washy practical stuff, and they're over by the first week of June.'

'The twenty-eighth of May, actually,' said Marmion.

'I've got nine,' said Judith. 'Nine. And one of them is constitutional law. I rest my case.'

Bill put an arm around Marmion. 'Don't rest it on Marmion,' he said.

'I've got a proposition for you all,' Fay said, when there was a lull in the conversation. 'Would you like to come up to my house in the Lake District in June? After Finals?'

They looked at her, eyes wide.

'After Finals and before graduation,' she said. 'There's a little music festival in the village. You could sing.'

'After May Week, do you mean?' asked Marmion, a little anxiously.

'Yes,' said Fay. 'I'll check the dates, but I'm sure it's after May Week. You can't miss that.'

'I didn't know you had a house in the Lake District,' said Stephen.

Fay looked at him: dear Stephen, she thought. That sombreness, that diffidence. They were all so different; it was a wonder they got on so well. She had no idea how she was going to manage without them, next year. And then it occurred to her that she might not have to. She might not have to manage anything, next year.

'You'll like it there,' she said. 'I hope you'll like it.'

On Friday she sat in Mr Reynolds's office again. They had rung with an appointment, so eager to make sure the time was convenient that it had seemed churlish not to accept.

'Right,' he said, when she told him. 'If you're sure you're happy with that decision.'

'Yes,' she said. She suspected that he liked the patients who said yes to surgery better. What was the point of being a brain surgeon, after all, if everyone said no?

He nodded for a while, and then he shut her notes and smiled at her.

'Dr Oblonski will look after you, then,' he said. 'He's the best person to manage things from here.'

Dr Oblonski was the opposite of Mr Reynolds: a small man, very bald, who reminded Fay somehow of a hedgehog. No prickles, though. It was his face, small and pointed, that accounted for the resemblance.

Dr Oblonski asked her a lot of questions she'd answered already, and others she hadn't.

'You have a son, Mrs McArthur?' he asked.

'Miss,' said Fay.

'I apologise.'

He waited.

'Yes,' said Fay. 'Yes and no. I had a son, but he was adopted.'

Did he really need to ask all this? she wondered. Was some kind of psychological therapy required, perhaps, in this sort of case? But if he knew she had a son, then it must be recorded in her notes. Everything must be recorded in her notes.

'You were unwell, after he was born.'

'Yes,' said Fay.

'But there have been no – recent recurrences?'

'Of what?' Fay asked. 'Of pregnancy, or . . .'

Dr Oblonski made a little sound that might have been a laugh. A hedgehog laugh, Fay thought.

'There have been no recent recurrences,' she said. 'I have been quite well for the last few years. Quite well.'

Dr Oblonski prescribed steroids and said he would see Fay in six weeks. Perhaps it was the steroids, perhaps it was the six weeks' respite, but after that the world slid back into focus and the radio interference stopped. When she went back after Easter he said she looked well and she told him she felt fine, absolutely fine. She went to evensong at St Anne's that evening and the choir sang 'God Be in My Head', which struck her as a nice piece of divine wit. She sat in the stalls in the half-dark with her eyes shut and thought, everything is all right now.

It was the things other people did that had made her unwell; that was something she held onto. People leaving or dying or not coming back when she hoped, hoped that they might. The last time . . . She couldn't blame him, her son. She'd been foolish, imagining he would come and find her, but somehow she had allowed herself to believe it. She had allowed herself to count down the years and then the months and weeks until he was eighteen, and then the days, weeks, months afterwards, until she hadn't been able to bear it any longer. But she didn't blame him. He didn't know how much she'd missed him. And she'd learned to live without him, after that. She'd done what they told her, tried not to think of him. And she was quite well now. She felt better than she had for a long time, and the headaches had stopped. *My spirit hath rejoiced in God my saviour*, the choir sang, and she rejoiced with them. With Marmion and Bill and Judith and Stephen and Cressida, her dear friends.

But a couple of weeks later she felt sick one morning, and again the next, just as she had when she was pregnant. She rang her GP, who sent her back to Dr Oblonski.

'Things will go up and down,' he said, in the same tone of voice in which he'd said how well she looked, a fortnight before.

'More down than up, I suppose,' said Fay. It seemed better for her to take the pessimistic line and for him to reassure her.

'In the long term, yes. But there will be ups. And we can do something about the downs.'

'What is the long term?' Fay asked. 'How long, I mean?'

For the first time Dr Oblonski didn't meet her eyes. 'It's hard to say,' he said. 'My advice is to concentrate on the ups. You seem to be good at that.'

That, Fay thought, was the nicest thing any doctor had ever said to her, even if it did skirt away from an answer.

'You live alone?' Dr Oblonski asked now.

Fay nodded.

'Do you have . . . friends? People around you?'

'Yes.'

He looked a little troubled, but he didn't press the point.

'Are the headaches under control?' he asked.

'Yes.'

'I will give you something for the nausea. Have you had any drowsiness? Dizziness? Blackouts?'

Fay shook her head. He looked at her notes for a few moments.

'For the moment I see no reason why you shouldn't drive,' he said. 'But perhaps not long distances, hmm? Don't push yourself too hard.'

'No,' said Fay.

It wasn't a long distance to High Scarp, she thought.

September 2015
Cressida

They were all torn, Cressida thought, between wanting the lawyer to leave now and wanting him to stay. They needed to talk without the constraint of his presence, but while he sat at the table, papers spread before him, they were each safe with their own emotions.

Her own abiding feeling was one of relief: relief and gratitude, and a touch of guilt because she had imputed to Fay motives that were less straightforward and less generous-minded than now seemed fair. There was bewilderment too, of course – although certain things made more sense, now, than they had before. She could still remember vividly that last encounter with Fay on her doorstep, when she had presumably had not flu but – whatever had killed her, Cressida thought, with a pang of retrospective distress. And of course Fay hadn't shunned her out of boredom or disapproval or for any other reason. Fay hadn't been there the next time she had called because she'd been dead by then.

'I shall leave four copies of the will,' Giles Unwin said. 'Please let me know if you have any questions. When we have written confirmation from each of you that you accept the terms of the bequest, we can proceed.'

'What happens if not all of us accept?' Cressida asked.

'I'm afraid it's necessary for all four of you to do so,' said Unwin. 'Should that not be the case, the entirety of the estate passes to St Anne's College.'

'What was Fay's connection to St Anne's?' Stephen asked. 'Do you know?'

'I understand that her cousin was Master of the college at the time of her death,' said Unwin. 'I understand that he was her only living relative.'

'The Master?' Stephen frowned. 'Hardwick?'

Unwin flicked through the sheets in his file. 'Harding,' he said. 'Professor Jeremy Harding. Professor Harding died last year, but the bequest is to the college, not to him personally.'

'But he was new that year,' said Stephen. 'He arrived at the same time as us, and Fay had been associated with St Anne's before that.' He looked out of sorts, Cressida thought. She wondered whether there were legal details that worried him.

'We're curious, that's all,' Bill said. 'It's all very curious.'

'Indeed.' Unwin continued to look through the file, but Cressida had the impression that he was thinking rather than reading. Eventually he looked up, and spoke with what seemed intended to be a note of finality. 'Miss McArthur had been an undergraduate at St Anne's for a period of time,' he said.

'A period of time?'

'Her studies were interrupted, I understand.' Unwin smiled.

'By what?' asked Stephen.

'I cannot enlighten you on that point,' said Unwin. 'It seems her loyalty to the college was not affected.'

'And you have no idea why the bequest was – what the twenty-year delay was for?' asked Stephen.

Unwin met Stephen's eyes, and held his gaze for a moment. Then he said, 'I cannot enlighten you on that point either, I fear.'

'And there are no further details in the papers you're leaving for us?'

'No.' The lawyer got to his feet now, and the rest of them followed suit. Stephen's face was moving, as though there were other questions he wanted to ask. What was he getting at? Cressida wondered. Did he know something the rest of them didn't, or was he just curious? Presumably they would never know any more about Fay now. Presumably she hadn't wanted them to.

'Thank you,' said Bill, holding out a hand across the table. 'It's clearly been an unusual instruction, this.'

'Very unusual,' said Unwin. 'But interesting. More interesting than a run-of-the-mill probate case, as you can no doubt attest, Mr Devenish.'

Cressida went with Bill to see the lawyer out, and when they came back, Stephen was bending over the turntable that stood on a shelf in the corner. There was a rustle and a series of clicks and cracks, and then an orchestra filled the room, followed by a woman's voice. 'O Thou That Tellest Good Tidings to Zion', thought Cressida: that was appropriate, if a little corny, especially for Stephen.

'Kathleen Ferrier,' he said, as he straightened up.

'It still works, then,' said Bill.

'Maintained in the same condition,' said Judith, with an unattractive edge to her voice. 'We should have guessed, you know. Nothing new, nothing changed, everything replaced like for like. No wine younger than 1994 in the cellar: why didn't that strike us, Stephen?'

'We didn't make an exhaustive survey of the wine stocks,' said Stephen.

He was standing by the mantelpiece now, listening to Kathleen Ferrier singing with that wobble that always sounded so heartfelt. Cressida tried to remember whether Fay had played them this record. She felt a quickening of her pulse at the thought that Fay's will tied them all to each other – tied her to Stephen. A small voice in her head told her that her interest in him was hopeless, that it had always been hopeless, but another voice said *never say die*, and she couldn't but admire its spirit. If nothing else, there would be the prospect of seeing him again next year. Assuming they all . . . She glanced at Isabel, who was still sitting where she'd installed herself when Giles Unwin arrived. She had the impression that Isabel liked High Scarp, but she might not like being forced into close association with the rest of them. And Judith was a concern. Stephen, too: he had least need of the bequest, at least in material terms.

Cressida felt suddenly despondent. It all seemed less promising than it had at first sight. Outside Dickens novels, wills weren't supposed to be so convoluted, nor to require so much of the beneficiaries. Clearly Fay had been ill, but wasn't it the lawyer's job to make sure the provisions were sensible?

Bill was leaning over the table, reading the will.

'What do you think, Bill?' Cressida asked.

'It's not complicated,' he said. 'Very simply written, in fact.'

'I meant more the motivation behind it. The – delay. Why make us wait twenty years?'

'That's anyone's guess,' said Bill. 'But if she was ill . . .'

'I don't know if it makes it better to write it off to insanity or to conclude that she wanted to teach us a lesson,' said Judith, 'but either way it's spooky to think that she died with us on her mind.'

She looked at Bill, and then at Cressida, and Cressida blushed. *She died with our behaviour on her mind*, Judith seemed to imply – and to remind Cressida that she, too, had been critical of that.

Judith had been moving around the room in a fidgety manner, picking things up and putting them down again – ornaments, books, the candlesticks on top of the piano. She stopped now, and lifted a glass vase off the mantelpiece. It was heavy, with a wide belly and a thick lip, slightly stained with age. 'I'd like this to be the first thing to go,' she said, 'if we're spared a Miss Havisham clause.'

Bill looked up from the papers on the table. 'I think we are,' he said. 'Good.'

'But only if we all sign on the dotted line.'

Judith brandished the vase in the air. 'Anyone object?'

There was another silence then, in which Cressida had no idea what anyone else was thinking; no idea at all what Judith was going to do next. She looked for a moment bizarrely like the Statue of Liberty, standing in the middle of the room with the vase held aloft in a gesture of defiance or affirmation, or perhaps of ridicule. Bill stared at her, then shook his head. Stephen frowned, murmuring something that Cressida couldn't hear.

'All right,' said Judith. She strode over to the open window and hurled the vase out onto the terrace. There was silence again inside the room as the sound of glass shattering, scattering, skittering on stone echoed back through the window.

'*Mazel tov*,' said Stephen, with a snorting laugh that seemed to encompass both admiration and reproof.

Turning back towards them, Judith smiled, and in that moment Cressida could see the old Judith, the hopeful, confident, resourceful, daring Judith, in her face. Stephen was smiling too, and as she caught his eye she felt hope flare inside her.

'Good,' she said. 'That's settled, then.'

They should open a bottle of champagne now, she thought, or perhaps sing again, or . . . But even as the moment of familiarity and togetherness blazed, she could feel it ebbing away. Like a match struck in an airless room, she thought. None of them knew what this was going to mean: sharing High Scarp, staying in touch. It didn't come with any guarantees.

'Would anyone like a cup of tea?' she asked.

But they were all shaking their heads.

'Later, perhaps,' Stephen said. 'I really need to get to my email.' His smile made the statement less convincing.

'I'm going down to the shop,' Judith announced. 'I feel an over-whelming need for a cigarette.'

For a moment Cressida thought Bill might make an excuse to follow, but instead he nodded towards the table where the lawyer's documents were lying. 'I might have a proper look at the will,' he said. 'No time like the present.'

But Isabel smiled at Cressida. 'I'll have some tea,' she said. 'We could take it outside.'

*

The terrace was very damp, but Isabel brought out two cushions to put on the ancient wooden chairs. Cressida set the tea tray down on the table. She wasn't sure whether this was a gesture of kindness on Isabel's part, or a request for kindness from her. Or perhaps for information. As she poured the tea, she looked at Isabel out of the corner of her eye, detecting a watchful, focused look that belied her casual manner.

'Have you ever been married?' Isabel asked.

'No.' A roundabout route, Cressida thought. A few home truths; an explanation of her position.

'Never too late, I suppose, if you . . .'

Cressida didn't reply. The tea steamed, fragrant, in her hand. She'd never really liked lapsang, but the smell was powerfully evocative.

'It's odd, being the outsider among you,' Isabel said now. 'I'm not sure how much –'

Cressida put her cup down. 'Isabel,' she said, 'if you're wanting to –'

'My intuition isn't always right,' Isabel said, in a sudden rush, 'but you've been very kind to me, this weekend, and I'd like to . . .' She paused. Cressida watched her, puzzled. Was this about the bequest, then? she wondered. About how the house would be managed?

'Bill said something about you and Stephen,' Isabel went on. 'About you liking Stephen. And I thought – as a friend, I thought I ought to tell you that I'm almost certain, I'm afraid, that he's gay.'

Cressida stared at her. *How dare you*, she wanted to say. *He can't possibly be. What the hell do you know?* But she felt too numb to speak. Too angry.

'I see,' she managed eventually.

'I know it's none of my business,' Isabel said. 'Perhaps I shouldn't have said anything, but I thought –'

She broke off, looking anguished. Not anguished enough, Cressida thought, but the rising tide of fury in her chest wasn't directed just at Isabel. Isabel was right. Of course she was bloody right. Right that

Stephen would never have her, anyway, whatever the reason. And what the fuck did it matter, in that case?

'I'm not sure if the others realise, even,' said Isabel. 'He's –'

At that moment Bill appeared at the back door, and Cressida sprang to her feet. She wasn't sure how much he'd heard, but the idea of Bill and Isabel discussing this, turning over her private hopes, was more than she could bear. They might have their difficulties, but they were a pair, and that set them apart from her. Pairs reminded her of what she had never had; what she had lost, what she might never have now. Michael, who had been a fantasy, an illusion, for so many years. Heming, who had written her a letter of flawless Scandinavian courtesy from Trondheim, but had been a fantasy of a different kind and was best left as such. And Stephen: another illusion. She was such a fool. She'd put too much trust in poetry, all these years.

'I might . . .' she began. 'I rather feel like a walk, while the rain holds off.'

June 1995

Fay

Something was up, Fay thought at breakfast. This was their last day at High Scarp, and she badly wanted everything to be well, to end well, but a shadow of doubt and secrecy hung in the air this morning. Looking round at the five of them, she wondered whether there had been a row – and then, with a plunge of dismay, whether they had guessed that she was ill. She'd done her best to conceal the headaches, the dizziness, the blank moments, but if they'd been observant . . .

She knew she ought to tell them the truth, but there was nothing they could do, nothing anyone could do, and she so much preferred their blithe ignorance to their sympathy. All she wanted was the last measure of enjoyment from this trip. It had been an effort, a real effort at times, but it had been exactly what she'd hoped, every detail as she'd imagined it: the singing, the walks, the meals on the terrace, the games by the fire – as if it were part of a long tradition that would carry on unchanged in the years ahead. She liked that idea. She had a notion, half formed, that gave her fierce consolation when she lay awake in the middle of the night. But just now, sitting around the breakfast table, thinking about the future, the years in store for the five of them, was horribly painful. Thinking about all the things she wouldn't do again.

Stephen started gathering up the plates, and the clatter of crockery caused a jab of pain in Fay's head. This was new, this sensitivity to noise. A distressing new symptom: even some of the music, these last few days, had caused her pain. She had a suspicion that things were moving faster than she'd expected inside her head. Perhaps she wouldn't come back to High Scarp again. She should have come more often, after her parents died. She felt another wash of sorrow, not just for the future but for the past: for the losses unaccounted for and the possibilities unexplored.

In the three months since her diagnosis she had never cried, but she could feel a pricking heat in her eyes now that filled her with alarm. She'd never been a crier. Perhaps that hadn't been good for her, but she was damned if she was going to succumb now. She turned her gaze deliberately towards the window. It was a beautiful morning, the sky streaked with lambswool clouds and the tops sharp and vivid. She could see St Sunday, Fairfield, Hartsop Dodd, Nag's Pike: she'd climbed each of them, once upon a time. Forced up them, the first time, by her father, but she'd tackled most of them again later under her own steam. Nag's Pike only once, though: she remembered that walk, the storm that had brewed up, the perilous descent. That had been living. Not that she'd thought so at the time.

'What time are we leaving?' Cressida asked.

Feeling another pulse of pain, Fay turned to look at her.

'Leaving?' she asked.

'For Cambridge.'

Fay pushed back her chair and stood up. She must get some pain-killers, she thought. But then an idea slid into her head: a way to defy her illness as well as to extend their stay in the dale for another few hours. A mad, marvellous idea.

'I thought we'd climb Nag's Pike this morning,' she said.

'Nag's Pike?' Cressida looked horrified. 'This morning? I thought we were going back to Cambridge.'

'There's no point spending the whole day in the car,' Fay said. She put a hand to her forehead to steady her skull. 'We always climb Nag's Pike with new visitors. It's a wonderful walk.'

'It looks rather steep,' said Marmion.

'You've had a few warm-ups,' said Fay. That was hardly true, but if she could do it, they certainly could. They would thank her when they got to the top. Her last gift to them, she thought, and she managed a smile. 'Don't worry. You'll be fine.'

She had taken them the wrong way, Fay knew. She should have brought a map. That was the first rule: always bring a map, even if you know the route well – and she didn't know this route well. They had come through a bog, encountered a barbed-wire fence, scrambled their way over loose scree. None of them except Bill had proper walking boots, and his looked too new to be comfortable. This grand idea of hers had proved more mad than marvellous, but she certainly wasn't going to give up, and nor were they. Once or twice Bill had suggested turning back, but she'd held fast. And now, she thought with a burst of exultation, they were on a path, a rather narrow path winding round the side of the steep slope, but one that would surely lead them to the summit.

The great thing, Fay thought, was that she felt so well. She'd taken a double dose of painkillers before they left, and an extra anti-emetic, and a couple of steroids for good measure, and the cocktail had definitely made her feel better. The fresh air, too. The exercise. *Don't push yourself too hard*, she heard Dr Oblonski saying. What did he know? Pushing herself seemed to be exactly the right thing to do. That slight light-headedness was surely no greater than you'd expect, the result of exertion and ascent.

Far below, the valley glistened in the sunlight. Fay could see three or four farms, each squat and grey and compact, and the silver slug-trail of the river. She felt a sense of triumph that wasn't just about conquering the tumour, dispelling her symptoms, but about conquering Nag's Pike, too. She'd always been afraid of it, but here they were almost at the top. The sun was shining and all was right with the world.

The group had strung itself out along the path, each of them finding their own pace. Fay found herself walking with Stephen, neither of them speaking much, but his proximity gave her pleasure. She'd always been especially fond of Stephen. It wasn't simply the fact that he was adopted, although that – she'd hugged that to her, sometimes, hoping that her boy, her precious lost boy, was as happy and as promising as Stephen. But more than that, she'd recognised in him something of herself: that sense of not belonging, of secrets fiercely kept, questions unanswered, hopes barely acknowledged. He stopped now to take a bottle of water out of his backpack and offered it to her.

'I don't know quite how I got to carry this all the way,' he said. 'I should have palmed it off on Bill when we stopped.'

'He can carry it down again,' said Fay, handing the bottle back. 'Thank you; that was a good idea.'

While Stephen drank she gazed out at the expanse of air between here and the next peak – the playground of falcons. Her father had taught her to recognise the different species that frequented the dale: the larger size of the peregrine, the smoother flight of the merlin, the effortless hovering of the kestrel. They had stood for hours, his hand on her shoulder. Fay felt an urge now to pass on this knowledge to Stephen; to all of them. She loved them all, she thought suddenly. She loved them almost too much to bear. Marmion with her wide eyes and Judith with her sharp tongue, Cressida who had turned out to be cleverer than she could have guessed and Bill who could sing anything, anything you put in front of him. Shining lights, all of them, but she couldn't feel easy about them; couldn't help wishing there was more she could do for them. There wasn't much time left, but today she would like to point out a silhouette dark against the sun, so that they could stand together and watch as it crested the valley, riding on the vectors of the wind. So that they would remember her whenever they saw a falcon in flight. But there were none around today; nothing but emptiness to fill the heat of the day.

'Ready?' Stephen asked.

'Yes.' Fay pushed away the image of wings spread, spirits soaring. Perhaps on the way down, she thought. Perhaps there would be a raptor to point out then. 'Yes, let's go on.'

She was glad now that there wasn't far to go. She felt weary all of a sudden, her legs reluctant to move without a conscious effort. Soon, she was sure, they would see the little cairn that marked the summit. She imagined them all standing round it, posing for a photograph, beaming with pleasure at their achievement.

'Steady,' said Stephen, as she stumbled over a loose stone, and she smiled to conceal the jab of pain in her head.

After a few more yards they came round a large boulder that blocked the path ahead from view – and there, taking advantage of its shelter, was a couple pressed together in a frantic embrace.

For a second Fay stared. Bill and Judith. Judith and Bill, clasped together like lovers. She just had time to register the shock of seeing them, and to hear her voice calling out in surprise and protest, and then the image dissolved, and – her mind operating, it seemed, in some kind of slow motion – she understood that they had lost their footing and slipped, that Judith was falling, falling, falling.

Standing over the calamitous scene, Fay could feel her brain condensing, focusing in on one thing. She was in charge; it was her responsibility to act. It was necessary to put everything else aside – the guilt and horror and disbelief, the fear for Judith's life, the fierce throbbing that had started up in her head – and plot a course through the next minute, the next hour. Judith was alive, but unconscious. They couldn't afford to wait and see whether she came round. There were other things happening, a thread of violent distress that had nothing to do with Judith's condition, but she must keep all that out of her mind for now.

'I'll go for help,' she said. 'Someone needs to come with me.'

'I'll come,' said Cressida. She looked resolute: the right expression, Fay thought.

'They'll send a helicopter,' Fay said. 'When you hear it, wave something. Make sure it sees you.'

'I could come too,' Stephen offered, but Fay glanced at Bill and at Marmion and shook her head. For a moment her eyes held Marmion's, and in them she read both shock and accusation. It was her fault, she thought: her fault that Judith had fallen, that Marmion had discovered . . . But again she wrenched her gaze, her focus, back to what must be done.

'We'll be as quick as we can,' she said.

She and Cressida set off at double the pace they had managed before.

'Careful,' she said, as Cressida stumbled. 'We don't want another accident.'

She had an idea where the closest farm was, a remnant of memory she wasn't sure she could trust. But what was she to trust, otherwise?

'Let's cut down here,' she said, when they reached a dry-stone wall. 'Can you manage?'

'Of course.' Cressida's face was scarlet: hers must be too, Fay thought.

Miraculously, serendipitously, the wall ran straight down to a farmhouse half hidden in a fold of the landscape. Fay had lost all sense of time by now, but surely they had been quicker than anyone could have expected. They ran across the last field, through the farmyard and up to the front door. An old, old man opened it, and the story poured out of them.

'There's been an accident, up on the fell. We need to use the phone. Someone's injured and we need to call for help.'

September 2015
Stephen

Through the window, Stephen could see Bill and Isabel wandering in the garden, stopping now and then to inspect a plant. Taking an inventory, he thought. This was certainly the moment for that, for all of them.

It seemed to him that although they'd dispersed after the lawyer left, moving off to separate rooms and separate pursuits, they were connected now – reconnected – in a way they hadn't been earlier. They'd all been drawn back within the compass of Fay's gravitational pull – or perhaps their own. Perhaps what they shared had finally come to bear its full weight.

He examined that idea for a moment. Maybe it was no more than the sense of connection you sometimes had with the rest of the audience at the end of a play – or an opera, indeed. The Valkyries had done something similar for him, hadn't they? But this was the beginning, not the end, he thought. When they all left this evening, or tomorrow morning, it wouldn't be to part from strangers they had no expectation of seeing again. They would have to communicate, to negotiate. They would have to meet, every year.

It would be odd to share something as solid as a house with other people. He and Suky had only managed a rented flat, and since then – since then he had been very careful what he shared with anyone. Which of them would take the lead? he wondered. He could imagine Isabel directing things rather effectively from behind the scenes. She and Bill lived the closest; presumably they were most likely to use the place. And Cressida, of course: Cressida might bring study groups up here for earnest weekends of poetry.

And as for Judith, who knew? He still wasn't sure what to make of that impulsive gesture half an hour before: whether it was a glimpse of suppressed passion or the reckless performance of a toddler confused by its surroundings. It had seemed to indicate a willingness to throw in her lot with the rest of them, though, and he had found it persuasive in a way that histrionic scenes rarely were. He'd been surprised that he was still capable of making decisions on emotional grounds, of assenting without a proper weighing of pros and cons. No doubt he'd resort, as he often did, to substituting his credit card for his time, making a semi-detached commitment to this joint venture – but would it be like that? he wondered now. Would it be possible to remain at one remove?

He ought to be a little closer now to knowing what it really meant, all of this. Meeting the others again, revisiting the past, reopening questions he'd closed off a long time ago. When he'd thought about them all, over the years – and God knows he hadn't done it very often – there had occasionally been a brief, sharp pang of yearning, as though they were his family: another family he'd turned his back on, or who had turned their backs on him. The same yearning he got listening to Kathleen Ferrier, and for no more rational a reason. He had always . . . This was absurd, he knew, but he had a memory, perhaps a faux-memory, of her voice, that particular aria, from his very early life, and there had been no records like that in Surbiton. Finding it here, in the shelf beside the turntable, immediately after Giles Unwin's departure, had felt like an intervention of providence, though perhaps it was merely an example of divine irony.

He'd wanted Fay's will to explain things, he admitted. He'd wanted a denouement. Instead there was only further mystery, in the shape of that twenty-year delay – and certainly no mention of Fay having a child. Stephen had to accept that that idea had been a fantasy, wishing into existence a connection between him and Fay, however tenuous: she a lost mother, he a lost son.

It would be easy to allow himself to feel lost again now. Let down again. It would be easy to feel angry at the sense that they were being played with from a safe distance, from twenty years in the past. But couldn't it also be read, this bequest, as an attempt to make them into a family? Fay's family, left behind to keep High Scarp going?

He almost laughed, then, at his perversity. His sentimentality, buried so deep he could almost pretend it wasn't there. Foolishness, he told himself. Nostalgia. He flipped open his laptop then and started scanning through the ranks of messages in his inbox. Here was reality, he told himself: a hundred and twenty new emails on a Sunday afternoon. A hundred and twenty decisions, suggestions, opportunities. This was what he was good at, what gave his life direction and purpose.

When Cressida came into the room twenty minutes later he was deeply engrossed, drafting a memo about the proposed expansion of an infrastructure project in China. He registered a dash of irritation at being interrupted, but after a moment's reluctance, a moment's hesitation, he shut the lid of the computer and smiled.

'Good walk?' he asked.

'Lovely. You should have come.'

Cressida looked better for the fresh air, her cheeks pink and her hair dishevelled in a way that made its artificial colour less apparent.

'I should,' he said. 'I've been dealing with email.'

She leant against the back of a chair, but made no move to sit down. 'I can't quite imagine you as a mogul,' she said. 'Is that what you are?'

Stephen laughed. 'That's one word for it, I suppose.'

'I didn't mean – I'm sure you're very good at it. It must be exciting, your life.'

'Not as exciting as it sounds, perhaps.' Stephen hesitated. 'It's . . . I don't know. What's life for? How do you know if you're any good at it?'

Listen to him, he thought: he never spoke like this. It was the effect of that mawkish introspection earlier – and of Cressida's questions;

her cool gaze. She'd always made him feel as though he ought to be somebody slightly different. Looking at her now, he recognised something else that made him uneasy: an expression he'd seen too often recently on other faces. Women of forty, seeing him as a last chance. He wouldn't group Cressida with them, but . . . Cressida was the only woman he'd ever slept with, he reminded himself, apart from Suky. So long ago that the memory was barely a shadow, but he was sure she hadn't forgotten. Poor Cressida: he was sure she hadn't forgotten how callously he'd treated her afterwards, either.

'It's been good to see you again, Cressida,' he said, warmth and reason carefully titrated in his voice. 'I can just imagine you as the Professor of Poetry.'

'I'm certainly not that.' She looked affronted: that was unexpected. She stared out of the window for a moment, then turned to look at him.

'What you said just now – about what it means to be good at life. That's something . . . It's the question for all of us, isn't it? We've all done well enough, but none of us . . . Well, I can't speak for you.'

She frowned. The luminosity the walk had given her skin had faded again, and Stephen felt a sudden compassion for her. Would it be so very wrong, he wondered, to offer what he could see she wanted? Might it even . . . He could recall the reasons for marrying Suky more clearly, just now, than the reasons for separating, although of course – but a *mariage blanc*, he thought. Would that be enough for Cressida? Would it give him . . .? And then, like the flick of a switch in his head, reason returned. No. No, no. What had he been thinking? He felt dizzy for a moment at the thought of the precipice so narrowly avoided. Cressida's eyes were on his face still, and he had the impression that she had followed, had understood, every nuance of his train of thought. She looked steadily at him for a moment longer, and then she smiled: a smile that contained both sadness and prudence and a flicker of amusement.

'I don't have any chance with you, do I, Stephen?' she said.

'I'm very much afraid you don't,' he said. 'Not that it's – anything personal. A general preference rather than an individual one.'

Cressida nodded. She looked suddenly younger, he thought. 'I rather wish I'd known that twenty years ago,' she said. 'It would have made life simpler. But there it is.'

She made a little movement, a little sound that could have been a laugh or a sob, and he felt it echoing inside him, finding similar empty spaces in his head, his chest, and illuminating them for a moment before it died away.

Cressida turned back to the window, where the great panorama of the valley was laid out, Nag's Pike sharp and clear in the centre of it.

'But you'll sign the document?' she asked. 'You'll come back next year?'

'Yes,' he said. 'I'll come back.'

'Good.' Her shoulders dropped; a visible discharge of tension. 'Good. I'm very glad.'

'Might you come up here before then?' he asked. 'In the Christmas vacation, perhaps, if everything has gone through by then?'

'Possibly.' She swung back to look at him, and he had the impression that she was seeing him clearly for the first time; seeing other things, too, perhaps. There was an animation in her face now that he hadn't seen for a long time, a glimmer of possibility that lent grace to her features. 'But I might go to Norway,' she said.

'A conference?'

'No.' She smiled. 'Just a holiday. And to look up a friend.'

Left alone again, Stephen felt deflated. That wasn't what he should feel, when the encounter with Cressida had been resolved so easily and so cordially in the end, and when his rejection seemed, perversely, to have left her happier. But perhaps it was that glimpse of happiness in her face, wherever it had come from, that had left him feeling the opposite.

His sexuality had never been publicly declared, even if it had never been actively concealed. Turning it over in his head now, he understood that he'd always thought of himself as someone without much appetite for that aspect of life – and that he'd been reassured by that judgement. His marriage had demonstrated quite clearly his unsuitability for heterosexual partnerships, and the occasional brief forays in the other direction, whilst headyingly pleasurable at the time, had left surprisingly little regret when they were finished.

But that moment when he'd conjured a shared future for him and Cressida, however outlandish the idea had been, had made him feel ... enlarged, he thought. A sensation Wordsworth would have been able to express better than him. An elevation of the spirit; a sense of possibility and connection. Possibility and connection were his bread and butter in the world of markets and finance, but it seemed to him suddenly that something else had been offered to him this weekend: that this was the moment to seize a commodity that had eluded him all his life.

An image of Suky in that white dress at Micklethorpe came into his head at that moment – and then, like the detail in a photograph that he had failed to see properly before, the boy with the handbell, ringing the audience in from their picnic. A dark-haired boy a few years younger than him, in a dinner jacket a couple of sizes too big. He shut his eyes for a few moments and let his mind drift back to the warmth of that summer evening, the faint smell of roses, and the sound of that bell, summoning, summoning.

October 1995

Fay

Looking out of her bedroom window one morning, Fay saw that the summer was over. The first scatter of leaves lay across the lawn and the sky had the grey, flat look of a sheet that has been washed too many times. Beside her bed was a calendar on which she was trying to keep track of the passage of time, but sometimes she couldn't remember whether she'd already crossed off a particular day; wasn't sure, when she woke from a long sleep, whether another night had passed. But this day, this grey day, seemed to be a Friday. The Macmillan nurse came on Fridays, and it was important that she remembered that. It was necessary to give a good impression or they would try again to take her off to the hospice.

There had been other visits over the summer, some of which Fay remembered better than others. Stephen had come one day: that had been a good day, nearer the beginning of the summer than the end. The roses had been at their best, and she had made him tea. Jeremy had come, and that had been a less good day. He had said he would come again, but Fay had known he wouldn't. She thought Cressida had come too, maybe even yesterday, but she wasn't certain of that. Sometimes, some days, it was hard to distinguish memories from dreams. But other things she knew were dreams: Marmion in the garden eating gooseberries that were as small and hard as peas. Such a vivid dream, that, but there were no gooseberries in the garden here, only at High Scarp. No, Marmion had not come, but she had written a thank-you letter in her little-girl handwriting on a postcard of Helvellyn.

Fay was very much troubled about Marmion. On her clearer days she could see that what had happened wasn't her fault, but on other days Marmion's grief pressed upon her. She had provided the occasion for Judith and Bill to betray Marmion, after all. She had taken them all to High Scarp, and then – for her own gratification – she had taken them up Nag's Pike. No good ever came of climbing Nag's Pike; she ought to have known that. And certainly she had been irresponsible in letting them walk so far without proper footwear. That memory dragged at her conscience: feet tramped through her sleeping mind, pressing on through bogs and thorns and landslides. Judith wouldn't have fallen if Fay hadn't shouted out when she saw them; if they had been on a proper path; if they had not been there at all. Marmion might never have known.

No; she couldn't bear Marmion's sadness, and she was sorry, deeply sorry, for Judith's injuries, and for the damage to the whole group. She could conjure still the memory of them in the Master's Lodge in their first term, that shining innocence and promise they had all had. And she could see them picnicking above Griseley, talking lazily about the future, so happy and certain that she, too, had felt confident of the future for that hour. She'd destroyed all of it, she thought. It was what she had feared at the beginning: she'd been too greedy, too intemperate. She had brought them all down with her.

She shut her eyes again, and floated back into the space in her head where sleep and waking were less distinguishable than they used to be. There was something else she'd been thinking about last night, something important, and if she floated for long enough it would come back to her and she might be able to tell whether it was real. Something she'd read. Her eyes opened again abruptly. Yes, something she'd read in a newspaper. A politician, a woman whose name escaped her now, who'd been reunited with her baby. A woman whose baby had been adopted when she was young, at university, and had come to find her. Was that true? Could such a thing have happened, or had she dreamt it?

She had certainly dreamt, these last weeks, about her own son. All these years she'd tried not to think of him, as they'd advised her, but now that she was dying she couldn't prevent it. Sometimes it seemed to her, just as she woke, that he was there beside her: some mornings the pleasure and pain of it cut through her consciousness before she remembered about the tumour. A picture of him came into her head now with startling clarity. He looked just like his father: he had that same edge of irritability; that same way of resting his eyes on her absently, casually, until his attention was suddenly snared; that same light in his face when he was happy. The love of her life. How desperately she'd wished that he could have been less honourable, less prominent, less stubborn. How painfully she'd mourned him when he died, still in the grip of that loveless marriage. How very much she'd longed to know his son, and regretted parting with him. If he – if her parents – if she hadn't been ill . . .

Circumstance was everything, she thought. Luck and chance gave you one life and not another. Lucky politician, lucky mother, to find her son again. But Fay had been lucky to find Marmion and Stephen and Cressida and Judith and Bill. She'd been luckier than she deserved, and then she had spoiled everything, for them and for herself, and there was nothing she could do about it now.

Except that perhaps there was. Someone else was coming today, she remembered: Edward Boreham, her solicitor. She manoeuvred herself carefully upwards and sat on the edge of the bed for a few moments, overtaken by a swell of emotion. Of course, she thought. This was the day when she could set in train the only kind of reparation she had to offer.

'How are you?' asked Edward.

Fay made a dismissive gesture with her hand. 'As you can see . . .' she said.

He nodded slowly. He was a big man, close to retirement: he'd been her father's solicitor, and had helped her through the legal tangle her parents had left behind them.

'So,' she said, 'you've brought the new will? As we discussed?'

He didn't answer at once: there was a hesitant look on his face that made her uneasy.

'We did discuss it, didn't we? A bequest to St Anne's, and the rest – High Scarp –'

'Yes,' said Edward. 'I have the names; I have all the details.'

'Good,' said Fay. 'Then I shall sign it. Please don't . . . I've made up my mind, Edward. I'm still compos mentis.'

'I wouldn't dream of trying to change your mind,' said Edward. 'But there is a problem. There's something you have to know.'

'What?' Fay frowned. Lawyers, she thought, always produced problems, when they were paid to solve them.

'One of the legatees,' he said. 'Marmion Hayter. I'm afraid she's dead.'

Fay stared at him. Until now she'd been certain she was awake, that this was a good day and she was in the real world rather than a dream.

'I'm very sorry,' Edward said. 'I hate to bring such bad news. It was a plane crash. Maybe you saw, on the news . . .? A terrorist attack, they think. A British Airways flight on the way to New York. Everyone was killed.'

'But Marmion wasn't going to New York,' Fay said. This seemed her best chance: hanging on to the facts she knew to be true.

'It seems she was,' Edward said. 'Her name was . . . I saw it, in *The Times*. An unusual name.'

Everything was swaying and bending in Fay's mind now, as though a strong wind had got up from nowhere and was trying to uproot things and carry them away. She had seen a newspaper, not so long ago; it had told her about the politician and her baby. Perhaps there had been – perhaps she had seen – a story about an aeroplane, too. But she hadn't known that had anything to do with her. She hadn't wanted to know about people dying, strangers dying. She hadn't known one of them wasn't a stranger.

'She's dead?' Fay said. 'Marmion's dead?'

'I'm afraid so.' Edward was looking at her now with a compassion she didn't want, certainly not from him. 'Shall I make a cup of tea?' he suggested, and the absurdity of this, the glaring cliché, forced the truth into her mind at last.

Marmion was dead. Sweet Marmion, shining Marmion, wronged Marmion. No one could make amends to her now. For a few moments Fay sat, looking past Edward into the garden, still and solemn at the turning point of the day as it waited for autumn to unclothe it. She would be dead herself soon: it was strange to find that she could feel such sorrow for Marmion. She'd had plenty of disappointments of her own; she'd failed to make of herself all that she might have done. But for Marmion there was a pure, clear river of grief, an outpouring augmented by the terrible certainty that she had died unhappy.

Edward had left the room. She would have preferred him to stay: the room felt strange, all the familiar things in it a long way away from her. Marmion had left her too, now – her face and her voice, which had been so vividly present a moment ago, were fading from view. In their place Fay saw something else: Judith and Bill, clasped together on the side of Nag's Pike. Judith jumping back when she saw Fay, then falling, falling, falling.

Out in the garden a magpie stalked across the lawn and a little gust of wind caught up a few leaves. It was an effort to place her thoughts in line, to make a different story with them, but she must do that while Edward was here.

If Marmion had lived, surely there would eventually have been healing, and a return of happiness? The same purity of mind that had caused her to suffer so deeply would have equipped her to love and be loved again. Whereas for Judith and Bill . . . What they were guilty of could multiply now into something that might feel – might be – irrecoverable. Something that might consume their lives just as surely as this thing multiplying inside her head was consuming hers. What they had done – all they had done, Fay thought – was to fall in love. Everything else was circumstance. She of all people should understand that.

Edward came back into the room, carrying two mugs.

'Thank you,' Fay said, as he set one down beside her. She could hardly stomach tea now, but this cup – milky and sweet, no doubt – was welcome, nonetheless.

He sat a little further away this time, as though to emphasise that the business he had come to discuss was not pressing; that there was still plenty of time. Or perhaps because he was afraid of her illness. She avoided mirrors herself, now.

'Tell me something,' she said. 'No: let me think for a minute.'

'Of course.'

Once more she dragged her thoughts into focus. She couldn't count what they had meant to her, those five; what she had felt for them. And they were so young. It shouldn't be the case that life was irrevocably altered by something you did at that age. Marmion was dead, that was a terrible thing, but Bill and Judith . . . It was too painful, too awful, to be dying just when there were people who needed her, whom she cared about, who might let happiness escape them. What she had planned seemed less certain now. There seemed less point to it. But might it help them? Could she do what no one had been able to do for her, by showing them a future that was still there, still possible?

But the face of her son came back to her again now – that little boy, that little baby she had held in her arms – summoned, perhaps, by the depth of her sorrow, or the faint flickering of hope. She couldn't help feeling it must mean something, his visiting her in her dreams, and his claim, surely, was . . . That other son had found his mother. Hers wouldn't come now, not before she died, but one day he might. Like the politician's child, he might try to find her when he had children of his own. He might need her help too: she couldn't bear him to be left empty-handed.

Could she do both, then? How could she help all of them? Not by selling High Scarp; she couldn't do that. High Scarp was what she had to give: it was what meant something to Bill and Judith and the others. And if he never came, her son . . .

Desperation made her voice stronger and her mind more resolute. 'Tell me, Edward, is it possible to arrange things so that . . .' How long? she wondered. How long for the son who might never come: how long so that it wasn't too late to give the others another chance? 'Is it possible to delay a bequest?' she asked. 'To allow time for someone to . . . come forward?'

'Most things are possible,' he said. 'Property can be held in trust, for example.'

Time slipped by: she wasn't sure how much. Was ten years enough? she wondered. What if he came in eleven or twelve? Twenty years, then. Her head ached and ached. She couldn't imagine herself dead for twenty years.

'Everything must be kept just as it is,' she said. 'At High Scarp. Is that possible?'

'Someone can be appointed to look after it,' he said. 'Funds can be set aside. Our Manchester office, perhaps, could –'

'Exactly as it is,' Fay said. She could feel fervour building inside her now, and she knew she must be careful not to let it spill over. She couldn't have him doubting her sanity, the clarity of her intentions. 'For twenty years. Not a word. They shouldn't be told I'm dead, even. And then bring them all back to High Scarp. Make sure they all come.'

'Very well.'

Was he humouring her? Fay wondered. She must be sure he wasn't. She had a picture in her head now that made her feel peaceful: her friends happy, and High Scarp too. That lovingly constructed past she had given the house coming true, and her ghost, her spirit, infusing the place.

'Come back tomorrow,' she said. 'I want to see it all drawn up. I'll sign it tomorrow.'

He smiled at her then. 'I'll come back tomorrow with a colleague. A witness.'

And so this afternoon she must rest, Fay told herself, as the front door shut behind him. She must be sure of tomorrow.

September 2015

Bill

Bill slept badly, the first week back home. Several nights in a row he lay sleepless for hours, watching the clock flick from eleven to twelve, one to two, three to four, before dropping into a dizzy, dreamless slumber from which he woke each morning feeling worse than he had the night before. Once or twice, in the depths of the night, he wondered if the lymphoma was coming back. It had been in his mind a good deal since he'd learned that Fay had been ill that summer, careering towards the end of her life despite seeming so full of life and vigour. But there were no night sweats, no aches and pains. His symptoms, he thought, were due to something else that simmered and propagated in his blood.

Most nights Isabel slept deeply beside him, oblivious to his restlessness, and he was grateful to be spared her questions and her worry. But one night as he turned once more from his back onto his side, adjusting his pillow with a surreptitious tweak, he felt her moving beside him and then, without a word, climbing out of bed. A moment later the bedroom door opened and closed quietly. Bill lay still, listening. She was gone longer than he expected, and he wondered what she was doing; how long she'd been awake.

Irritated with Isabel – irritated with himself, too – Bill turned onto his back again. It was hot tonight: the air was very still, the white walls of the bedroom pressing in out of the darkness. The door clicked open again, and he shut his eyes. Better to pretend to be asleep, he thought. Better to lie still and let Isabel slip in beside him. But she didn't get back into bed. For a few moments he heard nothing, and then a rustle near his shoulder alerted him to her presence on his side of the bed. There was a smell in the room that he couldn't immediately identify – a musky, heady scent. Isabel was leaning over the bed now; he could feel her breath on his neck. Terror flushed through him: perhaps she meant to murder him as he slept. Perhaps she'd seen through his perfidy and decided to put an end to it. He opened his eyes again and looked straight into her face: not the face of a murderer; of course not. It looked very round and smooth in the half-light.

'What are you doing?' he asked.

'I picked lavender for you.'

'Lavender?'

'It's still in flower, along the path at the front.' She showed him the stalks, then laid them beside his pillow. 'I thought it might help you sleep.'

Bill felt something entirely unexpected then. Surprise, relief, perhaps a whiff of amusement – but he was painfully touched, too. The lavender smelled of the night: he imagined her unlocking the front door and padding out into the garden barefoot, the dew on her ankles and the moonlight catching a faint shimmer of purple in the border. It was the gesture of someone in love, he thought.

'Isabel –' he began.

'Ssh.' She crumbled the final head of lavender between her palms and sprinkled it over the bed. 'My poor Bill; what a time you've had.'

'What do you mean?'

She took his hand. 'That weekend,' she said. 'All that trauma from the past. It had to be got through, but I could see how hard it was for you.'

'Isabel –' he tried again. He felt peculiarly powerless now, lying flat and looking up at her. He wondered if she was slightly mad, but all he could see in her face was compassion.

'It'll be all right,' she said now. 'It's a lovely house, and when we can go there on our own it'll feel quite different. We can make it ours; take some of our own friends.'

Bill could think of nothing to say. Which friends could she mean? he wondered. His head spun: it felt as though two things that wouldn't mix were being swirled into each other in an attempt to make them look like part of a whole. Isabel's view of the situation and his, he thought: oil and water.

'Come and get into bed,' he said. 'You'll get cold standing there.'

She laughed. 'It's awfully warm in here. Aren't you hot?'

But even so she climbed in and stretched out beneath the sheets with a little sigh.

'Thank you for the lavender,' he said. 'That was kind of you.'

'Oh, Bill.' She rolled towards him and propped herself up on one elbow. If only she looked a little troubled, he thought. If only she showed some sign of understanding. 'I love you, you know,' she said. 'Don't you – I've always loved you. Surely you know that?'

'No,' he said.

'No?' She looked puzzled, as though she wasn't sure whether he was teasing her.

'That's the thing, Isabel,' he said. 'I never thought love came into it very much.'

The words seemed to float for a moment, suspended above them like little puffs of smoke. As though his next words might set light to them both, Bill thought, burning to the ground this marriage they had both lived in for fifteen years. Isabel's face had shut tight: he couldn't be sure she'd understood, but it was said now, irrevocably, and his mind felt suddenly gloriously clear. Everything had fallen into place, the muddy emulsion of oil and water separating smoothly into two discrete layers.

Other people, he thought, might see things differently. Isabel's declaration might have summoned nobler instincts, a recognition that what he had given her all these years was worth more to her than he'd realised. But all he could see was the deadening effort it had taken to achieve a convincing equilibrium between them. He had thought they had an arrangement they both understood: that they had settled for each other, fifteen years ago, on equal terms. But if she loved him, and

he didn't love her – if they had lived on a false premise all this time –
surely that altered things?

There was a sense, he thought, in which she had not been honest
with him either. And he couldn't sustain the illusion under any longer.
The damage that might be done to Isabel must be weighed against the
damage that had already been done to him and to Judith: and surely,
surely, his love for Judith had just as much right to flourish as Isabel's
for him.

'Isabel –' he said.

'Don't say anything,' she said. 'I don't want to talk about this now.'

Her voice was calm and firm, as it was when she urged him not to
dwell on work, not to talk about his illness in the middle of the night.
But he knew now that she had heard, and that she understood, and
that things would never be the same between them again.

Judith had identified a pub two miles from the motorway, halfway
between London and Shrewsbury. It would have been simpler for
each of them to catch a train to Birmingham, Bill thought, but there
was something powerfully transgressive about driving towards each
other along the busy midday trunk roads and then parking side by
side in a place neither of them knew. There was no explanation for this
behaviour except the correct one – except that Bill had no idea, really,
what the explanation for their behaviour was; what the purpose of this
meeting was.

They arrived within five minutes of each other. Judith was wearing a thin wool dress with a silk scarf around her neck: she shivered
slightly as she got out of her car.

'It's colder here than in London,' she said. 'God, this place looks a
dump.'

Inside the pub, there was a smell of stale beer. A man with a red
face looked up from the till.

'Are you doing food?' Bill asked.

'Only sandwiches, midweek. Chef's not here until six.'

Bill looked at Judith. In the dim glare of the fluorescent light her skin looked like an oil painting, its texture lovingly evoked by Rembrandt or Holbein. He felt as though he'd stolen her; as though it should be blindingly obvious to anyone that she didn't belong to him.

'A sandwich is fine,' she said.

When they'd ordered, Bill looked around at the empty tables, inviting her to choose, but Judith demurred.

'Let's go outside for a bit,' she said. 'All that time in the car . . .'

The garden was planted in the style of a municipal park, beds of red flowers breaking up a lawn that looked as though it had been cut too short, like a little boy's first haircut. A path led to a row of fledgling leylandii, with a brook half-visible through it.

'What a place,' said Judith. 'I'm sorry.'

'It's fine,' Bill said. 'It's a place.'

He had almost given up hope when she'd rung, a week after he'd written to her. A phone call on his mobile, one lunchtime. She'd sounded chary, non-committal, but she had rung, and music had filled his head for the rest of the afternoon. *Can you get away?* Yes, he could; yes, he would, of course, at the click of her fingers. Four more days had passed in painful suspense, and now here they were at last, peering through the leylandii at the water as though the glint of light on its surface might help them through this encounter.

'This doesn't feel like I expected,' said Judith.

His heart bumped. He wanted very badly not to disappoint her. 'Worse?' he said. 'Better?'

'Neither. No, not worse. But it's . . . I've been trying to see things separately, but they're not separate, are they?'

'What things?' he asked.

'Oh, you know. Time, distance, age. Fay.' She paused, not looking at him. 'Isabel. Marmion.'

'They sound quite separate when you list them like that.' He bit his lip, not quite on purpose. Should he tell her about Isabel? Was it better to tackle her worries one by one, or roll them into a single will-we-won't-we decision?

'I don't know.'

But you wanted to meet, he thought.

'Now we're here, isn't it worth . . .?'

Judith made a sudden movement that reminded him of a bird lifting from a perch: a flutter of feathers that might indicate a decision to take off, or merely a resettling of wings.

'Was Fay trying to reproach us?' she asked. 'I feel as though that must be the answer, but it seems an odd way to go about it.'

'I don't think we'll ever know,' Bill said. 'I think of it as providence. Whatever she meant, that was the effect.'

'But it matters what she meant,' Judith said.

'It doesn't need to.' Bill's eyes lingered on the contour of her neck. He'd never forget that moment, that glimpse of a triangle of skin at Townend. The way it had seemed to hold the key to the rest of her.

A wisp of wind cut through the garden, and Judith shivered.

'Let's go back in. The sandwiches might be ready.'

While they ate they spoke of other things: the rugby World Cup, Judith's involvement in a recent asylum case, Housman and Shropshire. The sandwiches weren't bad, although Bill longed for a steak pie, something with more substance. All this time they were skating, skating, he thought, and the minutes were passing. He couldn't bear the idea that there might be nothing to show for this meeting. Why hadn't they . . .? He felt suddenly frantic. They could have gone anywhere, done anything, and they had chosen lunch in a third-rate pub.

'Judith,' he said. 'There don't need to be any obstacles, if you . . . Certainly not Isabel. I've already . . . We made a mistake, you and I. We should have hung on.'

He could see his face reflected in her eyes, and the pub folded in around him. Like looking at himself in a crystal ball, he thought. That was something he'd never managed, though: his failure of imagination had always been part of the problem. His failure of conviction, too – but just now, with her face so close, he was consumed by a fever of yearning, by disembowelling lust. He would risk anything, he thought, pay any price.

Judith pushed her plate away.

'I shouldn't have suggested this,' she said. 'I got your hopes up. Mine too, if it's any consolation. But at least this way you won't be left wondering.'

'Please,' he said, as she reached for her handbag. 'Please don't go yet. If you don't love me, I'd rather you told the truth, but if you do . . .'

'For heaven's sake, Bill,' Judith said. 'We're not students any more. You can't invoke love like that, like a trump card. It sounds ridiculous.'

'Not to me,' said Bill. 'Why are we both here, otherwise?' He gazed at her, desperate to prevail. 'I can't find the magic words, Judith. I can't explain things well enough to convince you, but I'm sure of what I feel, and I can't bear to let it go again.'

Judith looked down at the table, picking up crumbs with her fingertip.

'Love *is* a trump card,' Bill said, 'but we failed to play it last time. This is the truth, Judith: if Marmion hadn't died, we'd have ended up together. We were all so young; everything would have settled down.'

'But she did,' said Judith. 'That's the way it is. Believe me, I've been bloody furious about her dying, but that only makes it worse.'

Bill stared. 'But you're a rational person. How can you allow something totally beyond our control to ruin both our lives?'

Perhaps he'd gone too far, he thought: perhaps her life hadn't been ruined. But she didn't deny it.

'My darling,' he said, 'won't you let me –'

'Stop,' she said. 'I can't think. I don't know. I've got my life . . .'

He waited, fighting down an urge to grab her hand and hold it tight. And then, with one of those fluid, decisive gestures, she stood up.

'I can't do this any more,' she said. 'I'm going to go now.'

'What does that mean?' Bill asked. 'Can we –'

'Don't ask anything else,' Judith said. 'Please don't.'

Bill watched her put on her coat and slide her bag over her shoulder. He hadn't been able to believe she wanted to meet, and now he couldn't believe she was leaving. There were two stories, he thought: the one that should never have happened, and the one that looked as though it never might. Had it ever been possible that this meeting would change the course of things? If he'd behaved differently – said different things . . .

He waited a few minutes before following her out to the car park. There was another moment of wild hope then, but the space where her car had been was empty. His mind spun as he started the engine, retraced his steps to the motorway junction – past the garage on the corner, the farm gate – and rejoined the traffic heading north.

So that was that: that was the end. The fourth time, he thought, that she'd said no: he'd have to accept that she meant it now. She'd come all this way to tell him, perhaps not knowing what the answer would be until she got here.

Would it have been better, he wondered, to leave things as they were, with enough uncertainty, enough possibility to sustain him?

Would Judith come to High Scarp next spring, as they had all undertaken to do? He should at least have asked her that.

Into his head, just then, came Marmion's voice, clear and fresh across the decades. *For God shall bring every work into judgment, with every secret thing.* Could he believe that, now? That behind all this heartache and misadventure was divine judgement? The irony was that the nearest he'd ever come to God was in Marmion. The only time he'd ever believed in goodness and mercy.

He hadn't quite reached Birmingham when he heard his phone buzzing. Isabel, he thought, and he felt a clutch of dread. He had offered his heart to another woman and been refused, and he couldn't bear the thought of going home to Isabel tonight.

But when he glanced down, waiting for the answerphone to kick in, it wasn't Isabel's face that looked out from the caller ID screen. It was Judith's.

Epilogue

Heathrow airport, October 1995

As she approached the passport control desk, Marmion turned one last time to wave to her family, waiting in a little cluster beyond the barrier that funnelled passengers towards the departure zone. Pip, Maggie, Becky and her parents, all of them here to see her off as though she was going for good, rather than just a few months. *I'll see you at Christmas*, she'd said, and they'd smiled and hugged her – everything calmly managed, of course, with no embarrassing excesses of emotion, but even so their being there, their insistence on coming with her so early in the morning, touched her deeply. Especially, she thought, since – no use pretending – a little part of her was glad to be leaving them. Leaving the close, familiar embrace of her family, the house she'd grown up in, the weight of love that filled it, as well as leaving Cambridge and her friends. It was complicated, of course; that spark of impatience to begin the next chapter of her life was set against sadness and apprehension – but she felt certain that the spark would take, that the dry tinder of hope and expectation would burn brightly over the weeks and months to come.

One thing troubled her still, and she hoped she would find it in herself, before long, to set it right. She was bidden to live at peace with the world, and she was not at peace with everyone in it. She had seen Stephen; she had written to Cressida and to Fay; but she had not settled things with Bill or Judith. She wasn't ready to do that, to find the right words and to say them wholeheartedly, as she must – but that responsibility hung over her. Once she was in America, she thought, things would shift in her mind, in her heart. Another few days couldn't matter.

When she reached the departure gate, she squeezed into one of the last free seats, her hand baggage tucked against her knees. It seemed to her that she was already in a different world: a world populated by people more various even than those she had lived among in London. People of all ages, races, dress, expression, emotion. Opposite her sat a Scottish family with four small children who danced and chattered and tugged and argued while their parents remonstrated gently, and then less gently. To her right an elderly Indian couple waited patiently for the boarding instructions to be announced. On the other side a young man in Arab dress was absorbed in a book, his lips moving as he followed the words, and opposite him two American teenagers in short tartan skirts talked loudly about the excitements of their trip to London, watched by a boy a little older whose shaven head and tattoos made him seem, Marmion thought, vulnerable rather than tough. Further along the row of seats there was a woman with two tiny babies, a very old man with a shock of white hair and a Chinese woman in a black suit with bulky headphones clamped over her ears.

All these stories, Marmion thought, some of them almost completed and others barely started. All these people, gathered at random, an almost perfect cross-section of humanity. She felt, sitting among them, draughts of love and of anger, of acceptance and of resistance, of hope and of despair – and she felt an answering surge inside her soul. Shine like a light in the darkness, she thought. Shine for the good of the world.

Acknowledgements

As ever, my greatest thanks go to my husband, Richard Pleming, for his unstinting succour and support and his boundless wit and good humour – all blessings daily renewed. Love and thanks also, once again, to my parents and my lovely children, who make life worth living.

I'm ever grateful for the wise guidance and sanity of Joel Richardson at Bonnier Zaffre, and for the efforts of the rest of the team, especially Rebecca Farrell and Emily Burns. And of course for the marvellous Patrick Walsh, agent extraordinaire.

Cordelia Hall not only read early drafts of this novel but provided expert legal advice – as did Esther Millard. Thank you to them both. Geoffrey and Diana Manning – and before them, John and Kate – sowed the seeds of my abiding affection for Cumbria by allowing us to stay in their cottage for many, many years. I'm hugely grateful to them and to all our friends in Patterdale, and apologise for the shameless way I've altered their beautiful landscape.

This book is dedicated to the many friends with whom I sang in the chapel choir at Clare College, Cambridge between 1983 and 1986, but I would also like to thank everyone else with whom and for whom I've had the good fortune to sing over the last forty years or so – from the *Messiah* in the Albert Hall with the massed choirs of Buckinghamshire schools in 1978 to many memorable (and sometimes scary) concerts with various grown-up choirs in London and Oxford, and of course Bel Canto. These days my contact with choral music is mostly as a member of the congregation at Guildford Cathedral, and my final thanks go to the clergy and choir there – and especially to Daphne and Rowena – for bringing us such joy.

If you enjoyed *Every Secret Thing* by Rachel Crowther, then you'll love her novel

The Things You Do for Love

An elite surgeon with a brilliant but philandering husband, Flora Macintyre has always defined herself by her success in juggling her career and her marriage. Until, all at once, she finds herself with neither.

Retired and widowed in the space of a few months, Flora is left untethered. In a moment of madness, she realises there's nothing to stop her running away to France.

But back home her two daughters – the family she's always loved, but never had the time to nurture – are struggling. Lou is balancing pregnancy with a crumbling relationship, while her younger sister, Kitty, begins to realise she may have to choose between love and her growing passion for music.

And even as the family try to pull together, one dark secret could still tear them all apart . . .

Read on for an exciting extract . . .

March 1995

As Flora drives away from the hospital, her mind is full of heroism. Waiting at the traffic lights, then heading out onto the dual carriageway, she relives the hours under the lights, the glint of instruments, the counting in of swabs – all the rites and pageantry of the operating theatre, brought to bear on the body of one ordinary citizen. She conjures up the face of her patient, a young man with a faint tinge of green in the hollows of his cheeks, being coaxed back to consciousness among the reassuring paraphernalia of drips and drains and monitors.

And then she remembers the size of the tumour, the length of gut they had to remove, the bleakness of the prognosis. As the orderly lights of the ring road give way to unlit country lanes, Flora feels the adrenaline ebbing away. There is always this moment, this crunch of reality, when the elation of exercising her craft evaporates and the patient comes back into focus, a person with a life that has been interrupted by medical catastrophe. She never deceives herself about such things, but it's necessary to put them away while you get on with the job, focussing on the gaping abdomen before you.

Flora slows for a difficult corner then picks up speed again, shifting into fourth for the straight run along to the final crossroads. But, she tells herself, it's the person who wakes up in the recovery room, whom she'll see tomorrow morning on the ward, that she's made a difference to. She has done what she can to help him beat the odds. She thinks again of the hours of concentration and the expertise of her team: five hours multiplied by five, six, seven people. It's more than going through the motions, surgery. It's always more than that; always a battle fought to the last ditch. This afternoon they halted two hours in, wondering whether to abandon the resection, but they were right to go on. There are always the cases that turn out better than you dare expect, she tells herself, as well as those who do worse.

The village is quiet this evening, but the lights are on in the house, and a cheerful glow filters through the curtains as she turns into the drive. Flora thinks of Henry and the girls inside, cooking supper or watching television or finishing homework.

But in the moment between turning off the engine and opening the car door, the complications of home creep back into her mind: an almost tangible shift from comforting allegory to untidy reality. She recalls last night's row, left hanging this morning, and her earnest assurance to the children that she'd be home early tonight. It's her birthday, she remembers. They promised her a cake. She glances at the clock on the dashboard – it's almost nine. Will Kitty still be up? Will Lou be sulking by now?

There's no one around when she opens the door, just a hushed murmur of voices which she takes for the television. But in a moment Lou rushes down the stairs and throws herself against her chest.

'Mummy! You're back!'

Lou is twelve, and not much given to throwing herself at her mother anymore. Holding her tight for a moment, Flora can feel her small heart thudding.

'I'm so sorry I'm late,' she says. 'I really meant not to be, today of all days.'

'It's OK,' Lou says. 'We've got . . .' She draws away now a little awkwardly, as though she's not sure how she found herself plastered against her mother. 'Daddy's in the kitchen,' she says. 'I was on look-out.'

Flora catches a note of something – warning? – in Lou's voice. Her eyes sweep round the hall, halting for a moment on the portrait of her husband that hangs at the bottom of the stairs: a handsome boy of nineteen, drawn by his friend Nicholas Comyn during a tour of Italy, smiling at the world in the assurance of a warm reception.

'Is Kitty still up?' she asks – but before Lou can answer, Henry appears from the kitchen, carrying a bottle of champagne and some glasses on a tray. Henry resplendent in silk shirt and cravat, every inch the elegant host, the eminent critic, the reassuring Radio Three voice-over.

'Darling,' he says, 'Happy Birthday. Has Lou . . .?'

He leans forward to kiss her, swinging the tray to the side so he can get close enough to reach her lips. Last night's row hovers between them, less easy to dodge than the tray. Flora can smell wine on his breath, and can detect it, too, in the flush across his cheekbones. The soft skin there is a reliable barometer for excess consumption of several kinds.

'Sorry I'm late,' she says. 'Unavoidably detained at the operating table.'

'You're here now,' he says. 'Let me pour you a drink.'

Flora's eyes are caught now by another picture, another Comyn, of Kitty and Lou on the beach last summer. Something about it lights a fuse inside her: the image of happy family life. The same image she almost allowed herself to believe in a few minutes ago. She's been fobbed off too often with a glass of wine, she tells herself. She glances towards Lou, but Lou has vanished again. She's become an expert at vanishing, Flora thinks, with a flash of pain.

'Wait,' she says, as Henry moves towards the sitting room door. 'We need to talk.'

Henry halts, but he doesn't turn to face her. 'Not now,' he says, his voice almost jovial.

'Why not?' Anger has flared more quickly than usual, provoked by the way Henry's dress and demeanour speak of an evening of celebration, and by her guilt about Lou. By the too-familiar chain of complication and compromise. The last vestiges of surgical adrenaline urge her on. 'It's always "not now",' she says. 'Perhaps this is the moment, Henry. We can't simply –' She raises a fist, half-clenched – not as a threat, not exactly, but as evidence of her strength of feeling, her seriousness of intent.

And then the sitting room door bursts open. The murmur of voices swells suddenly and Kitty flies towards her, pink tutu fluttering, full of the wildness of a not-quite-three-year-old allowed to stay up beyond her bedtime.

'We've got a party for you!' she shouts.

The room behind her is full of people, looking nervously, smilingly, in Flora's direction. The smell of festivity is unmistakable: wine and perfume and the pepperiness of hot breath billow out into the hall.

Caught in the dismay of an ill-timed surprise, Flora can't muster the appropriate response. Memories of her mother's parties swim into her mind, and she feels suddenly very tired. Henry looks at her, raises an eyebrow infinitesimally, and then he goes on into the sitting room, and there is nothing for it but to follow him.

'What a nice surprise,' Flora says.

The guests – mainly from the village: not many of them friends, to be honest – are clearly embarrassed by the anticlimax, after keeping quiet for so long. They glance at Flora as though they know they should be pleased that their hostess is here at last, but are not sure they are. Why on earth has Henry invited them? To create a party, she thinks. A diversion. Because it would be hard to muster a houseful of people, otherwise, with whom they could go through the motions. Goddammit: and it's she who looks ungracious now. Heartless, even. Well, she'll show them. She scoops Kitty up and swings her round, kissing her hot little face.

'My darling,' she says, 'how beautiful you look.'

'You haven't got your party clothes on,' says Kitty. 'Have you been in the hospital all the time?'

'All the time.' Flora settles Kitty on her hip and turns away from Henry, who is coming towards her with a glass of champagne. 'All this long time. Now, Kitty, come and help me say hello to everyone.'

OUT NOW IN PAPERBACK AND EBOOK